Ashes on the Waves

For Karren Lynch,
who told me I could do it

PHILOMEL BOOKS
An imprint of Penguin Young Readers Group. Published by The Penguin Group.
Penguin Group (USA) Inc., 375 Hudson Street, New York, NY 10014, USA.
Penguin Group (Canada), 90 Eglinton Avenue East, Suite 700, Toronto, Ontario M4P 2Y3,
Canada (a division of Pearson Penguin Canada Inc.). Penguin Books Ltd, 80 Strand,
London WC2R 0RL, England. Penguin Ireland, 25 St. Stephen's Green, Dublin 2,
Ireland (a division of Penguin Books Ltd). Penguin Group (Australia), 707 Collins Street,
Melbourne, Victoria 3008, Australia (a division of Pearson Australia Group Pty Ltd).
Penguin Books India Pvt Ltd, 11 Community Centre, Panchsheel Park, New Delhi–110 017,
India. Penguin Group (NZ), 67 Apollo Drive, Rosedale, Auckland 0632, New Zealand
(a division of Pearson New Zealand Ltd). Penguin Books South Africa, Rosebank Office
Park, 181 Jan Smuts Avenue, Parktown North 2193, South Africa. Penguin China, B7
Jiaming Center, 27 East Third Ring Road North, Chaoyang District, Beijing 100020,
China. Penguin Books Ltd, Registered Offices: 80 Strand, London WC2R 0RL, England.

Edited by Jill Santopolo. Design by Amy Wu. Text set in 10-point Old Style 7.

Library of Congress Cataloging-in-Publication Data
Lindsey, Mary, 1963– Ashes on the waves / Mary Lindsey. p. cm.
Summary: Expands on the Edgar Allan Poe poem "Annabel Lee," as Liam and Anna
reunite on an isolated Maine island where they were children together and fall so deeply
in love they provoke a wager between Otherworld creatures from Celtic mythology.
[1. Love—Fiction. 2. Supernatural—Fiction. 3. Mythology, Celtic—Fiction. 4. People with
disabilities—Fiction. 5. Superstition—Fiction. 6. Islands—Fiction. 7. Maine—Fiction.]
I. Poe, Edgar Allan, 1809–1849. Annabel Lee. II. Title.
PZ7.L6613Ash 2013 [Fic]—dc23 2012026920

ISBN 978-0-399-15939-8
1 3 5 7 9 10 8 6 4 2

MARY LINDSEY

Philomel Books | An Imprint of Penguin Group (USA) Inc.

Also by the same author:

Shattered Souls

ANNABEL LEE

It was many and many a year ago,
    In a kingdom by the sea,
That a maiden there lived whom you may know
    By the name of Annabel Lee;
And this maiden she lived with no other thought
    Than to love and be loved by me.

I was a child and *she* was a child,
    In this kingdom by the sea;
But we loved with a love that was more
        than love—
    I and my Annabel Lee—
With a love that the wingéd seraphs of Heaven
    Coveted her and me.

And this was the reason that, long ago,
    In this kingdom by the sea,
A wind blew out of a cloud, chilling
    My beautiful Annabel Lee;
So that her high-born kinsmen came
    And bore her away from me,
To shut her up in a sepulchre
    In this kingdom by the sea.

The angels, not half so happy in Heaven,
    Went envying her and me—
Yes!—that was the reason (as all men know,
    In this kingdom by the sea)
That the wind came out of the cloud by night,
    Chilling and killing my Annabel Lee.

But our love it was stronger by far than the love
                Of those who were older than we—
                Of many far wiser than we—
And neither the angels in Heaven above,
                Nor the demons down under the sea,
Can ever dissever my soul from the soul
                Of the beautiful Annabel Lee:—

For the moon never beams, without bringing
                        me dreams
                Of the beautiful Annabel Lee;
And the stars never rise, but I feel the bright eyes
                Of the beautiful Annabel Lee:—
And so, all the night-tide, I lie down by the side
Of my darling—my darling—my life and
                        my bride,
                In her sepulchre there by the sea,
                In her tomb by the sounding sea.

                              —Edgar Allan Poe, 1849

The death, then, of a beautiful woman is, unquestionably, the most poetical topic in the world—and equally is it beyond doubt that the lips best suited for such topic are those of a bereaved lover.

—Edgar Allan Poe,
from "The Philosophy of Composition," 1846

1

There is no passion in nature so demoniacally impatient, as that of him, who shuddering upon the edge of a precipice, thus meditates a Plunge. To indulge, for a moment, in any attempt at thought, is to be inevitably lost; for reflection but urges us to forbear, and therefore it is, I say, that we cannot. If there be no friendly arm to check us, or if we fail in a sudden effort to prostrate ourselves backward from the abyss, we plunge, and are destroyed.

—Edgar Allan Poe,
from "The Imp of the Perverse," 1845

She looked like something out of a dream . . . or a nightmare. Simultaneously, so terrible and beautiful, it made me ache.

Waves pounded against the jetty, shooting geysers of frigid salt water into the air as she leaned into the wind, her long hair whipping in all directions.

"No. Stop!" I shouted, but the howling gale and crashing waves consumed my words.

She took a step closer to the rocky edge and held her arms out to the side as if she were going to fly. But she wasn't going to take flight. She was going to die.

"No!" I leapt onto the boulder at the base of the jetty and fought the wind, picking my way over the slick, moss-covered surface. "Don't do it!"

Arms still spread, she tipped her head back, letting the spray from the waves shower her face, like a lover embracing the rage of the sea itself.

A huge wave slammed the rocks to my right. I crouched and gained a fingerhold on the rough surface to keep from being washed away.

Just a little farther and I'd be past the wave break point.

She turned toward me, her glassy eyes unfocused. I'd been there. I knew what she was experiencing in that trancelike stupor. *Don't do it,* I bid her silently. She teetered for a moment and I felt certain she would fall backward. I was so close— within steps of reaching her. I couldn't lose her now. "No! Hang on!" I shouted.

As beautiful as I thought she was before, it was nothing compared to seeing her face. Fine and delicate, bathed in the rich, caramel glow of the setting sun, her brow was drawn in concentration as she seemed to grasp the reality of her situation. She'd reached the point of no return. If she didn't jump now, it was clear I wouldn't let her. How badly did she want this release? How deep was the pain?

Not deep enough, I realized with relief as I wrapped my good arm around her waist and pulled her to me.

"What the hell are you doing?" she screamed, shoving against my chest. "Are you freaking nuts? Let me go!"

If I had been whole, I could have reasoned with her while standing. Instead, I was forced to sit, pulling her down with me in order to gain enough control to keep her from hurting herself—or me for that matter. As hard as she was struggling, we were both likely to end up in the sea.

"Stop," I said in her ear as I forced her to her back and pinned her body with my own. She needed to be calm in order to listen to reason. The frigid water crashed against the rocks on all sides as her warmth seeped through our clothes into my skin.

"Oh, God," she cried. "What are you doing?"

Lying on top of her, I trapped her legs between mine and held her arm over her head by her narrow wrist, the full length of my body immobilizing her except for her free arm, which she was using to beat the side of my head. I lowered my mouth to her ear. "Stop, please," I said. "I just want to help you."

She went still.

It felt like her flesh melted into mine as the tension ebbed from her like an evening tide. We remained like this for a while, breathing in unison and saying nothing, her body pliant beneath mine.

Sensing she had calmed, I lifted my weight from her slightly. In one swift movement, she shifted higher and slammed her knee into me.

Part of me marveled at her cleverness. The other part struggled to remain conscious through a wave of pain so intense I couldn't breathe.

She muttered something indecipherable as I rolled onto my side and she pushed to her feet. Perhaps she had spoken clearly and it was just the sound of my pulse in my head that muffled her words.

Unable to move, I could only watch as she picked her way over the rocks toward the shore, never once looking back, now released from the call of the sea.

By the time the pain had subsided enough for me to get to my feet, she had cleared the jetty and was climbing the rocky path toward the mansion.

The structure loomed ominous and foreboding at the apex of the hill. The bottom half was shrouded in the dense fog that crept across the land from the water. Illuminated by lightning flashes, the mansion appeared alive—like a breathing stone monster waiting for the opportune moment to lay siege to our tiny village below.

I watched from behind a boulder marking the corner of the property as she raked the rain-soaked hair from her face and studied the stone beast as if she, too, sensed its mal-intent.

With her delicate, slender hands, she yanked the iron gate, but it only gave a few inches. The hinges screamed in protest as she gave it another tug and then another, until it finally yielded enough for her to squeeze through.

Inside the gaping mouth of the overhang at the front of the house, huge oak double doors with hand-hewn black metal hardware stood more like soldiers' protective shields than a welcoming entrance. Everything about the place screamed "go away," and I would have, but that wasn't an option . . . not yet, anyway. Not until I was certain she was safe.

She banged ineffectively on the doors several times, then slapped her palms against them—her softness in complete opposition to the unyielding harshness of the structure.

She turned and I ducked behind the huge stone. I thought for a moment she had sensed my presence, but to my relief, she was simply looking for something on the path just off the porch. With almost unnatural grace, she descended the few steps of the porch and picked up a fist-size stone. Rolling it in her fingers, she climbed the steps and slammed it against one of the iron straps across the door.

The sharp raps reverberated against the stone of the mansion and echoed into the fog that had all but enveloped the island. As if in reply, lightning split the sky, making the house appear to lurch as it reflected off the leaded-glass windowpanes that shone like the eyes of a hundred night animals.

The doors groaned as they were drawn open from within. I didn't see Miss Ronan, but I recognized her deep, liquid voice. "You should not be outside after dark, Anna," she warned. "Bad things happen after dark."

Anna shot a look over her shoulder toward the sea before running into gaping jaws of the mansion.

She was safe inside the belly of the monster: safe from the storm, safe from the call of the sea, and most of all, safe from me—a monster of another kind entirely.

A scream shattered Muireann's sleep. She nudged her sister. "Wake up! Something's going on." Her sister responded by snorting twice, then rolling over.

There it was again, louder this time. They were torturing someone. She crawled to the edge of the rock ledge and put her head underwater.

"Please, please," a youthful male voice pleaded. "Give me another chance."

"You had your chance," an older man answered. She recognized that voice. It was their leader.

"It wasn't my fault," the young male cried. "I had her. He severed the connection. No, please . . ."

Then the screaming began again.

Muireann lifted her head from the water and took a deep shuddering breath. She glanced over her shoulder to find her family still huddled comfortably together, deep in slumber.

Again, she put her head underwater, praying the young male would be released.

"Who severed the connection?" the leader's voice boomed.

"The broken one did it. He's the reason she got away. Please don't kill me."

There was a long silence. Muireann's lungs ached. She should have taken a deeper breath.

"If we become too weak to remain in this realm, you will *wish* I had killed you," the leader said. "There are things worse than death, son, as the broken one will soon discover."

Muireann pulled her head from the water, filling her lungs with a gasp. He had tortured his own son, she realized with horror. Muireann had no idea who the broken one was, but she knew he didn't stand a chance.

2

From childhood's hour I have not been
As others were—I have not seen
As others saw—I could not bring
My passions from a common spring—
From the same source I have not taken
My sorrow—I could not awaken
My heart to joy at the same tone—
And all I lov'd—I lov'd alone—

—Edgar Allan Poe,
from "Alone," 1830

*A*nna Leighton is on the island," Francine called from the storeroom behind the counter. "I saw the helicopter come in between storms yesterday afternoon. Polly told me the girl was the only passenger."

I tugged open the lid on a small box of washers with my teeth and dumped them, letting the aluminum disks crash to the bottom of the bin in a shimmering metallic shower.

Francine emerged in the doorway, wiping her hands on her apron. "I know you've been keeping up with her through those magazines you get from the vendors."

I shrugged, attempting nonchalance. Francine not only possessed a good heart, she was a keen observer. Every time an outsider came with a delivery, I'd ask if they had any old newspapers or magazines on their boat. Some had even begun saving them up for me, giving me sizable stacks when they delivered goods or picked up catch from the store. Most were local Maine newspapers, but the man who made the delivery this morning had left me a stack of magazines and newspapers from all over. I could hardly wait to look through them after work.

"Maybe I could arrange for you to make a delivery to Taibhreamh," she said with a wink. "I'm sure they need supplies of some sort up at the mansion."

I crushed the empty box into the garbage and placed another on the edge of the counter. "Maybe they need some two-inch marine-grade hex bolts to display in one of their lovely hand-cut crystal decanters." I sliced the seal with a knife and turned the box over, letting the weight of the bolts push the lid open. As they clattered and crashed into the bin, I glanced up to find Francine studying me. She did that frequently, as if she were decoding a puzzle. In my case, the puzzle was destined to remain forever unsolved. There were too many missing pieces.

"You have enough food at home, Liam?"

I nodded, relieved she'd changed the subject.

The cowbell on the door clanged, and six-year-old Megan McAlister skipped into the store followed by her mother. I'd seen Megan around. She was sort of a celebrity in our tiny village, being the youngest resident and the only child. This was the first time she'd been in the store since I'd begun working here.

"Hi, Miss Francine!" Megan said, standing on her tiptoes to peek at the candy jars behind the counter. "You got any salt-water taffy? 'Cause I need some." She opened her mouth and pointed at a bottom tooth. "It's wiggly and Mommy says I can have a piece of taffy since I lost my last one that way."

Francine patted her head. "I most certainly do. We had a delivery this morning, and it just so happens, candy was in it." She reached in a jar and gave the little girl a piece of taffy.

"I hope flour and cornmeal came too," Mrs. McAlister grumbled. "You've been out for a week."

Francine opened a cabinet and hefted out a ten-pound cloth bag of flour. She dropped it on the counter with a thud punctuated by a puff of white powder. "Weevils got in the last batch and this shipment was late because of the storms. Cornmeal will be here in a day or two, weather permitting." She wiped her hands on her apron. "Need anything else?"

Mrs. McAlister leaned closer. "I hear the Leighton girl flew in yesterday. Miss Ronan had Polly and Edmond come up to Taibhreamh to help clean out the cellar and load the supplies off the helicopter. They said there was lots of it. It looks like she's staying awhile."

My heart stopped beating for a moment. She would be here "awhile."

Mrs. McAlister glanced over her shoulder at me, so I occupied myself by sorting hardware that customers had dropped back into the wrong bins.

Megan came over and tugged my shirttail. "Can I help?" She picked up a handful of sixteen-penny nails from the bottom row of bins. Obviously, she hadn't been told about me yet or she'd have never gotten this close.

"Sure," I said. "Those go . . ." I pointed to the bin from which they had come. "There."

She gave me a gap-toothed grin and dropped the nails back into place. Other than my ma and Francine, this was the first time someone had actually smiled at me.

"Well done."

"Megan! Come away from him!" her mother shrieked.

As if electrocuted, Megan ran to her mother's side.

By this point in my life, I'd discovered that it was not possible to truly become desensitized or accustomed to discrimination. It is something one endures—and I had suffered it since my unfortunate birth almost eighteen years prior. Even my pa considered me an outcast.

Other than Ma, Francine was the only person who had ever treated me with respect. Well, other than Anna Leighton. But that was a long time ago; she probably didn't even remember. She certainly hadn't shown any signs of recognition last night on the jetty.

I took a deep breath and resumed sorting.

"With only one good arm, he can't be much help to you, Francine. Why do you keep him on here?" Mrs. McAlister whispered just loud enough for me to hear. I'd learned that statements intended to cause hurt could be excused if "accidentally" imparted.

"Why would I not?" Francine's voice was level, but her Scottish burr had deepened. I was familiar with this tone. She was angry.

"Because he's . . ." Mrs. McAlister looked at me, then at Megan.

Another thing I'd learned about discrimination is that the perpetrator often dons a mask of false politeness to obscure the ugly reality of fear and hatred.

". . . He's, you know . . ."

Francine leaned over the counter so that her face was quite close to Mrs. McAlister's. "I don't know. Why don't you enlighten me, Katie lass?"

The woman's face flushed crimson.

Were it not for the fact I'd witnessed this scenario played

numerous times, I'd have found solace in her discomfort. Instead, I knew it was yet another of Francine's valiantly fought battles in a war she could never win. Neither of us could.

"He's cursed. He's human flesh worn by a demon!" Mrs. McAlister blurted out.

My heart sank as Megan, still clinging to her mother's leg, stared up at me. She no longer wore her prior look of wonder and joy. Instead, she chewed her taffy, deep blue eyes brimming with distrust. The loathing her mother harbored would come later. Fear is instinctual; loathing is ingrained over time.

3

They who dream by day are cognizant of
many things which escape those who dream
only by night.

—Edgar Allan Poe,
from "Eleonora," 1841

on't think on it." Francine lowered herself
into a chair across from me at the round table
in the storeroom. "The old ways are hard for
folks to shake off. It's simple ignorance."

There was nothing simple about this. The lore of my people
was complex and ran as deep as human imagination allowed.
I accepted the cup of tea she pushed toward me. "Thank you."

Ordinarily, my situation was tolerable. In this case, it riled
me to see a gentle child's spirit tainted. Megan was as much a
victim as I.

I'd learned long ago that I couldn't stop it, but if I began to
believe the stories, I would become as lost as they expected; I
refused to let that happen. So instead, I had developed the ability to tune out the ugliness and bring beauty into focus. If that
part of my soul remained dominant, the darker side of me could
not advance.

My antidote? Anna Leighton. I hadn't seen her close to
twelve years, but she had sustained me since childhood. And

she was here. Last night I'd seen her. Heard her voice. Felt her warmth seep into my own skin heating my very soul.

"Liam? Are you okay?" Francine's pale eyes searched my face. "You're trembling."

So I was. Perfect concentric circles vibrated inward across the surface of the tea in the cup clutched firmly in my palm. I released the cup and leaned back in my chair. "I'm fine."

She reached across the table and patted my hand. "For all the reading you do, you certainly aren't one for words, are you?"

Words were inadequate. They never came out as intended. "No." I gave her a smile.

The bell clanged, followed by a light creaking of the floorboards. "Hello?"

I stood so abruptly, I knocked my chair over. That voice. *Her* voice. All night, I'd run it through my head. Over the years, I'd often imagined what she'd sound like grown up. The reality exceeded expectations.

"Hello?" she said again. "Is anyone here?"

"Just a moment," Francine called. She lowered her voice and leveled her gaze on me. "Well, don't just stand there with your jaw hanging open, Liam. Go help the girl."

No. Not now. Not yet. I shook my head.

Francine stood. "For the love of heaven, lad. Make things happen." She patted my cheek. "Just a moment. I'm coming!"

I remained momentarily frozen in both mind and body. Last night, I'd come upon her by accident and had acted out of necessity. She'd been about to succumb to the call of the sea. Today, she was simply . . . here. Touching things I'd touched. Breathing the same air.

For so long I'd held on to her as a concept. Now she was tangible.

Her voice drifted through the air like music. "I'm told you have a phone. My cell doesn't work on this godforsaken island and I really need to make a call. It's kind of urgent."

"Well, I have a satellite phone, but it is quite old and awkward; I'll have to work it for you," Francine answered.

"I don't care if you have to use smoke signals; I need to get hold of my parents."

I smiled. She was quick-witted. Taking a deep breath, I silently moved to the doorway and peeked into the store.

There she was—hands on hips—the most beautiful creature I'd ever seen. Ebony waves cascaded over her shoulders, and her clothes, unlike any worn here on Dòchas, clung to her slender form like those from the etching of Venus in my book of nineteenth-century French poetry. I covered my mouth to stifle a gasp.

"And, I'm afraid I'll have to charge you. I have to pay two dollars and fifty cents for each minute. Sorry, lass."

"Whatever it takes. I just have to make this call."

Francine led her to the phone in the corner. After turning some dials on the console and entering the number Anna recited, she handed the receiver over and walked to the counter.

"Hello, Mom?" She shifted her weight from foot to foot. "Oh. Hi, Aunt Susan. I need to talk to Mom or Dad." She brushed her hair over one shoulder. "Is Charles there, then? . . . Good, I'll talk to him instead. Thanks." She examined her pink fingernails and tapped her foot.

"Why don't you come on out here?" Francine whispered. "You've pined for this girl for over a decade."

I had not pined for her. Pining suggested sorrow or angst. My thoughts of her were never sad. I dreamed of her. Not about being with her, just . . . of her. Who she was, what she was doing.

I stepped just inside the doorway.

"Charles!" she said. "You've gotta send someone to come get me. . . ." She twirled her finger in her hair while the person on the other end spoke. "I know it's Mom and Dad's decision, but it's because of you and your stupid wedding. . . . That's not true! Come on. Give me a break. The people here are nuts. . . . No, really. The old bat that runs Taibhreamh is totally out of her mind talking about evil spirits and supernatural stuff. She really believes it, too. They *all* do. . . . Charles. You're not listening. None of you ever listen. I think I'm in danger. And a guy jumped me last night . . . Charles? Are you there? Hello? Dammit." She slammed the receiver back in the cradle.

"Careful there, lass," Francine said. "It might be old, but it's all I have."

She turned to face us. "Sorry, I just—"

Her eyes locked onto mine, and the world stopped.

"You," she gasped.

"I didn't jump you." My voice was barely above a whisper. I hadn't even intended to say it out loud.

She yanked the straps of her handbag higher on her shoulder. "What would you call it, then?"

She was in denial, which wasn't uncommon. I denied it myself the first time the sea tried to lure me to my death. "I was keeping you safe."

"Well, in keeping me safe by pouncing on me, you gave me bruises all down my back. Wanna see?" She stuck her chin out in magnificent defiance and turned, lifting the bottom of her shirt. Angry, violet-tinged bruises marred the perfect alabaster skin on the small of her back. I winced at the thought I might have been responsible for the marks. Still, she would've been much worse than bruised had I not come along. She lifted her shirt higher still. From what I knew of her from the tabloids, she did things for shock value. This was certainly no exception, and it worked. My body reacted viscerally to the sight of her bare expanse of flesh and black lace bra.

Two could play this game. "I'm bruised as well. Would you care to see?"

She looked over her shoulder and lowered her eyes to the area in question, then back to my face. And then she did the most remarkable thing: she laughed. As if the sun had emerged from behind a cloud, her laughter lit my soul. That singular sound wielded far more power than any cutting remark uttered by Mrs. McAlister, and for a brilliant moment, my dreams and reality collided.

"I'm sorry I frightened you last night," I said. "I didn't intend to injure you."

"Sorry I racked you," she replied. "I *did* mean to injure you."

"Anna Leighton, this is Liam MacGregor," Francine said with a wide grin. "But you've already met."

"Yes, last night was quite an introduction," Anna said, meeting my eyes directly. "You should really adopt an introduce-yourself-first-then-tackle-later policy."

Francine shook her head. "No. I mean before that."

Anna's brow furrowed. I hadn't truly expected her to remember me, but somewhere in a recess deep in my being, I'd hoped.

"Princess Annabel," I said, bowing.

She took a step back. "Oh, my God. You're . . ." She looked me up and down. "You're Prince Leem. Whoa. You've gotten . . . tall."

My heart felt too large for my chest. She remembered. "Growing up usually yields that result."

"And you talk funny—like somebody out of an old book."

"Yes, that too. Puberty rendered me tall with peculiar speech patterns."

She laughed again, and I was in bliss. This was the Anna I'd imagined for all those years. Not the one from the tabloids, but the one who spent a summer long ago on the beach with me, chasing crabs on the rocks and building sand castles. *My* Anna.

Her laughter faded and silence stretched between us as we simply stared at each other. Surely, memories of childhood were swirling through her brain as well, finding their correct slot and slipping into place, reconciling past with present.

She reached into her handbag. "So, how much do I owe you?" she asked Francine.

"Oh, nothing right now." Francine looked pleased with herself. "You'll probably be needing to use the phone again, so I'll just keep a tab. You just come on down whenever you want."

"Thanks." Her eyes met mine briefly before she lowered her gaze to the floor at my feet, as if hit by a wave of sudden shyness. "Well, bye, Prince Leem."

Then she was gone, cowbell clanging in her wake, leaving behind the ghost of her laughter and the scent of fresh-cut lilies. I filled my lungs with the smell of her.

"Well, what are you doing just standing there, boy?" Francine said. "You can't let an opportunity like this pass you by. Get your carcass out there and walk her home or something."

Muireann had never been all the way into the humans' harbor before. A delightful thrill shot through her body as she watched a male with red hair and a matching red beard untangle buoy lines on some lobster traps on the wooden pier.

"Dad would be really angry if he knew you were here," her sister, Keela, whispered from behind, causing Muireann to flinch and reflexively duck underwater. Staring up, she noticed Keela's head was still above water. She relaxed and allowed her body to float back up to the surface.

"How did you find me?" Muireann asked.

Keela rolled her eyes. "It wasn't much of a challenge. I simply followed you."

The human with the red beard whistled a lighthearted tune as he hefted a trap onto the front end of a fishing boat tethered to the pier. Another man tromped up, his heavy footsteps cutting the whistling short.

"Quick, over here," Keela whispered, bumping Muireann to steal her attention away from the humans.

Muireann ducked behind a boat tied to a buoy a little farther out from the pier and peeked around to watch the humans. "Why must we hide?"

"Because Dad says the harbor is dangerous. The boat motors can hurt us and there are too many humans in one place."

"They seem harmless enough," Muireann said.

"We should go back." Keela nudged her.

"Fine." As Muireann reached the mouth of the harbor, she turned back for one last look. Her breath caught as a human female she'd never seen before strode down the pier on long, slender legs.

4

*Just as the day dawns to the friendless and
houseless beggar who roams the streets
throughout the long desolate winter night—
just so tardily—just so wearily—just so cheer-
ily came back the light of the Soul to me.*

—Edgar Allan Poe,
from "The Premature Burial," 1844

y the time I caught up with her, Anna was
halfway down the harbor pier. She didn't
appear surprised by my presence. She simply
turned and smiled as if she knew I'd come. I
suspected this should shame or humble me, but instead, I was
emboldened. She wanted me to follow her—expected it, even.

She paused to look over the edge of the pier at a barnacle-
encrusted piling. "This place stinks."

"Stinks literally or figuratively?"

One of her perfectly arched eyebrows shot up and she studied me for a moment. "Both." She resumed her stroll toward the
end of the pier and I followed. "How do you stand living here?"

"Is your question rhetorical or do you really want an answer?"

She glanced at me over her shoulder. "Do you have an answer?"

"No."

"Rhetorical, then." She stopped short when a sand louse

darted across the planks in front of her and slipped between the boards near the edge. "Yuck."

"I assume you don't have many of those in New York City."

She stopped beside an empty boat slip and leaned against a piling. "We've got creepy-crawly things that make that bug look like nothing. We have rats the size of small house cats."

I wanted desperately to close the distance between us but stopped well outside of arm's reach. "Sounds lovely."

She brushed aside the hair the wind had blown across her forehead and gave me a leisurely, thorough perusal from head to toe and then back up again. "You grew up good, Liam. And you're educated. There's no school on this island, so you must have been sent out. Where did you go?"

"No one born here leaves. I suppose you could say I'm self-educated."

Again, the eyebrow lifted.

"Liam! What the hell are you doing down here?" Pa's voice shattered the first joy I'd had in a long time as easily as if it were a piece of brittle glass. Wearing his usual flannel shirt and waders, he glared at me, fists clenched. "Get back up to the store and make yourself useful."

His boat was docked in the last slot, and his fishing partner, Johnny, was loading some mended lobster traps on the deck. The storm had prevented them from going out last night, which would put Pa in an even fouler mood than usual. At least he was heading out and not coming in. Still, I wasn't in the mood for an altercation, or a black eye for that matter. Since Ma's death a year ago, he'd had little patience with me.

Anna caught my sleeve as I turned to leave. "Wait. Who is that jerk?"

Jerk was a good word. Not exactly the one I had in mind, though. "That jerk is my foster father."

She had to practically run to keep up with me. "You're just gonna let him talk to you like that?"

"Absolutely." I realized with some amazement that it was she who followed me this time. I shortened my strides slightly to allow her to keep pace without running.

"Why?" She was a little out of breath, which added a whole new appeal to her voice.

The bell on the door of the store clanged as I opened it for her. "Because I have a very strong survival instinct and that 'jerk' controls whether or not I starve or freeze to death. Also because he can overpower me and it's unpleasant when he does. I avoid it whenever possible."

She stopped just inside the door. "He hits you?" She actually looked concerned, as my Anna *would*.

I walked past her to sit on a stool near the counter. "Sometimes."

Her endless blue eyes met mine. "That's not right."

"Most things aren't."

She stared at my face as if searching for something lost. Her brow furrowed as her mind toiled. Undoubtedly my situation made no sense to her. She lived in a world of unfathomable privilege. Yet, from the tabloid accounts I'd read, that luxury didn't bring her happiness. This beautiful creature suffered too, and based on the fact she'd almost succumbed to the call of the sea, she was likely equally miserable. Time expanded infinitely as we stared at each other, souls communing on some level beyond earthly. I thought perhaps only I felt it, but she returned my gaze with equal intensity, as if she too were under the spell.

"Well, you two are back fast," Francine said, jerking me back to reality. She stopped in the doorway to the loading dock behind the store. "Are you hungry? I've got chowder on the stove."

"I . . . um . . ." Anna looked from Francine to the phone. "I appreciate your offer, but I really should go. I'd like to use the phone again first if that's okay."

"Certainly, dear." Francine led her to the console. "What number?"

After dialing, Francine joined me at the counter. Out of politeness, we should have given Anna some privacy, but I felt compelled to stay near her, as if she would dissipate like a dream if I left her presence.

She shifted her weight from one slender foot to the other in nervous anticipation. Perhaps, for different reasons, she feared her parents just as I feared Pa.

"Dad," she said, turning her back to us. "Sorry to leave a message on your cell, but I couldn't reach you at the house. I need to come home. I have to get out of this place. I'm . . ." She glanced over her shoulder at us. "I'll just call back later." Her voice became soft and tremulous. "Please don't leave me here."

I feared for a moment she would cry, but instead, she stood straighter and lifted her chin before placing the handset gently in the cradle. After a deep breath, she faced us. "Thanks."

"It's no trouble, dear," Francine said. "Are you sure you don't want to join Liam for a nice bowl of chowder?"

Her smile was an admirable effort, but clearly forced. "No. I should really go."

"Why?" I asked on impulse. I didn't want to part from her yet. Not when I finally had her near. Not when I felt alive for the first time in years.

"Miss Ronan doesn't know I'm gone."

Francine snorted. "I'm quite certain she does. She doesn't miss anything, the nosy old . . ." Francine cleared her throat. "Never mind. Bad words, thoughts, and deeds come back, you know."

Anna pushed the door open. "Thank you for letting me use

the phone." Her eyes met mine briefly and a lovely flush of pink moved up her neck. "Bye, Liam. It was great to see you again."

"Wait!" Francine trotted behind the counter quicker than I'd ever seen her move. "I need Liam to take something to Taibhreamh."

She pulled out a large burlap bag of coffee beans and set them on top of the counter, giving me a look I knew well. It was the do-as-I-say-and-ask-no-questions look. I'd received it week before last when she bargained with a vendor. "Here. Go with Anna and deliver this to Miss Ronan." She shoved the bag closer to the edge of the counter.

I thought for a moment that Anna would protest, but she shrugged instead. Maybe she wasn't ready to part company yet either—or maybe she was just too polite to object.

Regardless of her motivation, I slid the bag of coffee beans off the counter onto my good shoulder and fell into step beside her, thrilled at the prospect of being in her presence all the way up to Taibhreamh.

5

There are surely other worlds than this—other thoughts than the thoughts of the multitude— other speculations than the speculations of the sophist.

—Edgar Allan Poe,
from "The Assignation," 1834

*T*he path to Taibhreamh, once well worn by villagers walking to and from work at the vast estate, was now overgrown—almost obliterated in some areas like the cliff-side section we were currently climbing. When the Leighton family stopped summering on Dòchas over a decade ago, Miss Ronan let all the villagers employed there go. On rare occasions, she brought in a few for odd jobs, but the only permanent employee other than Miss Ronan was Connor MacFarley, the groundskeeper.

Anna stopped when we reached the top of the first hill. Her shoulders rose and fell as she breathed in the ocean air. She hadn't said anything since we left the village, so I remained silent as well, waiting for her to lead.

The waves, which had been so menacing during last night's storm, lapped the jetty below in gentle foamy caresses. During the day, it was hard to believe the lore—hard unless you had experienced it firsthand. Living on Dòchas had taught me that things were never what they seemed. Something darker always lurked under even the most placid surface.

Anna opened her mouth and then clamped it shut, evidently deciding the words were wrong. I shifted the bag of coffee beans on my shoulder closer to my neck and waited.

Still, she stared over the cliffs at the jetty, her expression as turbulent as the sea had been last night. Without a doubt, she wanted to talk about what had happened but wasn't ready, or perhaps just didn't know how to begin a conversation that unconventional. In her world, things like that didn't happen.

"I hate this place," she said finally.

I did too, but that wasn't what she wanted to talk about. I shifted the bag of coffee again.

"It makes me jumpy—not right, you know what I mean?" She sat on a large stone a few feet from the path and stared at the jetty below.

I knew exactly what she meant. The Otherworlders' presence on Dòchas was strong. Humans have a natural instinct to deny things that are not of the human world, which in most places shuts them out. Dòchas was different: the villagers' beliefs gave the Otherworlders enough power to transcend their plane and interact in ours.

I squatted down and let the bag of coffee fall from my shoulder, then sat on a rock on the opposite side of the trail. "Why are you here, Anna?"

"As a punishment. More like a banishment, really," she said with a shrug, still looking over the cliff at the water. "I pissed my family off."

"Ah." In a way, I was banished as well. We had that in common.

"It's stupid, really." She picked up a small stone and pitched it over the edge to the water below. "My brother's getting married, so they want me out of the way until it's over. The wedding is a big deal because my brother has political aspirations and is marrying the daughter of a governor." She brushed away the hair that had blown across her face. "You know this already, don't you?"

"I know about the wedding because of the newspapers. I know nothing about why you were sent away."

She laughed—not a genuine laugh—it was melancholic and full of pain. My chest pinched at her misery.

"If you read the papers," she said, "then you know exactly why I'm here."

Poor Anna. No wonder the Na Fir Ghorm had almost claimed her. The sorrow ringing in her voice was almost palpable.

"There's a significant delay in my news. The boats only come once every other week in these warmer months, weather permitting. Once a month if we're lucky in the winter, so I'm not very current on the big city happenings."

"That makes sense," she said. "It must drive you crazy to be isolated like this."

"It's all I've ever known. I suppose the lack of comparison to other places and lifestyles keeps me sane." I couldn't help but smile when her beautiful brow furrowed in concern. She was exquisite. Only a fool would send her away. "What did you do to anger your family so?"

"You really do talk funny," she replied.

"You're being evasive. The paper will eventually arrive and I'll read about it. I'd rather hear it directly from the source."

One side of her mouth turned up in a half smile. "It's silly, really. I got carried away at a friend's party at a hotel and ended up . . . a little underdressed." She looked back out over the sea and pitched another rock over the cliff.

"If the tabloids are correct, you've done that before," I answered.

"Yeah, but this time I got arrested and they mentioned my brother's wedding and his fiancée's father's name in every article about it. When the local news showed shots of me wrapped in a blanket in the back of a police cruiser, my mom packed my bags." Her eyes met mine. "And here I am."

"And here you are." Her misfortune had created my luckiest day. "Dòchas isn't really all that bad. Not as bad as jail, right?"

She turned her head back to the sea. "I'm not sure. Jail might have been safer. Things aren't right here."

Perhaps she trusted me enough to talk about what had driven her to the water last night. "I know," I almost whispered, willing her to confide in me. "Dòchas is unique."

After what felt like an eternity, she tore her eyes away from the jetty and leveled her tear-filled gaze on me. "I thought I heard something last night out on those rocks."

She was holding back—testing me to see if I would mock her claim. I'd done the same thing when it happened to me the first time. Fortunately, Francine had been the perfect confidante. "Yes, I know."

"What . . ." Her voice trailed off. I understood her struggle. It was difficult to reconcile the fantastic with reality, hard to accept that things we can't see exist—terrifying, in fact. Anna had every right to be afraid. The fear was good. It would keep her alive. "What did I hear? What was that?"

"The Na Fir Ghorm."

She twisted her fingers together in her lap. "The blue men that wreck ships and stuff? My uncle told me stories about those when I was a little girl. Miss Ronan mentioned them last night."

I nodded.

She sat very still, probably reliving last night's terror. Then she shook her head and stood. "Miss Ronan is nuts and my uncle's stories were nothing but fairy tales." She shook her head and started back up the path. "It's all total crap."

Denial was natural and would weaken the lure of the Na Fir Ghorm. She was emotionally fragile right now and an easy target for them. Best to leave it like this. Francine had allowed me to accept it gradually and I would extend Anna the same courtesy.

Most people on Dòchas had been told the stories from birth. My ma had kept them from me, probably to protect me, though I'd heard parts of stories on the wharf and when people spoke in hushed tones about me. But it wasn't until the sea first called that I became aware of the reality of the Otherworlders' existence. I hadn't been prepared, and neither was Anna.

I got on my knees and shoved my forearm under the bag of coffee. I wasn't sure if I could pick it up from this angle or not. I pinned the bag by closing my bicep over the top, but it was too bulky and awkward to roll up on the first try. I repositioned my arm underneath it.

"Do you need help?" Anna called from up the path.

I did need help, but Pa had trained me to never ask. Self-sufficiency was strength. I positioned myself better to lift and stand at the same time, squatting instead of kneeling this time and placing my feet far apart. Sliding the bag off the counter to my shoulder at the store was one thing. Picking it up from the ground was another thing entirely. I should never have put it down.

"Hey, let me help," she said, lifting from the bottom and lessening the weight of the bag as I stood and rolled it to my shoulder.

Our eyes met, and again it felt to me as though our souls touched, just as they had in the store. Perhaps it was her proximity that induced the spell; most likely, it was my own overactive imagination.

Her gaze dropped to my left arm hanging uselessly at my side and then back to my face. "What happened?"

No one had ever asked me that before. Everyone on Dòchas just knew. If she wasn't ready for the reality of the Na Fir Ghorm, she certainly wasn't ready for the truth about me.

"I was born this way."

She nodded and started up the path again. I let out the breath I'd been holding. She had accepted my answer without issue, buying me more time with her. Time I didn't have a lot of. As soon as she knew the truth, she, like almost everyone else on this island, would have nothing to do with me. She would mock and fear me—but not nearly as much as I feared myself.

Still, I had this moment with her. This brief, brilliant moment to cling to when she was gone again.

"We don't need coffee," she said over her shoulder.

"I know."

"Why do you think Francine sent it?"

She paused briefly at the top of a rise and I caught up. "I wouldn't even begin to try to decipher Francine's intentions. She's a very deep well."

Tilting her head, she crossed her arms over her chest. "You are too, aren't you, Liam?"

I said nothing, as her question wasn't intended to elicit a response.

She captured a strand of hair that had blown across her face and tucked it behind her ear. "Prince Leem was so skilled and brave, he fought off a dragon with only one arm. I remembered that part, I just didn't remember why."

She didn't remember because at the time, it didn't matter. Children look for the good and are not yet tarnished by the darkness. To the residents of Dòchas, darkness was often realized at a very young age. In my case, it had been a part of me since birth.

I attempted a smile. "That dragon didn't stand a chance."

"No, it didn't." She smiled and headed up the trail again.

The path turned northeast and cut through the woods. Dòchas was small but had rugged and varied terrain. When I was a child, this was my favorite part of the island. Like something out of *A Midsummer Night's Dream,* the woods had allotted me hours of fantasy and pleasure. More than that, they had offered me a place to hide.

Sun flitted across the leaves and boughs as the wind caught the branches, giving the woods life and the magical quality I'd always loved. Flecks of light bounced off of Anna's long, silky hair, making her appear as ethereal as Titania.

A high keening pierced the air. The wailing was unmistakable. Once you've heard a Bean Sidhe, you can never forget it. Their mournful wails were singular and I'd heard them all my life. It was part of my punishment, but I'd never heard them during the daylight hours before.

Anna froze and her breathing increased in pace. She'd heard them too. "Oh, God," she whispered.

Why she would hear them was unknown to me. Only those bound to the wrongfully dead could hear their cries.

She bolted up the path without warning, as if she hoped to outrun them. But Bean Sidhes couldn't be outrun. Like all Otherworlders, their powers transcended our feeble human abilities. As expected, the wails became louder. Anna covered her ears and continued to run. I had no choice but to lay chase. If the Na Fir Ghorm tried to claim her when she cleared the woods, they would no doubt have an easy time of it as frightened as she was. "Anna, stop!" I shouted. "They mean no harm."

She didn't slow until she burst out of the woods and into the brilliant sunshine. Even then, she only reduced her pace slightly. Bag of coffee bouncing on my shoulder, I finally caught up. She gradually slowed to a walk, but her features remained ashen.

"Truly, they mean you no harm," I said, catching my breath.

Her lips drew to a thin line as she began the final ascent to the mansion. "I don't know what you're talking about."

"They favor dark places," I said. "In fact, it's rare to hear them except at night."

She slapped a bug away from her face before gracefully picking her way over the low rock wall marking the estate grounds. "I didn't hear anything."

So be it. If she needed to maintain her denial a bit longer, I'd let her. Acceptance is never instantaneous. It took me a considerable amount of time to embrace it myself. Part of me still held out hope it was all just a terrible dream. The other part of me knew better.

6

~

I know not how it was—but, with the first glimpse of the building, a sense of insufferable gloom pervaded my spirit.

—Edgar Allan Poe,
from "The Fall of the House of Usher," 1839

Taibhreamh means "to dream" in Gaelic. Perhaps Anna's ancestors had a peculiar sense of humor because no name could be less fitting for the mansion.

From the highest point on the island of Dòchas, the building, with its sharp, pointed spires, numerous chimneys, and jutting battlements, loomed like an enemy armed for combat. I swallowed the lump of dread in my throat and fell into step beside Anna when the path widened at the base of the hill.

Villagers talked about how beautiful the mansion was with its imposing size and carved marble accents, but I found no beauty here. Whenever I was near, the hairs at the base of my skull tingled. Something instinctual in me sensed evil in the house. Perhaps it spoke to my own darkness.

Anna stopped outside the black iron gate but made no move to open it. Her shoulders rose and fell with a deep breath.

The door to the mansion opened and Miss Ronan stepped onto the porch. She didn't say a word at first; she didn't need to. Her expression said it all. She was furious.

"I went to the village store to make a phone call," Anna said, tugging on the gate. I wanted to help her open it, but I was still balancing the bag of coffee beans on my shoulder with my only functioning arm. The feeling of inadequacy was overwhelming as I watched her pull on the bars. Finally, the door opened enough to give her access.

"You were instructed not to leave the grounds," Miss Ronan said.

I followed Anna up the path to the porch steps.

Miss Ronan looked me up and down as if I were pestilence embodied. "What are *you* doing here?"

"Francine asked me to deliver this coffee," I answered, avoiding eye contact just as I would with an aggressive dog.

I hadn't seen Miss Ronan in years, but she looked exactly as I remembered her: abnormally menacing for such a diminutive woman. She wore an austere black ankle-length dress with her sable hair pulled severely back, making her brown eyes look enormous. Brigid Ronan was the sole witness to my birth and she hated me. "We don't need coffee," she said. "Take it back . . . and yourself with it, Liam MacGregor."

Anna's face flushed red. "I wanted it, and I asked him to carry it here for me."

Miss Ronan pulled her piercing gaze away from me and leveled it on Anna. A myriad of emotions played fleetingly across her features before she resumed her mask of stoic indifference. "Very well, Miss Leighton. You are my superior, of course, as I am in the service of your family. He can leave it here on the porch."

I bent down and slid the bag off my shoulder, letting it fall the rest of the way with a thump.

"Thank you. Now go," Miss Ronan said.

I turned to leave, but Anna grabbed my shirt. "No, Liam."

There was desperation in her voice and eyes. Fear. But just as Miss Ronan had done, she almost instantly slipped an expression of indifference over her features. The only indication of how affected she was could be felt in her trembling fingers entwined in my shirt. She addressed Miss Ronan with a leveled, smooth tone. "I invited him, and he's my guest. Please treat him as such."

Miss Ronan's huge dark eyes bored into mine with such intensity, I was compelled to lower my gaze. She, more than anyone, was aware of the danger I posed.

"I should go back to the store, Anna."

"You were nice enough to lug that coffee up here," Anna said, releasing my shirt. "At least have a cup of it with me. Just a cup, okay?"

Miss Ronan's eyes narrowed. "I will have Mr. MacFarley retrieve the bag." She stiffly nodded to Anna and disappeared into the house.

The air felt lighter once she was out of sight. I took a deep breath and noticed Anna had done the same.

"She creeps me out," Anna said, rubbing her upper arms as if cold.

"She has that effect on everyone, I believe."

"Why on earth does my family keep her on? They fire people all the time at home. Total hard-asses with employees—except with her. It's like she has something on them."

Probably. She had something on everyone. Especially me.

"You wanna come in?" she asked, gesturing to the formidable wooden doors.

I took an instinctual step back. "No. Thanks. I can't stay long. Francine expects me back."

Anna gave an unfeminine snort. "As if! She was practically throwing us at each other. Having you bring coffee? Come on.

We've got coffee and anything else we need up here and she knows it. She wanted you to come with me. She doesn't expect you back soon, Liam." She punctuated her statement by lowering herself onto a wrought-iron bench, arms over her chest.

I leaned against the pedestal of a huge urn near the steps.

"I will not let crazy Miss Ronan tell me what to do or who I can talk to," Anna said with a smirk.

My heart dropped a bit. I was a pawn in her game of chess with Miss Ronan and no more. Still. I was here in her presence, spending time with her. Memorizing her. And that was enough.

Anna jumped to her feet at the sound of boots on the stone walkway at the side of the house. Connor MacFarley came around the corner dressed in overalls and heavy rubber boots. He removed his hat and wiped his bald head with a handkerchief. "Hullo, miss. I've been sent to fetch a bag of . . . Oh, there it is." He easily hefted the bag onto his shoulder and, upon turning, spotted me. "What 'er you doin' here, MacGregor?"

"He's my guest," Anna answered before I could draw breath.

"Guest?" Connor adjusted his eye patch and scowled. "Careful the company ye keep, Miss Leighton."

He made a growling sound and lumbered back to the side of the house and out of sight. Anna said nothing until the clomping of his boots on the stone faded into silence.

"Asshole," she muttered. "And what's with the pirate look? What happened to his eye?"

I relaxed a little when she sat back down, relieved she hadn't heeded his advice and sent me away. "No one knows for sure, but it's rumored his wife did it one night as he slept."

"Ew. Really?"

"So they say. He won't talk about it, so we'll never know for sure."

She leaned back and crossed her legs. "Well, what does she say happened?"

"She accidentally fell from the cliff trail the next day."

Anna gasped. "Accidentally?"

I shrugged. "No witnesses, so yes." I wanted to sit next to her but found it hard to conjure the nerve.

"Wasn't there an investigation? Seems awfully convenient for her to die after poking his eye out."

"This is Dòchas, not New York City. We don't have prisons or police. What happens between a husband and wife is their business. The elders intervene if property or another family is involved."

She draped her arm over the back of the bench. "So who are the elders?"

"Any male over fifty years old." I moved several steps closer. "Connor MacFarley is on the elder board."

She rolled her eyes. "Figures. No women?"

"No."

"Why?"

I leaned against the pillar closest to her. "Our ways are old-fashioned, Anna. All of the villagers are descendants of Scotch and Irish immigrants. They've clung tight to their roots and traditions. Perhaps too tightly. Outside influence and learning is discouraged and in most families forbidden."

"So, you're telling me that if we were married, you could fling me from a cliff and nobody would do anything about it?"

The thought of being married to this magnificent creature seemed too fine a fantasy to cast off quickly, so I paced the porch for a moment, letting the images of us together fill my head as I pretended to consider her question. "Yes."

"That's barbaric. And wrong. You know that, right?"

"Were I your husband, Anna, I would never throw you off a cliff or harm you in any way."

She stepped in front of me to stop my pacing. "That's not what I meant and you know it. I meant letting somebody get away with it is wrong."

"I believe the act of murder is far more egregious than the deception that follows." And I would know. Yet, unlike Connor, there had been a witness to my crime and everyone in Dòchas knew of it. "I firmly believe that evil is punished and crimes are vetted naturally." I was punished every moment by guilt, and the Bean Sidhe made certain I would never forget it. "Sometimes natural and self-inflicted atonement is more severe than that of mankind's devising."

She put her hands on her hips. "Wait a minute. You're telling me that Connor MacFarley is being punished for murdering his wife by some kind of cosmic karma or something?"

"I'm saying that in some cases, being locked up or executed would be a relief. Guilt is a heavy burden, Anna. It weighs down not only the mind, but the soul itself to the point of intolerability. Connor MacFarley must live not only now on earth with what he's done, but in the hereafter."

She strode down the steps of the porch toward the opposite side of the house from Connor MacFarley. "That's seriously messed up, Liam."

I rounded the corner after her. "I'll acknowledge that, from your point of view, it must seem less than perfect."

She made that peculiar snorting sound again, like a laugh in her nose. "Well, if his punishment was perfect, he would be forced to look at *that* day and night." She pointed to a grotesque, winged gargoyle statue perched atop the keystone of a tall arched window. It reminded me of the etchings in my copy of Dante's *Inferno*.

"Ugh," she said with a shudder, still studying the gargoyle. "My great-great-grandfather was a nutcase." She sat on the lip of a round, multitiered fountain and stared up at the gargoyle. "This place was built as a gift to his wife." She choked out a laugh. "Ha! Maybe he should have just shoved her off a cliff instead."

I laughed and sat near her. "It would have been much cheaper and less drawn out a torture, to be certain."

She dipped her fingers gently into the fountain, skimming the surface just enough to cause shimmering ripples in the wake of her fingertips. "He was a total recluse and she was a social-ite. Both of them were loaded from real estate and railroad money. She wanted a castle to rival those of her friends and all he wanted was to get away from the society his wife adored." Anna pulled her fingers out of the fountain and flicked the water off. "Voila! Taibhreamh. Built miles and miles from the Maine coastline on the tiny island of Dòchas. A retreat for the recluse and a prison for his wife."

"And a prison for his great-great-granddaughter, as well," I added.

"More like a reform school, really."

"For those with tendencies to disrobe in public?"

She laughed, and the world stood still. I closed my eyes to focus on the sound. It was like a brilliant tinkling of bells in my ears. The laughter stopped abruptly and I opened my eyes to find her staring at me.

"Are you imagining me naked, Liam?" she asked.

From what I'd read in the tabloids, Anna Leighton was any-thing but shy, but this was unexpected. In retrospect, perhaps

I should have been imagining her naked, but at that time, her laughter was entrancing enough to fill my thoughts. "Um. No. No, of course not."

"What were you doing?" She scooted a few inches closer.

"Listening."

"To?"

"Your laugh. It's beautiful."

One side of her mouth pulled up in a quirky smile. "You're a strange one, Prince Leem."

"So I'm told." Her reference to our childhood relationship made my spirit soar, as did her nearness, but the elation was short-lived. The clatter of Miss Ronan practically dropping a tea tray on a small iron table near the fountain pulled me back to reality. We weren't children now, and I was way out of my league sitting in the garden of a mansion with this beautiful girl.

"I assume you can serve yourselves?" Miss Ronan said before stiffly striding back to the front of the house. She didn't want me near Anna, and who could blame her? I was much worse than Connor MacFarley and she would undoubtedly tell Anna all about me at the first opportunity. All the more reason to enjoy the here and now. I knew I might not get another chance to be alone with her, and that thought emboldened me.

Anna stood and poured a cup of coffee. "What do you put in it?" She was so graceful as she set the silver decanter down on the tray with barely a clink of metal upon metal. Such a difference from my one-armed awkwardness.

"Anything. Whatever you put in yours."

She scooped sugar in both cups and a bit of cream, then stirred them before handing me a cup and sitting back down even closer than before. It felt as though a small electrical storm raged between us and my senses were heightened by her every move. I watched with fascination as she lifted the cup to her lips and blew before taking a sip—so soft and feminine. How would it feel to touch those lips, to feel them on mine?

"Kiss me," I whispered, unsure whether I'd actually said it out loud. "Kiss me, Anna, and I swear I'll never ask it of you again."

I had indeed said it out loud because she lowered her cup and met my gaze straight on. "Well, this is unexpected, Prince Leem. What brought this on?"

"I . . ." What a fool I was—a desperate drowning person grabbing for one last moment of life. I stood and placed the coffee cup on the tray. "I apologize. I don't know what came over me. Thank you for the coffee and the company." How could I have been that stupid? I so rarely got to talk to anyone and I had let my guard down and allowed my base instincts to take over. Base, animal instinct and nothing more. With Anna of all people. Shame rushed through me in a torrent, forcing reason from my head and driving me to leave in such haste, I didn't spare a second look back.

Instinct, so far from being an inferior reason, is perhaps the most exacted intellect of all.

—Edgar Allan Poe,
from "Instinct vs. Reason—A Black Cat," 1840

The ceiling of my birth mother's shed held no great wonders, but I had memorized it to the finite detail. The morning sunlight crept in around the curtains from the only unboarded window, illuminating every familiar imperfection and knothole. This had been a tool-shed to a small house owned by Francine's aunt. Francine had taken pity on my mother and had begged her elderly relative to allow her to live here. It was just big enough to hold a tiny bed, a small, wood-burning stove that could also be heated with propane, a table, and my mother's prized possession, a copper bathtub that was hidden by a curtain tacked to the ceiling. The tub was a luxury few on Dòchas had and no one knew where she had gotten it. There were a lot of unanswered questions about my mother. Thanks to me, they would never be answered.

My foster parents had adopted me on the day of my birth, and I'd lived in their house near the harbor until my foster mother died. After that, my relationship with Pa became so contentious, I had to leave. My birth mother's abandoned shed seemed like the perfect refuge.

Out of honor to his wife, Pa still supported me in a sense. He provided enough propane to keep me alive in the winters, which were brutal on Dòchas, and for that I was grateful.

Dòchas. I laughed out loud. Naming the island Dòchas was a joke of some kind, surely. "Hope." The island of hope. No more hopeless a place existed on earth, I was certain of it. Or had been until yesterday, when a gorgeous ray of hope fleetingly entered my life for a brilliant few hours. I rolled over in bed and touched the small charcoal drawing I'd made last night. The curve of the throat, the sloping shoulders. Such hope. Now gone because I'd allowed thoughts to become words. *Careless fool.*

The wooden planks leading to my door creaked. I held my breath and listened. No one had ever come to my shed before. Even Francine allowed me privacy and never intruded. Perhaps I'd imagined it. Things were always muddled after a bad night from the Bean Sidhes and last night had been the worst ever. It was almost as if they were trying to tell me something rather than just punish me. Their cries had been more panicked than mournful, which was unusual.

No more noise from outside. It must have been my imagination. I tucked the drawing under my pillow and rolled over. I never slept in. Nobody on Dòchas did. Laziness meant death from starvation or cold, so it was a luxury no one could afford. Still, this morning, it certainly was tempting.

The creak sounded again. Someone was definitely outside. "Hello?" I called. I was answered by a delicate rapping against the wood. "Just a minute," I shouted, grabbing my trousers from the floor and slipping them on. The shirt was another issue. Putting it on one-armed took a little longer. "I'm coming," I said, holding the collar in my teeth as I fumbled to get the shirt turned right side out so I could put it on. It had to be Francine coming to check on me. She had instructed me not to come in until lunchtime after I told her about my visit to Taibhreamh.

Rap, rap, rap.

"Hold on." I tugged the sleeve over my bad arm and reached around behind my neck to pull it to my good side. The buttons would have to wait; it took me a while to button a shirt.

Fully expecting to find Francine, I yanked the door open. "Anna." It came out almost as a gasp.

"Heya, Leem," she said with a half smile. She looked tired— as tired as I felt. Her pale skin was marred with dark circles under her red-rimmed eyes. Most people wouldn't have noticed this, but I'd memorized her yesterday. Something had happened last night.

"Are you all right?" I asked.

She scanned me head to toe. "I might ask you the same thing."

I pulled my shirt closed and ran my hand through my bed-tousled hair. I probably looked a mess. "I'm fine."

She leaned to look around me into the shed. "Are you going to invite me in or are we going to stand out here like a couple of losers?"

I shot a look over my shoulder at my shed. "You might prefer it out here. It's not much."

She answered with an arched eyebrow.

I stood aside. "Come in, please." I groaned inwardly as the beautiful creature entered the monster's cave. She looked anomalous among my things—like precious art amid ruins.

She took a deep breath through her nose. "It smells good in here. Like wood and nature."

"Cedar," I said. "The walls, ceiling planks, and beams are cedar."

She studied my bookcase by the door. "All classics. Don't you read anything recent?"

"The books were my mother's. I don't have access to any

43

others. My ma gave them to me saying my mother would have wanted me to have them. Since there's no school on Dòchas, these were my education."

"Who is Ma?"

"My mother died at my birth. Ma was my foster mother. She passed away a year ago."

"I'm sorry, Liam." She resumed her study of my bookcase. "Yuck. Tennyson, Shakespeare, Keats, Milton, Poe, Hugo? Well, if these are what you grew up on, that explains a lot." She ran her fingers over the paint-stained easel in the corner. "You paint?"

"Sometimes." Having her in my space felt wrong. She didn't belong here any more than I belonged in her world.

She studied the splattered tabletop and floor. "You paint a lot." She ran her forefinger over the corner of the table and held up the blackened tip toward me in question.

"Charcoal. I sketch occasionally."

"May I see?"

"No." The word came out louder and quicker than I'd intended, and she winced in response. "I'm sorry. It's just not a good time."

She peeked behind the bathtub curtain. "I did sort of ambush you. Francine said you wouldn't mind, though."

"Why are you here, Anna?" I don't know what answer I was anticipating, but it certainly wasn't the answer she gave.

"To kiss you, of course."

I'd never fainted in my life, but I was certain I was on the brink at that moment. "I'm sorry about that. It was wrong of me."

She smiled. "I thought it was adorable."

Adorable. I stood stunned in the middle of my tiny shack staring at the most beautiful girl in the world, unable to move— hardly adorable at that moment.

She approached my bed and my heart rate doubled. "Okay, how about breakfast, then?" she said.

Breakfast I could manage. Being alone and this close to her would kill me outright. "That sounds perfect. I need to take care of some things first if that's okay."

"What kind of things?"

It was my turn to answer with an arched eyebrow.

"Oh," she said. "I'll just wait outside, then." She flashed me a brilliant smile and slipped out the door.

After taking a deep breath and waiting for my heart to slow to a non-lethal rate, I splashed water on my face, combed my hair, and brushed my teeth using the basin and pitcher on the table by my bed. After a bit of fumbling, I managed the buttons on my shirt and joined her outside. "One more moment, please," I said as I headed to the outhouse.

"Well, that answers that," she said when I joined her on the path in front of my shed. "I noticed you didn't have a toilet."

"The only structure with indoor plumbing on the island is the mansion," I replied.

"Well, that kinda sucks," she said with a smile. "I bet you don't stay in there reading the paper like my dad does."

I laughed. "Certainly not in the winter anyway."

She became serious all of a sudden. "How do you stand it, Liam? Living in a place like this, so isolated and cut off from the real world. So backward."

To me, this *was* the real world. It's all I'd ever known. And all I ever would know.

I inserted my key in my lock. I had installed the lock, probably the only one on Dòchas, after someone had broken in and written threats on my walls last year.

"You don't even have running water," she said. "I'd go nuts."

I stepped past her and struck out on the path toward the

pond. "You don't miss what you've never had, Anna." And at this moment, no words had ever been truer. After my blunder yesterday, my pain and longing had grown far more intense than it had ever been over the years—almost untenable. As much as it thrilled me to experience her in this grown-up state, it might have been better left as it was: a childhood love in a pretend kingdom by the sea—the imaginings of my fanciful mind.

We stepped into the clearing next to the pond and she gasped. "It's gorgeous! I had no idea this was here." It pleased me she found one of my favorite places beautiful.

"It's our ice pond. In several months it will be completely frozen over. The freshwater ice is cut and used by the villagers."

"That makes sense," she said. "No electricity means no refrigerators or freezers."

Several ducks paddled lazily across the mirror-like surface, unconcerned by our presence. The trees reflected in a ring, making the pond appear to fold in upon itself in vivid shades of emerald. A log made a natural bench and I gestured for her to sit.

"So, breakfast?" she said with a grin that exposed her perfectly straight, white teeth.

There were no restaurants on Dòchas. I could have gotten breakfast at the shop with my work credit, but at this time of day, I might run into Pa on the dock and wanted to avoid that at all costs. "We need to discuss our options," I said. "Would you prefer something from the sea or the earth?"

"Anything that works for you, Prince Leem. You should know, though, I don't eat flesh."

Oh, God. She'd heard the rumors. My pulse hammered in my ears and I fought to control my breathing. "Nor do I."

"Cool! So you're a vegetarian too."

Ah, I had misunderstood. Relief ran through my body in a warm cascade. "No. I eat meat."

"But you said—"

"I misspoke."

She absentmindedly picked a piece of bark from the log. "You're kinda weird, you know."

Weird was an understatement. "So, breakfast from the sea is out," I said. "Please wait here. I'll be right back."

The apple trees were full of fruit this time of year and the one on the far side of the pond was laden with them, even on the low branches. I twisted a couple off and slid one into my shirt pocket. They were small compared with the ones we got in the shop, but two should be sufficient.

Across the pond, I met her gaze. It was strange knowing she was watching me. I was unaccustomed to companionship and didn't like the feeling of self-consciousness and inadequacy her scrutiny invoked. What did she see when she looked at me? To her, I probably looked like a pitiful disabled eighteen-year-old stuck in a world inferior to her own. Just like when she gazed from the cliff at the sea, she had no awareness of the opportunistic evil under the surface, just waiting for the right moment to assert power.

I will never give evil the opportunity, I swore inwardly. I would fight it with everything in me.

I lowered myself beside her on the log, far enough away to stave off my impulse to touch her. The impulse was strong— almost overpowering—and based on last night's "kiss me" debacle, I needed to be wary of my weaknesses.

She reached over and slipped an apple out of my pocket, remaining close for a moment—just long enough for her floral scent to fill my nose and unravel me slightly. "You've got it bad, Leem, don't you?" she whispered in my ear.

She had no idea.

I'd read in the tabloids that she was notorious for saying out-landish things to get a reaction. She told the reporter it was her "shock and awe" approach, and I was experiencing both shock and awe at the moment.

I cleared my throat and shifted slightly away. "Be real, Anna," I whispered. "Don't play with me. You sought me out for a reason and this isn't it."

She nodded and took a bite of the apple. "Way to cut through the BS. You're right: I did come for a reason. But I'm right too. Admit it." She took another bite.

Admit I wanted her? I couldn't. It would give the impulse strength, thereby reducing my control. "Why did you seek me out?" I took a bite of the apple in my hand despite my complete loss of appetite.

"Because you know stuff I don't. Because I'm scared and need your help." She placed her fingers on my arm. "Help me, Liam."

Her complete and total candor surprised me. I'd expected her to keep puffing off squid ink to obscure her real motive, but instead, she cut right to the reason for her visit.

"I'll help you any way I can. Always." I pitched what remained of my apple into the pond and a duck pecked at it.

"Weird things are happening. I—"

Pa's voice cut through the trees like an ax. "Liam, you no good loafer! Where the hell are you?" I knew this tone. He'd been drinking. "Get out here!" He banged on my door hard enough to splinter it. The knocks bounced off the trees surrounding the pond. He must have gotten to my shed via the cliff trail. Only a small copse of trees separated us from his rage. "Francine said you weren't coming in this morning. You'd better have a damn good reason if you don't want to freeze this winter. You'd better be in there half dead. If not, you're gonna be."

"Let's go," I whispered, taking her hand.

"Go where?"

I pulled her to her feet. "Anywhere but here."

8

"Invisible things are the only realities."

—Edgar Allan Poe,
quoting William Godwin,
from "Loss of Breath," 1832

Slow down, Liam. I can't keep up." Still clutching her hand, I lifted my arm to prevent her fall as she caught her toe on a root in the path. She was unfamiliar with the landscape and wore a ridiculous pair of shiny shoes that barely covered her feet. "I mean it. Stop!" she shouted.

I stopped.

"What's wrong with you? That guy bellows, and you run like a scared rabbit."

She didn't understand, and there was no time to explain. "Please, Anna. I'll tell you why when we are out of view."

"But I—"

"Please. Indulge me."

She nodded. "Fine, but don't drag me, okay?"

I released her hand and started back up the trail to the lighthouse. She followed along behind me, picking her way over the rocks and roots. Pa's shouts rang in the distance. He'd probably figured out I wasn't in the shed by now.

When we reached the top of the hill, we sprinted behind the lighthouse and I had Anna duck down to stay out of view while

I retrieved the key from where I'd hidden it behind a loose brick in the retaining wall. We pressed flat against the back of the lighthouse and crept to the front. The metal door opened easily and I pulled Anna in with me before locking it tight. The walls of the lighthouse were thick enough to drown out Pa's yelling. In the complete darkness, Anna's fast-paced breaths mingled with my own over my hammering heart.

"Wow. You went all James Bond on me there, Leem," she whispered.

I had no idea who James Bond was, but the sound of her breathy whisper was entrancing. And she was close. If I had leaned forward, we would've made contact. I took a small step back to prevent what would have been a certain disaster.

"How long do we have to wait here?" she asked.

"Not long," I answered. Soon, our breathing slowed and her nearness was no longer painful. Surely Pa had given up his pursuit and had returned to the harbor by now. I felt my way around the brick room until I found the wooden ladder to the observation deck.

"Where are you going?" she whispered.

"Up. Follow me."

"I can't see you."

"Follow my voice. I'm over here." I kept talking until her hands met my chest. "There's a ladder behind me." With one hand still on my chest, she felt for the ladder.

"Got it. Going up." To my surprise, she climbed up into the darkness without hesitation. "I'm at the top. Now what?"

I was right behind her on the ladder. "There's a trapdoor above you. There's no lock. It's a bit weighty, though."

She grunted and then light burst through the widening crack of the hatch as she pushed it open. I admired her graceful ascent into the now-perfect square of sunshine. When I emerged, she was sitting on the deck, leaning back against the casing that used to hold the lamp when the lighthouse was operational.

"If we stand, we'll be spotted," I said, joining her.

She flashed a gorgeous grin. "No duh. Leave the Sherlock Holmes stuff to me and you stick to Bond, okay?"

"You're making pop culture references. I'm not familiar with those men." I peeked over the edge just enough to see Pa staggering down the final hill to the harbor.

She folded her legs under her. "Is he gone?"

"Yes." I leaned back against the casing.

"So dish."

"I beg your pardon?"

Her blue eyes appeared endless in the sunshine. "Why do you run from him? You told me he hit you when we talked in the store, but there's more to it than that, isn't there?"

"Yes."

She waited, but I was unwilling to reveal more.

Her eyes narrowed and she crossed her arms over her chest. "Oh, no way. You don't get off that easy. You said you'd explain why you bolt every time he raises his voice."

A gull screeched in the distance, barely audible above the sea wind. "Pa has a terrible temper and doesn't approve of me in any way." That was kind, actually. He hated me. "When he drinks, he . . . he's not himself."

I'd hoped that would satisfy her, but it didn't.

"And . . . ?"

"And I'd rather not end up at the bottom of a cliff like Connor MacFarley's wife." Though I was sure the entire island would applaud that outcome.

She brushed aside some hair that had blown across her face. "My God. You think he'd kill you?"

I knew he would. "Perhaps, but that's not an issue now. You said you needed my help."

"Yeah, well, that seems unimportant now. I don't have a crazy guy out to kill me."

"Nor do I. He's gone. Please tell me what's troubling you."

She hugged her knees to her chest, put her chin on her knee, and closed her eyes. She said nothing for a long time—so long, I thought she had dozed off. Finally she opened her eyes and spoke. "I think I'm going crazy." The wind whipped her hair across her face again and I resisted the urge to pull it aside. Poor Anna. She looked so tired. "Honestly, I think I'm losing it."

"Dòchas will do that."

She pulled her hair back and held it. "What? What does Dòchas do? How? Why?" Her eyes pooled with tears. *"Why?"*

My own eyes stung in sympathy. "I don't know why." In her case, it made no sense. "What's happening that leads you to believe you're going mad?"

She released her hair and it blew in all directions, obstructing my view of her face. "I'm hearing stuff—voices and screaming." Her shoulders rose and fell with a deep breath. "All night at the mansion, something screams. Terrible, terrifying screams. And when I get near the water, voices call me to join them—and I *want* to." She swept her hair away and met my eyes. "I'm scared, Liam." A tear breached her lashes and shimmered as it made its way down her flawless skin. Unable to help myself, I brushed it away with my thumb. She leaned her face into my touch.

And I was undone.

I pulled my hand away and held my breath. It was essential I focus. She wanted my help. What was it she needed? Certainly not what my instincts were dictating. I stood and grasped the railing, deliberately keeping my back to her so she couldn't tell I was shaken.

From this height, I could see most of the island. At the docks a few fishing boats bobbed next to their buoys. Seal Island was the only thing that broke the expanse of blue sea beyond the yawning mouth of the harbor.

"You think I'm crazy, don't you?" she asked.

"No."

"Ronan does."

I spun to face her. "You told her?"

She pushed to her feet. "I asked her what the screaming was at night and she acted like I was a total nutcase. Told me it must have been something I ate or the caffeine in the coffee you brought."

"Brigid Ronan knows exactly what you heard."

She joined me at the railing. "What was it, Liam?"

It was safer for her if she knew and she was ready now. "Otherworlders. The Bean Sidhes, in particular. You heard them in the woods as well."

"And the voices when I get near the water are really the blue guys that sink ships my uncle used to talk about?"

I nodded. "The Na Fir Ghorm."

"You think they're real."

"I know they are."

Her brows drew together. "You believe there are things communicating with us that we can't see."

I turned leaned against the railing. "Without a doubt."

She shook her head and strolled to the other side of the deck, overlooking the estate and cliffs. I joined her and we stood side by side in silence while she processed. She was smart. This would be hard for the intellectual and analytical sides of her to accept.

"Don't you think there are logical explanations for this? I mean, have you ever seen one of these things?" she asked finally.

"I've never seen an Otherworlder, but many have."

She put her fists on her hips in defiance. "Who? Some whacked-out ignorant villagers?"

I moved to the side of the lighthouse overlooking the woods. "What is the shape of the earth?"

She followed. "What does that have to do with anything?"

"Just answer me. What is the shape of the earth?" In the distance, Megan was playing with a dog on the path. It bounded through the underbrush to retrieve whatever object she'd thrown. It was too far to see her face, but since she was the only child on the island, it was certainly Megan.

Anna made that peculiar laugh-through-her-nose sound. "The earth is round—spherical."

I faced her. "How do you know?"

She rolled her eyes. "Because I've seen it."

"Have you?"

She threw her hands up. "Oh, come on! Are you telling me the earth is not round?"

"No. But imagine the reaction when scholars, with no satellite images to prove it, told people the truth they'd been taught all along was wrong. They were asked to accept that mankind was residing on a spinning ball in space when in fact the earth appeared flat." I gestured to the horizon all around us. "The proposed reality was based on something that was invisible."

She made a frustrated huff. "This is different."

"Yes, but the analogy works."

"No, not really. This isn't science."

"It is, nonetheless, reality, whether it be scientific or otherwise."

She ran her hands through her hair. "You could be wrong."

"So could you."

In the brilliant morning sunshine, her eyes flashed the dazzling azure of a tide pool, nearly taking my breath away.

She stomped her foot. "You're frustrating, Liam!"

"You're beautiful, Anna." Time stopped—as did my breathing. *Oh, God.* I'd done it again. Without waiting for a reaction, I retreated to the other side of the light housing. *Stupid, stupid, impulsive idiot.*

She approached from the opposite side of the deck. "I think I know why you do that," she said with a smile, running her fingers along the rail.

I did too. "Enlighten me."

"Well, I thought about it a lot last night." She clasped her hands behind her back. "You've never been around a girl, have you? I mean a girl your own age."

Unwilling to make eye contact, I stared out at the harbor. "No."

"So, you're just kind of freaking out because you're outside your comfort zone. You've never been up against the real deal before."

The real deal. I smiled in spite of my mortification. "That sums it up well. My interaction with people has been limited, to put it mildly." No one would dare get near me except my ma and Francine. "I'm way outside of my comfort zone. I apologize."

"It's all good. You'll get better at it."

"One can always hold out hope for improvement."

I glanced over and she winked, causing my heart to stutter in my chest.

She spread her palms wide on the railing. "So, why the screaming things? What do they want?"

I was relieved she'd moved the topic away from my faux pas. "The Bean Sidhes wail in mourning for the wrongfully dead."

She continued to stare out at the horizon. "Like murdered people or something?"

I took a deep breath. "Yes, they mourn the murdered."

"So does everybody here hear them?"

I glanced over. She was leaning forward, eyes locked in the distance, which made it easier to talk to her. "No. Only some people hear them." If I were lucky, she'd leave it at that.

"Who?"

So much for luck. "Those with ties to the dead."

She stood up straight. "So, I'm tied to somebody who was murdered?"

"It would appear so."

"Who?"

I shrugged. "I have no idea."

She paced in small, agitated circles. "But you hear them too."

There was no need for acknowledgment. It was a statement, not a question. *Please leave it at that,* I begged inwardly.

She stopped pacing. "Why do you hear them? Who was murdered?"

I closed my eyes and held my breath, willing her to let it go.

"Who?"

I met her eyes directly. "My birth mother."

"Oh, my God. Your mother was murdered? I'm so sorry, Liam." She placed her hand on my arm. "You said she died at your birth. Who killed her?"

I stared down at the patch of trees where she had died. Even from this distance, I could spot the simple cedar marker I'd made as a boy to honor her.

I did, I confessed in my head. It was an answer I prayed Anna never discovered.

An uncomfortable silence stretched between us and I was desperate for a change in topic. "I should get down to the shop," I said.

"But what about your foster father? Won't he be at the harbor?" Anna tucked a strand of hair behind her ear.

"He'll most likely be pulling traps by now. I'm surprised he wasn't out there before daylight."

"It's probably because he was hammered."

My face must have shown my confusion at her words.

"He sounded drunk," she clarified.

"Ah. Yes. He usually is . . . 'hammered.'" I moved to the hatch and stepped down onto the first rung.

The strand of hair blew across her face again, and she placed it back behind her ear. "So, can I come with you? I've gotta make a phone call."

She had asked my permission to join me. This had to be the best and most unusual day ever.

"Of course." I took another step down on the ladder.

She crouched down and touched my hand. "These screaming things and the guys in the water—are they trying to hurt me?"

"The Bean Sidhes are only making noise. The Na Fir Ghorm are dangerous. They derive strength and enjoyment from luring humans to their deaths. As long as you're aware they're trying to trick you, you'll be fine. They prey on emotions. Use your mind . . . and stay away from the water at night."

She nodded and squeezed my hand. "Thanks . . . really."

"For what?"

"For what you did out on the jetty . . . for stopping me from, well . . . from whatever. And for not treating me like a nutcase."

I took another step down. "You are simply 'outside your comfort zone.'"

Her musical laugh filled my ears as I proceeded down the ladder. Before I got to the bottom, the interior of the lighthouse fell into blackness. She had shut the hatch on her way down.

The sudden plunge into darkness startled me. Adrenaline surged to my extremities in a rush, causing an overall tingling sensation. I backed away from the ladder and felt my way around the wall to the door. When my fingers brushed the cool metal door casing, I reached into my pocket for the key, keenly aware of Anna's breathing nearby. I fumbled with the key, trying to orient it in my hand so that I could engage the lock—easier said than done with one hand—and dropped it. The clatter of the metal bouncing across the stone floor sounded almost deafeningly loud in the tiny, light-deprived space.

"Uh-oh," Anna said. She sounded amused rather than alarmed.

I bent down and ran my hand across the stone floor, feeling for it. "I dropped the key. Would you please open the hatch so that we have some light to find it?"

She made no sound. No move to climb the ladder. Nothing.

I turned my head in the direction from which her voice had come. "Anna?" There was a rustle, then light footfalls behind me. "The ladder is the other way," I said.

"Really?" Her voice sounded on the verge of laughter.

I sat back on my heels and listened in the blackness.

When her fingers touched my arm, I startled and gasped involuntarily.

"Shhh," she whispered, running her warm hand over my shoulder and down my good arm to my fingers. She must have been on her knees too because she pressed her body against my back as she entwined her slender fingers through mine.

I froze.

Her breath on my neck was hot. *This can't be happening,* I thought, trembling. Then her warm lips caressed the skin just under my ear, and I was certain my heart would stop.

"Oh, God, Anna."

She released my fingers and crawled to where she faced me. I couldn't see her, but I was keenly aware of her location, as if

I were a compass needle and she true north. My sense of smell was heightened as well as my hearing in the darkness. Her fast breaths and floral scent were intoxicating. I became dizzy as she ran her hands up my chest and around my neck, weaving her fingers into my hair. Her body met mine and her breath caressed my lips, rendering me too stunned to do anything but remain perfectly still, praying the world would stop spinning and suspend me in this unexpected, glorious moment forever.

"Yes?" she whispered almost inaudibly against my lips.

"Yes."

Yet what business had I *with hope?*

                    —Edgar Allan Poe,

        from "The Pit and the Pendulum," 1842

I was certain I'd walked of my own volition from the lighthouse to the harbor, but I didn't have any recollection of it. My bliss obliterated all memory and reason. My mind held no thoughts but of Anna, my childhood dream—now my living fantasy. But I knew deep down that was all it was: a fantasy.

Halfheartedly, I restocked canned goods while Anna talked to someone on Francine's phone. Occasionally, she would grin at me over her shoulder and I'd forget how to breathe.

"Are you going to tell me about it, lad?" Francine asked with a wink, putting another box of canned corn on the counter.

"Not a chance."

She cut the top of the box with a knife. "Your pa was here."

I shoved the cans further back on the shelf and grabbed another. "I know."

"Are you okay?" She held a can out to me.

"Yes. He didn't find me."

"But Anna did." Her grin was enormous.

I took the can and placed it on the shelf. "Yes, she did. Subject closed."

"If I didn't know better, I'd say it looks like you . . . um, bit your lower lip." Francine chuckled and wandered back into the storeroom.

I ran my thumb over my lip where Anna had playfully nipped me—just barely. Her kisses had tasted of apples and sunshine and . . . *hope,* something I'd never tasted before.

At the phone console, Anna twirled a finger in her hair. "So, since I can't have my party in the city, I figured you guys could come here," she said to whomever was on the other end of the line. "The helicopter holds three plus the pilot, Suz." She shot me a look. "It'll be great. . . . Um, Nicky?" She turned her back to me and lowered her voice. "Yeah. Invite him too, I guess. Otherwise he'll be pissy for a month." She shifted her weight from foot to foot. "See you guys tomorrow, then. Bye."

She turned and we stared at each other and I wondered if the scene in the lighthouse played through her mind as well.

She shifted uneasily and brushed her hair behind her shoulder. "So, I guess I should leave you to your work?"

I had no idea what to say. I wanted to beg her to stay for fear the memory of what we had shared would disappear along with her. I placed the can I was holding on the counter.

"Well, I had fun." She gave a half smile. "That sounded pretty stupid, huh?"

Not as stupid as anything I would utter at that moment, so I remained silent.

She took a step toward me, and my heart raced. "Are you okay, Liam?"

I picked up the can and moved it to the shelf. "Beyond okay."

"Oh, good. You got all quiet on me."

I remained with my back to her, reticent to meet her eyes. I wanted to thank her. Tell her she'd forever changed my life, and even if we never spoke again, I was better for her attention, but the thought didn't transfer to speech. "I'm not sure what words are appropriate . . . or adequate for that matter."

"How about saying you'll walk me home or something like that." When I didn't immediately respond, she took a step closer. "Come on, Liam. I know you want to."

Of course I wanted to, but I was also scheduled to work in the store. I hated to ask Francine for favors, as she'd already been so kind to me.

"Francine doesn't mind, Liam, if that's what's hanging you up. She'd like nothing better. We had a nice long talk this morning before I came to your place."

My startled expression caused her to smile.

"Oh, don't worry. It was all good. She's a big fan of yours." She winked, then shouted, "Hey, Francine! Is it cool if Liam walks with me up to the mansion?"

"Of course, lass," Francine called from the storeroom. "I'll just see you tomorrow then, Liam."

"Pardon me for a moment." I strode into the storeroom to find Francine entering stock on her clipboard. "Take the whole day off? Are you sure, Francine? I missed this morning already. I don't want to let you down."

She placed the clipboard on a box. "Liam. You have always struck me as a smart boy. Don't get stupid on me now. That girl likes you. She came looking for you this morning."

"Why?" I hadn't intended to actually say it out loud.

"*Why* doesn't matter. Don't you see, lad?" She reached up and took my face in her palms. "There's a beautiful girl out there who wants to be with you. Go with it. *Run* with it, for God's sake. We're only here on earth a very brief time and should grab every opportunity to be happy. Even if it's fleeting." Tears filled her eyes but didn't spill. "Now go."

She turned her back and picked up the clipboard. Subject closed.

I placed my hand on her shoulder. "I love you, you know, Francine."

"Yes, lad, I know." She shrugged my hand off. "Shoo! Off with you."

Anna was leaning on the counter when I returned. Just the sight of her made my chest tighten.

"See?" she said. "What did I tell you?" She smiled and strolled to the door and I rushed to open it for her.

The sun was shining, but the wind had picked up to the point I had to place my foot against the door to keep it from slamming shut. "A storm is coming," I remarked as she passed.

I followed as she led to the path to Taibhreamh. She was uncharacteristically silent, so I occupied myself with memorizing her as she picked her way up the obstacle-laden path. When she reached the fork for the woods, she turned left toward the jetty instead. I didn't question her or point out the woods path was shorter.

"I'm not ready to deal with Ronan yet," she said, nimbly navigating rocks blocking the path. "Can we hang out down there awhile?"

"Of course." I climbed down the trail to the ocean behind her. She paused briefly to look out at the jetty before sitting on a large boulder near the water's edge. I sat on the opposite side from her. The sun had warmed the stone to where it felt heated from within. The brisk wind coming off the Atlantic Ocean was chilly, so I pressed my palm flat against the stone, letting the heat transfer into my fingers.

"So Miss Ronan says I should avoid you no matter what, but she won't tell me why."

I was too stunned to even reply. Why would she be alone

with me after Miss Ronan's warning? Why had she *kissed* me? I knew I should tell her the truth, but my selfishness prevented me from doing so. Too ashamed to meet her eyes, I stared out over the ocean in silence.

"Francine says Ronan is full of crap. Well, she didn't say it in exactly those words, but that was the essence of it."

Still, I stared out over the water, unable to provide an adequate response.

She scooted closer. "Francine says you are simply a victim of superstition and rumor."

I took my first breath since she had mentioned Miss Ronan. "Francine is a kind person."

A pod of half a dozen harbor seals that had been playing in the cove jettisoned from the water one and two at a time onto the rocks of the jetty to sun themselves. Two emerged from the water and pulled themselves onto a flat, low boulder only a few yards from us.

"Wow! Look at that!" Anna gasped. "They're amazing." One made a grunting sound similar to a belch and Anna giggled. I noticed she was shivering.

"Come," I said, sliding off the boulder. I sat with my back against it facing away from the water, effectively shielded from the wind. Anna lowered herself next to me, eyes still on the pair of seals.

"It's like they're checking us out or something," she said. Both of the small females were watching us warily. "It's like they're listening to us."

"Some believe they are capable of that—understanding human speech."

She rolled her eyes. "More villager superstition."

"Celtic lore, actually, not just local village superstition."

"Unlike the rumors about you, right?"

I gained the courage to meet her gaze. "Those are definitely homegrown."

She searched my eyes and her brow furrowed. "You're different—not like them. Is that why the villagers are scared of you?"

"The fear of something unfamiliar is the source of most types of discrimination, and in my case, it certainly contributes."

She took my lifeless, non-functioning hand in hers and turned it over, palm up. "So the fact you have a paralyzed arm probably freaks them out, huh?"

"I suppose that doesn't add to my appeal."

She pressed a kiss to the inside of my palm, and I imagined I could feel her warm, soft lips there. I stifled a groan. "You don't feel anything at all?" she asked.

"No, but by all means, feel free to continue your experiment."

She laughed. I loved her laugh.

She pulled my arm into her lap. "You also look different than they do. Most of the villagers are pale-skinned and fair or red-haired. You have dark hair and very dark eyes. It's like your parents were Italian or something instead of Scottish or Irish. What did your mom look like?"

I stared at my hand in her lap. What would I not give to be able to feel the warmth of her gentle touch as she ran her fingers over my forearm? "I have no idea what my mother looked like. She had dark eyes, I'm told."

"And your dad?"

"No one knows who he was. She would never reveal his identity. She worked for your family as a maid and then was fired when it was discovered she was with child."

Anna gritted her teeth. "See, they'll fire a poor pregnant girl, but they won't tell that crazy old hag Ronan to hit the road." Her eyes flitted past me to the two seals sunning on the rock. "I swear they're listening to us. It's kinda creepy."

"It's said many seals are Selkies: Otherworld creatures who can change form to that of a human. That they can live in our world."

She stared at the pair of seals, who rolled over and closed their eyes as if ignoring us.

"This exact species of seal lives in Scotland and Ireland, and it's said that they followed our village's ancestors over to the New World to care for us."

"Care for you how?"

"There are stories of them pulling children to safety from the sea. The most prevalent stories are of Selkies shedding their pelts and appealing to humans as lovers."

She stopped moving her fingers over my arm and stared at the slumbering pair of seals. "Those? They're all hairy and pudgy."

I smiled. "Yes, but according to legend, under those pelts are creatures who in human form are so painfully beautiful, they're irresistible."

"Like you," she said with a shy smile.

"Me?" I was so astounded, my question came out as a choked gasp.

"Yes, you." She shifted to where she faced me on her knees. "You're totally clueless, aren't you? Don't you have a mirror in that shed of yours? You're hot, Liam. Hot in a *wow* kind of way." She grabbed my good hand. "I couldn't believe it when I saw you. You're one of the best-looking guys I've ever seen and you've been totally wasted here."

Surely, I was hallucinating. I shook my head and refocused on her perfect face. "God forbid I be wasted," I uttered in amazement.

"That's exactly what I'm thinking," she said as she wrapped her arms around my neck.

...

Muireann kept her eyes closed, feigning sleep until she was certain the couple was no longer aware of her presence. Her older sister, Keela, lay beside her on the rock enjoying the last bit of sunshine before the storm hit. Selkies were masters at predicting the weather, masters unless the Na Fir Ghorm were involved. Storms caused by the Na Fir Ghorm's power were as nasty as their tempers. This was a naturally occurring storm, though, so she knew she still had a bit of time before she had to return to the sea.

She rolled over and watched the couple as they embraced, and her heart sank. She would never experience anything like that—never feel human passion.

She was familiar with most males on this island because she had watched them pull traps for years. This one, though, never came out in the boats, and she'd only seen him once before when she was just a pup. He had been a child at the time, ineffectively pulling lines with one tiny arm, trying to yank the traps that were as big as he was into the boat. The man he called "Pa" became so frustrated, he beat the child. She had considered turning the boat over and would have had she not feared drowning the boy. Instead, she'd bumped the boat and interrupted the beating before the man killed the boy. She'd never forgotten the human child and wondered about him often. And here he was, the most beautiful human she'd ever seen, tangled up in the arms of a human girl. A girl that should be *her.*

Keela stretched and rolled over. "Mmm. Look at them go!"

"Who is the girl?" Muireann asked.

"The youngest of those in Brigid Ronan's care," her companion answered with a yawn.

"Care!" Muireann snorted. "In Brigid's care, she'd better watch her back."

"Well, the male seems to be watching her back—and all the rest of her—just fine, so no worries."

Both Selkies laughed, then froze as the humans paused to look at them.

"I swear they're watching us," the human girl said.

"Let's give them something to watch, then," the boy answered, pulling her back down with him.

A crack of thunder sounded over the horizon. The storm was close.

"Have you ever considered shedding your skin?" Muireann asked, unable to pull her eyes away from the couple.

Keela scooted to the edge of the rock in preparation to wiggle to the water. "You bet. For *him* I would. He'd totally be worth the trouble and risk. You?"

"No," Muireann lied, following her sister into the sea. "Never."

10

It is not impossible that Man, the individual, under certain unusual and highly fortuitous conditions, may be happy.

—Edgar Allan Poe,
from "The Landscape Garden"
(The Domain of Arnheim), 1842

The thunder rumbling in the distance was barely discernible over my pounding heart. It wasn't until a sprinkle of rain hit my face that I was able to force myself away from bliss back to reality. "Anna, we need to seek shelter," I whispered against her lips.

She sat up and stared at the ominous inky clouds poised to overtake the island. "Crap! When did that happen?"

"Somewhere between here . . ." I kissed her lips. "And here . . ." I lifted the edge of her shirt and ran my mouth along her ribs.

She giggled and stood, crossing her arms against the chill in the air blowing off the water. "We'd better get a move on before we get drenched."

"I'm afraid a drenching is inevitable."

My shed was easier to access because the trail leading to it was downhill as opposed to the route to Taibhreamh, which involved a significant climb. I would have preferred to take her to the mansion, but the storm had traveled rapidly and appeared fierce.

The rain didn't begin in earnest until we we'd almost reached the shed. The drops fell in frigid, stinging sheets, making it difficult to see. Anna grabbed the back of my shirt, which made me feel better as I could be certain she was close without having to look back.

Pa had indeed cracked one of the boards in the door earlier, but it could be easily patched. I unlocked the door and Anna ran inside with me close behind. The shed wasn't warm, but at least it protected us from the wind and rain. I threw some branches and kindling into the stove and lit them. "The place will warm up right away," I said.

Anna stood shivering near the bookshelf, arms crossed over her chest, a puddle forming at her feet. I grabbed a towel from behind the curtain surrounding the tub and handed it to her, then used another to towel off my own clothes.

"Thanks. Would you mind if I . . ." She looked down at herself, then back at me, blushing.

Her demeanor was a complete surprise. My understanding of her doubled in that one moment. "Would I mind if you what?"

"If I get out of these wet jeans."

I fought a smile. "Not at all." I turned back to the stove to give her some privacy. The "shooshing" sound of the denim as she peeled it off her legs nearly drove me mad, but I resisted the urge to watch. I focused instead on the fire that had emerged in the stove. I placed the water kettle on the burner.

"Okay," she said. "All clear."

I purposefully only met her eyes, not allowing myself to drop my gaze, but peripherally, I could see that she had left her wet shirt on and had wrapped the towel modestly around her waist. "Are you hungry?"

"Starving."

"I'm afraid I don't have much here." A mental inventory revealed only a couple of options. Biscuits were out of the question because my only flour was the bag Francine had rejected days before because of a weevil infestation. They didn't bother me because I could pick them out and the flour was fine. Food was food, but picking out bugs would undoubtedly be bad form in front of Anna.

I listed off our viable options. "I have jerky, a sleeve of crackers, two eggs, a can of beans, canned corn, and some Chips Ahoy! cookies."

"How about some crackers and cookies?"

My non-canned items, except the flour, were all kept in a metal bucket with a lid that lard had been shipped in. It kept the bugs out, which was why the flour wasn't in there at the moment. I put the crackers, cookies, and jerky on the table along with my metal mug. "Fine china," I said.

Once the tea had brewed, I joined her at the table and filled the mug. "Do you want sugar?"

"No," she said. "This is great."

I unrolled the sleeve of crackers and opened the cookie bag, turning them to face her, then pulled two pieces of jerky out of the bag, offering her one.

"No, thanks," she said, taking a bite of cookie. "I'm a vegetarian."

She had used the same word at the pond. "I take it that means you only eat vegetables? So cookies are a vegetable in New York?" I couldn't keep a straight face and eventually burst out laughing.

She joined me in laughter. "No. It just means I don't eat meat."

"Why not?"

She finished her bite of cookie. "I'm an ethical vegetarian. I don't eat meat because I'm opposed to killing things. It's wrong. If we can live without doing harm to other creatures, we should."

Her stand was admirable but utterly impractical. "I'm opposed to killing as well, but there is nothing unethical about staying alive. I don't have the luxury to turn down food of any kind. I'll starve to death during the winter if I do. Your choice is honorable and practical where you come from. Here, it would never work."

"Wow. I hadn't thought of that," she said.

"The concept of not eating meat for ethical reasons had never crossed my mind, so we've both been enlightened." I placed the jerky back in the bag.

"No, it's cool if you want to eat it in front of me. Most of my friends eat meat. It doesn't bug me; I just choose not to."

"Out of deference to your sensibilities, I'll save this for later. Cookies taste better anyway."

"You are so strange," she said.

"As are you."

She leaned back. "Me?"

"Absolutely."

"How am *I* strange?" She crossed her arms over her chest, which didn't bode well.

"You act as two people. There's the person you pretend to be, and there's the person you really are."

"I don't *pretend* to be anything."

I knew I was treading on thin ice. "I'm not being critical— quite the opposite. I'm simply trying to solve a puzzle."

She rolled her eyes. "I'm the same all the time. I'm not fake,

Liam. There's no puzzle to solve." A crash of thunder caused her to flinch.

I decided I'd pushed her too far and should drop the subject entirely. "Fair enough. Would you like some more tea?" I stood to retrieve the kettle.

"No. I want you to explain what you're getting at." She left the table and paced a circle, clutching the towel at her waist.

I sat and waited for her to calm.

She stopped pacing. "What?"

"Why the towel?"

She made the snort-through-her-nose sound. "Because I don't have any pants on. Duh."

"I understand, but still, why the towel?"

"You'd love it if I lost the towel, wouldn't you, Liam?"

She was completely missing my point. "Of course I would, but that's not my assertion. Please sit down. It's warmer over here by the stove."

After glaring at me for a moment, she acquiesced. "Okay. Let's hear it, then." She pulled out a cracker and nibbled the edge.

"Very well, I'll start with what I've read, then I'll move on to what I've observed firsthand." I grabbed the box of magazines and newspapers by my bed and dragged it across the floor to the table. I selected the tabloid on top, placed it on the table with the cover facing her, and recited the headline, 'NYC Socialite Bares All—Humiliates Family.'"

"That was almost two years ago," she muttered, stuffing what remained of the cracker in her mouth.

I rotated the magazine on the table to face me, flipped to the article, and read from it. "'So what?' said sixteen-year-old Annabel Leighton when we caught up to her the following day at the horse track. 'It's not like I've got anything different than everyone else has.'"

"True," Anna said with a shrug.

I pitched the magazine into the box and pulled out another. "You didn't make the front page this time," I said with a wink, turning to the article. "The headline is 'Leighton Heir Out of Control.' Shall I read from it for you?"

She reached for the cookie bag. "Is that from last Christmas?" I nodded.

"Nah. It's boring. I got a little crazy at a fund-raiser. Too much eggnog."

I put the magazine back in the box. "Were your parents there?"

"Yep. That's not the best one, though. One tabloid's headline was 'Leighton Heir Out of Her Noggin.' Get it? Eggnog?" She broke the cookie she was holding in half.

"I missed that one," I said.

She leaned over to look at the box. "Doesn't look like you miss many, though, huh? Looks a little obsessive or stalkerish."

Her tone was mild, but the words had negative connotations. I knew I had to be very careful or she'd leave and never look back. "You were the only person I'd ever met from the outside world. You were my only connection off this island. My interest in you was . . . and is acute."

She arched an eyebrow and then smiled. "Fair enough. I'll give you a free pass on the box-of-all-things-Anna. Now, what's the point of your show-and-tell?"

"Do you really want to know?"

"Yes." She took a bite from the piece of cookie.

"My theory is not intended to offend in any way."

She pointed at me with the remaining cookie half. "Stop with the disclaimers. I'll let you know right away if I'm offended."

Of that, I had no doubt. "Why did you conceal yourself with a towel today?"

She leaned back and didn't answer.

"Two years ago, you got completely undressed in front of strangers, just as you tell me you did recently, resulting in your current . . . captivity on this island."

Still no response, just a smirk.

"You undress, pull pranks, indulge in all manner of chemical substances, and say outrageous things." I ran my hand through my hair, hoping she'd respond instead of stoically stare at me. Perhaps I'd gone too far.

She leaned forward and put her elbows on the table. "Yep. I sure do."

"And yet, you wrap your body in a towel today."

Shrugging, she popped a piece of cookie in her mouth.

"And you don't act like you reportedly do in the tabloids. You are deep, sincere, and caring—caring enough to not want to harm another living creature."

"Get to the point, Liam."

"There's an element missing on this island that causes you to behave differently. Do you know what I think it is?"

"Logic?"

"No. Your parents."

She pushed to her feet and moved to the other side of the room. "That's bullshit."

"You and I are very much alike. You want more than anything in the world to be noticed by your parents—to garner their love. Just like me."

She turned away, closing me off the only way she could in my tiny shed, so I spoke to her back. "Here's where we differ, though. Since you can't get their attention by being excellent, you do it by acting out. You *demand* to be noticed. I, on the other hand, become invisible. Different tactics to achieve the same desired end result. Only neither of us is effective, are we?"

Her shoulders rose and fell several times, but she didn't respond. I held my breath, hoping she wouldn't leave. I knew my conjecture was right.

"You have no idea who I am," she whispered, still facing away.

I turned her to face me. "I want to know who you are. Everything about you."

She searched my face for a long time, as if an answer were written on my features. "I believe you, Liam. You're the first person who's ever really wanted to know me. Everyone else wants something. Even my friends."

"Even the friends coming tomorrow?"

She walked to my desk. "Oh, you heard that."

"I'm sorry, I wasn't intentionally eavesdropping."

"Yeah, especially them." She pulled a fleck of paint off the surface of my desk.

"Why did you invite them, then?"

"Because tomorrow's my birthday. I was supposed to have a party in the city, but obviously, that plan changed. If I couldn't go to my party, I'd bring it to me."

"I wasn't aware tomorrow was your birthday."

"Ah, so there's something about me you didn't learn in the tabloids."

"There are many things about you left to learn."

"Wanna learn some now?" She let the towel fall around her ankles, and I couldn't keep my eyes from taking in the perfect alabaster skin of her long, slender legs.

"My God, Anna. You're so beautiful."

She wrapped her arms around my neck and I was certain my heart had stopped. Her grin was gorgeous. "Well, like I told that reporter two years ago, 'It's not like I've got anything different than everyone else has.'"

"I'm certain that's not an accurate statement." I planted my feet when she gently pulled me in the direction of the bed. "Wait. No, Anna. Not now."

Her eyes opened wide. "Are you crazy?"

"My body certainly thinks so and may never forgive me. But, no, I'm completely sane."

She dropped her hands to her sides. "You're going to reject me, *really*?"

"No. No, Anna. Just the opposite. I'm in no way rejecting you. I'm accepting you—all of you. The intimate moments you've already given me have surpassed anything I could conjure in my wildest imaginings. Let me learn who you are inside your head and your heart first, then everything else will be even more amazing."

"You're scared, aren't you?"

"Terrified."

She picked the towel up from the floor and wrapped it back around her waist. "Offer rescinded, then," she said with a wink.

"Not forever, I hope."

"No. Just for the next ten minutes or so."

I groaned. She had absolutely no idea how difficult this was or how badly I wanted her, but I wanted no regrets from her. She was operating on habit and past expectations. The desire was uneven. I wanted her to want me as much as I did her—to need me as much as she needed to breathe.

For the first time in my life, I felt like there was hope for happiness. Not hope just for me, hope for both of us. She'd been living a desolation of her own, equally miserable to that of mine. And I knew that when she ultimately returned to her life, leaving me alone in mine, we would both be stronger and better for having shared our souls with each other.

"The rain has stopped. May I walk you home before the next band of showers moves ashore?" I asked.

She lifted an eyebrow. "So formal. I suppose I'll need pants for that."

"Miss Ronan would appreciate it, probably."

Still holding the towel, she picked up her wet jeans. "Getting into these will be a challenge."

I turned my back and stared out the foggy glass of my window at the blur of trees swaying in the strong offshore winds. "You strike me as a girl who's up for a challenge."

She made a grunting sound as she dealt with her uncooperative wet jeans. "You certainly threw the gauntlet down in challenge today, Liam MacGregor." The zing of her zipper was followed by the click of the snap at her waistband. "I hope you know you're going to lose."

"I certainly hope so."

11

*The fury of a demon instantly possessed
me. I knew myself no longer. My original
soul seemed, at once, to take its flight from
my body; and a more than fiendish malevo-
lence . . . thrilled every fibre of my frame.*

—Edgar Allan Poe,
from "The Black Cat," 1843

I remembered seeing helicopters come and go from the mansion when I was younger, but this was the first time I'd been close to one.

Like a fantastic, terrifying dragonfly, it hovered overhead before descending on the circular landing pad, creating gale-force winds.

I shouldn't be here, I told myself.

When I walked Anna home yesterday after the storm, she insisted I come today to meet her friends. I knew our worlds were incompatible and wanted no part of this gathering. Then she kissed me with such passion I would've agreed to most anything—and I did, so here I was, full of dread, bracing myself against artificial wind and outsiders.

The first person off the helicopter was a thin, short, blond girl who ran to Anna and tackled her in a hug. They were joined by a much taller girl with short brown hair who embraced her in a similar manner. Last off was a tall, fair-haired guy about my age. He had broad shoulders and wore a dark green sweater and jeans. I recognized him from the tabloids. He was in many of the pictures with Anna. Unlike the girls, he didn't run; he strolled slowly over to the group, pulled Anna to him, and kissed her on the mouth.

This was the first time I'd ever felt the demon inside me stir. Until this moment, I'd always held out hope it would remain dormant forever. A buzzing filled my head and a sickening churn consumed my stomach, making it hard to breathe.

Anna pushed away from him and immediately sought me with her eyes. I pretended to study the helicopter, walking behind it to put more distance between the group and myself, desperately attempting to force the demon back. *I shouldn't be here.*

The helicopter engine roared and the wind increased until the machine lifted off and eventually zoomed out of sight. The silence it left behind was almost hollow.

I swallowed the lump in my throat as Anna led her group of friends my way. Everything in me wanted to run away as fast as possible—to run and keep running. But I held firm. She had asked this of me, and I had agreed.

The short blonde took rapid steps much like a sandpiper in order to keep up with her long-legged companions. Anna and the taller girl walked arm in arm, and the boy trailed behind them, shoulders back, looking directly at me. Again, the demon stirred, causing the hairs on my neck to stand on end.

"Hey, guys. This is Liam. He lives here on the island," Anna said. "Liam, this is Suzette."

The short girl stepped forward and extended her hand. "Hi, Liam. You can call me Suz."

I'd never shaken a girl's hand. In fact, Anna was the only girl I'd ever touched. Tentatively, I held out my hand and she placed hers lightly in it. When I just stood there, stupefied, she squeezed my fingers and smiled. "Nice to meet ya."

"This is Mallory," Anna said. The tall girl smiled and waved. Relief washed through me when I realized I wouldn't have to shake her hand.

"Nicholas Emery." The boy extended his hand. I took it and he squeezed so hard while shaking it, I was certain my bones would break. The demon surfaced and I squeezed back with equal force until the guy let go.

"Let's go inside," Anna suggested, tugging Nicholas by the sleeve. "We have this freaky housekeeper, but she can really cook and she's putting dinner out."

"There's no way she cooks as good as you do, Annie," Nicholas said. "Nobody does."

My demon rolled over.

"I can't wait until you open your restaurant," Mallory said, stepping up on the porch.

Anna shrugged. "Dad hasn't even agreed to culinary school yet."

I stood frozen. I had no idea Anna wanted to open a restaurant. My feeling of being an outsider doubled. I didn't belong here.

Suz paused at the stop of the steps. "I'm starving. Come on, Liam."

I'd never been inside the mansion and had always hoped to keep it that way. The entry was tiled in dark marble with wood paneling stretching upward to the arched ceiling. The dominant feature was an ornately carved wooden staircase originating from the second-story balcony and parting in a curved V to form two symmetrical arches—the result reminiscent of mandibles on an enormous spider.

At the top of the staircase, an oil portrait of a man I assumed to be the mastermind behind the building's construction, Anna's great-great grandfather, stared down with indifference.

"Oooh. Cool place," Mallory said, rotating in a circle in the middle of the room.

Nicholas was studying a device in his hand. "I'm not getting any signal."

The petite blonde, Suzette, rubbed her arms as if they were cold, but if the house were affecting her as it did me, her goose bumps were not a result of the temperature.

Anna paused in the arch to the left of the stairs. "Phones don't work here. There's no cell tower on the island, Nicky."

He shoved the phone into his back pocket. "That explains why you haven't answered my texts. I just thought you were being a bitch."

My vision blurred momentarily and my jaw clenched so tightly, it ached.

"Well, I *was* being a bitch, but I never received any messages," Anna said with a smile, disappearing into the next room.

Mallory and Nicholas followed her, but I stayed just inside the entry, feeling completely outside myself.

"You coming?" Suzette asked, pausing in the archway.

"In a moment," I answered, feigning interest in a tapestry over the doorway until she disappeared into the next room.

I took a deep breath and let it out slowly. When Nicholas had called Anna a name, the beast inside me stretched again, inspiring the impulse to charge him. I was reticent to join Anna's party until I was certain I had control over it.

"Hey." Anna's gentle touch on my shoulder dissipated whatever darkness had overtaken me. "What's going on?"

"Nothing. I . . ." Her cobalt blouse accentuated the darker ring around her irises. I longed to hold her, to kiss her, to drown in those eyes and keep the demon inside me locked away. "Anna, I have to leave."

"Why?" Her brow furrowed.

"I don't belong here. I shouldn't be here."

"He's right," Miss Ronan said, causing both of us to jump. "He does not belong here." She was carrying a large silver tray with a domed cover and didn't even pause on her way through the entry hall to the room where Anna's friends were laughing and talking.

Anna shuddered. "Oooh. She gives me the creeps. I need to put a collar with a bell on it around her neck like a cat so she can't sneak up on me like that. She does it all the time."

The image of Miss Ronan with a bell around her neck made me smile.

"Really, what does she have against you, Liam?"

The truth. "The same thing everyone else does, I suppose."

"Not me." She stood on her tiptoes and brushed her lips across mine. "Please stay. Just for dinner, okay? Then you can take off if you still want to."

"Anna, I—"

"I have a very good argument to convince you." She circled her arms around my neck and pulled my lips to hers. In a few moments, any objection I had to staying dissipated. She released me and we stared at each other, breathing heavily.

"Well?" she said.

"Your logic is irrefutable."

She winked. "Thought so."

Taking my hand in hers, she led me through the arched doorway into a large dining room. It had a high vaulted ceiling and parallel vertical support beams that made it look as though we were inside the rib cage of a huge beast. At the end of the room, there was an enormous, ornate fireplace with flames blazing to the top of the opening, which was tall enough for a man to walk under—like a passage to hell.

I shuddered.

A long, dark wood table was covered in dishes containing more food than I'd ever seen in one place—even village gatherings. Five of us couldn't possibly eat this much.

"We're going super casual and eating over by the fireplace," Anna said. "Go ahead. Dig in!" Her friends picked up plates from the end of the table and filled them with pork, turkey, fresh vegetables, and bread. My mouth watered and my stomach rumbled, but I waited, watching to see how they managed the food so I wouldn't do something wrong. They held their plates with one hand and procured food with the other. Because I only had one functional arm, I would have to set the plate down and bring the food to it, and there wasn't enough room to set it down except at the end, which would make it awkward. I would certainly drop the item from the serving utensil before I made it back to the plate.

"Go ahead, Liam," Anna said as her friends moved to the fireplace.

"No, I'm fine. I ate before I came." My stomach rumbled again, exposing my lie.

Anna's brow furrowed, then relaxed. She glanced at my useless arm and smiled. "Come with me." She handed me a plate and grabbed one herself. Wordlessly, bringing no attention to us at all, she led me down the table, heaping my plate with large portions of meat along with the side dishes but only fruit, vegetables, and bread on her own. Her friends were deep in conversation in a sitting area by the fireplace and didn't even notice she was assisting me.

Nicholas gestured for Anna to sit next to him on a small sofa facing the fire, but she plopped down in an overstuffed chair next to Mallory instead. I chose the chair opposite Anna since my only other option was sharing the sofa with Nicholas, who was glaring at me like he wanted to throw me into the fireplace.

"I love this place," Mallory said, cutting a carrot with her fork. "Why haven't you brought us here before?"

Anna shifted uneasily, meeting my eyes fleetingly before she answered. "Well, we don't come here anymore. My parents used to when I was a kid, but we stopped when my uncle died."

"So, this was your uncle's house?" Nicholas asked.

Anna shoved some rice around on her plate with her fork. "No. It's my mom's. Her grandfather built it, so it passed from her mom to her. Uncle Frank just lived here."

I'd never tasted turkey like this. It practically melted in my mouth. I fought the urge to gobble it as fast as possible and instead cut off small bites with my fork, emulating my companions.

"So, why don't you come anymore? Does it make your mom sad?" Suzette asked.

Anna shrugged. "I don't know. We just don't."

"Man, if I had a place like this, I'd be here all the time," Mallory said.

"Me too," Nicholas agreed. "Hey, why don't we go check out the cliffs and jetty tonight? It looked cool from the helicopter."

"No!" Anna said, then tempered her tone with less panic. "No. I'd rather just hang out inside tonight and catch up with what's going on at home. I'll give you a tour in the morning."

My hackles stood at the sensation of being watched. I looked over my shoulder to find Miss Ronan lurking in the doorway. She met my gaze directly, her dark expression unchanging. "Will you be needing anything else, Miss Leighton? If not, I'm going to retire for the night. The new maid will clear the dishes when she comes in the morning," she said.

Anna flinched at the sound of her voice, catching her fork before it slid from her plate. "No. Thank you. That's all."

Miss Ronan slipped from view.

"God. Why does she sneak up like that?" Anna said through her teeth. "I hate it."

"We had a housekeeper like that when I was a kid," Mallory said. "Mom fired her."

"We have one that sings all the time," Nicholas said from the table, where he was loading his plate with seconds. "It drives me crazy. My little sister loves her, so my parents make me be nice to her."

"It's really hard to find good help," Suzette said. "At least she's an excellent cook, Anna."

"Yeah," Anna agreed. An awkward silence filled the room. I felt certain the mood and conversation would be much different were I not present.

I was content the demon was dormant at the moment. It seemed directly tied to Nicholas, so my strategy was to avoid him at all costs so as not to awaken it again.

"So tell me what's going on back at home," Anna said.

Her friends then launched into animated descriptions of parties, people, and events so foreign to me, I had no desire to keep up. I focused instead on the amazing feast in my lap. I could have lived for a week on this amount of food. As much as I disliked Brigid Ronan, I had to admit the food was delicious and I'd never tasted anything like it. Occasionally, I would look up to find Anna watching me. She always responded with an encouraging smile.

"So how long are you going to be here?" Mallory asked, setting her plate on the low table in front of us and folding her napkin.

Anna shrugged. "Until my brother's wedding's over, I guess."

Mallory laughed. "Yeah, you can't very well embarrass the bride from here, can you?"

"Who cares if she's embarrassed?" Nicholas said, putting another slice of roast beef on his plate. "She's a bitch."

"You don't even know her, Nicky," Suzette said, clutching her plate tightly. "Anna's brother likes her."

Nicholas strode to the sofa. "He likes her money and connections. Both sets of parents had this marriage worked out from the time they were born." He walked behind Anna's chair and placed his hands on her shoulders. "Just like you and me, huh, Annie?"

Anna's eyes narrowed. "Shut up, Nicky."

A prearranged marriage? The demon roiled inside. No longer hungry, I set my fork down.

Nicholas looked right at me as if issuing a challenge. He was handsome, rich, and educated. What threat could a one-armed, destitute villager pose? None. I didn't belong in this world.

"I need to go, Anna." I stood. "It was nice to meet all of you." Not wanting any objection from Anna, I strode to the exit as quickly as possible, trying not to run like the coward I was.

"Leaving so soon?" Miss Ronan said, opening the door for me.

"Liam, wait!" It was Suzette.

From the dining room, Anna's and Nicholas's angry voices filled my ears.

"Nick was just trolling you. Don't let him get to you like that. It's a game to him," she said.

"I don't play games."

"Look. Anna will set him straight and it'll all be good. Come on back in. We didn't even get to know you."

"There is nothing to know," I said.

The smirk on Miss Ronan's face made my stomach churn.

Suzette glared at her, then walked through the door she held open. I followed her out. "Excuse us," Suzette said, taking the door handle from Miss Ronan and pulling it closed behind us.

"Come talk to me, Liam," she said, stopping next to the fountain at the side of the house. I hadn't really paid attention to it when I saw it before. I had been too distracted by Anna. Grecian dolphins spit water from the top level, and the water trickled over the edge of three bowls, flowing finally into the large basin at the bottom with a bench-like ledge making the surround. I imagined Anna's slender fingers trailing lightly along the surface as she had done when we were here the other day—trailing lightly over my skin as she had done on the rocks yesterday. *Anna. Promised to Nicholas.* My heart sank.

I had no right to brood. She could never be mine. Deep down, I knew this. Still, somewhere in that deep recess of my heart I kept secret—even from myself—I had hoped. But I hadn't even realized it until now.

Ridiculous, I told myself. She was as far out of my reach as the full moon over our heads.

"How did you meet Anna?" Suzette asked, strolling to the opposite side of the fountain.

"When we were children, her family came here frequently. Her nanny allowed her to play with me on the beach. We played together every day for an entire summer."

"So you've known each other a long time, then." Suzette sat on the ledge of the fountain. "Sort of grew up together?"

"Not really." The next winter, her uncle disappeared. The commonly held belief was that he drowned. The family only visited a couple of times after that and didn't stay more than a couple of nights. "We haven't seen each other since that summer."

I liked Suzette. She seemed genuine and kind. I stared up

at the gargoyle glaring menacingly at us. Suzette didn't belong here either. "How about you? Did you meet Anna at school?"

"Yep. We go to school together. She was the first friend I made there." She took a deep breath. "It's hard breaking into that world."

I was certain it was. My island was grim, but at least I knew its perils. A world as complicated and vast as Anna's would be untenable.

Suzette tucked her straight blond hair behind her ear. "My dad came from a poor family and made it big in computer software and games. We moved from California to New York a couple of years ago when his company expanded, and he enrolled me in the same elite private school as Anna and the gang. I told him I knew I'd hate it and begged him not to. I'd gone to public school in California."

"Why did he do it, then?" I asked.

She shrugged. "Because he wanted me to have all the things he didn't have as a kid. All the best things, and this school is the best."

"He must love you very much."

She smiled. "Yeah, I guess he does. Anyway, I didn't think I'd find a single friend. But then I met Anna and she just kind of pulled me in."

She had pulled me in too.

"Nicky isn't a bad guy." She folded her hands in her lap. "He's just spoiled. He's used to getting what he wants. And honestly, you're in the way of getting what he wants tonight."

He wanted Anna. The beast inside me growled and my head buzzed. "I have to go."

She stood. "So, you'll just let him get his way as usual."

"If Anna wishes it, yes." I was completely out of my element, and the strange sensation of my demon awaking made me uneasy. The urge to get away from Taibhreamh was bordering on a frantic need. "Good-bye, Suzette. It was a pleasure meeting you."

"She likes you," Suzette called to my back as I rounded the corner of the house. "A *lot*."

I stopped, allowing her to catch up.

"I can tell by the way she looks at you and acts around you. I've never seen her like this. And you like her too, don't you?"

"Of course I do."

"But not enough to stay?"

It was wrong of me to interfere in her life. If I stayed, it would be because of selfishness. Besides, I didn't know how much longer I could keep the beast at bay. "I like her enough to leave."

12

A feeling, for which I have no name, has taken possession of my soul.

—Edgar Allan Poe,
from "Ms. Found in a Bottle," 1833

Muireann swam closer to the source of the voices, careful to stay out of sight. The Na Fir Ghorm were frantic to take a human life. After hearing the leader berate his son, she knew it was because they were growing too weak to remain in the human realm. It was rare for the humans to get near the water at night, but evidently, one had and they were making the most of it.

"Come," one called. "The water is peaceful and warm. Your mother's arms await."

"Yes. Be with her in a heavenly embrace," another said.

The water was freezing cold and nothing waited but a horrible death for the benefit of these despicable creatures. Muireann hated them with their blue skin and black hearts.

"Nothing holds you here," one called to the human making his way along the trail. "Be released from your mortal bonds. Join us."

Muireann rose to the surface to take a breath. It was *him*. Her human. So beautiful, walking along the cliff-side trail. The moon was full, so she could see him easily. She wanted to interfere but knew it would mean disaster for her pod. *Please be strong,* she thought.

"I will never join you," he shouted.

Muireann swam closer, relieved he was not in a suicidal trance as the Na Fir Ghorm wished. They had the ability to hypnotize with their voices, and it worked on the weak of mind and sick of heart. Her human was still strong. Why was he wandering the island at night?

"Your mother waits to hold you in her arms," one called to him.

"My mother is dead," the human yelled back.

"Find her killer!" a Bean Sidhe shrieked in the ancient tongue.

"Yes, only you can reveal the wrongdoing!" another wailed.

Muireann swam parallel to the shore, staying even with the human as he stomped along the path.

"He can't understand you, idiot creatures!" a Na Fir Ghorm said. "Stay out of this. The broken one is ours."

The broken one! Muireann's heart raced. It was *her* human the leader wanted dead. The one on whom he had sworn revenge.

Still, the Bean Sidhe moaned and shrieked, drowning out the Na Fir Ghorm.

The human covered an ear with his good hand and pressed the other against his shoulder but didn't falter from his progression down the path, which veered inland, taking him away from the shore and out of harm's way.

I pounded on the store door again—harder this time. I had no idea whether Francine could hear me from her upstairs bedroom or not.

The harbor lay eerily calm, and the full moon reflected off

the mirror-like surface of the water, making the middle of the night seem like dusk. I had wandered the dock for a while, trying to decide what to do, and this seemed to be the best course of action. It was unfair of me to wake her up, but I needed answers before something awful happened.

Her window slid open with a bang. "What in the name of heaven are you doing out there, lad? Are you in trouble?"

I backed several steps away from the door to get a better look at her. "Yes. No . . . I don't know."

"Stay there." She slammed the window shut and soon opened the door for me.

I followed her into the storeroom behind the counter and sat at the table while she put the teakettle on. We didn't talk for a while as she bustled about collecting cups, sugar, and tea. She placed leaves in the little metal diffuser and dropped it into the kettle. "Now, tell me what's going on." She joined me at the table, placing the sugar bowl between us.

"The demon inside me has awakened," I blurted out, not knowing how else to put it.

"I've told you all your life that there is no demon. It's only a vicious rumor started by a miserable woman."

I ran my hand through my hair. "No. I'm telling you, it's there. I felt it. It made me crave violence, just like everyone has predicted."

Francine wrapped her robe closer around her. "How's it going with the Leighton girl?"

"Francine! Did you hear me? The demon has emerged."

She smiled. "Yes, I heard you loud and clear. We'll get to your demon, but first I want you to calm down and talk to me. How's Anna?"

"She's good."

"Just good?"

I took a deep breath. Being around Francine made me feel safe again, and her lack of panic over my revelation brought me a modicum of comfort. "She's great . . . amazing. Beyond amazing."

Francine grinned. "And?"

"She's beautiful and brilliant, and when she kisses me, I swear I can do anything. I can fly, Francine."

"That's how love makes you feel, lad. Like you can fly." The teakettle whistled, and Francine left the table.

Love. That was the problem. On my way from the mansion, several things occurred to me. One was that the demon was real, two was that I was in love with Anna, and three, the two things were somehow related.

Francine returned to the table with two cups of tea. "Now, you and I have never really talked at length about this, Liam. I simply told you my theory and I stand by it. The demon is a rumor."

I shook my head. "It's real."

"Tell me first, who did you hear it from and what you know about it?" She spooned some sugar into her tea.

"I've heard—"

Francine interrupted me by making a tsk-tsk sound. "First, start with the source."

"Well, villagers. I've overheard it my whole life. Everyone knows about it."

She took a sip of her tea. "So nobody has told you directly."

"Well, no, but—"

"So you've overheard gossip and rumor."

She was trying to make me feel better by discounting the source, but I had *felt* it. "The story is consistent regardless of the source."

She added another spoonful of sugar and gestured to my cup with her spoon. "That's getting cold."

I picked up my cup. "When I was born, it's said that a demon possessed me. That it put on my human skin but did so erroneously or was interrupted before it got its left arm in correctly, which is why my arm doesn't work. That my flesh is animated by a demon and when I reach my prime, the demon will emerge, taking over my ability to reason, and kill those I love, just like it did at my birth when I murdered my mother."

"Oh, my God." The sound of Anna's voice caused me to drop my tea, spilling it all over the table and floor. I jumped to my feet, wanting more than anything to run.

"We didn't hear you arrive, lass," Francine said, sopping up my tea with a towel she had pulled from the stove handle.

Anna twisted her fingers in front of her, clearly uncomfortable. "When I came in, I said hello, but the teakettle was making a racket. You just didn't hear me."

I took several steps back.

"I didn't mean to sneak up on you. I'm really sorry." She met my eyes, but I looked away, focusing on the utensil jar on the counter instead. How could I face her now that she knew the truth?

"Well, you might as well join us since it concerns you too. Would you like some tea, lass?" Francine asked, dropping the towel in the sink.

"It doesn't concern her," I said, a little louder than intended.

"No, thanks." Anna sat in a chair at the table.

I gave Francine a pleading look.

"It's my home, lad. I invited her, so she stays."

I closed my eyes and leaned against the wall. She knew. She would hate and fear me now, like everyone else. "Well, I suppose it's best you found out now, before we . . ." I glanced at her briefly, then lowered my eyes to the floor. "Before we continued our friendship."

"Well, this certainly explains a lot," Anna said.

Francine sat back down and picked up her tea. "You sure you don't want some?"

"Positive," Anna said. I could feel her looking at me, but I was too ashamed to meet her eyes. "So, Liam, do you really believe that story?"

"How did you get here?" I asked. It came out harsher than I'd intended, but it occurred to me that she could have died on the way had the Na Fir Ghorm discovered her.

"I flew. Can't you fly, Liam?"

She'd heard more than she had indicated. My face grew hot. "It's dangerous walking near the water at night," I said. "The Na Fir Ghorm—"

"Yeah, those blue guys are a pain in the butt, I know. I went through the woods so I only had to deal with the shrieking things. You said they were harmless, remember? I never got near the water until I reached your shed."

My stomach lurched. "You went to my shed?"

"Well, yeah. Where would *you* have looked for you? When you weren't there, I came here, hoping you hadn't listened to the blue guys and offed yourself. You were acting pretty weird."

I approached the table and stood behind my chair. "Anna. I cannot impress upon you enough the dangers this island holds. You must try to stay indoors at night."

She laughed. "That's pretty hypocritical coming from demon dude. And weren't you going to turn me out just a minute ago?"

"Well, no, I—"

Francine chuckled.

"It's not funny," I said.

"No, it's not," Anna answered. "It's twisted and screwed up. It's one of those laugh-or-you've-gotta-cry situations. Could you sit down, Liam? You're making me uncomfortable."

I slid into my seat.

Francine moved to the stove and refilled my cup, poured a fresh one, and returned, placing the cups in front of us. "What kind of hostess would I be if I didn't insist? Tea is calming, you know."

"I guess it's best you hear the truth from me," I said, spooning sugar into my cup.

She made that peculiar snorting sound. "That's not the truth. That's a bunch of crap. It's nonsense. And don't give me the flat-earth analogy again, MacGregor. It's not going to work this time. You are no demon."

"No, that's not the assertion," I said. "A demon lies within, wearing my skin, waiting to overpower me."

Francine shifted in her chair, as if settling in for a long story.

Anna picked up her teacup. "Are you aware that since the beginning of time, all over the world, babies with disabilities have been rumored to be evil or wicked because of deformities when, in fact, it is just a natural defect or condition?"

"No."

She returned her cup to the table and ran her finger idly over the rim. "It's true. We studied it in Sociology my junior year. In most cases, the superstitions came about as a way to justify killing babies that would be a hassle for their tribe or family to raise. I suspect since your arm doesn't work right, they used that to prove the story they'd been told about the demon when it's probably some totally normal birth defect. I bet if you hadn't been born with a bum arm, they wouldn't have held on to the demon story all this time. It's nothing more than fear of something different."

Francine poured herself more tea but said nothing.

"I would like nothing better than to believe fear of a deformity is what has perpetuated the rumor of the demon, but I can't," I said. "I've felt it. It awakened today."

"Aye, you said that," Francine said. "Tell me about it. When did it happen?"

I closed my eyes and relived the day. "The first time was when I met Anna's friends."

"I need a specific moment," Francine said.

I was embarrassed to bring it up, but it bore revealing because even the memory caused the beast to stir. "When Nicholas kissed Anna as he got off the helicopter."

Francine's expression did not change. "Did it happen again?"

"Yes. When I shook Nicholas's hand and he tried to crush mine, and again when he called Anna a name. That was the worst. I almost lost control to the demon that time. It's why I left. I was afraid it would take over."

Anna and Francine exchanged a look as if they had shared an amusing secret.

"You're right," Francine said. "That was a monster."

At least I'd been vindicated in my belief. I knew I was right.

"A green-eyed monster." Anna appeared to be fighting a smile.

"One of the most dangerous monsters of all," Francine added.

"Enough. What are you talking about?"

Anna reached over and took my hand. "That was jealousy, Liam. Pure and simple."

"No. I felt different. Evil."

Francine leaned forward. "Yes, Liam. Jealousy is dark. It's perhaps the most powerful emotion and the hardest to control. You've never felt it before. You are such a kind, loving lad. You've always been happy for others' good fortune and have never had anything worth being jealous over." She looked at Anna. "Until now."

Anna squeezed my hand.

It couldn't be that simple. "What about my mother?"

Francine leaned back in her chair. "Ah, well, now. That's a bit more complicated, you see. But you are not a murderer. Of that I am certain."

She might have been certain, but I wasn't. "There was a witness, and the whole village saw her mutilated body. And what about my hearing the Bean Sidhes?"

Anna entwined her fingers through mine. "I hear those things screaming and I certainly haven't murdered anyone. Hey, I don't even kill animals."

Francine placed her warm hands over both of ours. "Liam. I held you in my arms less than an hour after your birth. You were a lovely, wee babe, not a vicious demon. I've no idea what happened to your mother, but I'm certain you didn't do it. The only person who really knows is Brigid Ronan, and she'll never tell the truth."

"What does she say happened?" Anna asked Francine.

Francine removed her hands, waving her question away. "It doesn't bear repeating."

"No, really. What did she say?" Anna pressed, squeezing my hand. I gently unlaced my fingers from hers, wishing for a way to end the conversation. She stood, hands on hips, eyes focused on me. "Look, just like you told me when I didn't want to explain why I was exiled here: I'm going to find out anyway, so it might as well be from you."

I closed my eyes and took a shuddering breath. I'd never given the story words before—never given it the power of being said aloud. "Miss Ronan says that she ran to help when she heard the screaming and that when she got there, my mother lay dead in her own blood and I was asleep against her with my umbilical cord severed."

Anna shrugged. "So, she gave birth to you, cut the cord, and died. It doesn't happen much anymore because of modern medicine, but it could certainly happen in this backward place. That's not murder."

Francine, clearly uncomfortable, cleared her cup and the sugar bowl from the table, busying herself at the sink.

"There was more to it than that," I whispered. "The body was mutilated. She was ripped and torn—I had clawed my way out, shredding her to death. I killed her."

Anna covered her mouth, but her eyes never left my face. I saw neither fear nor disgust, just shock and something else . . . pity?

Francine slammed her hand on the counter. "It doesn't add up. It never has." Then she muttered something in such a heavy burr I couldn't understand her. She turned from the sink to face us. "You were framed, but I can't for the life of me figure out why. Why an innocent babe?"

No longer able to sit still, I paced a triangle from the doorway to the sofa in the corner to the sink. "Francine, you've seen and interacted with Otherworlders. Why can't you accept that I'm possessed by one? Why believe all the other stories, but not this one?"

"Why would you choose *to* believe it?" Anna asked.

"Because there's evidence."

"No, there's not. I bet I could hire a detective and a forensic expert and we could solve this."

I stopped pacing. "How?"

"Well, we'd exhume your mother's body, and I bet on examination, we'd find the injuries don't match Ronan's story."

"There is no body. No bodies at all on the island. There's

not enough room and much of the year, the ground is frozen too solid to dig a grave. We cremate on pyres."

Anna wrinkled her nose. "Well, there goes that idea."

Francine cleared Anna's empty cup, shaking her head. "It has never added up. Babes are born with fingernails; long ones sometimes, but they're soft. The marks were deep and far apart. Liam's tiny fingers couldn't have spread that wide. Also, he couldn't have bitten through his own cord like she said. He didn't have any teeth."

"Didn't anyone point that out?"

"I did, but no one would listen. They were afraid of empowering the demon by giving it an alibi."

Anna snorted. "That's ridiculous!"

"I agree," Francine said. "Worse than that, they were going to just leave him there in the snow to die. But sweet Erin Callan couldn't stand it and convinced James to let her take him home since she couldn't have children of her own."

I'd never heard this before. I had no idea Francine had refuted the evidence. Nor did I know that they were going to leave me to freeze to death.

Francine sat back down at the table next to Anna. "And let me tell you, Brigid Ronan whipped them into a frenzy. I was worried they were going to execute the baby in some violent way on the spot."

"Oh, my God," Anna gasped.

"And they chose to believe her. *Her!* An outsider and all."

This was absolutely news to me. "Ronan isn't a villager?"

Francine leaned forward. "Heavens, no. She appeared out of nowhere. We assumed she was brought in by the old man." She nodded to Anna. "Your uncle. She was never part of our village, though she's familiar with the lore, which means he didn't bring her in from the city. Perhaps she came from the old country."

"Well," Anna said. "This calls for some sleuthing. And I know just where to start. I think it's time I become very close friends with my housekeeper."

"Be careful," Francine warned.

"Oh, don't worry. I'll just express my concerns about our demon here and see what she says."

"Well, I for one would like to see this put to rest," Francine said. "So Liam can get on with something more important—like flying." She winked at Anna, who flushed a beautiful shade of crimson.

13

There are some secrets which do not permit themselves to be told.

—Edgar Allan Poe,
from "The Man of the Crowd," 1840

hile Francine cleared the table, I could feel Anna looking at me. She knew. She knew who and what I was. More than that, she now knew how I felt about her.

Francine rinsed and dried a cup. "Anna, I don't think it's a good idea for you to go back to Taibhreamh tonight unless Liam walks with you there. The Na Fir Ghorm are restless for some reason."

"So are the screaming things. I thought my eardrums would break on the way here," she said. "Don't worry. There's no way I'm going back out there alone."

Francine stared out the tiny window at the end of the room. "Something is happening with the Otherworlders. It might be because of the upcoming Bealtaine celebration. They are always strongest when belief is highest."

"I'll walk you back," I volunteered, dreading the possibility of seeing Nicholas again. What if Francine and Anna were wrong? What if it were not jealousy, but the monster emerging instead?

"You're welcome to stay here," Francine offered a bit too

eagerly, "until the sun comes up and the Bean Sidhes and Na Fir Ghorm are weaker. Sunrise is in a few hours anyway. Why don't the two of you just relax? I'm going back upstairs."

Why, I wondered, was Francine throwing us together and encouraging a relationship when heartache was all that could result? Didn't she see the impossibility of it?

Anna looked from me to Francine and back again. I had no idea what to do. The fact that she would even consider more time with me was remarkable. Perhaps that wasn't the reason. Maybe she didn't want to be alone with me on the way back to Taibhreamh.

"Sure. I'll just hang out here, then, if that's okay," she said.

"What about your guests?" I asked.

She shrugged. "They know I won't be back tonight. They're cool. Nicholas found the wine cellar, so he and Mallory won't even know I'm gone." She rolled her eyes.

Francine didn't even try to conceal her grin. "Well, I'm off, then. You two make yourselves at home. There's food if you get hungry. I'll see you in the morning."

"Um, would you mind if I used your phone again?" Anna asked.

"This late, dear?"

"I'm going to leave a message for someone on voice mail."

Francine shrugged. "Of course."

In only a few moments, Francine returned. I could hear Anna's voice but couldn't discern the words. Perhaps she was again appealing to her father to bring her home away from this loathsome place. I certainly wouldn't blame her.

Before long, she returned to her chair and Francine bid us good night.

We remained at the table, silent for a long time after Francine's footsteps reached the top of the stairs and her door closed. Unable to find a suitable starting point, I waited for Anna to lead the conversation.

Wordlessly, she stood and moved to the sofa, brow furrowed, clearly struggling with her new information. I understood her difficulty, as I'd struggled to make sense of it since childhood.

"You should have told me," she said. "You had lots of opportunities."

I couldn't bring myself to meet her eyes. "Some things are best left unsaid."

"Not something like this. I asked how your mom died. I asked a lot of things and you didn't answer truthfully. I've been totally honest with you."

I met her eyes. "And I with you."

She crossed her arms over her body. "No. You've hidden things from me. What else do I not know?" She stood. "God, Liam. I wanted to . . ."

"But we didn't."

She paced in a circle around the table. "Yeah, because I thought you were shy and scared and had some kind of self-image problem we needed to work through first."

"I *was* scared. Terrified. I still am."

She stopped pacing and faced me from the other side of the table. "Of what? Of turning into a demon and killing me or something?"

I pulled my eyes away. She remained silent, and my chest felt as though it would cave in on itself. This was the moment I had dreaded. The moment when she would turn like the rest, hating and fearing me for my destructive potential. She had expressed her doubts about the demon, but certainly the possibility gave her pause.

She placed her hands wide on the table and leaned toward me. "I was scared too. You want to know why?" I met her eyes but said nothing. I slid my hand off the table into my lap so she wouldn't see I was shaking.

"I was scared, Liam, because I've never felt like this." She didn't move but stayed on eye level. "Never. You do something to me. I can't explain it." She stood up straight. "And honestly, it's disturbing."

Before I could speak, she returned to the sofa and buried her face in her hands. Too stunned to form words, I focused on breathing in a regular rhythm.

Her voice came out muffled through her hands. "I really wish you'd say something, Liam, because I feel pretty stupid right now."

I had no idea what to say. I wanted to laugh and rejoice. *She feels it too.* I took a calming breath, slowing my heart rate. "It is the belief of my people that certain souls are created specifically for each other and that if one is fortunate enough to meet his or her perfect match, their souls will commune on a level beyond earthly. It is called an *anam cara,* or 'soul friend.'"

She lowered her hands. "Are these the same people who say you're possessed by a demon?"

I shook my head. "No, that's a local belief. This is Old World lore."

"Good, because the demon thing is way off."

"I sincerely hope you're right," I said, sitting on the opposite end of the sofa.

We stared at each other, and again, as on several occasions before, it felt as though our souls touched.

She looked away, breaking the link, and picked at the fabric of the cushion. "Please don't keep stuff from me anymore."

"I'll endeavor not to, but I'm not the only one with secrets. You've withheld information as well."

She shook her head. "Nope."

"You didn't tell me you were practically engaged."

A perfect eyebrow shot up. "I am?" Her eyes opened wide. "Oh. You're talking about Nicholas." She rolled her eyes. "He's full of crap. No way would we get married. He's way too selfish. Dream on, Nicky."

"Why did he allude to an arrangement, then?"

"Because he's an ass and was trying to rattle your demon's cage." Her expression grew dark. "Wait. You don't think I'd mess around with you if I was in a relationship with someone else, do you?"

"Honestly, Anna, I'm unfamiliar with the rules of your world. My knowledge of you is based on what I've read and what I feel when I'm with you."

She crawled from her side of the sofa, stopping inches from me. "What do you feel when you're with me, Liam?"

I breathed in her lily fragrance. "Overwhelmed."

She moved closer still, until her warmth fanned across on my skin. "And?"

"Honored," I whispered as her lips almost touched mine. "Amazed."

"Like you can fly?" she said, brushing her lips along my neck.

"Absolutely."

The shrieking began the moment her warm lips met mine, jerking me from heaven into some kind of hell.

"Crap!" Anna covered her ears. "The timing sucks," she grumbled. "Why are they here?"

I dropped my head against the back of the sofa and groaned. "I have no idea."

Anna curled against me, hands still over her ears. "There has to be a way to get them to shut up."

I wished I knew how.

"What do they want from us?" she asked.

I smoothed her hair from her face. "I have no idea. In some stories I've heard, they're warning of an impending death. In others, they're mourning for the wrongfully dead, as we discussed. I hear them because of my mother. I've no idea why they are appealing to you as well."

"My uncle, maybe?"

"Possibly. It would mean foul play, though."

She pressed closer. "It sounds like they're screaming words. Can they understand us?"

If only my left arm worked, I could have put it around her. Instead, it lay uselessly by my side as she leaned against my chest. "I have no idea. I've never attempted to communicate with them."

"Shut up," Anna yelled. They got louder. "Well, that didn't work." She winced.

If they were speaking a language, it was one I'd never heard. "Please. We want to help you. Listen to us," I implored. They fell silent.

Anna sat up on her knees. "Whoa. It worked."

"Are you punishing me for my mother?"

Silence.

"Are you warning us?" Anna asked.

I flinched at the chorus of screams.

Anna grinned. "They understand us. Maybe they'll shut up if we can figure out what they want." She sprang from the sofa and walked in a circle around the room, leaving my chest, where she had been leaning, cold and empty.

"So, was someone murdered? Was it on this island?" The shrieks increased with each question she asked. "Is the murderer still alive?"

The volume was too much and I could only cover one ear. "Stop, please!" They obeyed.

Anna joined me on the sofa again. "So, there's a murderer on the island and they want us to do something about it."

"That fits the lore I've heard," I said. "We need to find out whose murder links us together since we both hear them. Are you here because of the death of my mother?" I asked. They wailed in response. Well, the entire village knew who her murderer was, but it didn't link me to Anna in any way I could imagine. My mother died when Anna was an infant.

"Was it my uncle who was murdered?" The wailing got even louder. "Please stop." The Bean Sidhe fell silent at Anna's command. "Well, we need to figure out how he died and who did it, huh?"

An incredible golden glow emanated from the corner opposite us. A beautiful woman materialized as if created by fireflies from the forest. She gazed at us as she stroked her long, golden hair with a silver comb. Her dress of a clinging gauze material moved about her legs like seaweed in a current. She smiled, and then the luminescence intensified until she was as brilliant as the sun and it hurt to look at her. Despite the pain, I was unable to avert my eyes.

"An angel," Anna gasped.

At that moment, I realized what it was, the Washerwoman. The Cailleach. "No." I pulled Anna to me. "Look away!" I tried to shout, but no sound came out. It was too late—we had been entranced.

The shimmer faded and the woman transformed, darkening and stooping over to become as terrifying as she had been beautiful just moments before. No longer did her skin luminesce; it writhed and boiled as if crawling creatures cavorted just under the surface. Her lush, sleek hair dulled to a knotted, gray tangle and the front of her dirty smock was covered in gore, as was the garment she held in her gnarled hands. She stared down at the bloodstained rag she clutched, then raised her black, hollow eyes to us. Her mouth gaped open, and a horrible shriek issued forth, sending shudders to my very core.

Anna went limp against me and slumped to the floor. I couldn't move, still caught up in the enchantment of the creature keening in the corner.

"What in the name of heaven is going on?" Francine's voice snapped the spell, dissolving the Cailleach and freeing me from my paralysis.

I dropped to my knees by Anna's side. *Oh, God,* I pleaded in my head. *Please, no.* I pulled Anna onto my lap. My insides folded in on themselves, causing an ache in my chest so intense, I couldn't breathe. A silent sob racked my body as the horrible truth burst in my brain, shattering all reason. Seeing the Cailleach meant death.

Francine placed her palm against Anna's neck, then patted me on the shoulder. "She's fine, lad. Just passed out cold."

I sucked in a rush of stinging air and shook my head to clear it. Placing my palm over her chest, I reveled in the miraculous thump of her heart that traveled up my arm, wrapping itself around my own heart. She was alive.

"Anna, wake up," I said, cradling her head with my hand.

"No. Let her sleep." Francine stood. "Sometimes our body shuts down to help us cope with things our mind can't handle. Help me move her to the sofa."

Anna looked so fragile, lying under the quilt Francine had draped over her.

"Now, tell me what happened," Francine whispered, motioning for me to join her at the table. I hesitated, reluctant to leave Anna's side. "Come on, Liam. She's only sleeping. Let her rest."

The chair seemed unnaturally hard, and my heart still raced. I looked over my shoulder at Anna, wishing to be closer.

She had felt it too—the strange, more-than-earthly connection we shared. She acknowledged it—her proclamation followed by the closest thing to a death sentence the lore provided. Her words were appropriate: the timing "sucked."

"Tell me, Liam," Francine pressed.

She patiently waited while I untangled the unintelligible chaos swirling through my brain. "It was the Cailleach," I whispered. "It was a beautiful, ethereal being—too beautiful to behold—and then . . ." I shuddered at my recollection of the gore-covered hag.

Francine's brow furrowed. "The girl saw it too?"

I nodded.

She grasped my hand between hers. "Liam, the Cailleach brings an omen, not a curse."

That was not the case and we both knew it. "Everyone who sees her dies."

"Liam, lad. Everyone dies no matter what. It's only an omen. It is not a certainty."

I pulled my hand away. Had I seen the Cailleach before Anna's return into my life, it wouldn't have mattered. Imminent death would have been a relief in a way. Not now. Not when I'd finally found a reason to live.

"Look at me," Francine said. "You need to really hear me. Are you listening?"

I nodded, numb and cold, as if I'd been submerged in the icy ocean.

"We all die—some sooner, some later. How or when we die doesn't matter; what's important is how we *live*."

I looked away.

"Live, Liam. Live in the moment. Treat each second like it could be your last."

It could be my last. I had been doomed. So had Anna. "How do I tell her?"

Francine leaned across the table and took my face in her hands. "You are not hearing me."

I pulled myself out of my ice-cold numbness and focused on Francine's face.

"You cannot tell her," she said. "It's only a myth, a story."

I shook my head.

She moved her hands to my shoulders and squeezed, as if trying to wake me, her blue eyes boring into mine. "There are things that should be kept secret. This is one of those things." Francine's intensity was alarming. "I know what I'm talking about. I've been in your shoes."

"You've seen the Washerwoman?"

She dropped her hands. "No, but someone I . . ." A pained expression crossed her face. "Someone I knew did."

"How long before death?"

"You are missing my point," she whispered.

"How *long*?" My voice cracked.

"Not long, but his death could have been unrelated to seeing the Cailleach."

I put my head down on the table. Anna would be leaving Dòchas soon. Maybe off the island, the spell would be broken and she would be spared. My heart lifted slightly.

"Don't make the mistake I made," Francine said. "Time is precious. I lost sight of that. I only focused on how to beat it. All my thoughts went to preventing his death rather than celebrating the time we still had together."

It dawned on me that I truly knew nothing about Francine. Who had she lost?

She took my good hand. "Live, Liam. For the first time in your life, really live. Consider this a gift, not a curse. Perhaps that is the way to beat it—to really *live*."

14

Thou wouldst be loved?—then let thy heart
From its present pathway part not!
Being everything which now thou art,
Be nothing which thou art not.

—Edgar Allan Poe,
from "To F— — s S. O ——d," 1835

iam." Anna's voice was barely above a whisper.

Francine smiled. "Even in sleep, your name is on her lips."

Anna's words from earlier played through my head. *Please don't keep stuff from me anymore.* "I have to tell her," I said.

Francine shook her head. "To what end? To worry her when it's naught but a story from our homeland? There are cases where people live many years after seeing the Cailleach. It's only rumor, Liam, and I've never heard of it affecting an outsider."

After glancing over my shoulder to confirm Anna still slept, I leaned across the table, closer to Francine. "How many do you know personally who have seen it?"

She lowered her eyes to her lap. "Four. My parents, my brother, and my . . . friend."

"You told me about your friend. How long did the others live after the sighting?"

"I've heard of cases in which people live full lives," she said so quickly, the words tumbled over themselves.

"How long for the people you knew personally?"

She sighed. "All of them died inside of sixty days."

I glanced over my shoulder at Anna. "I have to tell her the truth."

"Suit yourself, but take my advice. You have no control over death, only life. Make it count." With that, she rose and disappeared up the stairs.

"Liam," Anna called again.

"I'm here." I sat on the edge of the sofa. She stirred and rolled on her side, her arm draping over my lap. I took her hand in mine and her eyes fluttered open. "I'm here," I repeated.

She shot upright with a start. "Oh, God. The thing. The old woman." Her eyes darted around the room.

"It's gone," I assured, squeezing her fingers. "You've nothing to fear."

"You saw it too, then?"

I nodded.

"I don't know whether that makes me feel better or worse." She curled her legs underneath her.

"Nor do I."

"So, it was real?" she asked, not pulling her hand away. I was glad she didn't. I needed to touch her.

I stared down at her slender fingers in mine. "Reality on Dòchas often borders on the fantastic; it's hard to determine where illusion ends and reality begins."

"That was a well-spoken non-answer." She slipped her hand from mine. "Okay, then, Mr. Riddle, did I pass out?"

Her color had returned to her face. Perhaps she would not go into shock.

"Francine says our mind protects itself that way sometimes."

She gave the snort-through-her-nose sound. "Like I tripped a breaker in my head or something." My confusion must have shown on my face because she clarified. "With electricity in houses or appliances, there's a switch that shuts down the current if there's an unusual spike in energy. It keeps things from overheating or burning up."

So smart, my Anna. "I know nothing of electricity."

She swung her legs off the couch, sitting close enough to me to touch all the way down the thigh. "Yeah, but you know all about creepy Celtic creatures. What was it?"

"Celtic lore varies from region to region. Dòchas is no exception. Here, this particular creature is called a Cailleach, or the Washerwoman." Hoping she would accept that as a complete answer, I got up and pulled a cup out of the cabinet. "Would you like some water?"

"Please," she said as she stretched.

I filled it from the cistern tap, handed her the cup, and returned to the cabinet.

"So, what did the thing want?"

I filled a second cup, relieved this was an innocuous question. "No one knows what it wants. It just . . . *is*."

She shuddered. "Well, it's creepy as crap. I hope it stays far away."

"Me too."

Cup in hand, I sat beside her. She turned sideways facing me. "How long was I out?"

"I don't know exactly. Less than an hour."

Her eyes widened. "Did I do anything embarrassing?"

I set my cup down on the coffee table in front of us. "Like live up to your tabloid reputation of taking your clothes off in public?"

She put her cup next to mine. "Would that embarrass you, Liam?"

I smiled. She'd turned my joke back on me. "No. What were you worried about doing in your sleep?"

She fidgeted. "I don't know. Drooling, snoring, talking . . ."

"Well, now that you mention it . . ." I grinned as she squirmed. "You certainly snore loudly for such a petite girl."

She punched my shoulder. "I do not snore."

I pointed to her chin. "You have something wet right . . . there."

Her laughter warmed me. She rolled her eyes. "Ha-ha. Liam, the demon comedian!"

Now it was clear what she feared. "You didn't talk in your sleep." *Except for my name.* My heart tightened as I remembered Francine's remark, *Even in sleep, your name is on her lips.*

"Whew." She leaned back. "Good, because I say strange things sometimes. Do you talk in your sleep?"

I had no idea. I'd never slept in the same room with someone. Well, not since I was a little boy. "Not that I know of."

"I stopped going to sleepovers when I was in middle school because I'd say stupid stuff. Sleep is like a truth serum for me or something. I say what's on my mind. If I was mad at a friend, I cussed them out in my sleep. If I liked a boy, everyone at the slumber party knew about it." She shook her head. "So embarrassing."

Live for now, I reminded myself. "You need never be embarrassed with me, Anna."

She stared into my eyes for a long time and the world seemed suspended, frozen, as our souls touched, entwining. The effect was overpowering to the point I wanted to weep.

She ran her fingers down my cheek. "I really like you, Liam. I like who I am when I'm with you."

My voice was shaky. "Who are you when you're with me?"

A smile spread across her face. "I'm *myself*. The real me. And I kinda like her."

"I do too. A great deal."

I realized as her soft, warm lips met mine, I was happier now than I'd ever been in my life. It was better to have a brief time left with her in it than a long life without her. I would take Francine's advice and live for the moment and be sure as many moments contained Anna as was humanly possible. The prospect of imminent death was, in ways, liberating.

The glow of sunrise peeked through the curtains of the window. Anna was wrapped around me on the sofa, face completely relaxed in slumber. She hadn't spoken in her sleep but had smiled and laughed numerous times. Her dreams were pleasant, which brought me comfort. Perhaps she would not fall prey to the lore since she was an outsider.

"Tea?" Francine asked, entering the room.

"No, thanks."

Anna shifted and made an "mmmm" noise, causing my body to come fully awake.

Francine chuckled and put the teakettle on. "Did you tell her?"

"We didn't explore the topic fully."

"Ah, you explored other things fully instead." She winked and I groaned silently.

I attempted to sit, but Anna repositioned, effectively pinning me in place. "Anna," I whispered, brushing her hair out of her face. "It's morning."

"So what?" she mumbled.

"So, we need to get you back to see your friends off."

"Screw 'em."

Francine stifled a laugh. "She certainly knows her mind."

No doubt about that. It was one of the things that appealed most to me, perhaps because I knew so little of my own. "She does indeed." I pulled the blanket back and cool air swirled around us, causing Anna to furrow her brow. "Good morning," I whispered.

"It is good, isn't it?" she said, rubbing her warm palm up my chest.

I cleared my throat and stayed her hand. Francine laughed out loud, which finally snapped Anna into alertness. She sat up and ran her hands through her tangled hair, face flushed. I'd never seen anything as beautiful.

"Would you care for some tea?" Francine asked.

Anna shook her head. "No thank you. I need to get back."

I smiled. She must have been asleep when she spoke earlier. "I'll walk you back."

"Good. You need to say good-bye to Suz, Mallory, and Nicky, especially since you took off at dinner without a word."

I slid on my hiking boots. "I apologize. It was the best course of action at the time." The thought of facing Nicholas again made my stomach roil.

To my horror, Anna's gaze was locked on the painting over the sink. "That's the jetty near the mansion, isn't it?"

"It is." Francine stepped aside so she could get closer.

"Oh, my gosh. That's us!" She glanced at me over her shoulder. "The little kids are Princess Annabel and Prince Leem. I recognize my yellow sundress. I wore that thing every day that summer." She turned to me. "You did this, didn't you?"

I nodded.

"Liam is a talented painter. He sells his work to the vendors sometimes, and they in turn sell it to people on the mainland. He trades with one who supplies paint and canvas in exchange for a painting of his choice each trip."

Anna's expression was unreadable. I held my breath and waited as she studied the painting. Finally, she stepped back and stared at me in disbelief. Was she angry that I had painted her without permission?

"You're really good, Liam. I'm serious. Crazy good."

I let my breath out through my nose, heart singing.

"There are several more in here," Francine said, walking into the store. Anna followed, giving me a curious look over her shoulder as if she were seeing me for the first time.

One was of the lighthouse with a storm approaching, another was of Seal Island, capped with winter snow, and the last was a close-up portrait of six-year-old Anna in her yellow dress with a bucket and shovel, digging in the sand.

"That's me," she whispered.

"Most of his paintings are of you, lass," Francine said, wiping the edge of the sales counter with her dishcloth.

"They are?"

I cringed, leaning against the doorway from the kitchen.

"Where are they? The others?" Anna asked, still studying her portrait.

Francine spoke before I could answer. "He has dozens—maybe hundreds of them in his case. One of the vendors likes his work so much, he gave him a leather portfolio to keep his work in."

"Are they at your place?" Anna asked.

"Yes."

"Why didn't you tell me? Show me?"

I shrugged. "I was unsure of your reception."

She looked at me as if I'd lost my mind. "I need to see them." Perhaps my reaction affected her, but her tone softened. "Please, Liam."

"Not today. You need to get home to your friends." I would

as soon die as show her my work. It was so personal. *As soon die,* I played through my head. The new relevance of the idiom was almost funny. *Live for now,* I reminded myself. "Soon," I amended. "I'll show them to you soon. I promise."

Francine gave me a hug on her way into the kitchen. "In the moment," she whispered for my ears only.

The morning was peaceful and clear, interrupted only by the call of gulls. A couple of men were prepping their gear for the day, but Pa's boat stood empty in the last slot. There was no sign of either him or Johnny, which was unusual. He was probably nursing a monster of a hangover.

"It's beautiful here," Anna remarked, taking my hand.

"Just yesterday, you were saying how much you disliked it."

She squeezed my fingers. "It's growing on me."

Don't, I begged her in my head. *Go back to civilization, where you will be safe.* My heart, however, disagreed completely.

Being with Anna made me better—whole. I'd always been a mere reflection of what people expected me to be: a latent demon; a worthless, adopted burden; a leech on the community. Not with Anna. Like Francine, she gave me the freedom to explore my potential, which through her eyes seemed vast. My feelings for this girl made my chest feel too full and my body weightless—like I truly could fly.

Heavy footsteps farther up the path caused me to freeze. I recognized the cadence of the boots that had stomped toward me so many times in my life, only to bring terror or heartache. I cringed as Pa came into view over the rise.

I attempted to pull my fingers away, but Anna held tighter.

His house was south of the harbor, so why was he coming from the upland side of the island? I wondered.

He halted for only a moment, looking from me to Anna and

back again, and then, uncharacteristically, he shoved past me without a word. Not an insult, not a name, not a threat.

Stunned, I watched as he made his way down the path toward the harbor.

"That went well," Anna said.

The hair tingled on the back of my neck. "Something's wrong. Really wrong."

In silence, we continued up the path to the cutoff for the wooded section, which overlooked the cliffs. The jetty could be seen in the distance.

"Oh, my God. Is that . . . ? What is that, Liam?"

Amid a swirl of turbulence, a human form could be seen, facedown in the water, halfway down the jetty just off the edge. The movement of the water was unnatural, and my entire being shuddered with an unexpected chill. "Stay here," I said.

"Like hell I will," Anna answered, following me down the cliff-side path.

The strangeness of the current was explained when I neared the jetty. The body was being, for lack of a better word, herded along by a pod of harbor seals. Seals often play with their prey, but that was not what was happening here. They were keeping the body afloat, and it appeared they were trying to beach it on the rocks.

Being facedown, the man was dead, I had no doubt. Who and why could only be answered by retrieving his body. Carefully, I made my way to the midpoint of the jetty. Anna followed several steps behind.

I climbed onto the rock closest to the water, trying to figure out the best way to lift the body.

"You get an arm, and I'll grab a leg. We should be able to drag him up that way," Anna said.

It wrecked me that she had to be a participant in such a macabre event, but her suggestion was a good one. With only one arm, it would be difficult to do this alone. A seal took his wrist in its mouth and dragged him closer. The animal met my eyes as if it were trying to communicate. The Selkie myths made sense when interactions like this occurred. It seemed almost human beneath its pelt. Those eyes . . .

From the harbor, the bells clanged a slow dirge, announcing death.

I lay flat on the rock and reached to the hand being offered. The skin was ice cold and slick. I jerked it closer so that I caught it by the forearm and had the shirt as well as slippery skin. I pulled hard, and Anna grabbed the shirt, then the waist of the pants, getting a solid hold on the belt.

"On three," she said. "One, two, three."

We tugged the torso up onto the rock and she rolled the body over, face up.

"Johnny," I said. "Johnny O'Keefe, my dad's fishing mate."

His lips were blue and his skin puckered from being in the water, but it was easy to tell it was Johnny because of the red beard and dense freckles. Small, angry gashes covered the exposed skin, probably from being repeatedly washed against the rocks, which had rough edges covered in barnacles. Honestly, he looked much better than most of the bodies rejected by the sea. Many were mangled beyond recognition.

Anna covered her mouth and stared wide-eyed at the corpse. A loud sob rose from her throat. "His eyes!" she gasped.

Johnny's eyes stared lifelessly at the sky, pupils enlarged to completely fill the iris. I rubbed my thumb over one eyelid and then the other, closing them. I shouldn't have let her follow me here. I could have spared her this horror.

The harbor bells continued their proclamation of death. We might have retrieved the body, but someone else knew prior to our grisly discovery.

"You! I should have known you would be involved, Liam MacGregor. I've been saying for a long time you would kill soon."

I fought the urge to vomit and turned to face Mrs. Katie McAlister, Megan clinging tightly to her hand.

15

Oh, the bells, bells, bells!
What a tale their terror tells
Of Despair!

—Edgar Allan Poe,
from "The Bells," 1848

"It was . . . We . . ." I fell silent, deciding not to continue in my discourse with Mrs. McAlister. Words would only exacerbate the situation, which was worsening by the second. Half of the village was filing down the trail toward us, several of them already mounting the jetty.

The villagers' angry words were indistinguishable, but their intent was as clear as the tolling of the bells in the harbor. Anna crawled closer to me. "What the heck? All they need are pitchforks and torches and we'd have a witch hunt here."

"A demon hunt," I whispered.

"Oh, God. They don't think you—"

"Indeed, they do."

"I caught him red-handed!" Mrs. McAlister announced with a tone bordering on glee. "I found him in the act!"

Anna pushed to her feet. "In the act of pulling a guy that was already dead out of the water!"

Mrs. McAlister's face pinched up as if she smelled something foul. More of the villagers were picking their way across the jetty rocks to get a closer look at the demon and his prey. I saw no prospect of a positive outcome. Perhaps the Washerwoman's recourse would happen sooner rather than later. I hadn't envisioned my death at the end of a rope.

"Stop!" Anna shouted. "Stop right now."

The villagers fell silent. I looked up to the trail and noticed Anna's friends watching from the cliff above, not near enough to hear us. Miss Ronan stood slightly apart from them. It was too far to see her face, but I was certain Miss Ronan's expression was one of triumph. The evil seed she had planted in the villagers' brains eighteen years ago had taken firm root and was driving their actions and thoughts. She controlled them like a master puppeteer.

Anna took several steps toward Mrs. McAlister. "You caught him red-handed doing what?"

Mrs. McAlister's mouth opened and closed several times like a mackerel dropped into the bottom of a boat. Anna crouched down to Megan's eye level. "What did you see?"

"You will not speak to my child!" Mrs. McAlister shouted.

"You will not speak to me in that tone. Are we clear?" I marveled at Anna's forcefulness. "You are accusing someone of murder. This is not a game and you are not in charge." She acted as I would imagine appropriate for a great lady of a mansion such as Taibhreamh. In awe, I held my breath and waited for Mrs. McAlister to react. To my amazement, her shoulders slumped and her mouth clamped shut in a tight line.

For a moment, no one spoke, but the bells continued their monotonous drone, underpinning the scene with a rhythmic dirge.

Clang, clang, clang.

"Justice!" someone yelled from the back of the crowd. An angry unintelligible rumble resulted. These people wanted something—someone to blame. I was that someone. My greatest hope was that Anna would not be implicated as well.

"No!" The cry was followed by harrowing sobs only the truly bereaved can deliver. Johnny's wife pushed through the crowd. "No, Johnny!" She fell on her knees at his side, cries accompanied by the mournful tolling of the harbor bells.

Out of respect, I supposed, the angry villagers quieted.

Clang, clang, clang.

Once again, I scanned the crowd, including those on the cliff-side trail. I spotted my pa's unmistakable broad form at the top, arms crossed over his chest. He would be as willing to believe I had given in to my murderous demon as anyone else. My spirit shrank with regret at the relationship we never had and never could have.

"What happened?" Johnny's wife asked.

"I have no idea," I whispered.

"I know exactly what happened!" Mrs. McAlister shouted, surely with the purpose of inciting the crowd again. "We all know what happened, don't we?"

Several villagers shouted agreement, then were joined by others. I was most certainly doomed. Crowd mentality is powerful. Coupled with fear and grief, it's unstoppable.

"I have one question." I hadn't realized I could raise my voice that loud. The crowd hushed. "Who is ringing the bells right now?"

"Edmond Byrne," someone yelled.

"Why?" I shouted.

No one answered because everyone knew why. The bells only rang for fire, which was visible from anywhere on the small island; a birth, the last of which was Megan's, six years ago; and death—the bells we heard most often on Dòchas.

Emboldened, I continued. "They started to ring before I removed the body from the water. You know this is true because that's why Mrs. McAlister got here in time to see me pull the body out. She heard the bells and was told where the death had occurred. Who brought the news? That's the person who knows what happened."

A whispered murmur spread through the villagers.

"Who reported it?" I pressed.

"I did," Pa shouted from the top of the trail. "I reported Johnny's death."

My heart stopped. This was the worst-possible outcome, well, other than if the witness had been Miss Ronan or Mrs. McAlister.

Clang, clang, clang. It was my death knell too.

The villagers waited expectantly for him to offer me up. This was his chance. He'd told me my whole life he wished he could get rid of me—that the only thing keeping him from it was my ma. Now, without her, there was nothing to hold him back. He'd be free of his burden at last.

I closed my eyes and found myself breathing in time to the strike of the bells, waiting for the inevitable.

"Leave the boy alone," Pa yelled. "He had nothing to do with this." I opened my eyes. Based on their absolute silence, the villagers were as stunned by his response as I was. "Johnny went to the sea on his own in the middle of the night." Pa paused and wiped his face with his handkerchief. He was too far away to see clearly, but he appeared overcome with emotion as he pointed at the sea. "He said he heard his son calling from out there. I was too drunk to realize what he meant at the time."

Johnny's son had died three years ago when he fell off the boat while out pulling lobster traps with his dad. Neither could swim, so Johnny watched helplessly as his only child drowned just out of reach.

"Johnny answered the call of the sea," Pa said. "We've all heard it." He shook his head. "Let the boy be." With that, he turned and disappeared over the hill.

I remained motionless, frantically trying to form a cohesive stream of thought, but none came. I could only repeat one word in my head: *Why?*

Like children denied a bright plaything, the villagers filed off the jetty with the exception of several men and Mrs. McAlister, Megan in tow.

Mrs. McAlister's eyes narrowed as she studied me.

Anna slipped her arm around my waist. "Nice try, McAlister," she said through gritted teeth. "This jetty is part of the Taibhreamh estate. You're trespassing. Get off."

Other than her eyes opening so wide white was visible all around the iris, Mrs. McAlister made no response. She pivoted and retreated to the trail. Megan looked back at me several times, lip trembling.

The four men lifted Johnny wordlessly onto their shoulders without making eye contact. Was it shame or disappointment that caused them to look away? I wondered. Fear perhaps.

The bells still moaned as the macabre procession cleared the jetty and disappeared over the hill.

"Are you okay?" Anna whispered, rubbing small circles on my back.

I was stunned, but alive and free. Pa had exonerated me— something I would never have dreamed possible. "Yes. I'm fine."

Now that my shock was receding, my misery welled for Anna. She should never have been subjected to what she'd just witnessed. A battered corpse is traumatic even to one accustomed to death. For someone like her, it had surely been a living nightmare. And then the villagers.

I pulled her against me, breathing in the amazing scent of lilies and Anna. "I'm so sorry. I . . ." I shook my head. Words failed me again. My world was wrong for her and she needed to get out as quickly as possible. That's what I wanted to say, but somehow couldn't. "My world is complicated."

"Your world is screwed up," she said. "Majorly screwed up."

Pushing selfishness and desire aside, I vowed to myself that I would do anything in my power to ensure she returned to New York, where she belonged. She needed to shake free from this cursed island and evil it held, including me, before it was too late and her gentle spirit fell victim to the darkness here. "I'm so sorry," I whispered into her hair.

She ran her fingers up my stomach and slid them between the buttons on my shirt, her fingertips skimming my chest, leaving tingles in their wake. Her simple touch had more effect on my tortured soul than a thousand words. I sighed and relaxed, the terror of prior moments receding like the tide, my breathing once again taking the slow rhythm of the bells sounding in the distance.

"What the hell was all that about?" Nicholas shouted from far down the jetty. I lifted my head to find Anna's three friends awkwardly making their way over the rocks toward us. Miss Ronan was nowhere in sight.

Mallory jumped to the next rock. "Yeah, that was intense. Was that guy dead?"

Suzette was several feet behind, stopping on each rock and analyzing the best path to take to cross safely to the next.

Anna didn't respond to them, but slipped her hand from my

shirt and placed it on the side of my face. "Are you okay, really?" she asked, looking straight into my eyes.

"I will be."

"I can send them back to the house," she whispered.

"No. You've given too much already."

She dropped her hands. "You don't get it, do you?"

My mind raced to grasp her meaning, but found none. Almost imperceptibly, I shook my head.

She placed her lips against my ear. "Nothing is too much. I'm in love with you, Liam MacGregor."

The world around me melted into silence: the waves hitting the rocks, my breathing, the pounding of my heart . . . and the bells. No sound, no pain, no fear. Only Anna.

Muireann was shocked by the treatment of her human by his own kind. She thought only the Na Fir Ghorm capable of such callousness.

It was humans' unlimited capacity for love that appealed to Selkies. It was the reason they cared for humans and championed them with Otherworlders.

She rose to the surface and snuck another peek. The villagers had cleared, and he was with the girl she had seen him with before. He held her tightly as if his life depended on it. Maybe it did. No others of his other kind seemed to want him.

But Muireann wanted him. She'd been told about the lure of humans but had never experienced it until recently. She longed to shed her pelt and talk to him and get to know him.

Three humans she'd never seen before interrupted the couple's embrace. After sharing words, the tall girl and the boy touched hands with her human and the smallest one embraced him, and then the three of them along with the girl he favored took the trail that led to the big dwelling. Her human went the other direction toward his home.

The Na Fir Ghorm were still celebrating last night's victory. She could hear the revelry every time she put her head underwater. That poor man had honestly believed he was joining his dead son when he entered the water. Muireann recalled the horror on his face when the Na Fir Ghorm released him from the trance too early—but too late to save himself. He fought death until his last heartbeat.

It was her sincere hope that Manannán mac Lir had granted him passage and that he truly was with his son now.

Muireann swam toward Seal Island with her head above water. *The hateful creatures.* Their raucous singing and boasts made her feel sick to her stomach. If only there were a way to stop them from killing her human. From killing any human again.

Impossible. They were unstoppable.

16

I stand amid the roar
Of a surf-tormented shore,
And I hold within my hand
Grains of the golden sand—
How few! yet how they creep
Through my fingers to the deep,
While I weep—while I weep!
O God! can I not grasp
Them with a tighter clasp?
O God! can I not save
One from the pitiless wave?
Is all that we see or seem
But a dream within a dream?

—Edgar Allan Poe,
"A Dream Within a Dream," 1827

Elation and exhaustion swirled through me in equal parts. I hadn't slept a minute last night at the store, wanting to savor every moment with Anna. Being with her gave me the freedom to be what I wanted to be: whole, valuable, loved.

And she had told me that she loved me. Annabel Leighton loved me. *Me.* Unfathomable. I shook my head in wonder and checked the large pot of water on the burner. Tiny bubbles were just forming on the bottom.

The splash of the bucket echoed off the walls of the well. One more after this and the tub would be full enough. Johnny had only been in the sea a short while—six hours at the most—but I still felt tainted by the brush of death. I wanted to wash the entire event out of my mind and off my body.

I poured the bucket of water into the tub.

His poor wife. My heart ached for her. I couldn't imagine the pain of losing a lover or spouse. That was why it was imperative Anna return to New York City before this progressed any further. Surely the reach of the Washerwoman was restricted to this island and Anna would be safe once in her world and free of mine.

The well bucket splashed for the last time and I cranked the handle, winding the retrieval rope until I could balance the bucket on the ledge and unclip it. Francine had helped me devise this because manually pulling up the rope was not possible with only one arm. The crank had a brake that held it in place once I got the bucket to the top. Because it was difficult for me to transfer water from one vessel to another, she ordered a special clip that fastened through an eye bolted to the handle. It snapped open with a pinch of two fingers.

After dumping the water into the tub, I added the boiling pot of water from the stove.

Anna had asked me to come back to Taibhreamh when the helicopter arrived so that I could say good-bye to her friends. I hadn't heard it fly over yet, but I scrubbed quickly just in case it happened soon. After toweling off, I grabbed my dirty clothes from the floor and threw them in the tub. I then slid on my only other pair of pants.

I would tell Anna that she needed to go home. That we were too different and there could never be a meaningful relationship between us. I realized I wasn't scrubbing the clothes but rather pounding them against the side of the tub.

"No!" I shouted.

Why, when happiness was finally within reach, was it denied me? My chest felt as though it would crack in two. I took a deep breath and resumed scrubbing.

She told me she loved me. That would have to be enough to sustain me once she was gone.

After swirling the clothes in the water to remove the last bit of soap, I pulled the plug that allowed the water to drain out of a pipe through the floorboards to the slope behind the shed.

I stepped into the tub, rolled the pants into a tube shape, and put my foot on one end. Then I twisted the other end with my good hand to wring the water out.

I wondered if Anna would follow my advice and leave. What if the tables were turned? What would I do in her shoes?

The shirt received similar treatment to the pants, and I hung it next to them on the line strung above the tub.

I knew exactly what I'd do if the situation were reversed. Nothing and no one could induce me to leave her, not even the Cailleach. I'd stay with her every possible minute, even if it meant my minutes were limited.

I balled a sock up in my fist and squeezed the water out.

But she didn't really know the truth. I needed to tell her what seeing the Washerwoman meant.

I shook the sock and hung it over the line. After repeating the process with the other sock, I stepped out of the tub.

Maybe if she knew the truth, she'd do the rational thing and get as far away from this island as possible.

The conflicting desires of wanting her to leave but needing her to stay were ripping me apart. It was imperative I handled this today.

As I fastened my last shirt button, the distinctive sound of the helicopter's arrival ripped through the air. I swallowed the lump of dread in my throat. I'd have to face her friends again. I'd ruined her birthday party—first by my presence at her home and then by the nightmare on the jetty with Johnny. I hadn't even wished her a happy birthday or given her a gift.

Regardless, I promised her I'd come, and I always kept my word.

I paused with my key in the lock as Francine's words played through my head. *You have no control over death, only life. Make it count.* Somehow, knowing part of me could go with her when she left made the inevitable more palatable. I pulled my portfolio out from under the bed, then headed to Taibhreamh, my heart lighter.

"You made it!" Suzette called from the porch as I squeezed through the partially open gate. "I'm so glad."

The glare Nicholas delivered caused my demon to stir. Coming here was a mistake. Mallory looked up from the magazine in her lap and studied me with indifference. Anna was nowhere in sight.

"I was afraid we weren't going to get to see you again," Suzette said, trotting down the steps to meet me.

So was I. In fact, there were some moments this morning when I'd been certain I'd be hanging from a rope by now. Suzette stopped a foot or so from me and grinned. "I hope you'll come see us in New York soon. You'd love it there."

I would hate it there, but I smiled and nodded, pushing down the urge to look back up at Nicholas.

"What's that?" Suzette asked, pointing at the portfolio.

"Oh, it's um . . ." I shrugged. "It's nothing important."

"Looks like an art portfolio."

I nodded.

"May I see?"

"No, I'd rather—"

"Yeah, let's see it." Nicholas descended the steps two at a time.

Instinctively, I took a step back. I'd brought my art for Anna, no one else.

Mallory joined us. She circled behind me, which made me uneasy, but I was loath to take my eyes off Nicholas.

"You brought it for some reason, right?" Nicholas said.

I said nothing.

Suzette stepped between us. "Leave him alone, Nicky."

He smirked. "I'm not doing anything. I'm just talking to the guy. No harm in that, is there?"

"Don't be a jerk."

His face was all innocence. "Me?"

Mallory ripped the portfolio out of my hand. I spun to grab it back, but she had skipped out of reach. She ran up the porch steps and pitched the portfolio on the bench.

With calculated deliberateness, she unzipped the portfolio, watching me the whole time. "Wonder what our island boy has in here," she said. "Finger paintings? Stick figure cartoons? Perhaps we'll get a glimpse into how the other side lives."

Nicholas joined her. Suzette looked up at me, brow furrowed.

Mallory stared at the painting on top and her jaw went slack. Nicholas raised his eyebrows and stared from the painting to me, then back again.

"Wow," Mallory said. "Not quite what I expected."

Nicholas lifted the landscape painting of the harbor and flipped through several subsequent canvases underneath.

Stop, I willed him in my head. *Please stop.* It felt as though my insides were dissolving. Then it happened.

"Hey, that's Anna," Mallory said. "So's the next one . . . and the next."

Suzette ran up the steps to look as I felt myself shrinking into the ground beneath my feet. Soundlessly, they ravaged my privacy, scrutinized my very soul as they flipped through drawing after drawing after painting. I slumped to the ground, covering my face with my hand to mask my outrage and pain.

"What is going on? Why's Liam in the yard?" Anna sounded angry. "What are . . . oh, my God . . ." Her voice trailed off into a whisper.

I kept my head down, containing my anguish.

"He didn't want to show us, but we fixed that. They're all of you, Annie," Nicholas said. "Somebody's crushing bad. Nothing wrong with dreaming big, I suppose."

"Screw off," Anna said. The sound of the zipper on the portfolio was followed by gravel crunching underfoot. I stared at my trembling fist and held my breath.

"Hey," Anna whispered. "Are you okay?"

The smell of lilies filled my nose and her fingers raked through my hair, rendering me whole again. I nodded, my anger dispersing like sea foam on the shore.

She placed the portfolio in my lap. "I'm sorry they did that. I'm glad you brought your art. Will you show me some of it later?"

"Yes."

"Good." She brushed her lips across mine. "Look at me, Liam." I did. Free of makeup and hair still wet from a shower, she was too beautiful to be real—like a dream. "Remember what I said on the jetty?" she whispered. "Hold that in your heart and not what they just did. Keep that demon down, okay?"

I nodded and stared into her crystal blue eyes and something in me stirred. Not the demon. It was a flutter in my chest as beautiful and bright as the sun breaking through storm clouds.

Fists balled at her sides, she mounted the steps to the porch. She must have worn a fierce expression because Nicholas appeared genuinely unnerved.

They were too far away for me to hear her with her back to me, but I could hear Nicholas. "Look, I didn't take it, Annie."

Unintelligible angry words from Anna cut him off.

"We were only having fun. Come on. It's no big deal."

Anna's shoulders rose and fell as she took deep breaths but didn't respond.

"You can't really be mad. He's just a guy from the village. He's nothing. A nobody."

Anna's voice was raised enough for me to hear. "He's not a nobody to me."

Nicholas stood. "Look. I can totally understand the appeal of going slumming. We all need to walk on the other side sometimes, but you are taking this way too far. Nobody got hurt."

"Liam got hurt," Anna growled.

"So what?" Nicholas said, throwing his arms up. "It's not like it matters. What's gotten into you? It's like I don't even know you anymore."

"You don't," Anna said between gritted teeth. "You never have and you never will, Nicholas. You are too selfish to see me or anyone else. The helicopter is waiting. Go home."

Mallory grabbed the suitcase at her feet and descended the stairs without saying good-bye to Anna. Wordlessly, she passed by me through the gate. Nicholas was right behind her. I stood as he neared. He extended his hand and gave me a brilliant, straight-toothed smile. "No hard feelings there, Liam, right?" I shook his hand, looking over his shoulder to the porch, where Anna was hugging Suzette. He leaned closer. "You may have her right now, but she'll get bored with you soon. She always gets bored. And when she comes home, you'll be nothing but a failed experiment." He gave my hand a painful squeeze. "Enjoy it while it lasts."

My demon roused and I squeezed his hand back, causing him to flinch. "I will. I plan to enjoy every second of it. And trust me, Nicky; she won't get bored."

Practiced ease gone, he jerked his hand away and stormed out of the gate. My demon delighted in his anger and discomfort.

"Sorry about that nasty bit of business," Suzette said, slinging her tote bag over her shoulder. "Nicholas and Mallory can be thoughtless, but they aren't really that bad." She stopped near me and smiled. "I'm sorry they stole your portfolio, but I'm glad in a way because I got to see it. You're an amazing artist. Your work has sort of an Andrew Wyeth feel. Keep at it. You're really good." Then she hugged me. "Take care of Anna, okay?"

I nodded.

"Happy birthday," Suzette said as Anna reached us. "Thanks for having us to your island."

Anna gave a wistful smile. "Sorry I bailed on you guys last night."

"That's perfectly understandable. In your shoes, I'd have done the same." Suzette winked and headed out the gate.

Anna took a deep breath. "Are you okay?"

"Yes."

She made the snort-through-her-nose sound. "I'm not. Let's go wish them good riddance—I mean see them off."

By the time we reached the helipad, the doors to the vehicle were closed and the rotors were starting up. We shielded our eyes and closed our lids partially to keep out the whirling debris stirred by the enormous blades. With a deafening roar, the machine lifted off, removing Anna's friends from my life.

She waved until there was no possibility they could see us any longer and we were again alone. She wrapped her arms around my waist and I held her against me, willing the world to stop so that I could simply revel in the joy of her nearness.

"You smell so good," she said, nuzzling against my chest.

I conjured my best Francine accent. "Irish Spring soap, lassie."

She laughed and my heart leapt.

"Can you hang out with me awhile?"

"I can think of nothing I would rather do."

I followed her through the gate and stooped to pick up the portfolio.

"Are you hungry?" she asked.

I nodded and followed her up onto the porch, wondering if I would ever grow accustomed to the peculiar sensation that I was being swallowed whole by the house every time I entered. Probably not, I conceded with a shudder as we stepped into the entry hall. From the archway under the gaping mandibles of the double stairway, Deirdre Byrne appeared. I hadn't seen her in a long time. She shot us a frightened look, then scurried away.

"That's the new maid," Anna said. "She's a little freaked out, I guess. Understandable if you have to deal with Miss Ronan on a regular basis."

Instead of going left into the dining room, where we had been last night, Anna led me to a passage on the right. Wall sconces that looked like inverted raptor claws lined the narrow space, giving the impression they would grab a passersby if he got within reach.

Before my morbid imagination could get the best of me, we entered an enormous kitchen. The floor was the same black marble as the entry hall, and the cabinets that stretched all the way to the ceiling appeared to be made of mahogany. The stainless-steel-clad countertops matched the enormous double oven with eight burners on top. There was a sink big enough to bathe in and on the far wall, a rack held utensils and knives in a terrifying, deadly display. All those knives, I marveled, one of every shape and size. I had only one. I only needed one, but with this kind of wealth, it wasn't about need.

"I'm starving," Anna said, pulling a pot down from a rack above a gigantic chopping block table in the center of the room. "Miss Ronan has the day off, thank God, so we're on our own."

I wondered where Miss Ronan would go or what she would do on a day off.

Anna pulled a pitcher and a white paper package from the refrigerator and placed them next to the pot. She poured cream from the pitcher into a cup on the counter near the stove. "I've been dying to get in here and make something, but she's always lurking. She's like a disease or something."

Too bad there was not a cure to make her go away, I thought as I watched Anna return the cream pitcher to the refrigerator and remove a jar of amber liquid and some leeks.

Again, I marveled at the sheer size and extravagance of the room. The entire village could outfit their kitchens with what I could see on display alone. I could only wonder what was inside the numerous cabinets and drawers.

Anna walked to the utensil rack and selected a knife with a large triangular blade. After washing the leeks in the sink, she returned to the chopping block and removed and discarded the dark green ends. She just threw them away. On Dòchas, very little was thrown away. The tops were perfectly edible, and it seemed a waste. With incredible speed and accuracy, she diced the leeks into tiny pieces and scooped them into the pot, adding a chunk of butter from the white paper.

"So, you can set that down if you want," she said, nodding to the portfolio I still clutched.

I laid it on a table near a door that opened to the outside of the house.

Anna placed the pot on the stove and turned a knob. The burner under her pot lit as if by magic without a match.

"Any more fallout from the Johnny thing?" she asked, opening the lid to a bin in the corner.

"No."

She pulled several potatoes out and selected a funny-looking knife from the rack. "Good." She paused, a potato in hand, and simply stared into my eyes. "That was scary. I thought I was going to lose you."

"I thought you were going to lose me too."

She smiled and ran the funny knife over the potato, leaving a curled strand of peel in its wake.

"Can I do something to help?" I asked.

"Nope. This is my thing. I love to cook. Just have a seat and be amazed." She winked.

I sat at the table where I'd placed my portfolio and watched as she deftly removed the peel from the remaining potatoes. The sunlight slanted through the transom at the top of the room, illuminating her striking face from an angle, and I longed to pull out my sketch pad.

She paused in the middle of chopping the potatoes into cubes. "What?"

"Nothing."

"You're staring."

"I'm admiring."

She blushed and turned her attention back to her task, chopping with incredible dexterity and speed. She hummed lightly under her breath as she stirred the leeks around in the pot. "If I could, I'd spend all day doing this."

"I would assume you have staff to cook for you."

She smiled and slid the potato cubes into a bowl she held under the counter edge. "Yep. That's who got me interested at first. Our cook, Beth, used to let me help her when I was a little girl."

She poured the golden liquid into the pot. "Vegetable stock Miss Ronan saved from yesterday's meal." She stirred the contents with a big spoon.

My hackles stood on end at the mere thought of Miss Ronan. I remembered Anna's plan to pump her for information. "Did you speak with her about me yet?"

She put the lid on the pot and turned the dial on a timer. "A little. She wasn't very forthcoming. She just said to avoid you."

"Please don't."

She met my eyes directly. "I can't."

The metallic ticking of the timer matched the tempo of my aching heart. No matter how much I wished to halt time or pretend the Cailleach was but a bad dream, my moments with Anna were running down, just like the minutes on that timer. In order to save her, I would have to turn my back on the first happiness I'd ever known and persuade her to leave.

17

I have no time to dote or dream:
You call it hope—that fire of fire!
It is but agony of desire.

—Edgar Allan Poe,
from "Tamerlane," 1827

The soup has a bit to go," Anna said, pulling out a chair at the small table by the door. "Do you want something to drink?"

"No. Thanks." I sat across from her.

She rubbed her hands over the leather portfolio. "This was a surprise. It's hard for you to share your art, isn't it?"

"Yes."

She ran her fingertips along the zipper present on three sides. "I noticed how uncomfortable you were when Francine showed me your paintings at the store. What are you afraid of?"

What I always feared: rejection—the one constant in my life. I didn't answer but watched as her fingertips skimmed their way along the zipper to the end.

"Did you bring them to show me?"

I held my breath as she grasped the pull on the zipper. She met my eyes, asking permission without words.

"Yes," I whispered.

My heart raced as she traced the pull around the portfolio, laying it open.

She met my eyes again before turning her attention to the contents. She stared a long time at the landscape on top, tipping her head slightly as she studied it.

"You have a great sense of motion and color," she said. "Who taught you?"

"No one."

She flipped the page to the next landscape. "My parents sent me to art school every summer for three years."

"So you paint?"

She flipped to the next canvas. "Nope. I suck at it." She slid that one aside, revealing a portrait of her I had done last month based on a tabloid picture. "But you don't." Her crystalline blue eyes met mine and I held my breath, waiting for her reaction. I had taken some poetic license in this painting and had given it an impressionistic flair, using broad strokes and intensifying the colors.

She turned to the next, then the next and shook her head. "You are so wasted here, Liam."

As she flipped through the remainder of the paintings and sketches, I noticed her fingers trembling. I caught her hand in mine. "What?" I asked.

She didn't pull her eyes away from the watercolor of her in a party dress I'd painted years ago based on a photo found in a New York newspaper. "How long?" she whispered.

"I beg your pardon?"

"How long have you been in love with me, Liam?"

"Forever."

In silence, she examined the rest of my work. As she reached the last one, a practice sketch for the painting of us as children that hung in Francine's kitchen, tears filled her eyes. She gently closed and zipped the portfolio, not looking at me, and set it on the floor, leaning it against the wall.

I had no idea what was running through her mind that would cause such a reaction.

The timer gave a shrill series of dings and she moved to the stove to tend her creation. She added some cream from the cup she had poured earlier and continued stirring, keeping her back to me.

"Anna," I said, standing behind her. "I'm sorry if I upset you somehow."

She reduced the fire under the pot to a flickering blue ring, then turned to face me. "Sorry. You're sorry?"

I nodded.

"You've been stuck here in this godforsaken place suffering all kinds of abuse and neglect while I've been off running around not even aware you existed, and you're sorry?"

Stunned, I took a step back.

"I'm the one who's sorry, Liam. I'm going to make it right, too."

She had it all wrong. There was nothing to rectify. "I don't want your pity or charity."

"What do you want?"

I wanted *her*—body, mind, and spirit—all of her, and I wanted her now, but that was impossible. "I want you safe."

"Oh, brother." She pulled two bowls from the cabinet to the right of the stove and ladled soup into them, then placed a spoon in each. From a basket at the end of the counter, she procured two crusty rolls and put them on a plate. She carried the plate and one of the bowls to the table. "Let's eat."

I grabbed the remaining bowl and followed her. I had no idea potatoes could taste so good. She had thrown spices in, but I hadn't paid close attention. "This is amazing. Truly."

She beamed. "Thanks. I'm going to open a vegetarian five-star restaurant someday. Dad says he'll send me to culinary school in Paris next year if I stay out of trouble."

"S'cuse me, miss," Deirdre said from the doorway. "Miss Ronan told me to attend to you. Do you need anything?" Her eyes flitted to the roll in my hand. I knew that look.

Evidently, Anna recognized it too. "Come on in and join us," she said to the girl.

Deirdre shook her head so vigorously, a hairpin fell out. "Oh, no, miss. My mother and Miss Ronan told me to never fra—frat—um . . ."

"Fraternize," Anna said.

"Yes, miss. That. I'm not supposed to be doin' that with you."

Anna stood and pulled a chair over. "You wouldn't be. You'd just be following my orders."

Wide-eyed, the girl watched as Anna ladled another bowl of soup and grabbed a roll from the basket. She set them on the table and gestured to the girl to sit.

"No, miss. I couldn't." Saying no to hot, fresh food was certainly painful for her. She clutched the apron at her waist and twisted it in her fingers, never taking her eyes off the table.

Anna sat. "It is not a request; it's an order from your boss. Now sit."

"And . . ." The girl twisted her apron even more violently.

Anna shifted in her chair to see her. "And what?"

"Him." She gestured to me with her chin.

Just when I was feeling normal, reality crashed down upon my head. Who was I kidding? Myself, obviously. I put my spoon down, no longer hungry.

"Liam, you mean?" Anna left her chair and stood behind me, facing her. The girl nodded, avoiding my eyes. Anna ran her fingers through my hair. "Well, I wasn't offering you Liam, only a bowl of soup. He is delicious, though, huh?"

Anna must have made a face or gesture behind my back because the girl covered her mouth and giggled.

"He's not what you've been taught, Deirdre. He's just a person like you and me." Anna sat in the new chair by my side and left hers opposite me open. She switched the bowls so that Deirdre wouldn't have to sit next to me. "Who do you work for?"

"You, miss."

"Then do as I say and sit, please."

Deirdre obeyed, moving as if she were treading upon broken glass. Gingerly, she sat, stiff-backed and wary.

"Go ahead. I want your opinion on the soup," Anna said. "I think it needs something. What do you think?"

It needed nothing, but my clever Anna had found a way to entice the girl to eat without guilt. My chest swelled with admiration.

We ate in silence for a while. Deirdre struggled to not shovel the soup into her mouth as fast as possible. I knew that kind of hunger. I'd felt it much of my life.

"What do you think?" Anna asked.

"Oh, miss. It's wonderful."

"Well, I think you should test out another bowl for me," she said, taking Deirdre's bowl and filling it at the stove. "So, how did you come to work here?" Anna placed the fresh bowl in front of her.

Deirdre's eyes darted to Anna and then back to her bowl. "Since my dad lost his boat in a storm, we really need the money. My parents also thought it best I get some training to make me a good wife."

Anna dropped her spoon into her bowl. "Wife! My God. How old are you?"

Deirdre sat up even straighter. "I'm almost fourteen. I'm plenty old, miss. My mom married at barely thirteen."

Anna shot me a horrified look.

Her parents, Polly and Edmond Byrne, struggled hard to feed themselves, and the only reason they hadn't married her off already, lessening the burden, was because of the lack of eligible husbands.

Deirdre took another bite of soup. "You see, miss, if I get married, it'll be better for my family. My husband will provide for me and I'll have a warm place in the winter and a real bed."

"You don't have a bed?"

Deirdre put her spoon down and wiped her mouth. "My family does right by me, if that's what you're asking." She raised her chin and tucked a loose strand of auburn hair behind her ear.

Anna nodded and tore off a piece of bread. "So, if I needed an employee to live here and be my personal assistant, would that be something you'd consider?"

"Live *here*, miss?"

"With your own room," Anna added.

Her face lit like a lantern, then clouded over. "Well, I'd have to ask my parents. Are you sure it would be okay with Miss Ronan?"

Anna's expression didn't change, but her tone was as ominous as a threatening storm. "Miss Ronan works for *me*."

"Yes, of course, miss." Deirdre stared at her hands folded in her lap.

Anna carried her empty bowl to the sink and Deirdre jumped to her feet. "No, miss! Please, let me. It's my job."

"Great. If you'd clear the table, then, that would be great," Anna said, placing the pot in the refrigerator.

Deirdre reached for my bowl and then recoiled as if touching something I had touched would taint her somehow. Though it stung, I didn't fault her. She'd been systematically brainwashed from infancy. "It's okay," I said. "I'll get it."

After putting my bowl in the sink, I followed Anna back through the constrictive hallway into the entry hall. "Let's go outside," she said. "This place gets to me after a while."

As we descended the porch steps, the wind shifted out of the south. Anna covered her mouth. "My God! What's that smell?"

It was a smell one never forgot. It burned into the core of memory for eternity, permeating all senses to the point of being its own special sixth sense of sorts. It was the smell of Dòchas. The smell of the inevitable. The smell of death.

"Let's go back inside," I suggested.

Her hand muffled her words. "What is it? God. It's horrible."

"It's Johnny's funeral pyre. You can see it just there." I pointed to an area west of the lighthouse where a dark plume of smoke rose into the air. Like a terrifying specter, it writhed and twisted, bringing its inevitable scent with it, causing the living in its path to recoil in dread.

Anna, mouth still covered, ran back into the house.

I followed, but there was no sign of her in the entry. Eyes huge, Deirdre hovered in the archway leading to the kitchen.

"Where is she?" I asked.

"I won't tell you. I won't let you hurt her."

She must have thought it was I who had spooked her. "For God's sake, Deirdre. Tell me where she is."

"No."

"Liam!" Anna's voice came from upstairs. Without another glance at the girl, I ascended the stairs two at a time, calling out for her when I reached the top.

"I'm here." Her voice came from a room at the far right of the balcony.

I found her curled up in a window seat beneath an expanse of stained glass that stretched all the way to the ceiling. Sunlight refracted through the beveled pieces of glass, showering her skin and hair with flecks of color, making her appear Otherworldly.

"Are you okay?" I asked.

"Yeah. I just had to get away from the smell—that smell of burning . . . Ugh." She shuddered.

The room had a settee the color of the sea and a bed with spiral carved posts several feet taller than I was that tapered to sharp points. On a stand near the bed, an enormous suitcase stuffed full of clothes stood open.

Following my gaze, Anna remarked, "I didn't unpack. I hadn't planned on staying."

"Good," I blurted out before I could catch myself.

"Good?"

"Anna, I . . ." The hurt look on her face caused something in my chest to pinch. "I didn't mean that like it sounded."

"I'm glad because it sounded pretty crappy."

I sat next to her. "This isn't the place for you."

"This isn't the place for anyone, Liam." She traced a blue fleck of light on my arm, and I thrilled at the simple touch. I needed to tell her the truth despite my body's insistence otherwise.

"Why didn't they just bury him? Why burn him like that?" she asked.

She traced a different fleck of light higher up my arm, making it difficult to speak. "It's just how we do it."

"It's gross and wrong. He should be buried since the ground isn't frozen."

I stilled her hand. "It is not wrong. The spirit has long departed. It makes little difference whether the body left behind becomes food for the worm or ashes on the waves."

She said nothing for a long time, then took several deep

breaths before speaking. "Why did you say 'good' when I told you I hadn't planned on staying? Do you want me to leave?"

She stared straight ahead at a grim painting of what appeared to be one of Dante's circles of hell.

"What I want is irrelevant at this point. What's important is that I haven't been completely forthcoming about what happened at Francine's last night."

She shifted to face me. The strokes of color across her flawless pale skin took my breath away. "You're talking about the angel that turned into a . . . whatever that was."

"The Cailleach." This was it. In keeping her safe, I was ensuring my loss of the one thing I loved the most. I took a deep breath. "It brings death to those who see it."

"I don't feel dead," she said with a smirk.

"I don't mean immediately. It's a warning, Anna, an omen. You need to get off this island as soon as you can before it comes true. You saw it. No one sees it and lives."

She placed her hands on either side of my neck and the tension melted from my shoulders. "Listen to me, Liam. I'm not buying it. I don't believe in prophecies, omens, fortunes, palm readers, psychics, or creepy crones predicting death. I've never lived my life in fear. I won't begin living that way now."

"But—" She silenced me by placing a finger over my lips.

"Granted. Freaky things happen on this island. What you're telling me may be true, but I'm not going to run away because of a story."

"I'm begging you to leave, Anna," I pleaded. "Please go."

"You want me to leave?" She got on her knees, face only inches from mine. "Is that what you really want?" I nodded. She moved so close, our noses touched and her breath tickled my lips. "Really?" She pressed her cheek against mine and whispered in my ear, causing chills to race down my spine. "Because I don't believe you."

"Anna, please."

She caught my earlobe between her teeth and released it. "I can't leave," she whispered. "It's not possible." She trailed kisses down the side of my neck and I groaned. Her lips tightened into a smile against my skin. "I've found the best thing ever, and you expect me to just take off because of some bogus fairy tale?"

I was certain my heart would stop any second. I wanted to object, to beg her to listen, but I could only sit still, mesmerized by her touch.

"It's not going to happen, Liam. I'm not dying and I'm not leaving." She pulled away and stared into my eyes. "I didn't make up what I said on the jetty. I'm not going anywhere, so you're just going to have to deal with it."

As if under a spell, I could only stare in wonder at this beautiful creature. The light from the window reflected off her sleek ebony hair and flitted across her alabaster skin. The only sound was my uneven breath as I fought to control my desire.

"This is the part where you kiss me," she said.

Without hesitation I obliged.

18

Though I turn, I fly not—
I cannot depart;
I would try, but try not
To release my heart
And my hopes are dying
While, on dreams relying,
I am spelled by art.

—Edgar Allan Poe,
from "To Miss Louise Olivia Hunter," 1847

To my surprise, Francine didn't push or interrogate me when I finally arrived at the store that afternoon. She did, however, linger nearby pretending to be busy, undoubtedly with the hope I would volunteer information.

"The supply boat's not coming today after all," Francine said, putting the phone headset back in the cradle. "There's been foul weather on the mainland coast."

I squeezed the water out of the mop and moved to the section of floor closest to the cash register.

"That means we need to transfer the lobsters from the holding crates to the underwater pen." Francine sighed. "I was hoping it would be a lazy day so we could visit over some tea."

Her blatant nudge made me smile. I rinsed the mop and put it in the wringer attached to the inside of the bucket.

"I certainly hope the storm doesn't come this way and ruin the Bealtaine celebration tonight," she said.

I had lashed an extra two feet of dowel to the mop so that I could tuck it under my armpit for leverage and guide it with my hand and forearm, which made it easier, but it was still difficult for me. Balancing the mop handle on my shoulder, I pushed down on the wringer handle and gray water cascaded into the bucket.

Francine shuffled to the area I'd just mopped. "You *are* going to the celebration, right?"

I straightened and pulled the mop out. "I suppose."

"Well, you need to take the Leighton girl so you can ask for a blessing on your union."

I lifted an eyebrow. "Union?" I turned my back to her and ran the mop down the floor under the counter.

Francine blocked my progress. "Okay, Liam. Union, relationship, or whatever you two are doing, you can ask the Otherworlders to bless it."

"Whatever we are doing *is* blessed. We don't need Otherworlders to make it so."

I swiveled and pushed the mop in the other direction. Francine stomped around me and stepped on the soggy cords. "Best you do all you can to make good with them."

"Make good with them? There is nothing *good* in it. My entire life has been misery because of them, or rather because of the villagers' belief in them." I sloshed the mop into the water, surprised at my level of resentment. Ordinarily, I tempered my thoughts and feelings about Dòchas and my place in it because fighting it was as futile as attempting to stop the incoming tide. At this moment, though, nothing was tempered. I practically boiled with indignation. All my life I'd been pushed down, denied, and shunned because of things over which I had no control. Seeing the Cailleach had brought all the unfairness of my life home to me. Perhaps Anna was right and it was all "bogus." I dumped the mop back in the wringer. "I'll never ask them for anything. Ever."

Francine pulled the mop handle from my hand and let it fall to the floor. "Liam, lad." She took me by the shoulders. "Listen to me." She gave my shoulders a slight shake. "Do not anger them. You need them on your side."

"No one is on my side!" I shouted. "No one but you and Anna. Don't you see? Everything works against me, especially the Otherworlders. They scream at me at night. They taunt me from the sea. My own people want to kill me because of the things they do. Yet, you want me to ask them for a blessing on the only thing that has ever been right in my entire pathetic existence?"

Hands still gripping my shoulders, she stared into my eyes for what felt like an eternity. "Yes, I do."

Out of breath from my rant, I leaned against the counter, and something that sounded much like a whimper issued from my throat. I closed my eyes and gathered my composure. Francine was far older and wiser. She knew much more about the Otherworlders than I. What harm could it do?

"We'll set candles on the water and ask for their blessing," I whispered.

She patted my cheek. "That's a smart lad."

A sense of dread had been niggling at Muireann since before sunup. Perhaps it was because of the death of the human yesterday. Maybe it was because she knew the Na Fir Ghorm would derive power from the human worship tonight. Whatever the reason, she didn't share her pod's enthusiasm for the activities onshore.

"Will you look at that!" her sister, Keela, said. "The bonfire will be even bigger than last year!"

All day, the villagers had been combing the island for fallen wood to make the Bealtaine fires. They did this at the turn of the season every year.

Muireann swam from behind the harbor buoy to get a closer look. She had seen her human walking on the cliff-side trail several hours ago on his way from the big dwelling at the high point of the island. He had not stopped at his home, but he wasn't helping with the bonfire preparation. She slipped behind a moored boat and peeked around the bow.

"Looking for someone?" her sister said, nudging her shoulder.

"Don't sneak up on me like that!"

"You're so jumpy. What's wrong?"

Muireann slipped under the surface and glided into the shadows under the dock. She knew Keela would follow, but it gave her time to come up with an answer that would suit.

The Na Fir Ghorm were an everyday part of life for her pod. In the old country, they didn't interact much, as the Na Fir Ghorm stayed in caves deeper out in the sea and inhabited the straits and more remote areas. Here, they lived close in to shore among the Selkies.

Until now, the Na Fir Ghorm were not an issue for Muireann because they didn't affect her directly. She'd never had trouble adopting the Selkies' "live and let live" attitude. Her feelings for her human had changed everything. She could no longer remain impassive as they took human lives for their entertainment and enrichment.

There he was! Her human was dropping lobsters from plastic boxes into a wire pen in the water at the end of the pier. Her pulse quickened at the mere sight of him.

"He's quite beautiful," Keela said. "Too beautiful, really."

Yes, too beautiful, Muireann thought. This was the closest she'd ever been to him.

"He makes you want to change, doesn't he?"

"Yes," Muireann whispered.

"Listen to me, little sister," Keela said. "Father says human males are good for nothing but pain. They steal your heart, then they steal your pelt, leaving you in human form to die an early, miserable death, never to see your family again."

Muireann couldn't imagine her human being cruel. She'd heard the stories of humans hiding or stealing their Selkie lovers' pelts in order to keep them in human form. "He's not like that."

Keela gave a loud snort and ducked under the surface.

Her human looked over his shoulder straight into her eyes, and she melted inside.

"Hello, there," he said.

He was talking to her! She was too stunned to even move. She kept her head above water—a huge no-no when this close to a human—and simply stared back. His eyes were deep brown and rimmed with thick, black lashes. If only . . .

He leaned down to get a better look under the dock where she hid. Everything in her told her to flee, but she could not. She was frozen, mesmerized by his beauty.

"How's it going out here?" a middle-aged woman with graying red hair asked him.

He placed a finger to his lips. The woman nodded and joined him. "Ah. A Selkie girl," she said. Muireann knew she should swim away as fast as possible but could not budge.

"Do not encourage her, Liam. She'll only bring you trouble."

Liam! His name was Liam. Muireann rejoiced at this bit of information. Her human had a name as beautiful as his face. It was worth the danger of being this close just to know his name. *Liam,* she said over and over in her head. *My Liam.*

"It's just a harbor seal, Francine. It's probably here because of the lobsters," he said.

The woman narrowed her eyes and studied Muireann, who winced. "No. Definitely a Selkie. Be careful. There will be many here tonight. Bealtaine was when I . . ." The woman got a far-away look on her face. "Never mind. That was long ago. Are you almost finished here?"

He nodded. "One crate left."

"When you're done, come on inside. I have a gift for you. I was going to give it to you for your birthday next month but changed my mind." After shooting Muireann one last curious look, the woman wandered back to the shop.

"Selkie," he muttered under his breath as he pitched a lobster into the underwater pen.

Muireann swam out of the shadows, closer to the end of the pier—closer to her Liam.

"Well, look at you," he said. "Aren't you pretty?"

She felt as though her heart would burst. Her Liam found her pretty.

"Do you want one of these?" he asked, holding up a lobster with bright blue bands on its claws.

She shook her head. His eyes widened and he dropped the lobster on the pier, then scrambled to catch it before it skittered off into the water. He tossed it into the bin, followed by two others from the plastic crate before returning his attention to her.

Cross-legged, he sat on the end of the pier and stared at her. She stared right back. "It's almost like you can understand me."

"Liam!" the woman called from the back door to the store. "You need to get moving if you are going to the celebration. You can't go smelling like a lobster."

Yes, he can, Muireann thought. *He smells perfect. He is perfect.*

"I guess I'll see you tonight, then, little seal," he said. He lay on his belly to close and latch the wire lid to the top of the underwater bin, which was wise; her brothers and sisters would clean that out in seconds tonight if given the opportunity.

He glanced over his shoulder at her before disappearing into the store.

She would find a way to protect him, she vowed. She would keep her Liam safe even if it meant shedding her pelt. Her heart hammered at the thought of meeting him in his own form. Of wrapping her human limbs around him as his female companion had done on the beach that day.

Her sister must never know. Her pod must never know. She understood she could never keep him, but she could protect him from the Na Fir Ghorm, and at that thought, her heart soared.

19

The appearance of the ocean, in the space
between the more distant island and the shore,
had something very unusual about it.

—Edgar Allan Poe,
from "A Descent into the Maelström," 1841

Anna wore a dress with a sheer, silver gossamer overlay that shimmered and reflected the final rays of the sunset as it threw vivid streaks of magenta and gold across the placid water of the harbor. I'd never seen anything like it—or her—in my life.

"You are so beautiful," I said as she entwined her fingers in mine.

"You're looking pretty sharp yourself," she said with a grin.

I looked down at the new clothes Francine had given to me today after I'd finished transferring the lobsters. She insisted I shower at the shop and then presented me with a brand-new pair of blue jeans and a soft, pullover shirt, both of which felt foreign to me after wearing Pa's hand-me-downs for so many years.

"So, what can I expect at this soiree?" Anna asked as we stepped up onto the wooden sidewalk leading to the docks.

"Crazy people talking to Otherworlders around a couple of huge fires."

She laughed, and all my apprehension about bringing her here dissipated. "You're beginning to sound like me," she said.

"As long as I don't begin to look like you."

She stopped and pulled my hand so that I almost fell against her. "No, no. You keep looking just like you look and we'll be fine." She wrapped her arms around my waist and pressed her body close. "More than fine."

"Oh, Anna. What you do to me."

She grinned. "What do I do to you?"

The list was infinitely long, so I chose the most important. "You make me feel good about myself."

"You *should* feel good about yourself." She clutched my hand again and we continued toward the point of the beach past the harbor. "You're freaking amazing."

I'd no idea what I'd done to warrant the title "freaking amazing," but I liked it.

"There you are," Francine called from the shop door. "Come in here first. I have something for you."

She hugged Anna and ushered us into the store. "Tonight is very important. Liam has never been a big believer in tradition, but all things considered, I think it best the two of you participate."

"You said it was crazy people talking to Otherworlders around huge fires," Anna whispered when Francine went behind the counter to retrieve something.

"She's one of the crazy people," I said loud enough for Francine to hear.

Francine tsked. "Liam MacGregor! Mind your manners or I'll box your ears." She handed each of us a candle. "Crazy indeed." She winked at Anna. "He knows what to do with the candles. Make sure he does it." She wrung her hands in front of her body.

Anna took my candle and slipped both into her silver handbag. "Will do."

"Now, go," Francine said, pushing us out the door. "You don't want to miss the lighting."

Anna shifted her handbag to her right shoulder so that it wasn't between us. "I've never seen Francine that intense."

I nodded. Francine had always behaved in a peculiar manner at Bealtaine. It was the only celebration in which she did not participate. Something had happened years ago on this day, she'd hinted at that much, but I'd never had the nerve to outright ask her about it.

We reached the end of the wooden sidewalk and stepped off onto the dirt trail leading to the low area of beach that jutted out into the water where the logs and limbs had been piled for the fires. Most of the village was already there.

"So, are we going to have to kick somebody's butt tonight like we almost had to on the jetty yesterday?" Anna asked. "Because I'm really not dressed for it."

I chuckled. "No. This is the only day of the year that I'm left totally alone. Bealtaine was, in its origin, a time for tribes to come together with a love-your-enemy kind of mentality."

"You being the enemy."

"Exactly."

I stopped at a boulder with a flat surface on the top that was only a few feet tall. "Let's observe from here." I preferred not to press my luck by mingling just yet.

The sun was obscured by Seal Island at the mouth of the harbor, but its rays stretched out horizontally in crimson streaks that had the appearance of flames dancing across the surface of the water.

Connor MacFarley and Edmond Byrne held torches at the ready near the two enormous piles of wood.

"Wanna tell me what this is all about?" Anna said, smoothing her dress across her thighs.

"I told you."

She rolled her eyes and patted the stone next to her. "Get over here and tell me a story, demon dude. That or make out with me, because you are looking pretty fine in this light."

"I much prefer the latter option."

Something over my shoulder caught her eye and the smile melted off her face. I spun around to find Brigid Ronan dressed in black from head to toe standing only feet behind me. "I see you did not heed my advice." She looked me up and down with disgust. "You are playing with fire, Anna. But that doesn't surprise me. Some people like to play with fire, as you will see tonight. Just don't get too close. It's fatal."

In silence, we watched as she strolled down the beach and disappeared in the crowd of villagers.

"Was that a threat?" Anna asked. "Because if that was a threat, she'd better start looking for a new job."

I sat next to her. "It sounded more like a warning." I brushed her hair behind her shoulder so I could see her face in the last vestiges of light.

She took a deep breath. "I wish Mom and Dad would get rid of her."

"I wish I had my sketch pad."

A cheer rose from the villagers as Connor and Edmond touched their torches to the wood.

"Story time," Anna said, nestling against me.

"We have four seasonal celebrations: Samhain, Imbolg, Bealtaine, and Lughnasa. The traditions derive from our Celtic heritage, but they have been distorted over our centuries of isolation on Dòchas. The intent remains the same, though. We honor the pantheon of gods and creatures that our ancestors honored. It is said they followed our ships to the New World, invigorated and empowered by our worship. My people believe that the Otherworlders still heed our requests because we have not turned from the old ways."

Anna folded her legs to the side. "So, the creepies are hanging out on this island because you guys do this stuff."

"Yes."

She shuddered. "Oooh. Cut it out, then."

Several women gave shrill calls and held sheets above their heads.

"They've collected the evening dew on the sheets and will wipe their skin with them."

"Why?" The fires were taking hold, casting a golden glow on her skin.

"Bealtaine is a celebration of the fertility of the earth. It's believed that the nighttime dew has restorative qualities." The women wiped each other's faces with the sheets.

"Watch out, Noxzema corporation. We've got dirty dew sheets working here," she said with a giggle. "Oh, hey. That's Deirdre. She looks beautiful."

The women of the village formed a circle around Deirdre, whose auburn hair cascaded down her back in stark contrast to the pure white shift she wore. A woman with a sheet wiped all of the girl's exposed skin, including her legs and feet.

"So, why's Deirdre looking like a sacrificial lamb to me?" Anna asked.

The fire on the left flared from within as something shifted in the pile and the crowd cheered.

"Because she is."

Anna stiffened. "They're not going to—"

"No, no." I put my arm around her. "Not that kind of sacrifice. It is customary to perform handfasting ceremonies at Bealtaine. They must be promising her to someone tonight."

The women smiled and laughed, but Deirdre appeared miserable. She stood stiff and unsmiling in the circle, eyes unfocused as if she saw nothing.

"So, who's she marrying?" Anna asked.

"I have no idea. We have a great shortage of eligible males . . . and females for that matter. She's the only woman of childbearing age on Dòchas."

She pulled away. "Woman of childbearing age? My God, Liam. She's not even fourteen yet!"

"Remember where you are, Anna. Dòchas is not New York."

"We're not in Kansas anymore," she whispered under her breath.

It was another pop culture reference, I assumed, so I didn't respond.

Edmond held his torch over his head and gave a guttural cry, silencing the crowd. The sun had fully set, but the flames blazed, illuminating the scene in an ominous orange glow. He stepped to the space between the two fires and shouted a rhyme:

Strike the fire and let it rise
In cleansing flames to the summer skies.
Our ancient customs we now renew
Bathed in purest nighttime dew.
We invoke the spirits of olden days
By following our ancestors' ways
We affirm the power that you wield
Over the bounty of body, sea, and field.

He threw his torch into the fire and the villagers cheered. Mac and Ron Reilly pulled their fiddles from under their arms and struck up a feisty jig.

"Look at Deirdre," Anna said. "She's miserable. She was so happy about the prospect of having a husband at the house earlier today. I wonder what happened?"

Deirdre sat on a log near the water with her mother, Polly, who had an arm around the girl and was speaking in her ear.

"Perhaps she doesn't like her parents' choice of a prospective mate."

Anna stiffened. "You don't suppose it's you, do you?"

I laughed. "Not a chance. That would certainly bring her misery, though."

Her brow furrowed. "Why not you? Why is that funny?"

"I'm not eligible for marriage. I am, for lack of a better word, broken."

She stared into the crowd. "So who is eligible?"

I ran through the candidates in my mind. All were old enough to be her grandfather or great-grandfather. She wasn't going to like my answer, so I shrugged.

Sighing, she nestled back in under my arm. "Well, I'm glad it's not you because I'd have to take her down and stake my claim." She winked and I gave her shoulder a squeeze. "Hey. Ronan's looking at us."

With the firelight writhing across her face, Brigid Ronan looked like she belonged in the painting from Dante's *Inferno* in Anna's room. The hairs on the back of my neck and scalp tingled under her minatory glare.

"The mean old witch," Anna said under her breath. "Let's give her something to stare at." Anna captured my face in her hands and kissed me with such passion, it caught me off guard. I gathered my wits and returned her kiss with equal enthusiasm, finding myself light-headed after a few moments. She released me and we stared at each other, gasping for air.

"Whoa," she said. "That was . . . wow."

The strains of the fiddles and villagers' singing swirled through my head and everything seemed a blur except Anna. She was as crisp and focused as my desire.

A cheer rose from the crowd again. Someone had placed a burning plank on the ground between the two fires and men were jumping over it.

"Purification by fire," I explained. "In the old country, livestock was driven between the fires to ensure fertility and health."

"Let's go do it," she said, jumping to her feet.

"No, Anna, I don't . . ."

She grabbed my hand and tugged. "Come on, Liam. We only live once. Let's live well."

At this moment, I understood that she truly comprehended our situation. She hadn't completely discounted the possibility that we were doomed but had chosen to be with me over taking the safer path. This reality took my breath away. "Yes. Let's live well," I answered.

Laughing, she danced toward the fire, pulling me with her.

"Wait," I said as we neared the flames. "Your dress."

She grabbed it up from the bottom and tied the hem in a knot at the top of her thigh, exposing her pale, slender legs, nearly causing my heart to stop.

"Anna, I swear, the Cailleach's prediction is going to come true right now. You'll be the death of me."

She grinned and took my hand. "Ready?"

The music and singing continued, but many of the villagers closer to the horizontal plank simply stared at us. We must have looked quite the pair: the latent demon and the half-dressed eccentric socialite.

"Ready," I answered, and we laughed and laughed all the way over the flames to the water.

She untied the knot and the dress fell back in place to just above her ankles. Again, I longed for my sketch pad. The iridescent fibers of the dress caught the blue hues of the moon shimmering off the water from the front, and her back was bathed in orange from the fire behind us.

"Something is moving out there," she said, pointing to the water.

The surface that had earlier been slick was now churning. Perhaps it was just my imagination, but it also appeared that heads bobbed out of the water and then disappeared.

"Harbor seals, most likely," I said.

"So what do we do with the candles?" she asked, unsnapping her purse and pulling out one of the small, bowl-shaped candles.

"We light them, cast them upon the water, and ask the Otherworlders to grant a wish."

She handed me one. "So, what are you going to wish for?"

"All my wishes were granted the moment you returned to Dòchas."

Muireann had assumed the Na Fir Ghorm clan consisted of no more than a dozen of the hideous creatures, but she had been wrong. Everywhere she turned, she saw blue skin and gray hair as they filled the harbor, and more arrived by the hour; there were at least fifty of them now. The ones arriving must live in deep ocean caves and crevices like their Old World ancestors.

"They're at it again," Keela said. "Oooh. He really likes her."

The flames from the Bealtaine fires backlit the couple at the edge of the beach, rendering them silhouettes with shape and no features, but she'd know her human anywhere.

"Are you jealous?" Keela asked.

When the female had pulled up her garment before leaping through the fire, exposing her human legs, Muireann had been jealous, but only of her form and only for a moment. Having feet would be so much better than flippers. "No. She brings him happiness."

Keela snorted.

"It's true."

"Whatever you say," Keela said, rolling her eyes.

The Bean Sidhe drifted above the water like puffs of golden clouds. Muireann had always liked them. Too bad she was stuck in the ocean with the Na Fir Ghorm rather than with these lovely creatures. Well, lovely until they opened their mouths. Even when they whispered, their piercing voices made her uncomfortable.

"Come on," Keela said, "they're heading to the pier. Maybe he'll talk to you again."

Muireann hoped she didn't come to regret telling her sister about her encounter with him today, but she had been too excited to keep it secret.

They weaved their way among the Na Fir Ghorm assembled near the shore and surfaced at the end of the pier.

"My ancestors used to float burning reeds upon the water, but Francine makes these floating candles, which simplifies things," her Liam explained to the human female from the steps to the water. "Bealtaine is a time when the Otherworlders are close, so we make wishes and ask for their help or blessing."

Muireann gasped as he produced fire from a small object

in his hand. The human female tipped her candle and held the wick to the tiny flame.

Several Bean Sidhes drifted around them, but the humans did not notice. Like the Na Fir Ghorm closing in around the pier, they cloaked themselves with a glamour that made them invisible to humans. The Selkies had no glamour abilities. They had to hide in plain sight by adopting the form of a creature of the human world. Muireann had never been certain whether the seal was her natural form or the creature within the pelt. She just knew that the form within was fragile and in her seal form, she could live four or five centuries, which was why so few of her kind dared to shed their pelts.

"The selfish creatures will wish for wealth," a Na Fir Ghorm said, yellow eyes like those of a squid trained on the couple.

"Or children. These islanders always asks for children," another said. "Always thinking of themselves."

"Selfish and worthless," the first one replied. "And completely inferior to us."

A Bean Sidhe swirled above their heads. She spoke in the ancient tongue. "No! You are wrong. Humans have an infinite capacity for unconditional love. That is what makes them unique and precious."

The human female placed her candle on the water and closed her eyes. "Done," she said.

Liam kissed her cheek. "You have to make a wish."

"I did."

"Out loud, so that they can hear you."

"Oh." She stared out over the water at her invisible audience. "You go first."

He created flame from the object in his hand and held it to a candle on the step next to him. He placed the candle on the water and it bobbed for a moment before settling. "We'll make our wishes together."

Muireann held her breath. What would her Liam wish for?

"Here it comes. Money or children. I'll bet for this one, it will be money," the first Na Fir Ghorm said.

"His wish will be selfless," a Bean Sidhe answered.

"What will you bet?" the Na Fir Ghorm replied.

"The one who loses will grant his wish."

"Done. I hope you have some gold. Humans are the most selfish creatures in any realm."

Muireann's heart pounded. She hated that her Liam was the object of a bet.

"Ready?" Liam said to his human female. She nodded.

"I wish for . . ." he started.

"Your happiness," they said in unison.

The Bean Sidhes let out an earsplitting celebratory shriek only the Otherworlders could hear.

Muireann ducked underwater to mute the volume. When she surfaced, the couple was kissing . . . again.

"Now you must make good on your debt and grant his wish," the Bean Sidhe said.

A Na Fir Ghorm laughed, then responded, "We cannot grant happiness. That's preposterous. There is no such thing. Just as there is no such thing as love."

The Bean Sidhes swirled in a golden vortex over the group of Na Fir Ghorm. "You are wrong. Love is real."

"That's not love. It's lust," said a Na Fir Ghorm to Muireann's right, his gray beard swirling on the surface of the water. To her knowledge, all Na Fir Ghorm were male. She'd never seen a female.

"Love is the only thing that lasts forever," the Bean Sidhe replied.

"Love is fleeting and fickle. Humans only love when it is easy. If an obstacle were thrown in their way, they would cast this love aside like fish bones after the flesh is gone."

"Obstacles make love grow stronger," was the reply of the Bean Sidhe.

Muireann exchanged glances with Keela. She'd never heard the Bean Sidhes converse with the Na Fir Ghorm, much less debate with them. A queasy churning filled her stomach.

"We are never wrong. Everyone knows we are the smartest creatures in the Otherworld. Intellect rules the heart every time. Feelings and emotions are worthless," came the answer from a Na Fir Ghorm a little farther out. They all looked alike to Muireann, so she could only identify them by location.

"Love is the most powerful and valuable asset of any living creature, of this world or any other," said a Bean Sidhe.

The humans on the steps at the water held each other, talking quietly, oblivious to the battle of words waging around them.

"Prove it," said a Na Fir Ghorm close to the steps. Muireann recognized this one because of his distinctive voice and the long scar on his face. This was the ruler of the clan in her waters—the one who just days ago tortured his own son. A wide grin split his face, exposing sharp teeth like a shark. "Or rather, let *them* prove it." He gestured to the humans with a bony arm, pointing with webbed fingers. "The only reason these humans are feeling what you call love is because it is easy. I'll wager that this 'love' will falter at the first bit of difficulty."

The golden cloud closest to the Na Fir Ghorm leader defined itself into shape of a woman. "Love is strongest in adversity."

His eyes widened, exposing his horizontal pupils. "A wager, then?"

"The cost?" she replied.

"The losing species must leave this territory forever!" His

announcement was greeted with gasps and grumbles from both factions.

Muireann was torn. She was certain that the humans would pass the test, but at what cost? Ridding her waters of the Na Fir Ghorm would be a gift as long as it didn't hurt her Liam.

A Na Fir Ghorm from farther out shouted over the grumbling. "You cannot speak for all of us. You can only represent your own clan. Those of us who live in the deeper waters remove ourselves from this wager." With that, dozens of the horrible creatures swam out of the harbor.

Liam and his female cuddled on the steps, speaking in whispers. *Ignorance is bliss,* Muireann thought, quoting her father.

The leader of the Na Fir Ghorm stood on the lowest step in front of the couple. "So, is it a wager?"

The swirling gold clouds of mist congealed to form six iridescent women hovering over the harbor. "We exist to serve. Leaving will be contrary to our purpose," one said.

"We cannot lose," one of them said to her sister Bean Sidhes. "Their love is to the very soul. If we win, we could rid the island of these creatures that prey on humans at a rate greater than they reproduce. We should accept the wager."

The leader of the Na Fir Ghorm crossed his arms across his scaled blue chest as if daring his clan to object or speak up. As Muireann expected, the dozen or so remaining Na Fir Ghorm remained silent.

"We accept on the following conditions: First, the contest can last no longer than thirty days. Second, before any test is issued, both sides must approve it. Third, we must follow the rules of the Otherworld with regard to taking human life," the Bean Sidhe said, her brightness intensifying.

The grin on the Na Fir Ghorm leader's face made Muireann shudder. She knew what his motivation was. He had no interest in ridding Dòchas of the Bean Sidhes. He wanted to torture the broken one, her Liam.

"Let it begin, then," the horrible blue leader announced.

"Wait," Muireann said. "Maybe we—"

"Maybe *we*?" the leader shouted. "*We?* You are not part of this. You are simply a creature stuck between worlds with no say in anything. One more word from you and you will be tiny pieces of bait."

Keela sank below the surface, but Muireann remained, trembling, furious. On the steps behind the Na Fir Ghorm leader, her Liam laughed at something his female said, and her heart ached. He was about to be an unwitting pawn in a game of ancient malice and evil, and she could do nothing to stop it.

20

Near neighbors are seldom friends.

—Edgar Allan Poe,
from "Metzengerstein," 1832

Muireann's sister turned her back, something she had never done before. "Please, Keela. Try to understand," Muireann begged.

"I understand all too well." Keela moved farther up the rocks, closer to their sleeping family. "You put our entire pod in danger because of your attraction to this human."

"That wasn't what I was trying to do."

Keela stopped halfway up a rock. "What exactly were you trying to do, then?"

"Save him."

Keela grunted as she pulled her bulky seal body up onto the ledge below the sleeping pod. She glared over the edge at Muireann. "It was stupid and reckless. The Na Fir Ghorm hate us and would love to find a reason to kill us off."

"I'm sorry."

"You should be."

Muireann lurched and flopped her upper body and flippers on the edge of the rock shelf to join her family.

"There's no room for you up here," her sister growled. "Find another place to sleep. Maybe you can cuddle up with your human since he means more to you than we do."

Tears blurred Muireann's vision. No one had ever been unkind to her before. How did her Liam stand it? He was treated this way all the time.

"I'm sorry," she whispered as she slunk back to the water.

The Bealtaine celebration was still in full swing when she returned to the harbor. The villagers danced around the fire and candles littered the surface of the water. Her human was no longer on the steps, but a small group of Na Fir Ghorm congregated just at the end of the pier. Slipping behind one boat and then another, she snuck close enough to hear them.

"We have this wager netted," the leader said. "There is no way this couple can stay together. We could win without even adding to their troubles. I've learned a great deal about them tonight. The female's wealthy parents will find the broken one unsuitable and will not allow the relationship to continue. Even without the parents' intervention, my source believes it will end any day now. As soon as the newness wears off, the female will leave him for a more appropriate mate who can tolerate her lifestyle."

Muireann moved closer, hiding behind the pen of lobsters her Liam had filled earlier in the day. She took a deep breath and went back under to listen again.

"Just to be on the safe side, I think we need to help things along. To make the split happen faster, we will force him back into his foster father's home. Not only will the broken one be miserable, his foster father will keep them apart and the female will get bored."

A smaller Na Fir Ghorm spoke up. "How are we going to force him back to the foster father's home?"

The leader grinned and Muireann shuddered at the evil in his voice. "Let's just say, he's about to undergo a trial by fire."

···

I had never been happier in my life. I was madly and passionately in love with Annabel Leighton and she with me. Had the Cailleach's marker been called at this moment, I would have died willingly, having experienced joy few mortals had ever known.

The bonfire flames still raged and the villagers sang and danced madly in a whisky-induced frenzy. Amid this surreal scene of fiery jubilance and revelry, though, was one dark miserable being. Deirdre Byrne's tear-stained face drew my attention like a magnet to metal.

She sat in agonizing solitude as those around her rejoiced in spite of her misery—some perhaps because of her misery.

The part of the ceremony in which her betrothal would be announced would happen anytime now.

If my suspicion as to whom Deirdre would be bound was correct, Anna would not receive the news well. "Let's go," I whispered in Anna's ear.

She smiled. "It's about time."

"You're not enjoying my dear neighbors' celebration?"

Her smile broadened. "We could do better on our own."

"Wait here," I said.

I picked up one of the long, pale sticks that had been stripped of bark from the pile set aside for relighting home hearths. I stuck it into the embers of the north-most fire until the end ignited. Villagers watched, but none bade me good night or good luck as they would one another. It didn't matter to me this year. I had Anna, which was more luck than I deserved.

The boards of the harbor sidewalk creaked underfoot. A light still shone from Francine's apartment above the store. I briefly considered dropping in on her, but with her history of reclusive behavior at Bealtaine, I abandoned the idea.

"What's with the burning stick?" Anna asked.

Our pace was slow because with no second hand to block the wind, I knew it was likely to extinguish. "It's to relight the hearth fire as a symbol of renewal. All the villagers extinguish their fire in their home on the morning of the celebration and then relight it with the flame from the Bealtaine fire."

"Well, it's about to go out." She pulled it from me with one hand and cupped her other hand in front of it. The tiny flame flared and strengthened. "We'd better pick up speed or it'll burn down to nothing before we get to your place."

As I took one last look back at the harbor, I noticed the unmistakable shape of a seal's head poking from the water at the end of the pier and I wondered if it was the little seal from earlier in the day.

We took the cliff-side trail because it was a bit shorter. It worried me that Anna carried the flame while wearing her impractical slippers and lovely dress that could hang on bushes and branches. After just a few yards on the trail, the burden of maintaining the flame outweighed its benefits. I lifted it from her hands and extinguished it underfoot.

"What about the tradition?" she asked.

"It's not *my* tradition." I pitched the stick over the cliff into the water.

"Let's start a new one of our own, then." She struck back out up the trail, holding the front of her skirt. "What should we do in place of lighting the hearth with the Bealtaine fire?"

"How about I paint you by firelight?"

She stopped at the top of the trail and turned so that the sea wind blew the hair out of her face. The moonlight danced through the silver fibers in her dress, giving her the appearance of being lit from within. The gossamer fabric rippled, making the effect even more dreamlike.

Awed by her beauty, I could only stare, trying to commit her to memory: every curve, every plane, every shimmering ripple of her dress.

She smiled over her shoulder, fully aware of her effect on me, and kept walking.

"Or moonlight," I said. "I could paint you by moonlight."

I nearly tripped several times because I couldn't keep my eyes off her. I'd been completely entranced and captivated, body and soul.

Before we even made the turn to my shed, I knew something was wrong. The feeling wasn't triggered by any tangible thing, like a scent or sight; it was just an overall sense of foreboding that radiated throughout my body.

"Fire," Anna gasped when my shed came into view. "Oh, God, Liam. It's on fire."

Flames lapped out from under the back of the building, which was elevated on blocks. The fire had just started, but there was no hope of stopping it. In the time it would take to retrieve and deliver water in buckets from the well or the sea, the entire structure would be engulfed.

"My books!" I ran down the trail and yanked on the door. It was locked. I fumbled for the key in my unfamiliar, tight jean pocket.

"No, Liam. It's not worth it!" Anna shouted, grabbing my shirt.

Finally, my fingers skimmed the key in the deep front pocket.

The crackling and hissing of the cedar drowned out everything but one thought: I had to save the books.

"No!" she shouted again as I oriented the key in my trembling fingers. "Don't go in there."

Flames shot up the opposite side of the structure, stretching to the sky. The entire back half was an inferno. My time was running out. Searing chest pain resulted from each intake of smoke-filled air. I blinked hard, clearing my vision enough to insert the key in the lock. The tumblers clicked and I kicked it open, only to be driven back by a billowing cloud of black smoke. Coughing, I covered my nose and mouth with my shirt, squinted my eyes into slits, and bounded into the shed, Anna's screams ringing in my ears.

I had to release the shirt in order to free my hand to grab books. Coughing and gasping, I threw one out the door and then another. I was on my sixth when the heat became too intense and a horrible crash behind me sent me running out the door, slamming right into Anna.

"Your shirt!" she shrieked.

I twisted around to discover the bottom of my shirt had ignited. Anna pushed me hard and I landed on my backside. "Roll!" she shouted, shoving my shoulders. I obeyed, extinguishing the flames in the dirt.

She forced me to my side, examining my back. "Are you burned?" she yelled over the roar of the fire.

I shook my head. "My books," I said.

"Screw the books! Let's get away from the fire." She yanked on my arm hard. I marveled at her composure and physical strength. Once I was to my feet, she pulled me to a clearing a safe distance away from the flames, which now rivaled the Bealtaine fires in the harbor. Fortunately, the air was still as death, making it unlikely the fire would spread beyond my shed.

"Stay here," she ordered.

Racked by coughs, I watched as she retrieved the books I'd rescued, stacking them next to me.

"I'm not an invalid," I said between bouts of coughing.

She glared at me. "No. But you're stupid! You could have died."

I tried to answer but could only cough.

She dropped to her knees next to me. "What were you thinking?"

The flames reflected in her eyes, which brimmed with tears.

"Those books are all I have that are my own."

She brushed my hair out of my face. "No. You have me."

And at that moment the incredible truth hit. The future was all that mattered. The books, the shed, none of it would mean a thing in the end. Only Anna.

I pulled her to me and inhaled the scent of her, blocking out the acrid smell of smoke.

"No way," she said, looking at something over her shoulder. "Where did you put your Bealtaine stick after you put it out, Liam?"

"I threw it over the cliff."

She pushed away from me and dug something out of a bush. She held up a long stick similar to the one I had discarded. The end was charred and still smoldered. "Looks like someone lit your hearth fire for you."

21

Hear the loud alarum bells—
Brazen bells!
What a tale of terror, now, their turbulency tells!
In the startled ear of night
How they scream out their affright!
Too much horrified to speak,
They can only shriek, shriek,
Out of tune,
In a clamorous appealing to the mercy of the fire,
In a mad expostulation with the deaf and frantic fire,
Leaping higher, higher, higher.

—Edgar Allan Poe,
from "The Bells," 1848

M uireann could not see her Liam anywhere. She'd followed his progress from the harbor as he and his female climbed the cliff trail toward his dwelling but lost sight of him once he'd run toward the flames.

This must be what the Na Fir Ghorm meant by a "trial by fire."

Please let him be okay, she chanted in her head.

Something moved in the vegetation on the slope behind her Liam's dwelling. She squinted to make out what it was, but it was too dark to see clearly. Ducking under, she swam closer to shore.

A horrible clatter came from the harbor, startling her so much she breathed in seawater. The humans were ringing those awful bells again. She blew the water out of her nose in one hard puff, flinching at every strike of the bells. She could even hear them underwater.

As she neared the slope, the form moved again. It was traveling toward the beach away from the fire, which was raging, sending a black column of smoke to the sky. Eyes and nose barely above the surface, she waited.

The human burst from the bushes, looking over his shoulder at the fire on the top of the cliff. It was the human male she had seen the Na Fir Ghorm leader speaking with earlier in the day. It had struck her as odd the Na Fir Ghorm were talking to a human, but now it made sense. They were using him.

It was the same human she had seen talking to Brigid Ronan—the one with the black square covering his eye.

"Who do you think torched your place?" Anna asked, sitting down next to me, holding the Bealtaine stick she'd discovered in the bushes.

A choked laugh escaped my throat and then turned into a cough. "It would be far easier to list those I do *not* think did it."

The alarm bells sounded from the harbor. Someone must have seen the smoke. "They'll be here any minute," I said, pulling Anna against me.

"Who?"

"The villagers. They'll come to protect their property by containing the flames if necessary."

"Yeah, well, I bet they won't lift a finger to help *your* property," she grumbled.

"No. It's too late for mine."

"I bet they wouldn't help even if it weren't too late."

I shrugged. "I'm certain you're correct."

She jumped to her feet. "I have an idea. Let's hide and listen to who says what. We might be able to figure out who did it."

I ran my fingers over the cover of the book on top of the stack. *Les Misérables.* How appropriate. "What would we do with that information? We have no law enforcement. No one would ever take my side anyway."

She picked up the stack of books. "*We* would know. Knowledge is power, right? I'm all about being powerful."

Shouting came from the direction of the trail. They were close. More out of the desire to avoid confrontation than to accrue information, I led Anna behind a vine-covered heap of abandoned lobster traps, where we could hear what was going on without being detected. The traps had belonged to Francine's uncle, who passed away decades ago.

The gaps in the vines gave us a clear view of the burning shed and the clearing at the top of the trail.

Edmond was the first to the scene, followed Mac and Ron. "It's MacGregor's shed," Edmond yelled back toward the trail.

Mrs. McAlister and Polly were next to arrive, followed by a dozen or so others. No one said anything for a while. They just stood mesmerized by the flames consuming what was left of the shed.

"Good thing there's no wind," Edmond remarked.

"Liam!" I could hear Pa before I saw him. "Liam," he yelled, shoving through the crowd. Clearly intoxicated, he stood swaying, staring at the burning remains of my shed, wearing a horrified expression. "Where is he?" It was almost a whimper.

"If we're lucky, he was in there," Mrs. McAlister said.

Pa turned and charged her but was stopped by Mac and Ron.

"How dare you!" Pa slurred. "You'd really wish upon him the torture of being burned alive?"

Emboldened by the fact Pa was restrained, Mrs. McAlister took a step toward him. "I don't wish him burned alive, James. I just wish him dead. So do you. We all do."

To my amazement, Pa shook his head. His mouth formed the word "no," but no sound came out.

Mrs. McAlister took cover behind Edmond when Pa shook free, but he ignored her, shoving his way back through the crowd to the trail.

The villagers watched his retreat, the silence only broken by the clanging of the bells. Several shuffled their feet uncomfortably and exchanged glances.

I needed to cough but fought down the urge. Anna rubbed her hand reassuringly down my arm.

"Well, that's it, I guess," Edmond said. "We won't know anything until morning. If he shows up, there's that. If not, we won't know anything for sure until we can sift through the ashes."

"Let's just hope the Leighton girl wasn't in there with him. Her people will raze the whole island," Mac said.

As quickly as they'd arrived, they departed, leaving us with no clues as to who had set the fire. In fact, none of them had even spoken of how it had started, which was one of the first topics whenever anything burned down. Either they all knew or none of them wanted to know. Both scenarios were equally disturbing.

Anna turned around and leaned back against the wall of traps. "What a lovely group of people. They weren't worried that I was dead, they were worried my parents would be pissed off."

Finally, I could cough and relieve the unbearable tickling in my throat I'd endured for the eternity the villagers were near.

"You okay?" Anna's sweet voice was like music juxtaposed with the harsh clang of the harbor bells still ringing in the distance.

I nodded. Now that the shock was wearing off, the ramifications of the fire had moved to the forefront of my mind. I had no place to live—nowhere to go except back with Pa. The haunted look on his face when he called my name had nearly ripped my heart out. It was the same tortured look he had when Ma died. I took a deep, shuddering breath. It was probably the alcohol altering his reactions. He'd made it more than clear many times that he wished me gone.

They all wished me gone except Francine and Anna.

"I love you," I whispered.

She skimmed the backs of her fingers across my jaw. "Now you're talking. Keep that up and I'll take back my 'you're stupid' statement and forgive you for almost dying on me."

"I *was* stupid," I said. "I don't know what came over me."

"Shock. Fear. Losing what was left to you by your mother." Anna said. She stood and picked up the stack of books. The golden hues from the fire floated across her exquisite face, creating an effect so beautiful, it erased all my worries, replacing them with awe and gratitude.

The harbor bells fell silent, leaving no sound but the crackling fire as it consumed my past.

"We can figure all of this out tomorrow," Anna said, adjusting her purse strap on her shoulder. "Tonight, let's just head to Taibhreamh and steer clear of fire-wielding villagers, okay?"

For the first time, the thought of the mansion didn't fill me with dread.

22

No footstep stirred: the hated world all slept,
Save only thee and me. (Oh, Heaven!—oh, God!
How my heart beats in coupling those two words!)
Save only thee and me.

—Edgar Allan Poe,
from "To Helen," 1848

*T*aibhreamh was unattended when we arrived. Miss Ronan was probably still at the celebration, which no doubt found rejuvenation after the discovery I might have been destroyed along with the shed.

But I hadn't been destroyed. From those ashes, I'd been renewed. Without a past, I could focus on the future: Anna.

I followed her up the stairs to her room, where she placed the books on the window seat. My portfolio was there, leaning against the ledge.

She pulled her hair in front of her nose. "We stink like smoke," she said with a shudder. "It reminds me of the funeral pyre the other day." She slipped her handbag off her shoulder and pitched it on the bed. "We have to shower or I'll have night-mares."

The Bean Sidhes took that moment to shriek.

"Shut up!" Anna yelled. "Please. Give us just a little peace, okay?"

They fell silent.

I thought of all the nights I had lain awake tormented by their screams. Why had I never thought to talk to them? Probably because I knew they wouldn't listen. No one listened . . . until now. My whole life had built to this moment—to this girl.

"Follow me," Anna said. At the opposite end of the balcony overlooking the entry hall, she disappeared through an ornately carved alcove. "My great-uncle's rooms."

I hesitated in the doorway. Damask curtains the color of blood ran down either side of a tall, narrow window. Paneling almost as dark as the black marble on the first floor stretched up every vertical surface, broken only by occasional paintings in thick, carved gilt frames. Everything about the room was in equal parts opulent and oppressive, even the iron chandelier that looked to be ringed in sharp daggers with jeweled handles.

Unsure whether my inability to efficiently fill my lungs resulted from the smoke I'd inhaled earlier or the effect of the room, I drew a deep, slow breath through my nose, willing my heart rate to slow.

"The shower is through there." She indicated a door in the corner. "I'll find something for you to wear. And I'll put your clothes in the washer if you'll pass them out to me."

A washing machine. I'd seen pictures of them in the magazines.

I entered the bathroom and closed the door behind me. I slipped out of my smoky clothes, painfully aware there was nothing but a few inches of wood between us. After wrapping a towel around my waist, I opened the door enough to peek out. She stood just outside with a bundle of clothes. In awkward silence, I passed her my dirty clothes in exchange for the clean ones. Her eyes traveled up and down my body and she smiled. "Enjoy your shower."

I groaned and leaned back against the closed door. Nothing in this world, or any other for that matter, could be as alluring and desirable as Anna Leighton. I shook my head to clear it.

The faucet functioned like the one at Francine's, only it was ornate and gold—probably real gold. I would never get used to such decadence and waste. Steaming hot water right from the tap, though, I could learn to accept without issue.

Shampoos, soaps, and all manner of supplies waited on a shelf. In no time, I washed away the smoke smell that had clung to my body like a second skin.

The royal blue silk pajamas and matching robe felt foreign against my skin. Too light, too smooth, too . . . rich. But any reservations I had about them disappeared when Anna told me I looked "yummy."

"I have something for you," she said. "I had the pilot bring it when he picked up Suz, Mallory, and Nicky." She pulled open a drawer of the table next to her bed and withdrew a rectangular item with a glass front. "It's an iPad, which is cool, but what's coolest is what's on it." She patted the bed next to her.

It turns out, she meant the "coolest thing" was what was *in* it, because it contained movies behind that shiny piece of glass. I'd never seen a movie or any video media before, but I had read all about them. It was fascinating to see the concept translated into reality. It exceeded all expectations. *Sherlock Holmes* was the first we viewed and then *James Bond*.

She had called me Bond at the lighthouse. I smiled as I recalled that day—the overwhelming sensation of her touch and the smoothness of her lips. The smell of freshly cut lilies on her skin. Bond in the movie was kissing a scantily clad woman not half as beautiful as Anna. I looked over to find her staring at me, the look in her eyes as heated as my thoughts.

Just as our lips met, the Bean Sidhes wailed again.

"This is ridiculous," Anna said to the air above our heads. "You guys are the most effective mood killers ever." She paused the movie and slipped off the bed. "Talk about forced abstinence. Really."

She paced from the bed to the window and back again, running her hands through her still-wet hair. "Are you hungry? I am."

I nodded.

Watching her move about the kitchen was like witnessing a beautiful, complex dance. She was so graceful and confident—and skilled. The omelet she prepared with mushrooms, Swiss cheese, asparagus, and eggs was the most delicious thing I'd ever tasted.

"I feel better now," she said, taking her last bite.

"Because you were hungry?"

"No. Because I needed to *do* something." She put her fork down. "I feel so helpless here." She stared out the window at the sunrise.

Silence stretched between us. Her brow furrowed as she searched for something in her mind: a thought, a memory, the proper words perhaps.

"It's like everything is out of control on this island. Things happen to you and there is no power over it. At home, I know what's going on and what's going to happen for the most part. I control my life. Here, I'm clueless."

"Dòchas is a unique place," I said.

She made her peculiar snorting sound. "That's an understatement. And when I start to figure something out, craziness happens: somebody dies, stuff burns, freaks go on a witch hunt."

"Demon hunt," I corrected. "I'm not a witch."

"You're not a demon either." She took her dish to the sink. "And we're going to prove it. We're going to find out as much as we can about your birth. We're also going to figure out what happened to my uncle."

I placed my dish on top of hers in the enormous sink and followed her to a room off the kitchen that held a washer, a dryer, and a large table.

She moved clothes from one machine to the other and started it. A rhythmic rumbling filled the room, and behind the porthole of glass on the door, the clothes danced and leapt in a clockwise circle. She leaned against the machine. "What do you want, Liam?"

"You."

She rolled her eyes. "I mean what do you want from life?"

"My answer stands."

"Other than that."

There was nothing else. Anna was all I wanted. All I'd ever dreamed of—never expecting fate to be so kind as to allow me time with her. I had everything I could desire.

She threw her hands up. "You're not getting it. You've sold paintings to the guys on the delivery boats, right? What if we could get your work into a gallery back at home?"

It was too far-fetched. I shook my head.

"Why not? You're crazy talented. I know my dad could find a broker for your work." She took my hand. "You could get out of here. Live in the real world instead of this backward anachronistic hellhole."

I dared not consider so fine a dream for fear the Washerwoman would strike me down on the spot. I knew in my soul that I'd never leave this island. Functioning in any other world was impossible. "Let me draw you," I said. "Please, Anna."

Her smile was brilliant. "Don't you have enough drawings of me already?"

"Those are yours now. Happy birthday."

Her hand flew to her throat and she gasped. "Mine? Really?"

I nodded.

"All of them?"

"Yes."

She turned her back to me and clutched the top of the dryer. I had hurt her somehow.

"Anna."

"Sorry," she whispered. "This is all really new to me."

Afraid of saying the wrong thing, I remained silent and waited.

She turned to face me. "Everyone always buys things for me. No one has ever given me something they've made themselves." She wrapped her arms around me and leaned her head against my shoulder. Her tears soaked through the fine fabric. "It means a lot. Thanks."

She pressed against me, every curve of her body painfully defined through the loose silk pajamas.

"Will you draw me now?"

"Yes." My voice sounded as if it came from someone else— deep and far away. "I have art supplies in the outer pocket of the portfolio."

"I saw them there. I'll be right back." She pulled away and left me empty.

I leaned back against the table and watched the clothes tumble in the dryer as if under a hypnotic spell. I *was* under a spell of sorts: Anna had completely bewitched me.

"Dear gods of the ocean!" Brigid Ronan's thick voice startled me to the point of paralysis. I held my breath, unable to move. "You've returned," she whispered to my back. I shuddered as her cool fingers touched my shoulder. I turned to face her, and she screamed.

"You! What are you doing here?" Her eyes darted up and

down my body. "Where did you get those clothes?" The look of horror on her face mirrored my own.

"Anna gave them to me." I backed up against the dryer.

"How dare you! You have no right. No right to be here. No right to wear his clothes." She was shaking all over. "You have no right to exist. Get out!"

She shoved me hard and I almost lost my balance.

"Get out and don't come back. Stay where you belong!" she screamed.

The Bean Sidhes began to wail at that moment and I was overcome.

Miss Ronan's voice was barely discernible over the creatures' keening. "She doesn't really love you. She's only passing the time while she is here. You're not good enough for her—you and I both know that. Go back to your pitiful little life and stay away. You've done enough harm already. Now go!"

23

Our first impulse is to shrink from the danger.
Unaccountably we remain.

—Edgar Allan Poe,
from "The Imp of the Perverse," 1845

ilence!" I shouted. To my amazement, both Miss
Ronan and the Bean Sidhes obeyed. "You hold no
power or authority over me, Brigid Ronan." We
stared at each other, breathing hard, for several
moments.

"Heed my words," she warned, eyes narrowed.

"Heed your words? Your words have tortured me my entire
life through the villagers' mouths, but they no longer frighten
me. I believe it is *you* who is frightened." I took a step toward
her and she shuffled backward away from me. Something inside
me rejoiced at the tiny bit of ground I'd won. "Until Anna tells
me otherwise, I will remain."

"Liam! Are you still in the laundry room?" Anna called from
somewhere in the house.

"Yes," I shouted.

Miss Ronan's lips pulled into a tight line. "This is a dangerous game, MacGregor. You will lose her and your life as well.
Get out of this while you can."

"I wasn't aware we were playing a game." I ran my hand
through my hair. "My life is meaningless without her, so death

would be welcomed if you're correct." I took another step closer and lowered my voice. "We both know what's on the line for me, but what do you stand to lose, I wonder."

Her eyes widened, perhaps from fear. I hoped so.

"Hey," Anna said from the doorway. "Everything okay in here?"

"Perfect," I said, not taking my eyes off Miss Ronan. "Everything is just fine."

"Great. Well, um. I have the supplies." Anna looked from me to Miss Ronan. "You sure everything's okay?"

"Positive." I put my arm around Anna in a possessive display that wasn't wasted on Miss Ronan. She got my message loud and clear. She stormed from the room and I reveled in yet another tiny triumph.

"What was that about?" Anna asked, slipping out from under my arm.

"I'm not exactly sure yet. It was as if she thought I were someone else until she saw my face."

"That's weird. Who?"

"Your great-uncle, I believe."

"Well, I guess that rules her out as the murderer."

I took the portfolio from her. "At this point, I don't believe we should rule anyone out."

"Whoa. Listen to you, Sherlock."

"I would rather be—" I lifted an eyebrow. "Bond. James Bond."

Her grin was gorgeous. "You can be anybody you want to be. Who should I be?"

"You." I set the portfolio on the table. "Never anyone but you."

Her lips were warm. I thought for a moment my knees would give way when she ran her hands down my back, only a thin layer of silk between her touch and my skin. Time stopped every time she held me. Anna made me better. She made me whole.

"You damn well better let me in or I'll tear your eyes out!"

Francine! I pulled away to listen.

"She sounds really pissed off," Anna said, retying the sash on my robe.

I hadn't considered how the shed burning would affect her. She might think me dead. Anna pulled me by the hand through the kitchen toward the entry hall, where we found Francine in a standoff with Miss Ronan.

"Oh, lad. There y'are." Her accent was thicker than usual. "I knew you hadn't perished in the fire because there were no bones, but I worried you might have been called by the sea."

She shoved past Miss Ronan and joined us in the narrow hallway to the kitchen. "You were called by something else, though, I see." She winked and Anna grinned. "We need to talk," she said in a whisper. "Somewhere else, if you know what I mean."

Anna nodded. "Let us get dressed and we'll be right out."

"I'll wait outside." Francine eyed one of the claw-like wall sconces and shivered. "This place gives me funny feelings."

The jeans and T-shirt were still warm from the dryer when I pulled them on. I couldn't imagine what it would be like to live in this kind of luxury every day.

I found Francine sitting on the porch bench. "Anna's not out yet," she said. "It's going well, then?"

I nodded and sat next to her.

She nudged me with her shoulder. "How well?"

"Extremely well."

She gave an exasperated sigh. "You're not going to give me any details, are you?"

"Not a chance."

"Your new clothes look good on you." She patted my jean-clad leg.

I placed my hand over hers. "Thank you again for everything. The clothes, the friendship. I'm sorry about your shed."

"Don't think on it." She stood. "You had no control over that. I'm just glad you weren't in it. Got any idea who lit the fire?"

"It could've been any one of them." I shrugged. "Everyone on this island wants me dead except for you and Anna."

"And your pa."

"He's just like them."

She shook her head. "No, Liam. He's a mess over this. He came by the store this morning looking for you. He was covered in soot from searching for your bones in the ashes."

"So he could celebrate with the rest of them."

"No." She took my face in her hands. "Don't get hard like them. People change."

I closed my eyes and took a deep breath of the morning sea air.

"You're better than that. Stay above it like you always have." She released my face.

"It's hard," I said. "I finally have something good in my life and it's as if everything in the world is conspiring to take it away."

"So you fight for it."

Anna stepped out onto the porch like a ray of sunshine. She wore blue jeans and a bright yellow blouse. "You owe me a drawing, Liam," she said, patting her handbag. My metal pencil box and sketch pad peeked out of the top.

I followed her down the porch steps. "No. You owe me one. This one is mine, remember?"

Francine caught up and led us down the cliff-side trail.

...

Muireann had spent the night and early part of the day watching the female's large dwelling. She had seen her Liam go in last night but had not seen him come out until now. He was healthy and sound and still with his female. She made a celebratory twirl in the waves. The Na Fir Ghorm had lost this round, or at least they had so far.

"Where have you been?" Keela asked, swimming up from behind. "Mom's worried sick."

"Like you care." Muireann ducked under and swam closer to shore before her sister could tell how hurt she was. She had spent the worst night of her life, regretting the fact she put her pod in danger and worrying about her Liam. It was the first night she'd ever spent away from her family, and all Keela could do was lay on more guilt.

"Still stalking the human male, I see. Maybe you should just shed your pelt and get this out of your system," her sister said, popping up next to her.

"I've had enough of you," Muireann said. "They tried to kill him last night. Look at the cliff where his dwelling used to be."

Her sister looked up at the cliff. "Yep. All gone. You need to take a break from lusting and come tell Mom you're okay."

Muireann couldn't believe her sister's hard-heartedness. "Why don't you tell her you wouldn't let me join the pod to sleep last night? That should clear it up just fine."

"Your selfishness astounds me."

"Really? I was just thinking the same thing."

They stared at each other for a while, neither willing to back down.

"I have some news for you," Keela said, "since you are obsessed with this human."

Muireann wasn't sure of her sister's motive, but if it could help her Liam, she needed to hear it. "What is it?"

"Agree to come with me to let Mom know you're okay and I'll tell you."

"Fine," Muireann agreed.

Keela paddled a few yards in the direction of Seal Island. "Come on, then."

"No. Tell me first."

"You don't trust me?"

Muireann shook her head. "After last night? Not for a second."

A look of hurt crossed Keela's face. "I'm sorry."

Muireann heaved a sigh of relief. She'd never been at odds with anyone before and it made her insides churn. "Me too."

They swam in a tight circle, putting their chins on each other's necks in a Selkie hug.

"So, the news?"

Keela met her sister's eyes directly. "The Na Fir Ghorm are meeting after sundown to plan the next test for your human and his mate. They say it is a test of faith. It will be initiated before sundown."

A test of faith . . . "Is that all?"

"No. The human who set fire to the dwelling delivered an item to the Na Fir Ghorm last night. He took it before burning the dwelling."

"What was it?" Muireann asked.

"I don't know. It looked like a blue stick."

Muireann had no idea what the Na Fir Ghorm were planning, but she would do whatever it took to protect her Liam. She had to find a way to eavesdrop on that meeting tonight, even if it meant another night away from her pod.

We heard villagers' voices before we saw the shed, or what was left of it.

"Look, a fork and knife," a woman said.

"Don't pick it up," replied a male. "It's been touched by a demon."

"But it's been purified by Bealtaine fire," said the woman. "Surely it wouldn't be infected still, and we need another set at home."

They were picking through what was left of my possessions. I would have expected this to anger me, but it only brought sadness.

When we rounded the turn, Polly's, Edmond's, and Deirdre's startled expressions met us.

"Busted!" Anna whispered in my ear.

Deirdre was off to the side while her parents stood in the charred remains of my home. The wood was all reduced to ashes, but the stove and bathtub, completely covered in soot, appeared to have survived.

"Hello, Polly and Edmond," Francine said as if nothing unusual had occurred. "What brings you here this morning?"

I smiled inwardly at Francine's casual, veiled accusation.

"We, um . . ." Polly replied. "We were on our way to deliver Deirdre to Taibhreamh."

"We stopped here to see if there was anything to salvage." At least Edmond was honest.

"I imagine anything made of metal is still intact," Francine replied. "The shed was little and the fire couldn't have lasted long enough to melt anything. Why, look. There's a knife and fork. Why don't you take them? Liam won't need them anymore. He's going to live there." She pointed to her aunt's house.

"And it is fully stocked." She gestured to the knife and fork with her chin. "Go on. Take them."

Edmond flitted a glance to me only briefly before scooping up the knife and fork. "Thanks. Come on, Deirdre."

The girl joined her parents at the top of the trail.

"Hey, you start today as my personal assistant, right?" Anna called.

Deirdre nodded. "Yes, miss. Thank you." She grinned and ran after her parents.

I stood in front of the rubble. Nothing was left of the bookcase, bed, or table. The eight cinder blocks that had supported the shed remained in place. The tub was a bit askew and the stove had fallen to its side when the boards burned out from under it. I felt no sadness, no all-too-familiar ache of loss, as I would've expected.

"They were stealing," Anna said. "Why did you let them have the knife and fork?"

Francine strolled around to the back of the shed remains. "For the same reason you have the girl coming to Taibhreamh today."

"She needs help," Anna answered, shifting something in the ashes with her toe.

"They all do. Of all the families on Dòchas, they are the most in need. Edmond lost his boat and has no other way to make a living. I'm hoping now that Johnny has passed, maybe Liam's pa will take him on. If not, they might not make the winter."

Anna pulled her hair back and tied it in a knot at the base of her neck. "That's tough. Wouldn't someone help them?"

"We're all just trying to stay alive. The people here are proud. They will not take handouts if doing so will harm the donor."

Anna shook her head. She had never been subjected first-hand to abject poverty, and certainly the concept was hard to reconcile with her upbringing.

"I appreciate your generous offer, Francine, but can't accept it," I said.

Francine put her hands on her hips. "You'd best not be talking about this house that has stood empty for these last months since my aunt died, Liam MacGregor, or I'll take a switch to your backside."

Anna giggled.

"You've given me too much already."

She cocked her head. "Then where are you going to live? With James Callan?"

Pa would probably kill me within a month, but I had no choice. I nodded.

"You could move in with me," Anna suggested.

"Miss Ronan would love that plan," I said. "Besides, you'll be leaving soon, and I'd be back in the same position."

"You are so dense sometimes. I don't plan to leave as long as you are here." She took my hand. "So you'll just have to come to New York with me and get off this island forever."

"I couldn't possibly . . . I'd be—"

"That's a lovely idea," Francine said. "But for now, you are moving into my aunt's house and I'll have no more discussion on it. Understand? I need to get back to the shop and don't have time to dillydally with you." She climbed the porch and opened the closed house. We followed.

"I really like her," Anna whispered.

"So do I."

Francine opened all the windows, and she and Anna set about shaking out curtains and dusting furniture while I mopped the floor with my special mop and bucket Francine had evidently brought up from the store on her way to Taibhreamh. It was waiting in the center of the room when we came in. The house had a separate bedroom, which was bigger than my entire shed had been.

From the doorstep, Francine gave a round crocheted rug one last shake. "I would have offered to let you move in here when my aunt died, but I knew you enjoyed the tie to your mother in the shed." She placed the rug just inside the door. "And I didn't want to give anybody more reason to cause a fuss. You living in a nicer place than some of these villagers would have invited their ire."

"I believe that invitation was extended eighteen years ago," I said, wringing the mop in the bucket. "But you're right. I was comfortable in the shed." I carried the bucket out the door, tipped the water out, and set the mop and bucket upright.

"Also, unlived-in houses decline quickly. You're doing me a favor, see?" Francine pulled a set of sheets out of a chest in the corner of the bedroom. The bed was much wider than mine had been. It dawned on me as I helped her make the bed just how exhausted I was. I hadn't slept last night.

"So, you are all good now, right? I put some food in the cupboard for you, but you'll need to collect some firewood." Francine picked up the mop and bucket. "I'll see you soon. Our next delivery doesn't come until day after tomorrow, so feel free to take off work until then."

I put my arm around her shoulders. "I can't thank you enough. I'd be long dead if it weren't for you. You're better to me than I deserve. Better than a mother."

She sniffed and shrugged out of my hold. "Be good to him, Anna," she said. "They don't come better than this."

"I know," Anna said, kissing Francine good-bye. Finally

alone with me, she leaned back against the closed door and gave me a look that made everything inside me stir. She reached up and untied the knot from her hair and shook it free. Without a word, she strolled to the bedroom and, from the doorway, delivered a smile that left me gasping for air.

"I'll be right there," I said, washing the mop water off my hand in the kitchen sink.

Heart pounding, I entered the bedroom. The curtains were closed and from a small gap between them, a single shaft of golden light shone across Anna on the bed. I slipped off my shoes and padded closer. She lay on her side fully clothed, her glorious hair fanned out on the pillow, fast asleep.

I reached into her handbag on the chair and pulled out my sketch pad.

24

And the silken, sad, uncertain rustling of each
purple curtain
Thrilled me—filled me with fantastic terrors
never felt before.

—Edgar Allan Poe,
from "The Raven," 1845

The best sleep I'd ever had ended with earsplitting pounding on the door. "MacGregor! Do you got the Leighton girl in there?" a man's voice shouted.

Bang, bang, bang.

"Open up! She's gone missing and Miss Ronan sent me to fetch 'er back before nightfall."

"Crap." Anna covered her head with a pillow and then mumbled something indecipherable.

I attempted to disentangle my legs from hers, but she tightened her grip and grabbed my shirt. "No. Ignore him."

"I can't. There's no lock on the door of this house and he'll come in if I don't answer." I swung my legs over the side of the bed. "Just a minute," I called.

"So what? We've got our clothes on. Believe me, I've been in crazier situations than this."

I ran my fingers through my sleep-tousled hair. "Not with me. I won't do anything to compromise you."

She rolled over to face me. "Oh, my God. You are something else. My own hot time capsule."

"I don't know what that means, but thank you." I looked out the curtain to see the sun setting. We had slept all day.

Bang, bang, bang!

"I said I'm coming," I shouted, lacing up my hiking boots.

I closed the bedroom door behind me and opened the front door. Connor MacFarley, red-faced and sweating, stood on the porch. "Where is she?" He craned his neck to look around me into the house.

"She's inside. I'll bring her to Taibhreamh directly."

"Listen here. I've been instructed to bring her back myself without you. And you'd better watch your step. Next time, it won't just be yer home that's burned to ashes."

"Are you threatening Liam?" Anna asked from behind me. "Aren't you a Taibhreamh employee?"

Connor's mouth clamped shut and his face grew even redder, all the way up over his bald head. He adjusted his eye patch and shuffled foot to foot. The fear of starvation or freezing to death in the winter could shut down even the most aggressive of men.

"We'll both walk her back," I said.

"Yer to stay put here."

"I don't trust you to deliver her home safely," I said. "People tend to fall off cliffs when you're around."

"It'd be best you keep that in mind, MacGregor."

"Stop it," Anna said. "I'll go back, but I want Liam to come with us. He goes or I don't." She slammed the door in his face before he could react.

"I hate this place," she fumed, stomping to the bedroom. "People push each other off cliffs!" She picked up her handbag and slung it over her shoulder. "And they get away with it."

She paused, staring at the drawing on the floor I had made. She picked it up and sat on the bed. "You make me look like an angel."

"You are one." An angel sent to save me from the misery of this world where people do horrible things and get away with it. *My* angel.

She said nothing for a long time as she stared at the drawing. "I love how I look through your eyes."

My rib cage felt too small for my heart.

Bang, bang, bang.

Anna growled and set the drawing on the bed. "When I finally get to talk to my parents, old One Eye out there is top on my list of complaints."

As expected, Miss Ronan was waiting for us when we reached Taibhreamh. On the porch along with her was Deirdre Byrne, her dirty smock replaced with a black dress and a starched white apron. Anna smiled at her, but the girl couldn't take her eyes off Connor MacFarley, whose salacious stare held her paralyzed.

"I have told you that it is dangerous to be out after dark, Anna," Miss Ronan said. "I assured your parents you would always be home before sunset."

Anna smirked. "Oh, yeah. Well, it was okay. I was with Liam. . . . No, wait. He's one of the dangers, isn't he?" She pulled my face to hers for a kiss that left me breathless and stunned. "I love danger," she said, leading me up the porch steps by the hand. "Danger turns me on."

She yanked the door opened and slammed it behind us once we were inside. "I wish I could see Ronan's face right now," she said, running up the stairs. I followed, still a bit stunned.

"It is best not to incite her," I said. "We don't know enough about her yet to agitate her."

Anna flopped onto her bed. "She's always agitated."

I stopped just inside the room. "Yes, but until we know exactly who or what she is, it would be best to play by her rules."

"I know exactly what she is," she said. "She's a—"

"Stop. Francine believes words and actions come back. We need all the help we can get." A horrible sense of foreboding had haunted me all the way here. "We need to find out more about her and what happened to your uncle."

"And your mother."

"Yes. I think they're all linked." With that, the Bean Sidhes started up at a deafening volume.

"So, they *are* linked?" Anna asked the air. The wailing increased in volume, which I didn't think possible. "Linked to this house?" The pitch got higher and Anna stuck her fingers in her ears. "Okay, then be quiet so we can think."

The Bean Sidhes fell silent and I sighed with relief.

"Time to explore," Anna said, pushing to her feet.

Deirdre knocked gently on the door frame, eyes cast to the floor. "I'm sorry, miss. I've been sent to tell you that dinner is served and to ask if the . . . if Mr. MacGregor will be staying for dinner."

"He will, and so will you. Tell Miss Ronan to set three places."

Deirdre's eyes grew huge. "Oh, no, miss. I couldn't possibly. I'll be beaten for sure."

Anna strode through the door. "I'll tell her, then. If anyone raises a hand to you, they are fired."

Deirdre stood trembling in the doorway.

"Did Miss Ronan threaten you?" I asked.

She shook her head. "No. My da."

I nodded. "Mine too."

She met my eyes for only a moment, bobbed a curtsy, and

fled. At least it was something. She'd actually made eye contact. Though earning her trust might be next to impossible after thirteen years of brainwashing.

We dined in the huge room where Anna had entertained her friends. This time there was no roaring fire at the end of the room. The enormous fireplace stood cold and black like the entrance to a dungeon rather than the fiery gateway to hell.

The food was amazing, of course, though part of me pondered the grim possibility that Brigid Ronan might have poisoned it. This didn't give me pause for long because it smelled irresistible. Deirdre didn't eat at first but eventually agreed after Anna threatened to turn her out if she didn't clean her plate.

"Would you like some of the chicken, miss?" Deirdre asked, pushing the plate closer to her.

Anna met my eyes before answering. "No thank you. Not today."

"Fish, then?"

"No. I'll pass for now."

"My ma says that I have to eat meat so I'll be strong for my hus . . ." Her eyes filled with tears. "Excuse me." She shoved her chair back and ran from the room.

Anna dropped her fork. "A little girl shouldn't have to go through this." She scooted her chair away from the table. "Have I told you I hate this place?"

I set my fork down. "You have indeed."

"Good. I wouldn't want to give the wrong impression." She stood.

"You could never be accused of that." I smiled in spite of myself. She was gorgeous with heightened color in her cheeks.

She placed two more rolls on the girl's plate and covered it with a napkin. "Where do you suppose she went?"

"I have no idea. To her room, perhaps?"

Anna picked up the plate. "I'm going to go find her. You can stay and finish your dinner if you want to."

I stood. "And let you play hide-and-seek without me? We can start exploring right now. Maybe we can find some clues as well as your assistant."

Anna nearly slammed head-on into Miss Ronan as she burst from the dining room.

"Is something wrong?" she asked in her deep voice.

"Yeah. Where's Deirdre's room?"

"Through there." She pointed at the door under the center of the double staircase.

I shuddered. The staircases on either side of the door still looked like the jaws of a huge spider to me and we were about to willingly walk into its mouth.

Miss Ronan didn't appear the least bit ruffled at Anna's urgency. "The first door on the left."

When we reached the room, the lights were out. The white, gauzy curtains on either side of the open window fluttered in the evening air. "Deirdre?" Anna whispered. She flipped on the light switch. The door in the far corner was closed, as was the one to the left of the entrance door. She opened the one to the left first. It was a closet containing only a black dress, an apron, and Deirdre's clothes from earlier today. A muffled cry came from behind the other door.

"Deirdre?" Anna called again, setting the plate on a chest of drawers. There was a thumping sound and then a scream. "No! Please don't!"

Anna sprinted to the door with me on her heels. She threw the door open and gasped.

Connor MacFarley had Deirdre backed up against the wall with her skirt hiked up to her waist.

"Stop!" Anna shouted. "Let her go right now."

He released the girl and she slumped down to a heap on the floor, racked with sobs.

"What do you think you are doing?" Anna asked, fists clenched.

"I might ask you the same thing," MacFarley replied coolly.

Anna helped Deirdre to her feet. "It appears I'm stopping you from raping a child."

"What's yours can't be raped," he said, arms across his chest.

Anna's mouth fell open. "What do you mean by that?"

He yanked Deirdre back to him by the upper arm. Her only sign of resistance was a pitiful squeak. "She's mine. Her parents gave her to me. I'm to provide for her and take care of her any way I see fit."

"Oh, my God," Anna gasped. "You're her . . . They're marrying her off to *you*?"

Deirdre gave a pitiful sob that made my chest ache. My pa had beaten me, but I had never feared a lifetime of torture like this poor girl.

The grin on MacFarley's face exposed several missing teeth. "They are. We are to be wed on the next full moon, so you can leave now."

"Please go get Miss Ronan," Anna said to me.

I didn't have to go far. She was lurking right outside the door. Her completely unconcerned demeanor made the demon in me growl.

"Yes, Miss Leighton?" she said in an almost-bored tone.

"Here's the deal," Anna said. "From now on, this . . ." She pointed at MacFarley. "This *man* does not set foot inside the house. He is not to have access to Deirdre ever on this property. She is not to leave this house without me. Not even with her . . . no, *especially* not with her parents."

Miss Ronan simply lifted an eyebrow.

"If I find out he has laid a finger on her, neither Connor

MacFarley nor you will have a job. My family will close this house and throw you out, Miss Ronan. Do you understand?"

She no longer looked bored. With precise articulation indicating focused control, she answered. "You have made yourself perfectly clear. Yes, I understand."

"Let her go," Anna ordered.

MacFarley raised his hands in the air in surrender and the girl flew to Anna, clinging to her like a drowning person to a life ring. Anna's voice was low and measured. "Where I come from, there are laws against attacking children. You are despicable. Get out of my house."

MacFarley shot a glance at Miss Ronan, who looked away. Without a word, he stomped out of the room. No one moved or spoke until after the front door slammed.

"I'm sorry, miss." Deirdre sniffled, still clinging to Anna. Anna ran her hands through the girl's mess of hair that had been in a tidy knot at dinner.

"You didn't do anything wrong. You have nothing to be sorry for."

When I stole a look at Miss Ronan, she appeared to be moved. Her features had softened and her lip quivered. She caught me looking and immediately stiffened into her stoic self. "Will there be anything else, Miss Leighton?"

"Yes. I want her things moved up to my room. She's going to stay with me tonight."

The girl clung even tighter. Anna met my gaze over her head and I smiled. Her heart was so giving and strong. Never had I known anyone like her.

Once Anna had tucked Deirdre into her bed with the plate of food and the iPad playing a movie made of drawings about a mouse, she joined me on the upstairs balcony overlooking the entry hall. "I'm going to find a way to get her off this island before that monster hurts her." She glanced over her shoulder at the closed door. "Poor thing. She'll be asleep before the movie is over."

"You need some sleep too," I said.

"I slept all day."

"I know. I was there."

"Why didn't you wake me up?"

It had been almost impossible. "You were so peaceful."

She leaned her elbows on the railing. "So, did I do or say anything embarrassing?"

"I slept too."

"Not while you were drawing me."

I smiled.

"What did I say?"

I leaned my elbow on the railing next to her. "You told me that you wanted me forever."

She blushed and straightened. "That's so embarrassing."

"Why?"

"It just is."

I wrapped my arm around her and pulled her against me. "You only articulated my exact thoughts. I want you forever, Anna. In this world and whatever comes after."

She entwined her fingers in my hair and pulled my lips to hers. "Forever isn't long enough," she said just as the Bean Sidhes started up.

I pulled away laughing.

"It's not funny!" she said. "They're doing it on purpose."

"They're reminding us to stay true to our task. We need to solve the murders."

"This is making me crazy. You guys suck!" she shouted at the air. "Shut up. We're working on it."

"Where should we start?" I asked, chuckling.

She looked around and settled her gaze on the alcove to her uncle's room. "Where he hung out the most, I guess."

The room was even more oppressive than I remembered it—from the enormous carved bedposts with depictions of game hanging to dry to the grim paintings in the gilt frames. Most were still-life oil paintings, but something about the subjects unnerved me. They featured fruit or flowers past their prime in various states of decay and rot. Several had flies or worms. And everything about the room was dark. I felt certain that even in the daytime with the red curtains drawn open, it would still be gloomy.

I pulled one of the smaller paintings down and held it close to the lamp. "Whose initials are these: FMR?"

She continued rummaging through a desk drawer. "Uncle Frank's. Francis Michael Richards."

"Richards. Your mother's side, then?" I hung the painting back on the hook.

She closed the drawer. "No. He's not really my uncle. He was a friend of my grandfather's. We just called him Uncle Frank."

I examined another painting. The same initials were in the bottom-right corner. "How did he come to live here, then?"

Anna picked up a framed picture from the top of the dresser. "Because of her." She turned the picture toward me. It was a portrait in oil as well, but it depicted not elements of rot or decay, simply a lovely blond woman smiling out at me.

"That was his wife. When she died twenty-something years ago, he flipped out and my granddad let him move in here. It was supposed to be temporary, but he never left." She shrugged. "Or at least we think he didn't."

She stared at the portrait in her hands. "Wouldn't it be funny if he just left and hadn't died at all and all of this is just a wild-goose chase? Maybe he's hanging on a beach in the Bahamas laughing at all of us."

The Bean Sidhes screeched at such a deafening level, she dropped the portrait.

"Okay. I get it! We'll keep looking. Stop!" she said, ears covered.

The creatures ceased keening.

I took another picture down and held it to the light. This one depicted a large horsefly on a piece of half-eaten melon. The color he used for the melon flesh was a putrid shade of chartreuse that gave the entire piece a sickening feel. When I lifted the picture to replace it, I noticed something odd about the peg.

"Come look at this," I said, putting the picture on the floor.

She studied the peg. "What?"

"There are notches in the wood just above and under the peg. The other wasn't like that."

On closer examination, I noticed the joint between the molding and the wooden panel was not as tight as that of the panels on either side. Warily, I reached up and touched the peg. Nothing. I pulled down on it with no result. I pressed in with no effect, but when I pushed up from the bottom, a loud click sounded behind the panel.

"Oh, my God. It's like an Alfred Hitchcock movie!" Anna gasped.

"What's an Alfred Hitchcock movie?"

"It's probably better that you don't know." She ran her fingers along the crack that had widened when the panel clicked. "There's a latch or something." She bit her lower lip as she ran her fingers in the gap. "Got it." Another click and the panel swung open.

A musty smell wafted from the opening and we both took an instinctual step back.

"This is really creepy, Liam. We should get a flashlight or something."

"Agreed."

She started toward the door. "I'll go ask Miss Ronan for one."

"No, wait! We should probably do this without notice."

"Ahhh. Gotcha." Her brow furrowed in thought. "I know. We can go old school. There are candles in the top desk drawer and a lighter too."

I opened the drawer. "Probably kept for this very purpose." I pulled two candles out along with a lighter and closed the drawer. I passed Anna the candles and ignited both. After putting the lighter in my front pocket, I took a candle from her. "I'll go in first."

The floor of the passage was only an inch or so below the level of the floor of the room. We were on the second story of the structure, so it made sense the floor was wooden. The passage was narrow, but there was enough room for a full-grown man to walk upright.

"Wait," I said, squeezing past her to examine the closing mechanism on the panel we had just come through. "If we get closed in, I want to see how it works."

"How could we get closed in?" Her voice wavered a bit.

"We're on Dòchas. Anything is possible." The wall lever pulled up on a tongue-type lock, but the second latch was simply a safety catch that could be lifted with a finger. I pulled down on the lever from the back of the door and the tongue moved. It appeared impossible to be locked in or out. "It appears we can't be trapped."

"Well, that's a good thing, I suppose." She struck out ahead of me.

"Wait, Anna. Could you please tie your hair back?" I pointed to her candle. "The flame."

She handed me her candle. "Good idea. Like you said, 'this is Dòchas.'"

After tying her hair in a knot at the nape of her neck, she took her candle back.

"My freaky great-grandfather probably had these passages built so that he could cheat on his wife or spy on the servants," she said.

The passage took a sharp turn to the right. Anna stopped at a door similar to the one in her uncle's room. "This would be one of the bedrooms for guests. Mallory and Suz stayed in the blue room and Nicky in the green."

The demon in me roused a bit at the mention of his name. "Nicholas would've preferred to have stayed in your room."

She arched a brow. "No doubt. But I was with you, so it wasn't an issue."

"Would it have been an issue?"

"Not for me." She grinned. "Are you jealous?"

"Occasionally." I pushed up on the lever behind the door and the tongue slipped out. I flipped the second catch and the panel swung inward.

"Yep. This is the blue room," Anna said.

I peeked over her shoulder to find a room with wooden paneling and blue curtains and bedding. I pulled the door closed and it latched automatically.

"We don't even need to look in this one," she said, passing another door. "It's the green room. If there's a secret door to my room, I'm going to freak completely out."

"Get ready to freak," I said. "I have a feeling every room has a secret passage."

I was correct. We swung the panel open to find Deirdre sound asleep on Anna's bed, iPad on her chest.

"I want this sealed off," she said, pulling the door closed.

"It might come in handy." I examined a perfectly round hole in a floorboard. "You never know when you need to sneak out."

"I just don't want someone getting in."

"I think we can fix that." I stuck my finger in and pulled up on the hole and found it to be a trapdoor with a ladder descending into darkness below us. The air that gusted up smelled of ocean brine.

"Ugh. It smells like something dead." She touched my shoulder. "What if there *is* something dead down there?"

"Then perhaps we'll have discharged our duty and the Bean Sidhes will stop tormenting us."

Anna shivered and crouched down next to me and peered into the dark hole. "I'm scared."

"Kiss me."

"What? This is not a time to make out, Liam. It's a time to freak out."

"I need you to kiss me." I touched my lips to hers. "It makes me remember why we're doing this. It makes me willing to go down there even though I'm scared." I held my candle out to my side to be sure it wouldn't do any harm and kissed her again, more fully this time. She stretched far away, tipping her candle on its side, letting wax drip on the boards. When a pool of wax had formed, she placed the candle end into it, effectively making a candleholder. After gluing my candle in a similar manner, she returned to where I crouched at the opening to the tunnel below. With a gentle shove, she forced me off balance and pushed me until I was on my back.

She hovered over me until my breaths came in quick gasps.

Unable to stand it any longer, I pulled her down to where our bodies and lips and tongues met and I felt anything but fear. Everything but fear.

Muireann had watched the female's house for a glimpse of her Liam, but he had remained inside since he arrived just before sunset. Maybe he was going to stay the night . . . with *her*. She ducked under the water and swam farther north. She needed to head to the Na Fir Ghorm's caves to listen in on their meeting.

Something moved at the base of the cliff. Nose and eyes above water, she got close enough to tell it was a female human. It was Brigid Ronan coming out of a cave in the cliff under the house.

Muireann's heart almost stopped when she saw that Brigid Ronan met a Na Fir Ghorm who was just off the end of a boulder where the water was deeper.

She was afraid to get any closer. After last night, another slipup could mean the destruction of her pod. From too far away to hear, she watched as Brigid Ronan said something, nodded, then walked away from the Na Fir Ghorm toward the cliff cave entrance.

Anna tied her hair up again and grinned as she pulled the candle loose from its wax holder. "You're right. I'm not afraid anymore."

I took a deep breath, certain when I sat up, I'd be too dizzy to walk. She pulled the other candle out of the wax, keeping it upright, and held it out to me.

"I'll go first," she said, stepping down onto the ladder.

It was probably just as well that she went first because it took me a bit longer. Climbing down a ladder with a candle in my only hand was no easy task, and by this time, the candle was less than half of its original length. My feet hit dirt at the bottom.

"This'll be a lot more interesting," Anna said. "I'm not as familiar with some of the rooms downstairs."

The path split in three directions. We took the left branch of the tunnel. The first room was the dining room.

"This should be the library," she said, outside the second door.

I pulled the lever and entered the most amazing room I'd ever seen. Anna flipped on a light and I gasped. From floor to ceiling the entire space was lined with books. I'd never imagined such a place. Were there a heaven, I was certain it would look like this.

"We can come back in the morning," Anna said.

"Wait." I noticed that the books were organized by author. Hugo was at eye level. I blew out my candle and pulled out a book. *Les Misérables, Volume III.* "Anna. How . . ." I checked Tennyson. Sure enough, a book was missing. Likewise with Shakespeare and Poe.

"My books came from here. How did my mother get them?"

"Maybe she took them. She worked here."

I opened the volume of Hugo and something slipped out. Anna leaned down to pick it up. She blew out her candle and unfolded the piece of paper.

"It's another one of Uncle Frank's portraits," she said. "The woman is gorgeous. I have no idea who she is, though."

The woman who stared back at me from the small piece of folded canvas made me shiver. It was as if she wore suffering on the surface of her dark eyes. Draped over her shoulders was a spotted fur wrap and in the bottom-right corner were the now-familiar letters FMR. I put the folded portrait in my back pocket and returned the Hugo volume to the shelf.

"Ready?" Anna asked, holding out both of our candles. I pulled out the lighter and lit them.

"Ready."

The next room was the one in which we had discovered MacFarley with Deirdre, followed by several more small chambers similarly appointed. The second-to-last door was a bit different. It didn't have the second latch and there were oil stains down the back of the door as if it had been lubricated frequently. Whoever used it had wanted a silent entrance—perhaps to sneak up on someone sleeping or unaware.

I pulled down on the lever and the door swung open. The room looked just like the others before it with one exception. It had no windows. None at all.

"The door from this room into the house has a double dead bolt," I said. "The others had a thumb lock doorknob."

"What's the difference?" Anna asked, raising her candle to look at a painting.

"You can lock someone in from the outside."

She disappeared into the bathroom and flipped on the light. "Hey. Come look at this." She blew out her candle.

In the corner of the small bathroom where a shower should be, there was an empty space with a faucet sticking out of the wall. Protruding through the floor were four bolts that should have held a bathtub.

"Well, this explains where my mother got that bathtub," I said.

"And we know she didn't steal it. It would take several men and a wagon of some kind to get it down there."

I stepped back into the room and examined the art on the walls. All were paintings of the sea with Uncle Frank's initials on them. "Someone in the village has to know how or when it happened because one or more of them had to have helped move the tub."

Anna ignited my candle with hers and we stepped back into the tunnel. "One room left," she said. "Kitchen, maybe?"

I slid the lock and pushed the panel aside. "Not the kitchen."

"Oh, God," Anna said from behind my shoulder.

The long, narrow room appeared to be made completely of black stone and had a tall cathedral ceiling stretching to sharp points at the apex. Wooden support beams ran the length of the ceiling with intricate carved spires pointing down like fangs.

In the open windows, purple silken curtains writhed in a macabre dance to the ocean wind, creating an effect so terrifying all the hair on the back of my neck stood on end.

"I could use a kiss about now," Anna said, stepping into the room. "But I doubt it would help."

Nothing could help. The room we had entered was a cross between a dungeon and a sorceress's lair. Only one person could inhabit such a place.

Brigid Ronan.

"What do you think she does with all this stuff?" Anna asked, peering into a large glass jar filled with a brown substance.

"I couldn't begin to imagine." I closed the door to the passageway behind us. "I know she's considered to be a healer in the village. Maybe the jars and dried vegetation are related to that."

"She's a witch doctor. That certainly fits." Anna picked up a jar that appeared to contain a dead animal suspended in liquid and held her candle up to examine it.

An enormous painting hung over the bed. Barely illuminated by the distant candle flame, the man staring out at us with dark eyes seemed alive. I held my candle closer. He had dark wavy hair and a haunted expression of utter desolation. Chills coursed through me as I stared at what appeared to be a mature reflection of my own face.

"I think that's Uncle Frank when he was young," Anna said. "I only knew him as an old guy. Wonder why she has his picture?"

"Is there a light switch?" I asked.

"It should be by the door to the room."

I flipped on the switch and blew out my candle.

"Whoa. Check out the wall to your right," Anna said.

The entire surface of the black stone wall was covered in hash marks in groupings of five—four vertical marks with one diagonally across them. There were thousands.

"What do you think Ronan's counting?" she asked, extinguishing her candle.

There were long lines every now and then, like dividers between groupings. "I have no idea."

"I wonder where she is? What if she finds us in her room?"

I counted twenty-five longer lines. There were seventy-three sets of hash marks between them.

She ran her finger over the thumb lock on the door handle. "Liam. It's locked from the inside. She doesn't want visitors. We should go."

"I agree." Seventy-three times five . . .

There was a metallic scraping and a click behind the hidden panel from which we had come.

"We have to get out of here," Anna said, yanking my sleeve. "Now."

I reached for the doorknob.

"No. She'll know we were here. It's locked."

We sprinted to the window. Fortunately, we were on the first floor. I followed Anna out. Hiding in the hedge under the window, we held our breaths.

Anna pulled her knees to her chest and rested her head against the stone building. Flecks of moonlight shone through the bushes, gliding across her face. The exquisite beauty of the effect entranced me momentarily.

We needed to move in case Ronan looked out her window. Crawling on my hands and knees, I made my way out of the hedge. I could hear Anna following. Once we were several yards to the side of the window, I stood and we ran around the corner of the house.

"Three hundred and sixty-five," I said.

"What?" She was out of breath.

"Marks between the dividing lines." I shoved the bit that was left of my candle in my back pocket. "She's counting days—years—over twenty-five of them."

Anna's eyes grew huge. "Oh, God, Liam. I left my candle in her room."

25

The wild—the terrible conspire.

> —Edgar Allan Poe,
> from "Tamerlane," 1845

hen we rounded the front corner of the house, Brigid Ronan was standing on the porch, arms folded over her chest. "Bad things happen after dark," she said. "Very bad things."

Anna clutched my hand. "We went for a walk. I was perfectly safe. Liam was with me."

Miss Ronan gave no reaction at all. Like a statue, she waited for something.

"Well, we're going to bed," Anna said, mounting the porch steps, pulling me with her.

Miss Ronan blocked the doors. "Not him."

Anna opened her mouth to protest but was cut off.

"Your parents forbade him to stay the night. They were quite specific."

"It's fine," I said, giving her hand a reassuring squeeze. "I'll just see you in the morning."

"Wait. When did you talk to my parents?"

"On my day off. I called them from Francine's phone. I give them a weekly update. I have for years."

"What did you tell them?"

"The truth."

"Your truth and my truth are entirely different."

No good could come of this. Both of them had dug in and would never back down. I stepped between them. "Please. Let it go for tonight. I'll just see you tomorrow."

"First thing in the morning, I'm calling home to clear this up." Anna stood on her tiptoes and pulled my face down to hers. Miss Ronan never looked away as Anna kissed me in such a way it almost made leaving worthwhile.

Breathless, she smiled. "See you in the morning. There's nothing done at night that can't be done in the daylight." After flashing me a gorgeous grin, she brushed past Miss Ronan and into the house.

Miss Ronan stopped me before I even made it down the porch steps. "You forgot something." She dug in her pocket and pulled out the candle Anna had left in her room. She held it out to me. "You should never have come back here. I warned you, but you didn't listen to me, did you? Just like your mother, you can't stay away." She moved closer and I fought the urge to retreat. "What is it you're after? Money? Power? Sex, perhaps?"

"No!" I found myself backing up, despite my best efforts not to do so. "I love her. *Her*. Nothing else matters . . . and she loves me too."

She arched a brow. "Are you certain?"

"Positive."

"You'd better hope you're right. Go home, Liam MacGregor."

Muireann followed the Na Fir Ghorm that had met with Brigid Ronan back to his cave. Underwater, sound traveled great distances, so after he disappeared into the opening, she flattened herself against the rocks at the base of the entrance to listen.

So many of them were talking at once, she couldn't make sense of it.

"It is time!" the voice of the leader shouted above the rest. "Listen well. Our success depends on getting this right." The other voices fell silent. "Tonight is the night we win the wager."

Muireann's lungs ached. She was at the end of her breath of air. The Na Fir Ghorm had gills and didn't need to surface like she did. She zipped up, gulped air, and returned to the opening of the cave.

The Na Fir Ghorm were all talking at once again; this time, in loud, unhappy voices. It sounded like she had missed something important.

"What if she doesn't come this year?" one asked.

"She always comes on this night," the leader answered, "and we have been assured that the broken one will be alone at the right time to make it work."

"But what if—"

"Silence!" the leader shouted. "If you fail, this will be in your heart instead of hers! Now take it and go!"

Muireann shot from the mouth of the cave to a hiding spot behind a boulder on the south side. A half dozen of the horrible creatures emerged from the cave, heading in the direction of the harbor.

Thanks to her terrible timing, she had no idea what they were up to, but whatever it was, it couldn't be good.

Staying far enough back to not be seen, she followed them to the harbor, where they gathered under a pier. Swimming from the cover of one boat to another, she soundlessly slipped behind the lobster pen at the end of the dock to the store, feeling completely and totally helpless.

The Na Fir Ghorm hung out under the pier in silence and she struggled to stay awake. She hadn't slept for an entire sun cycle, and the exhaustion was overwhelming. She placed her chin on top of the pen, keeping her body in the water, and closed her eyes. If something happened, she'd hear it for sure.

But she didn't. By the time she woke up, it was too late.

Too late, at least, to do anything for the poor human floating facedown in the blood-clouded water, a blue stick protruding from her chest.

A lit candle floated on the surface of the water between the body and the human child who wept at the edge of the pier.

The nose of a mob is its imagination. By this, at any time, it can be quietly led.

—Edgar Allan Poe,
from "Marginalia," 1849

The sun hadn't even come up when someone rapped on the door. At first, I wasn't sure whether I'd dreamed the taps or had actually heard them. I pulled on my jeans and stood just inside the door. "Hello?"

"It's me, lad." Francine opened the unlocked door, still in a bathrobe, sucking in ragged breaths. "Are you alone?"

"Yes."

"Have you been here by yourself for long?"

"Yes—most of the night. Why?"

She stepped inside. "You need to get out of here and hide."

"What?"

"There's been another death."

"And? I'm blamed every time someone dies. What good will hiding do?"

She bustled into the bedroom and returned with my shirt. "It will buy you time and give us a chance to figure out what happened."

I took the shirt she thrust at me. "Who was it?"

"Katie McAlister."

My stomach dropped. I would naturally be suspect number one. She'd made no pretense of liking me, nor I her.

"She was called by the sea like the others, I'm sure." I pulled the shirt over my head.

She tugged my shirt down by the bottom hem. "This one is different."

"How?"

"Where are your shoes?"

I pointed to the bedroom. "How is it different?"

She returned with my shoes and dropped them at the foot of a chair. I sat and slipped my feet into them. I was able to lace and tie hiking boots one-handed, but as if I were a child, she laced and tied them for me. "You need to hurry. Can you hide at Taibhreamh? They wouldn't dare hurt you there."

"Yes." I placed my hand on her shoulder. "Francine. Tell me."

Her eyes filled with tears. "Oh, lad." She shook her head and wiped her eyes. "She was pulled out of the harbor with one of your paintbrushes stabbed into her heart . . . and they are coming for you. They're bringing a rope. You've got to get to Taibhreamh. Now!"

Shouting erupted from nearby.

"The kitchen window," she whispered. "Hurry."

I bolted to the window, threw it open, climbed over the sink, and practically fell out of it behind the house. Francine pulled the window closed behind me. "I love you," she mouthed.

The shouting was much louder outside the house. The villagers were close. In fact, it sounded as if they were everywhere. "We'll check the house. You go to Taibhreamh!"

The door to the house slammed open. "Where is he?"

"I don't know. I was here looking for him," Francine answered, her usual calm completely gone.

I had no idea who she was talking to. It didn't matter, really.

At this point, the villagers were all the same and of one mind: kill the demon.

"If we find out you are hiding him, you'll hang beside him," a male growled.

I crawled behind the lobster cages. Through the vines, I watched a group of men climbing up the trail to Taibhreamh.

"Spread out and search," another male voice shouted.

Darkness was the only advantage I had and it wouldn't last long. Already, a warm glow spread along the horizon where the sky met the sea. Climbing down the cliff and running along the beach would be the fastest route to Taibhreamh, but it would leave me visible and vulnerable. The woods were my best option.

"Stay here in case he returns," the man in the house said to another villager I couldn't see. "And be sure she doesn't leave to go warn him."

"He didn't do it!" Francine said. "He's incapable of such a thing."

"Shut up," the man shouted. "He should have been hung years ago. Hell, he should have been left to freeze as a newborn and burned alongside his mother. If it weren't for you, he would have been."

"He's probably with the Leighton girl. If he's in there, we'll have a hard time getting him out," said the man assigned to guard Francine.

"Ronan will make him available. She wants him gone more than we do," the first man replied. "The best thing that could happen would be if he's in the mansion."

Despite my desperate desire to see Anna and clear this up before she heard about it from someone else, Taibhreamh wasn't the most suitable place to hide. Brigid Ronan had the upper hand and she knew the insides of the beast far better than I. No place there would be safe.

Francine's store was out, obviously. My pa would never hide me, and when daylight came, even the woods wouldn't conceal me for long.

The lighthouse was the only location left. Unfortunately, it was on the other side of the island and the risk of being seen would be great.

The band of light that streaked across the horizon widened by the second. My time to make a move was running out. I scanned the trails to and from my location in all directions. No villagers were close enough for me to see or hear. Most of them had probably arrived at their designated search locations. I doubted any of them had been assigned the lighthouse. No one knew of the key. As a boy, I had pulled it out of the ashes after the sea captain's funeral, so it wouldn't be considered a hiding place.

Staying low, I crept from behind the lobster cages to the outhouse, then sprinted to the copse of trees near the ice pond. My arrival alarmed some ducks paddling on the surface. Their calls seemed deafening as they fled in a rush of wings. I held my breath and willed my heart to slow.

"The pond!" someone a considerable distance down the trail yelled.

Crashing through the thorny underbrush, I cut through the woods north of the pond and dashed toward the lighthouse.

The key was right where I'd left it behind the loose brick in the wall. Shouts sounded from the trail south of me and were answered by more from the direction of Taibhreamh. My heart fell into my stomach at the word "lighthouse."

I focused on not losing my grip on the key. If I dropped it, I was done. Now that they scented blood, the frenzy was unstoppable. Only stalling them long enough for reason to set in could save me now. And the chance reason would settle into the minds of a mob so revenge driven was slim.

Still, I wasn't ready to just give up. If the Cailleach had decided it was my time, she would have to work for it.

The lock clicked and I opened the door just enough to wedge my foot in the crack. I held the door in place with my shoulder while I slipped the key out. I shoved it in the knob on the inside, then closed the door, wrapping myself in a blanket of total darkness. Only when the lock tumblers clicked into place did I realize I'd been holding my breath. I took a shuddering gulp of air and turned my back to the door, slumping down to the floor in a moment of exquisite relief. I'd bought myself at least a few more minutes of life.

Through the brick, the villagers' words were muffled, but the tone was clear. Anger oozed through the lighthouse walls with increasing volume as more of them arrived.

My dark, safe cocoon became a torture chamber when they began striking the metal door with a hard object. A hammer, perhaps? I crawled to the ladder, certain my ears would bleed as the blows resonated around the cramped circular room and rattled through my skull.

Then the banging stopped.

I knew they hadn't simply given up. They were going to try something else, but what? There was no way in . . . or out, for that matter. Deaf and blind in a sense and completely helpless, I waited. And waited. And waited.

My thoughts turned to the last time I was here—to the first time I'd ever been kissed or touched by someone other than a caretaker. The smell of her skin, the smoothness and warmth of her lips. The one thing I had worth living for—or dying for—Anna.

Then it dawned on me: I might never be with her again. A panic so severe I was unable to breathe seized me. I had to see her whatever the cost. I refused to let this lighthouse become my tomb without seeing her again.

I climbed the ladder and pushed the hatch open. When I emerged into the morning sunlight and looked down onto the villagers surrounding the lighthouse, their next strategy became painfully apparent: they were turning the lighthouse into my funeral pyre—only the brick structure would never catch fire, it would just heat up like an oven and smolder, killing me slowly and painfully, as befitted a demon.

The screaming of the Bean Sidhes was the first indication something was happening on the south coast of the island. By the time Muireann got there, most of the Na Fir Ghorm had assembled near the shore under the lighthouse.

Villagers were piling lumber around and against the structure.

"You cheated," a Bean Sidhe screamed in the ancient tongue.

"We did no such thing," replied the Na Fir Ghorm leader.

In her golden, female form, the Bean Sidhe hovered just over the surface of the water. "You killed the woman by your own hand. She was stabbed."

He smiled, exposing his multiple layers of sharp teeth behind his blue lips. "She killed herself. We simply added the stabbing for effect after she was dead. A lovely detail, don't you think?"

"How does this test their love? You said it was a test of faith. This is going to result in his execution," another Bean Sidhe cried.

Several of the hideous blue creatures bobbing at the surface chuckled. "The event was received with more emotion and zeal than we anticipated," one said. "We assumed he would be blamed as usual and the female would have to determine whether or not she has enough faith in him to believe him even though the evidence is insurmountable."

"That is hardly a test. And now the contest is invalid because he will be dead."

The Na Fir Ghorm leader grinned. "What better test of love than death?"

Muireann sank under the surface and bit her lip to keep her sobs quiet. If only she hadn't fallen asleep, she could've done something to save her Liam. She could have pulled out the stick before the humans found the body or distracted the pitiful woman before she succumbed to the call of the Na Fir Ghorm. Anything. But now her Liam would die and it was her fault.

27

*Experience has shown, and Philosophy will
always show, that a vast portion, perhaps the
larger portion of truth, arises from the apparently
irrelevant.*

—Edgar Allan Poe,
from "Doings of Gotham [Letter VI]," 1844

The villagers were too swept up in their murderous frenzy to notice me observing from the deck. Almost giddy with purpose, they piled lumber against the aging whitewashed brick of the lighthouse.

Once the lumber had been lit, I'd only have two options: try to burst out the door through the flames, which would be nearly impossible considering the amount of lumber stacked against it and the inevitable heat of the door, or remain and be slow roasted. Neither prospect appealed. Somehow, the noose Mac Reilly had thrown over a large limb in a tree just west of the lighthouse seemed preferable—inviting, almost.

No. I would not go without a fight and I would see Anna first. I wanted to leave this world with her name as my last utterance, her face my last sight, and her sweet voice filling my ears.

"He didn't do it, I tell you!" Francine yelled as she emerged into the lighthouse clearing from the trail, Ron Reilly close behind.

"She climbed out a window," he shouted, catching up and grabbing her upper arm. "I tried to keep her put."

"Polly! Go get Anna Leighton!" Francine pleaded, trying to shake free of Ron. "Go quick."

Polly looked up at her husband, Edmond, and he nodded. Without hesitation, she lifted her skirt and ran toward the trail to Taibhreamh.

At this point, I suspected most every resident of Dòchas was present and pitching in to add lumber to the pile, except my pa. He was nowhere to be seen.

I shuddered at the grisly sight at the edge of the cliff. Katie McAlister's body lay twisted in an unnatural position in the grass, my long blue boar's hair detail brush protruding from her rib cage. No wonder they wanted me dead.

They must have combed the island for every fallen limb and piece of driftwood available because there was more stacked around the base of the lighthouse than in the Bealtaine bonfires. Because of the short stature of the structure and the height of the piles of wood, the flames would lick the bottom of the deck and set it on fire.

"It's time!" Connor MacFarley shouted, pulling a lighter from his pocket. "Time to rid our island of evil forever."

"What! Are you going to light yourself on fire, then?" I shouted.

There was a cumulative gasp and then a sea of faces turned to me.

"Because I haven't shoved my wife off a cliff or tried to rape a little girl. In fact, I've never committed any crime."

"Time!" he yelled again.

"Light that fire, and I'll kill you on the spot." My pa pushed through the crowd, knife in hand. "We'll not be killing him until we hear his side."

"What side is there?" someone in the crowd shouted. "His paintbrush is in her heart. He killed her."

Pa looked up at me as if seeking an answer.

"My paintbrushes all burned in the fire," I said. "Whoever burned down my shed must have taken the brush first. Nothing was left and I had no brushes with me at the time it burned."

"Prove it!" someone shouted.

Anna, Miss Ronan, Deirdre, and Polly entered the clearing. Anna ran to the base of the lighthouse.

"I can't possibly prove it. I can only tell you that I had no brushes left after the fire."

"But that's your brush?" MacFarley asked.

"Yes, but—"

"But nothin'!" he replied. "She was found in the water off the pier where you work with your paintbrush stabbed into her."

The look of horror on Anna's face made me feel as though a brush had been stabbed into my own heart.

"He wasn't there," Francine said. "He hasn't worked for me in days. He was home asleep."

"Were you with him?" MacFarley asked.

"Well, no, but—"

"Was anyone with him?"

"No. I was alone," I answered.

MacFarley struck the lighter and moved toward the wood by the door.

"I'll kill you dead right here and now, Connor," Pa threatened. "You'll not be burning him."

MacFarley released the thumb switch on the lighter and the flame died.

"I need to talk to Anna," I said. "I need to see her alone."

A grumble spread through the crowd.

Anna shook her head and my world collapsed. She didn't want to talk to me. She thought me capable of horrors. I had to get to her.

"Anna, please."

Her eyes full of tears, she again shook her head. "Stay where you are."

No. It would not end this way. I needed to touch her. To hold her one last time before leaving this world. The Cailleach might have won, but I would die on my terms.

I descended the ladder and unlocked the door. It wouldn't open because of the wood against it. With my shoulder I shoved and it gave an inch or so.

"He's coming out!" someone shouted.

"Get ready," another said.

I shoved again and gained a couple more inches. I could hear them moving the lumber that was blocking my way. In just moments, I would break free and be able to hold Anna one last time. If she let me.

Finally, the door burst open and I squinted against the brilliant sunlight. The villagers crouched in various states of readiness to snatch me. Slowly and deliberately, I took a step toward Anna. "I'm only going to speak with her. Let me talk to her and I'll peacefully succumb to whatever you wish." I took another slow step and none of them pounced.

"Back off!" Anna said to the villagers, then ran to me.

She wrapped her arms around my waist and her scent filled my nose. I breathed deep and sighed. I was complete.

"I said, back off!"

The villagers backed up, leaving a closed ring around us.

"I didn't do it," I said.

She buried her face in my shirt. "I know."

"You do?"

"Of course I do. You could never kill anyone."

"Why did you tell me to stay up there?"

"Stop! NO! He did not kill my mommy!"

It felt as though the ground came up to slam into me rather than my falling down to it.

"He didn't! He didn't!" Megan continued to scream.

I rolled to my side and loosened the rope around my neck, too weak to remove it over my head.

"Let me go," Anna said.

Anna. My Anna. I opened my eyes to find her on her knees beside me. She pulled the noose from around my neck and ran her hands through my hair.

"What happened, Megan?" Mrs. Byrne asked.

I sat up and MacFarley moved just behind me. "It is not over yet. You stay put."

"Mommy went to put a candle on the water for Daddy's birthday and she started talking to somebody. I couldn't hear who she was talking to, but I think it was Daddy. She walked down the steps to the water to go swim with him, but she must have forgotten how to swim because she splashed around and then stopped moving." Her eyes darted to her mother's corpse and she burst into sobs.

"How dare you subject her to this," Francine said. "All of you should be ashamed."

Polly Byrne crouched down to eye level with Megan. "How did the paintbrush get there?"

Megan shook her head violently. "I don't know, Aunt Polly. I thought she was waking up because she moved once, but I don't know. It was just there when they pulled her out."

"Did you ever see Liam last night?" Anna asked.

Megan shook her head. "No. The demon was not there. He didn't do it."

MacFarley threw the noose back over my neck. "Everything

she says is irrelevant. She's nothing but a child. We all know what happened."

"No!" Francine shouted. "We do *not* know what happened, but we do know it had nothing to do with this boy." She helped me to my feet and then pulled Megan close. "We know this child saw her mother die and we'll not subject her to another death." She put her hands on her hips. "Show's over. Everyone go to work."

28

We loved with a love that was more than love.
—Edgar Allan Poe,
from "Annabel Lee," 1849

*Y*ou left a witness!" the leader said. "You are never to leave a witness."

"We had no choice. We are forbidden to lure children and you told us the woman had to die no matter what."

Muireann closed her eyes and leaned against the cave entrance, ignoring the burning need to take a breath. She would not miss anything this time.

"They are stronger than I thought. Certainly not typical humans. There is one thing they cannot resist, though—something that makes even the strongest human male weak."

Muireann's lungs ached and she grew dizzy, but she knew she couldn't surface and let her Liam down again. She had to stay and discover their plan.

"No human can resist a Selkie."

Francine poured tea into three cups and delivered them to the table. I had a throbbing headache and my neck still burned, but other than that, I felt nothing but bliss. I'd been given more precious time with Anna.

"I don't want you alone anymore," Anna said. "It makes it easier for them. Please move into Taibhreamh."

Francine joined us at the table. "That's a wise proposal, lad. Taibhreamh is better fortified and you will have a full-time alibi if you are with Anna."

"I wouldn't want to impose."

"Impose! What part of this do you not get?" She stood and paced from the sink to the door and back again. "The crazy villagers want to kill you, which we would like to avoid, and I want to be with you. This takes care of everyone's business, right?"

"Right," Francine said, holding up her teacup in salute.

I almost couldn't bring myself to point out the real problem with the plan. Any time I had with her was a blessing, but I was becoming selfish. "What happens when you leave?"

She stopped pacing. "You'll come with me."

I shook my head.

"Why not?" She took my face in her hands. "I can go to cooking school and open a restaurant and you can paint."

"Your parents already hate me. You heard Miss Ronan."

She sat in her chair next to me. "Yeah, but they don't know you yet. Once they meet you, they'll love you, just like I do."

Again, I shook my head. I understood how deep discrimination could go. I'd experienced it all my life.

"Look, Liam. My trust fund from my grandparents vested a few days ago on my eighteenth birthday. I don't have to rely on my parents. We can buy our own place if that makes you feel better." She ran her finger over the burn mark on my neck. "Nobody will try to hurt you. No one will treat you badly ever again. You can leave this all behind and we can be together. Forever."

Forever. Surely I would be struck down on the spot if I even dared to entertain a dream so fine.

"Say yes." She leaned toward me. "I need you to say yes, Liam." Her lips met mine, and I was undone.

"Yes," I whispered, unwilling to resist her—un*able* to resist her.

Francine cleared her throat, bringing me back to earth. "Did you ever find out anything about Anna's uncle or your mother?"

"Yes," I said. "Not much, though. The books and bathtub she left came from the mansion."

"And there are hidden tunnels everywhere," Anna added.

"We found this." I pulled the folded portrait of the dark-haired woman out of my pocket. "Do you know who this is?"

Francine took the portrait from me. She stared at it a long time, brow furrowed. "Where did you get this?"

"It fell out of a book in the Taibhreamh library. Do you know her?"

She nodded. "I do. It's your mother."

My mother. The torment in her huge brown eyes spoke directly to my soul.

"I need to know everything about her. You've never told me a thing," I said.

Francine took a sip of tea. "You've never asked."

"I'm asking now."

She set her cup down and stared into it as if the answer were within it. "She just appeared out of nowhere one day. She was found on the beach by Brigid Ronan. Brigid took her in and she worked at Taibhreamh."

Anna took the portrait from Francine. "How long was she there?"

"Not long. Brigid brought her to me several months later

saying she could no longer stay at Taibhreamh because the Leighton family wanted her removed. The poor girl was with child and had no place to go, so I let her move into the shed. That's all I know."

Anna stared at the portrait. "What did the girl tell you?"

Francine shook her head. "She never spoke a word. It was as if she had no ability to speak."

I took my cup to the sink. "How did the bathtub get to the shed?"

"Ah, that was an unusual bit of business. Frank Richards hired a group of men from the village to deliver and install it for her. She filled it with ocean water and spent a great deal of time in it. I visited her daily to check on her, and she was either reading or bathing. Very strange, but then, she was a strange girl."

"What did Ronan say about her?" Anna asked.

Francine refilled her teacup from the kettle on the stove and topped Anna's off. "Not a word. Other than telling me the girl could no longer stay at Taibhreamh and spreading the awful lies about Liam being the spawn of a demon, she's never talked about her."

Before Francine sat, the phone rang in the other room. "Excuse me," she said, hustling out the door.

Anna kissed me and a soothing calm radiated out from where our lips met to my outermost extremities. "You'll love New York," she said, and every bit of calm fled as quickly as it had come.

"Anna, darlin', your mother is on the phone."

Her eyes flew open wide. "Wow. Perfect timing. I was just about to call her." She winked and ran to the phone.

Francine gestured for me to join her at the door. I felt awkward listening in on Anna's conversation. "Lovers have no secrets," Francine whispered. "You need to know what's going on."

"Today?" Anna said, twirling the phone cord on her finger. "That's soon."

She shifted her weight foot to foot as the person on the other end spoke.

"I want to bring someone with me," she said, shooting a look over her shoulder at me. "Yes. Liam MacGregor . . ."

Her rocking continued as she listened.

"Why not? . . . That's a terrible reason. I don't care what Nicky or his parents think."

She stopped rocking and her shoulders slumped. "Okay, fine. That reason makes sense. But I want to come back here the minute the wedding is over . . . Yeah, I love you too. I'm excited to see you as well. . . ."

She kept her back to us for a while after placing the handset back into the cradle. When she turned, her eyes were full of tears.

"They only have the two-person helicopter available because they're using the other one to bring in people from everywhere for Charlie's wedding."

I wrapped my arm around her. "But they want you there for the wedding. That's fantastic. Maybe this'll be the time to mend your relationship with your family."

"I wanted you to come," she said into my shirt.

"I think my presence would impair your ability to make it right between you and your parents, which is much more important."

She looked right into my eyes. "Nothing is more important than you."

And with those words, whatever minuscule remaining cautious part of me had been reserved fell the rest of the way in love with Annabel Leighton.

"I only have a little while before the helicopter arrives. The pilot left already. Will you come with me to get ready?"

I didn't want to yield a second of my remaining time with her. "Of course."

"I really want you to stay at Taibhreamh while I'm gone. You'll be safer, and you might find out something about my uncle or your mother. Besides, I need you to keep an eye out for Deirdre until I can find a way to get her off this island. I'm going to talk to some people about it while I'm home."

My first inclination was to say no, primarily because of Brigid Ronan, but on consideration, it was an excellent plan. The bedroom doors had locks, which the new house didn't, and Anna was right, it would give me the opportunity to look around. Miss Ronan, though troubling, didn't present any real danger that I could tell. She backed down easily when I confronted her. It appeared she derived some of her power from the fear of others. I would no longer give her any power.

Francine pulled out a package from behind the counter. "Here's the other set of clothes, and don't bother coming in to work. I'll be fine."

"No. I'll stay at Taibhreamh, but I want to come to work."

Francine nodded. "Suit yourself. I'll see you in the morning, then."

We didn't see a living soul on the way to Taibhreamh. It was as if all the angry people we had encountered hours earlier had dissolved into the rugged landscape of Dòchas. Even the mansion itself seemed devoid of life.

"I moved Deirdre into the green room this morning when we woke up," Anna said, pulling a long tube with caps on both ends and a duffel bag out of her closet. "I want you to stay in my room while I'm gone. Is that okay?"

I eyed the secret panel. "Yes. Any idea how long you'll be gone?" I shoved a dresser in front of it. If anyone wanted to sneak up on me, they would have to climb over the furniture to do so.

She put some folded clothes into the bag. "Only a couple of days. The wedding is the day after tomorrow and Mom said I could come right back after the reception." She zipped the bag. "I really want you to come with me," she said again.

"This is for the best. The transition would be difficult enough for me, but being thrown into a high-society wedding wouldn't be the best introduction to your world."

She crossed to me. "You are so smart."

I smiled and leaned back against the dresser. The light streaming in through the stained glass flitted across her skin like a rainbow. "I have my moments."

She ran her fingers over the rope burn on my neck. "This would've been hard to explain as well."

I laughed as she kissed my neck.

"I love you, Liam MacGregor. You know that, right?"

"And that makes me the luckiest person alive."

She looked at her wristwatch. "Mmm. Still some time. What on earth should we do to pass it?"

"I leave the pre-departure itinerary in your lovely, more-than-capable hands."

29

*There was something in the tone of this note
which gave me great uneasiness.*

—Edgar Allan Poe,
from "The Gold-Bug," 1843

lease don't make me do this," Muireann pleaded.

"If you want to survive the day, you will do as instructed," the Na Fir Ghorm said. "The next test is fidelity, and who better than a Selkie to test that?"

She couldn't believe her father was allowing this. They'd always lived in fear of the Na Fir Ghorm, but she never dreamed they held this kind of power over the pod.

"It's only for one night," Keela whispered. "Then everything will go back to normal. That's what they promised Dad."

"And you think they'll keep a promise?"

"Do we have a choice?"

The Na Fir Ghorm were watching them closely, but on land, the sound didn't travel well and they certainly could not be heard.

"This could be your chance to help him," Keela said. "Who better than you to go interact with him? All you have to do is spend until sundown tomorrow with him. Isn't that what you've been dreaming about?"

"No! I have not been dreaming about tricking him."

Keela turned so that her back was to the Na Fir Ghorm. "Listen to me, little sister. If you do not do this, they will most likely wage war on us. Is that what you really want? Is it so awful to have to go ashore and shed your pelt for some human you have already been longing for? Would you rather I do it?"

"Yes."

She snorted. "Well, that's not an option. They want you because you were a troublemaker in the harbor and defended him. Maybe next time you won't interfere."

"Your time is up," the leader called. "What will it be?"

Muireann searched her parents' faces, but all she found there was a pleading for compliance. Her father nodded.

"I'll do it," she whispered. Never had she imagined that her wish would turn into her worst nightmare.

I arrived at the store right as the sun broke over the harbor. I loved this time of day. There was so much promise in new beginnings, and daybreak always filled me with hope. Today was no exception.

Anna loved me, and that alone made my soul soar. As much as it pained me to be apart from her, the promise of her return made her absence endurable.

She would come back and we would leave together. We'd travel far away from Dòchas and the Cailleach. Far from misery and persecution. We'd be together forever. This thought made me want to shout and rejoice. I'd finally be free. Free and totally bound to Anna.

Something splashing off the end of the pier caught my eye. Perhaps it was a seal trying to break into the lobster pen.

I ran down the steps, ready to shoo the creature off, but stopped short about halfway down the pier. It was a girl about my age. She appeared to be unable to swim, clinging desperately to the wire pen.

"Hang on," I called. "I'll help you."

I grabbed a long-handled net from the rack and sprinted to the end of the pier.

By this time, she had made her way down the side of the pen and was close to the barnacle-covered piling.

"Wait," I said. "Stay there. The piling will cut you."

She froze, still clinging to the pen. In the morning darkness and murky water, it was hard to tell for certain, but it appeared she was naked. The water was cold year-round. Cold enough to induce hypothermia if someone were in it long enough. I had to get her out right away. Her lips were tinged with blue.

"I'm going to put the net in the water; hang on to it and I'll pull you to the stairs."

She nodded and grabbed the net I extended. As I pulled her along the pier to the stairs, her body rose to the surface. She was indeed naked.

"Francine!" I shouted toward the store. "Francine, I need your help!"

When the girl reached the stairs, she released the net and climbed out of the water, shivering. I ripped my shirt off and pulled it over her. "We need to warm you up," I said. "Are you okay?"

She nodded. At least she hadn't gone into shock yet.

"Can you walk?"

She shook her head and I caught her just as her knees gave way. "Francine!" With one arm, I couldn't carry her. I had to warm her up. I sat and pulled her against me, rubbing her frigid skin. "Francine!"

Finally, she burst from the store. "What in heaven's name?"

When she reached us, her jaw dropped. "Where did she come from?"

"I don't know. I found her in the water."

"Help me get her inside," she said, pulling the barely conscious girl to her feet. We balanced her between us and made it to the sofa in the store.

"Take off your pants and lie down," Francine ordered, holding the girl in an upright position.

"What?"

"Do as I say."

I slipped out of my jeans and lay on the sofa and Francine pulled my shirt off the girl and pushed her against me from head to toe.

"Wrap your legs over her. We need as much skin-to-skin contact as possible. We have to raise her core temperature."

When I hesitated, she shouted, "Do it!"

After covering us with a blanket, she put the kettle on the stove and pulled out two red rubber water bottles from under the sink cabinet. The poor girl in my arms shuddered and quaked to where it felt like her bones would rattle apart.

"Shhh," I whispered in her ear. "You're going to be okay now. Relax."

She muttered something through her chattering teeth that sounded like "Liam," but I was certain it had been my imagination.

Francine filled the water bottles and placed one against the girl's chest. "Hold this," she said. "For heaven's sake, lad. Hold it." She placed my hand over the bottle, then gathered the girl's hands and put them under mine. They were as cold as ice. She put the other bottle on the bottom of her feet and rubbed her toes.

"She's lucky you found her. Any longer in the water and she

might not have made it. She must have been out there awhile. She should have known better."

"Known better?"

Francine shook her head. "Never mind. I'm just rambling."

"Do you know her, Francine?"

"No."

The girl shifted slightly, and my heart stuttered. "Where do you suppose she came from?"

Francine frowned. "No telling. I have my suspicions, but let's wait and see what she has to say."

"What are your suspicions?" The girl made a moaning sound and pushed even harder against me.

"Lad, I've lived long enough to learn not to speculate out loud." She placed the water bottle between the girl's knees and continued rubbing her feet.

The bell on the door chimed. Francine got to her feet. "I'll be right back."

Somehow, my situation seemed more peculiar without Francine in the room. "Liam," the girl said as plain as day. "My Liam . . ."

"I'm here," I responded, sounding anything but comforting. Panicked was more like it. I was lying with a naked girl I knew nothing about who knew my name. I was certain my situation couldn't get any stranger, but I was wrong. At that moment, Brigid Ronan entered the room.

She squatted down in front of us and studied the girl's face. "Open your eyes," she said. I couldn't see her face but felt her eyelashes flutter against my arm.

Miss Ronan nodded. "I'll take her to Taibhreamh until we can piece her story together."

"Wait. You can't just walk in and take her away," I said.

"Exactly what had you planned to do with her, Mr.

MacGregor?" she asked, pushing to her feet. "You will have access to her since Miss Leighton commanded me to allow you to stay at the mansion. Unfettered access. Will that not be sufficient?"

I felt completely cornered. Not only was I pinned in physically by the girl, I was trapped by my own words. "That's not what I meant."

"Could I offer you some tea, Brigid?" Francine asked.

"No. I only came to drop off Miss Leighton's letter before the boat arrived. She asked me to do it the day her friends left, but I forgot about it." She dropped an envelope on the kitchen counter. "Mr. MacGregor can bring the girl when he comes to Taibhreamh this evening. Deirdre will enjoy having a companion . . . that is, if Mr. MacGregor is willing to share her." Stiffly, she turned and marched out of the room.

"I don't care for that woman," I said as the bell jingled.

"I think it's mutual." Francine patted me on the shoulder. "The girl's color looks good. We need to get her moving around. Let's see if she is warmed up enough to sit up and drink some tea." She pulled her to upright by the shoulders. "Here you go, lass. Let's have a nice cup of tea, now. Oh, my." Francine grabbed her apron from the oven handle, put it over the girl's head, and tied it around her back. "Well, there you go," she said. "Can you talk?"

The girl nodded.

"Can I get up now?" I asked. The girl turned her face to me and I was stunned. Her long, blond hair was matted with seawater and her skin was now a healthy golden hue. The eyes, though, seemed out of place with the rest of her—enormous, round, and very dark.

I realized that if I moved, it would shift the blanket and expose her, so I just remained still. "Never mind."

Francine handed the girl a cup of tea she had loaded with sugar. She took it but seemed completely confused. Maybe she hadn't recovered as much as I'd thought. Francine raised the cup to her lips and the girl took a sip. She grinned and gulped the rest of the tea in only a few swallows. "Good thing it was cooled off a bit," Francine said. "Now you'll be coming with me. We need to put you in a shower and get you warm and clean. Can you walk?"

"Yes," she said. Her voice matched her eyes: dark and rich.

Francine pulled off her bathrobe and wrapped it around the girl. The girl touched a flower on Francine's nightgown. "Pretty," she said.

"Yes, well. Let's get you up the stairs, then." Francine helped her to her feet and together, they climbed the stairs to Francine's apartment.

I slipped on my jeans and pulled my now-wet T-shirt over my head. The envelope Miss Ronan had delivered caught my eye. *Nicholas Emery* and an address were on the front with several colorful stamps. It was unsealed. I turned it over in my hand several times.

This was a private message from Anna to Nicholas. I would not invade her personal business.

"There are no secrets between lovers," Francine had said. There should not be. I would not hide anything from Anna. She would be welcome to read anything I wrote.

Still . . .

Leaving it unopened, I put it back on the counter and headed out to the pier, where I set about moving the lobsters from the holding pen to the plastic bins for transport to the mainland. They were marked with colored bands around their claws that indicated sizes for sorting. It was easy, mindless work, which was what I needed.

Every fiber of my being ached for Anna, and the appearance of the new girl made it worse somehow. It was as though I were being teased or tormented by the Otherworld.

"Haven't I suffered enough?" I shouted to no one. For some reason, my emotion surged and I was overcome. For the first time since I was a small child, I wept for my own condition. My loneliness. My misery. Myself.

After the woman named Francine helped Muireann shower, she gave her a gown with flowers on it just like the one she was wearing.

Muireann wanted to look pretty for her Liam.

Life as a human was different. She could move on land far better than she could in her seal form, but the water was terrifying. After she shed her pelt and hid it, her human form felt like a stone trying to pull her to the bottom. And she was cold. So cold.

But not now. Now, she smelled like her Liam and looked like his female in a pretty dress.

"Are you hungry?" Francine asked.

"Yes!"

"Liam! Come in for lunch," Francine shouted from the window overlooking the harbor.

She opened a can and it smelled heavenly. After mixing something up in a bowl, she spread it on a roll and put it in front of Muireann.

Hands were convenient. She didn't have to bite the food off the plate. She could pick it up and nibble like she'd watched humans do at the dock. She knew a lot about the human world because of the stories told by her relatives who had returned to the sea after shedding their pelts. It was fascinating to experience it firsthand. She could identify most human objects.

Her Liam came in from the back door and she got a funny feeling in her chest. Her human form was strange indeed.

"Her name is Muireann," Francine said. "She doesn't know how she got here, nor does she remember anything from her past."

Liam washed his hands at the sink and sat opposite her at the table.

"Hi, Muireann. I'm Liam."

Her face felt hot. Being human was confusing. "I know."

"Sometimes traumatic experiences keep us from remembering things," Francine said, serving her a second canned tuna sandwich. "Maybe your memory will return with time."

"Surely someone will come looking for you," Liam said.

She shook her head and took another huge bite.

"There's nothing wrong with her appetite," Francine said with a grin.

Her Liam laughed. "Apparently not."

Something about his eyes was not right. They were rimmed in red. This troubled Muireann. "You have shed tears," she said. "Why?"

He looked into her eyes, then down at his plate, saying nothing.

The rules of the human world were obviously different from her own. "I'm sorry," she said. "I must have misspoken."

Liam stood. "Excuse me, please. I'm almost finished with the bins." And then he left without touching his sandwich.

"How long will you be on Dòchas?" Francine asked.

Her heart hammered. What an odd question. "I don't know."

"Why are you here?"

She knew. Muireann tucked her hands in her lap to keep from fidgeting. "I have no idea."

Francine leaned very close. "Let me tell you something. If

you have been sent to do him harm, you'd better just collect your little pelt and dive right back into that sea. I'll not be tolerating it. Are we clear?"

Muireann nodded.

Slowly, she repeated her earlier question. "Why are you here?"

"I'm here to help him. I . . . I want to help him. I would never hurt him."

Francine pulled her chair very close and grabbed Muireann's chair when she tried to scoot away. "Who sent you?"

Tears stung her eyes. "I can't say. They will hurt my family. Please. I promise you, I won't hurt him."

"I'm going to make sure of that. Where is your pelt?"

"I . . . I . . ."

Francine yanked her up by the arm. "Tell me now, or I'll toss you back in the sea without it."

"It's under the stairs to the pier," Muireann sobbed. "Please don't destroy it."

"I'm only going to hold it for safekeeping. You don't harm him and I'll give it right back and you can go your way. How long will you be here?"

"Until sunset tomorrow. Please don't tell him. They will hurt my family if you do."

"Who will?"

"I can't say." The tears burned her human skin.

Francine released her and she slumped back into the chair. "Listen to me, little Selkie. You keep your hands and every other part of your body off him. Are we clear?"

"Yes."

"I love that boy and so does Anna. You'll not be messing this up."

Muireann trembled. This woman meant business and it was

terrifying. Terrifying and wonderful. They were on the same side, even if Francine didn't know it yet.

Francine nodded as if satisfied, then picked up an envelope from the top of the counter. She pulled out the paper inside and skimmed the contents. "Oh, God," she said under her breath. She shoved the letter in her pocket. "I have a job for you, Selkie."

30

Misery is manifold. The wretchedness of earth is multiform. Overreaching the wide horizon as the rainbow, its hues are as various as the hues of that arch—as distinct too, yet as intimately blended.

—Edgar Allan Poe,
from "Berenice," 1835

Staying in Anna's room was a mixed blessing. The sheets smelled of lilies and her very essence filled my senses, making it impossible to sleep. I could almost hear her voice at times. The Bean Sidhes had mercy and gave me peace, but so entwined was her soul with mine, I could find no rest.

Today was her brother's wedding day and she would return to me tomorrow, I realized with joy as the sunrise shone spectacularly through the stained-glass window. Only one more night without her.

"Come in," I called to whoever was rapping on the door.

Deirdre stuck her head in. "Miss Ronan is off today. Do you need anything?"

"No. Thank you."

She nodded and pulled the door closed. Giggles erupted outside in the hallway.

Another set of raps.

"Yes?"

The door cracked open again. "Are you going to come down to breakfast soon?" Deirdre asked. Over her shoulder I could see Muireann waiting in the hallway.

"Yes."

Again, the door closed, followed by giggles. What a change it was to hear laughter in this dismal place. Perhaps the evil would be warded off by such joy.

I threw off the covers, showered, dressed, and went in search of Deirdre and our new houseguest.

"Good morning," I said, finding them in the kitchen. Every available surface was covered with pots, pans, and various foods.

"I am making breakfast," Muireann announced.

"More like she's making a mess," Deirdre added with a grin.

"What exactly are you making?" I asked.

"Everything!" Muireann said.

I picked up a roll and cut off a piece of cheese, trying not to laugh at her utter enthusiasm. She was a delightful change of pace. Even Deirdre was brightening in her light.

"Deirdre says you paint people. Your female showed her lots of pictures you made. Will you paint me?" Muireann asked. She still wore Francine's floral cotton nightgown and no shoes. Getting her to Taibhreamh had been a challenge. She refused to wear the shoes Francine had given her because she said she liked the way her feet looked and she didn't want to cover them up.

I smiled. "Yes. After work."

She pouted. "Francine said you didn't need to come in until after lunch today since the boat came yesterday. Can't you paint me now?"

She ate like an animal and pouted like a child—such a

strange and fascinating creature. "Okay. Meet me at the fountain outside."

Armed with my sketch pad, I found her alone sitting on the edge of the fountain, dipping her fingers in, just as Anna had done. My heart ached. "This isn't a good idea," I said. I had never painted any girl other than Anna. It felt wrong.

"Why?" Her reactions were so innocent and childlike, it was disarming.

I shook my head and sat on a bench across from her. "Just sit still for a moment."

"Can I have it to take with me when I go away?" she asked.

I started with the general shape of her face. "Are you leaving soon?"

"I don't know." She shifted.

"Sit still, please." Then I roughly sketched the hairline. She had gorgeous golden hair that cascaded past her waist. I formed the eyes. Those strange eyes that seemed incongruous with her face somehow—too large and dark.

Then to my astonishment, she unbuttoned her gown and let it fall to her waist. "I want you to draw me in my human skin."

Before I could react, Brigid Ronan rounded the corner of the house. "Well, you work fast, Mr. MacGregor," she said. "Have you painted a nude of Anna yet?"

"What? No, of course not. Wait! It's not what it looks like."

She looked from Muireann to me and back again. "Of course it's not. It's . . . What exactly is it?"

"It's a mistake," I said, yanking the gown back up over Muireann's shoulders.

"It always is." She gave me a menacing smirk and then walked away.

"Did I do something wrong?" Muireann asked in complete innocence. It was as if she truly didn't understand.

I picked up my sketch pad. "No," I said. "Not intentionally. This was completely my fault." I should never have agreed to draw her. "I have to go now. I'll see you tonight."

"Can I come with you?"

"No."

Muireann knew she had made a huge mistake, but she didn't know what it was for sure. Obviously, humans had a strange notion about their skin. She found it beautiful, but they all kept it covered. Okay. Lesson learned.

She had to make this right. Francine had asked for her help and she would use the day to do just that. She would help her Liam. It would involve searching the room he was staying in, which would mean she would need to find the key.

For all their hang-ups, humans seemed friendly enough. Surely Deirdre would help her.

She stared out over the cliff at the water. Longing filled her from head to toe. She didn't belong here. She needed to be with her family in the ocean. It was worth it, though. She was helping her Liam.

"God, lad. What have you done?" The look on Francine's face said it all. Ronan had already been to the shop before I got there.

"Nothing. What did she tell you?"

She hung her dish towel over the oven handle. "She told me nothing. She called Anna. She told her all kinds of things and at first, Anna didn't believe her, but then she put Deirdre on the phone. Deirdre told her about you painting the girl by a fountain, and then Anna asked to talk to Miss Ronan again. I don't know what she said, but Ronan seemed pleased."

Unable to stand, I slumped into a chair.

"I warned that girl. I'll burn that pelt. I will!" She slapped her hand on the counter.

"What are you talking about?"

"She did this to you."

"Are you talking about Muireann? She didn't do anything. It was a big misunderstanding. She's strange and impulsive, that's all. Nothing happened. Ronan got it wrong."

"Strange is right. You need to steer clear of her. She's trouble."

I buried my face in my hand. "She's harmless."

"She's an Otherworlder, Liam. She's dangerous even if she doesn't intend to be."

I stared at Francine. Surely she was kidding. "An Otherworlder? Come on, Francine."

"She's a Selkie. I know what I'm talking about. I've had dealings with them. Be careful."

The phone rang and Francine left me alone with that shocking information bouncing around my head. The reasonable side of me knew this was nonsense, but were it true, all of Muireann's bizarre behavior and naïveté made sense.

"It's Anna," Francine said. "You need to read something first before you talk to her." She handed me the envelope Miss Ronan had left on the counter yesterday.

I slipped the letter out of the envelope. The writing was swirly and feminine. I had never seen Anna's handwriting, but it was how I would have imagined it. But within those swirls was a horror so deep, I was left breathless as I read them.

> Dear Nicky,
>
> God, I'm miserable. I'm so bored. I can't wait until my parents finally let me come home from this crappy place. I hope it's soon.

And when they finally do, I'm never coming back here. I hate it.

You were right about Liam. Slumming is fun, but only for so long.

I can't wait to see you again so we can make up for lost time.

Love,

Annie

Numb, I put the letter back in the envelope and dropped it on the table. I'd been played for a fool. All the things we'd done, the words she'd said, were nothing but pretense. She'd used me as a diversion to pass the time while I had hung my very soul on her every word, touch, and false promise.

"Now, lad. The timing on this is not right. Letters take time to arrive on the mainland. Why would she send a letter when she would beat it there?"

"Because when she gave it to Ronan, she didn't know she was going home. Her parents made her think she wasn't going to be allowed to attend the wedding." How pleased Nicky must have been when she told him in person.

Like a condemned man walking to his execution, I stumbled to the phone. I'd never spoken to anyone on it before and had no idea what to expect. The clarity of Anna's voice nearly drove me to my knees.

"So, I got a strange phone call today," she said. "Deirdre filled me in on what you've been up to since I've been gone."

I held my breath.

The acid in her voice burned through my heart. "Who's the topless slut?"

I wanted to scream and yank the phone console from the

wall, but I kept my voice low instead. "The better question is who is the biggest fool? That would be me."

"What are you talking about?" she asked.

At this point, confronting her about the letter would only exacerbate the situation. There was no desirable end goal. She had never wanted me, so I had nothing to win. I kept silent.

"I want her out of my house and you too."

The line went dead. That was it. Just like that. My entire life went dead along with it.

If only the hanging had been successful, I'd have never known this agony. I'd have left the world happy under the foolish misconception that my love was reciprocated.

Never had I felt like this. As if all my insides would implode at once. I fell to my knees, too overwrought to even make a sound. Francine ran to me and pulled me against her like she had done when I was a child. She held me and rocked while I hurt too much to even cry. Why had I been left alive for this torment? Hopefully, the Cailleach would take me soon and end my miserable existence.

*The angels are not more pure than the heart of a
young man who loves with fervor.*

—Edgar Allan Poe,
from "Byron and Miss Chaworth," 1844

Muireann had met with Francine and exchanged what she had found for her pelt. Sliding into it didn't bring the relief she had expected, though. The minute she submerged, she could hear the Na Fir Ghorm celebrating.

They were claiming victory, evidently because of something she had done. Instead of helping her Liam, she had destroyed him.

The Na Fir Ghorm sang her praises and chanted to her success while all she wanted to do was curl up and die. She hadn't even gotten to say good-bye to him.

"Human love is frail and fickle!" one shouted to the Bean Sidhes, who hovered over the water in golden clouds. "It has failed already."

"No. The contest is for thirty days. They might still reconcile. Humans have as large a capacity for forgiveness as they do for love. It is not over yet," a Bean Sidhe answered.

The leader grabbed Muireann by the scruff and pulled her underwater, where the Bean Sidhes could not hear him. "Now you listen to me. You are going to go back up there and take care of this. I want him to fall in love with you so that he won't go back to that human. Are we clear?" He put his terrible face right in hers. "You will go back up there or I will kill your sister."

From the corner of her eye, she saw two Na Fir Ghorm grab Keela and drag her under. They exposed their multiple rows of sharp teeth and made as if to bite her.

"What say you?" he asked.

She nodded vigorously.

"The minute we feel like you are not making your best effort to woo him, we will kill her. Do you understand?"

Again, she nodded.

They let Keela free and she darted to the surface and up onto the safety of Seal Island. Muireann knew that even though it was against their laws, the Na Fir Ghorm could go up and kill her anytime they wished, but for now, she was out of their claws.

"You will go now, before they have a chance to work this out. We will win this or you and your pod will die."

Deirdre met me at the doors to Taibhreamh. Her face was tear-stained. "Miss Ronan says you and Miss Leighton are not friends anymore and you are not allowed to come here."

"Sadly, that's the case."

Tears welled in her eyes. "I hope it's not my fault. Miss Ronan made me tell her about Muireann. I didn't know it would make her mad."

"No, Deirdre. This is not your fault at all. You did nothing wrong."

She attempted to smile and sniffed. "I've been feeling so bad and sorry."

"You've nothing to be sorry for. Sometimes things just take unexpected turns."

She handed me my folded jeans and shirt and held out my art portfolio.

"No. Only the clothes are mine." I nodded to the portfolio. "That belongs to Anna."

She shook her head. "Miss Ronan said Miss Anna wanted you to take that away too."

That was probably the worst blow of all. I put the clothes under my arm, took the handle, and tried to smile. "Thank you, Deirdre. I wish you the best."

"Mr. Liam. I know now that you are not a demon. Demons can't be nice like you."

Her words cut to the heart of the matter. I wasn't a demon. I never had been. I had been brainwashed like all the others. "Thank you."

She twisted her fingers in front of her apron. "I wish my parents had promised me to you instead of Mr. MacFarley. He really *is* a demon."

Poor Deirdre. My position was, in many ways, superior to hers. "Miss Leighton will find a way to help you out of that, Deirdre. She's a great person with a big heart. She won't let you be hurt."

At that, she ran to me and wrapped her arms around my waist, sobbing. I longed to join her, to just break down and cry until I ran dry. Instead, I remained passive, holding my clothes under my arm and my portfolio by the handle while she drenched my shirt with tears.

Storm clouds loomed low and threatened to break loose at any moment. I made it home before the first drops fell, which was good because the portfolio was not waterproof—not that it really mattered. I never planned to open it again. I tossed it in the corner and dropped my clean clothes in a chair.

The Bean Sidhes decided to shriek right about the time the rain started, which, of course, was when I had closed my eyes to sleep. I wanted just a small slice of oblivion, and instead I got bedlam. "Stop it. I'm done!" I shouted, sitting up. "I don't care who killed my mother. I don't care who killed Anna's uncle. It doesn't matter to me anymore." Nothing mattered to me anymore. "Leave me be." Through the window, a huge shaft of lightning spread in horizontal tendrils across the sky. In that flash, I saw something . . . or someone in the yard.

I slipped out of bed and pulled on my jeans. I hadn't barricaded my door on the premise that death would be preferable to living without Anna, but now that someone was outside, I regretted that decision. Maybe man's desire for existence outweighed his need for happiness after all. Perhaps my change of heart was due to some tiny kernel of hope deep in my soul that I was afraid to acknowledge—the hope that Anna would forgive me and come back—an impossible hope.

Another flash of lightning exposed my trespasser. Muireann, completely naked, was stomping around in the rain outside my house. I almost laughed. Francine was right. She was dangerous—probably more dangerous than Connor MacFarley with a rope.

I opened the door and watched her for a moment. She noticed me and stopped. "Hi," she said.

"What on earth are you doing?"

"I'm dancing in the rain."

"Why are you dancing in the rain?"

She shrugged. "Because I can and it keeps me warm. You should try it."

I leaned against the door frame. "Where are your clothes, Muireann?"

Holding her arms out, she grinned. "This is the way I come. Clothes aren't included."

I went to my bathroom and returned with a towel. "Come on inside before you catch cold."

She skipped up to the porch and I wrapped her in the towel. Her manner was so childlike and endearing. My heart pinched a little. She was definitely dangerous.

Clutching the towel, she wandered into the house. I lit several gas lamps and she began examining things. When she reached out to touch a curtain, the towel dropped. I grabbed my clean shirt from the chair and tugged it on over her head. After floundering for the armholes, she continued her perusal of the house. "It's very different from your female's dwelling, isn't it? You must be of a lower caste."

I sat on the sofa to watch her. She was fascinating. "Yes. Much lower."

"Why did you choose to be here rather than there tonight?" she asked, looking through a drinking glass in the light from the gas lamp on the table.

"It was not exactly my choice." The more I watched her, the more convinced I was that this girl was indeed a Selkie. Her manner was totally unnatural for a human. Why, I wondered, had she sought me out?

She put the glass down. "Was it because of me?"

"In part, yes."

"So does that mean I'm your female now instead of the one from the big house?"

Her forwardness was at the same time enchanting and terrifying. I had to be careful. Nothing from the Otherworld was benign, especially something in packaging this attractive.

"No. That's not how it works. Displacement alone does not ensure that status."

She cocked her head to the side. "I have no idea what that means, but it sounds very pretty. You are pretty, Liam."

"You're pretty too, Muireann. Why don't you sit down and

talk to me. That's how this works." She enthralled me. I actually had the chance to talk to an Otherworlder. To learn about things most humans never encountered.

"Teach me how it works in your world," she said. "I want to do this right this time. I hurt you last time and that was not my intention." She sat on the sofa right next to me.

I moved to a chair. "I'm going to sit over here so that I can see your face."

"Do you like my face?" She ran her fingers over it.

"Very much. Tell me about your family. Where you come from. How you came to be here."

"I can't answer most of those."

"Why not?"

"I'm under oath not to. We can't share with humans. Why don't you tell me what you know so far?"

I leaned forward, no doubt in my mind that what I knew was accurate. "I believe you are a Selkie. You are the seal I talked to off the pier. Am I right?

She nodded.

"What I don't know is why you are here."

She absently played with a lock of her hair. "I am here to help you."

"Help me what?"

A blank look crossed her face. Then her brow furrowed. "Well, my objective changed, actually. At first, I came to help you stay with your female. But that's not what I'm doing now."

"What exactly are you doing now, Muireann?"

I don't know what I was expecting, but it certainly wasn't what she did. She crossed to me and stood there for what seemed like forever, head tilted to the side, studying me with her huge eyes.

"Your female doesn't want you anymore, but I do. I've loved you my whole life, my Liam, from the first time I saw you as a child in the boat with the man you called Pa, I loved you."

I had only gone out with Pa a couple of times and only one was memorable. "You're the seal that nearly tipped the boat over. You kept me from being beaten."

"I am."

She felt for me the way I had always felt for Anna. My heart ached not only at my own loss, but also at her unrequited longing. I understood that longing.

She took my good hand and pressed her lips to the inside of my palm. Her breath was warm and sent tingles down my arm and along my spine. I closed my eyes, knowing I should stop her. But why? Anna didn't want me. She had used me and lied to me.

Muireann kissed her way up my arm, over my shoulder, and up my neck. When her lips met mine, she moaned and my entire body reacted. Anna didn't want me, but this girl did. She always had. Like I had always wanted Anna.

Like I *still* wanted Anna.

"Stop," I said, pushing her gently away. "I can't."

"What? Why? Am I doing it wrong?" She ran her fingers through her wet, tangled hair. She looked wild and exquisite and completely Otherworldly. Perhaps one of the most beautiful things I'd ever seen and my body ached for her. But my heart was an entirely different matter.

"You are doing it exactly right." I gestured for her to sit again and she did. "It has nothing to do with you. I love Anna. I always have. I always will."

"Like I have always loved you."

"Yes."

She stared at her hands in her lap awhile. "But she doesn't want you anymore."

"No. But I still love her. There will never be anyone for me but Anna. No matter how long I live or how I die, she will always be in my heart."

Her dark eyes met mine and I had to look away. Her pain mirrored my own and neither of us had the capacity to heal the other. Not without compromising ourselves.

She took a deep breath. "Human hands are fascinating. So useful. I like feet too. My feet are very pretty."

I laughed. "Yes, they are. You're a lovely human."

She smiled. "I am a lovely seal too. I much prefer it. Humans are confusing. You hide your feelings and thoughts like you hide your bodies."

"I've been very open with you about my feelings and thoughts."

"With me, maybe." She got up and walked straight to the portfolio. "But not with your female. You need to tell her how you feel. Maybe she would want you again." She ran her hands over the leather. "What's this?"

"Nothing important."

"Oooh. A zipper. My great-aunt told me all about zippers." She unzipped it and laid it open. It was empty except for a single small sheet of paper. "I can't read," she said. "You read it."

The handwriting was bold and tilted strongly to the right— very unlike the script in the letter to Nicholas.

Dear Liam,

I took your drawings to New York with me. I rolled them up and put them in a mailing tube because it was safer and easier to carry them that way. I hope you don't mind. I know our lawyer will find a broker for them. Like I said, you're crazy talented.

Know that I love you, Prince Leem, and can't wait to get back to this crappy island so I can be with you again.

Forever,

Anna

P.S. My cell number is below if you ever get bored.

"What does it say?" she asked, sitting on the floor and zipping and unzipping the portfolio.

"It . . ." The letter to Nicholas was not from Anna. It had been a trick. The whole horrible truth crashed through my mind. I had betrayed her by not believing in her when she stood by me at the lighthouse even in the face of overwhelming evidence. "It says I am a fool."

"Why would someone write that?"

"Because it is true." But fools could be redeemed. "Muireann, listen to me. I need to go do something right now."

She popped to her feet. "Oh, good. I'll go with you."

"No. You said you wanted to help me, right?" I folded the paper and put it in my pocket.

She nodded.

I considered telling her how charming I found her and that I hoped she would visit me in the harbor. But I was afraid my purely platonic sentiments would be misunderstood, so I simply stated the truth. "I need you to return to your world now."

The hurt look on her face cut like a knife in my heart. "It is because your Anna will not like me here alone with you. Because I am beautiful like she is and she wants you to herself."

"If I am very lucky, yes. She'll want me to herself."

She crossed to me and put her hands on either side of my face. "Your Anna is very lucky." She pressed her lips to mine, then walked out the door into the rain. I watched from the window as she made her way toward the sea until I could no longer see her through the downpour.

32

O craving heart, for the lost flowers
And sunshine of my summer hours!
Th' undying voice of that dead time,
With its interminable chime,
Rings, in the spirit of a spell,
Upon thy emptiness—a knell.

I have not always been as now.

—Edgar Allan Poe,
from "Tamerlane," 1827

Francine!" I burst into the store drenched to the bone. "Francine, where are you?"

"I'm here, what's wrong?" she called from the storeroom.

"*I'm* wrong. Anna didn't write that letter!"

She appeared in the doorway with a grin on her face. "I know." She reached around behind her and untied her apron. "Do you want some tea?"

"You know?"

"Of course I know. The Selkie girl brought me a recipe Anna had written and the handwriting didn't match. Now, do you want tea before or after you call her?"

"No, I don't want tea right now." And calling her was out of the question. On the way here, I had decided that my relief over her love being true wouldn't overshadow my consideration for her safety. "And I'm not going to call her."

Francine folded up her apron and dropped it on the table. "Why in heaven's name not? She didn't forsake you any more than you did her. You need to make this right."

I buried my face in my hand. She was away from here—safe from the Cailleach's curse.

Francine patted my shoulder. "Ah, I see how it is." She pulled my hand away from my face. "You're dripping on my floor. I washed your old clothes. Go put 'em on and come right back here. I'm going to tell you a story."

Something about putting on my old clothes seemed appropriate. I was returning to a pre-Anna life. Well, that was not exactly true. Because of Anna, I'd been empowered.

I tightened the belt on the too-loose trousers and hung my jeans on a hook in the corner to dry.

"There now," Francine said, placing a cup of tea in front of me. "Tea makes everything better." She sat in the chair across the table.

The silence that seemed to stretch on forever bordered on painful.

Finally Francine spoke. "You believe that keeping Anna away from here will keep fate from calling. That the Cailleach only can reach as far as this island."

I looked away. Francine, as usual, had cut right to the essence of the situation.

She leaned closer. "Your selflessness is selfish."

Unable to form an adequate or cohesive response to such a cryptic statement, I remained silent.

"Liam, lad. Did you tell her what seeing the Washerwoman meant?"

"I did."

She smiled. "Let me guess. She told you it didn't matter a hill o' beans to her."

I met her eyes. "In so many words, yes."

She leaned back in her chair and picked up her teacup. "And what *she* wants doesn't matter to you?"

I slapped my hand down on the table, causing my cup to rattle in its saucer. "Of course it matters."

"Yet, when she left, you were perfectly thrilled that she would be coming right back to you."

"Things were different." I stood, holding the back of my chair.

She set her cup down on the table. "Yes. You were thinking with your heart and soul, rather than your head. Sit down."

Not willing to cross her, I sat.

Again, she leaned in close. "Fate is a funny thing, Liam. You can't trick it. You can't outrun it. You can't change its mind."

"You said you didn't believe seeing the Cailleach meant certain death."

"My beliefs do not determine reality. Whether I think the Cailleach accurately foretells death is neither here nor there. What I know is that we only have so much time and that time should not be wasted."

"Keeping Anna alive is not wasted time." I shot to my feet, fully intending to leave the room and end the conversation before she changed my mind. I wouldn't allow myself to put Anna in danger. Before the phone call from Miss Ronan, nothing could have kept her away. Now, she was content to stay in her world, and that was a gift I could give her.

Francine pushed away from the table. "What you do with my words is your choice, but you'll hear me out, Liam Mac-Gregor."

In deference to her, I returned

"I promised you a story."

I picked up my tea and took a sip. Francine settled into her chair and cleared her throat.

"There was this girl, you see. She was young and full of dreams. The problem is that she was stuck on an island and she thought none of her dreams would ever come true."

"Is this an analogy for me?" I asked.

"I'd appreciate it if you would just let me tell my story and not interrupt. No, it's not you. You are a boy, not a girl."

I sat back, determined to hold my tongue. I couldn't recall a time since my childhood when Francine wanted to tell a story.

"It happened on Bealtaine. Several of her friends' handfasting ceremonies were to occur and she was terribly sad because she did not have a fine man to whom she would be tied. So, she set her candle adrift and wished for a beautiful man to come love her like no human had been loved before and she in return would reciprocate this love. She made this wish out loud, of course."

She took a sip of her tea and stared at me. It was unclear whether she was testing to see if I would interrupt or whether she was making sure I was alert. Either way, I remained silent and stared right back.

After nodding, she continued. "Well, an Otherworlder heard her wish. Out of the water came the most beautiful man she had ever seen." She patted the table. "You saw that little Selkie girl; well, let me tell you, the males are even more spectacular." She winked and I laughed.

"So, she looks at this man and realizes he is her *anam cara*."

"How did she know that?"

She smiled. "Well, she just knew. She felt drawn to him."

I laughed. "And being drawn to him had nothing to do with the fact he was a beautiful naked man."

She grinned. "That certainly didn't hurt. Stop interrupting."

I rolled my eyes.

"Now, they came up with all kinds of clever ways to be together without her parents knowing. She was worried her parents would figure out he was a Selkie and forbid her to see him. He would meet her on the jetty or by the cliffs in secret. But then the Cailleach appeared to her parents and then her brother, and all died of a fever within the span of two months, leaving the girl alone. Her lover no longer had to hide. He held her through the grief of losing her family and filled her nights with love." Francine's eyes filled with tears. "She would have died of grief were it not for him."

She rose and filled the teakettle with water. "They were united in a handfasting ceremony the following Bealtaine." Back still to me, she took a deep breath. "He saw the Cailleach that very night."

I studied the wood grain of the table while she lit the stove under the kettle. No wonder she stayed to herself on Bealtaine.

Wiping her eyes with the cup towel, she lowered herself into the chair next to me. "She had lost everyone she loved. She was determined not to lose him as well. Instead of loving him and spending precious time with him, she persuaded him to go away—to outrun fate and flee beyond the reach of the Cailleach. Out of love for her, he did."

For the longest time, she stared over my shoulder, as if seeing something play out in her mind. "He was dead within a week."

I had no idea how to respond. Obviously, the girl was Francine. Perhaps telling the story as if it were someone else's removed the pain to a degree.

I put my hand over hers. "You believe the Cailleach's reach extends to Anna in New York."

"I believe you would be foolish to assume it doesn't."

. . .

Muireann pulled herself closer to the edge of the rock. She had been preparing for this all night.

One gray head after another popped up only yards away, the yellow eyes sunken deep into the blue faces. The sun would be up soon, so she had to hurry. The Bean Sidhes did not tolerate daylight well.

"I have news for you," she said to the Na Fir Ghorm. "The human male rejected me and says he will have no other than his chosen female."

"You did not try hard enough!" the leader shouted. "You failed deliberately."

"I did not. He believes she will never return, yet he still remains true. Please do not put them through any more. Let them alone."

"Silence!" the leader ordered. "You will go back up there, Selkie, and finish this."

She stretched her neck up to make herself appear confident. "I will not."

The leader lurched up out of the water and grabbed her by the flipper. "Then you and your pod will die."

She held her breath, thrilled he had taken the bait so quickly.

"Stop!" screamed a Bean Sidhe, materializing overhead. "This is forbidden! Manannán mac Lir will banish you from this realm if he discovers you have taken a human or Otherworlder life."

"You knew they were here the whole time," the leader growled, digging his claws into her flipper. "You have allied with them."

She winced. "I have not. I asked them here like I asked you. They have agreed to drop the wager."

He released her and slid back into the water, beard drifting on the surface like seaweed. "Ah, well, then, our clan is willing to accept their concession and claim victory."

"But you haven't won," Muireann said. "You won't win. The human pair's love is strong. Give up before you do them harm. Let it go. No winners, no losers."

The Na Fir Ghorm leader looked above her head at the six golden forms that had materialized. "So, you are just willing to drop the wager?"

"Yes," they cried in unison

Silent, the Na Fir Ghorm clan bobbed on the surface, all eyes trained on the leader. Overhead, the Bean Sidhes swirled in a formless golden vortex. Muireann shifted on the rock, heart pounding. *Please accept,* she prayed. *Let this end.*

The leader turned to his followers and then back to Muireann. And then, to her horror, he threw his head back and laughed, bubbles spilling from the corner of his mouth. His laugh was shrill, bordering on a scream. "Never!" he shouted. "We will never step aside. We will not even entertain the thought of losing."

The Bean Sides took their female forms, hovering over the water. "Then we proceed," one said.

The leader continued to laugh as the Bean Sidhes evaporated from view. "It will be interesting, little Selkie, to see how far your allies are willing to go to win. How much suffering will they allow the humans to endure before they forfeit the wager?"

33

*We gave the Future to the winds, and slumbered
tranquilly in the Present, weaving the dull
world around us into dreams.*

—Edgar Allan Poe,
"The Mystery of Marie Rogêt," 1842

rancine dialed the numbers on the bottom of Anna's letter and handed me the receiver. I was so nervous, I could hardly breathe.

The phone rang for what felt like forever, then Anna answered.

"Hey," her voice said.

"Anna, I—"

"I can't answer my phone right now because I'm on an island with no cell coverage. My parents know how to reach me, so if it's really important, call them. Don't leave a message after the beep, because I won't be able to get it."

It was a recorded message, probably from her last trip.

"If this is Liam," the message continued, "I'm on my way back. I'm a lot of things, but stupid isn't one of them. Neither are you. We're just out of our comfort zone." Then there was a loud, metallic beep followed by silence.

I gently placed the phone receiver in the cradle. She was on her way back.

Francine studied me with a furrowed brow from the counter. "Are you all right, lad?"

"Yes, I'm . . ." I ran my hand through my hair. "I'm fine. Great, actually. I'm fantastic!"

"What did she say?"

I crossed to the counter, still a little stunned. "It was a message. It said she's on her way. She's coming back."

Francine grinned ear to ear. "*Anam cara* can't be parted for long."

The flying vehicle landed near the large dwelling with a roar.

"What do you suppose is happening?" Keela asked.

"I hope Liam's female has come to her senses and returned," Muireann answered. "And I hope she takes him away to her world right away so the Na Fir Ghorm can't hurt them anymore."

Keela's eyes grew large. "You want him to leave? I thought you fancied him."

Muireann swam close to shore and rested on the rocky bottom, head above water. "I do. I love him. That's why I want him to leave."

"That makes no sense at all," her sister replied, sliding next to her.

"Love doesn't make sense. Not human love anyway. It's all confusing and painful."

A man Muireann had never seen helped Liam's female out of the vehicle. After she had moved away from the machine, the man got back in and the thing roared and flew away. Liam's female stood still, looking from the dwelling to the trail leading to Liam's house, as if confused. Leaving her bag behind, she struck out on the trail toward the woods.

"She's looking for him," Keela remarked.

"I hope so," Muireann answered.

"You are really ready to give him up so easily? He's very pretty; I'd have a hard time doing that."

"He's even prettier than his skin." Tears filled Muireann's eyes. "And he was never mine to surrender. He has always been hers. He always will be."

"Are they bound?"

"No." *Bound*. Muireann's heart raced. "Wait! That's it. If they are bound to each other, then the Na Fir Ghorm will have to honor that and not interfere." Muireann swam in a tight circle around her sister. "You are brilliant! That's the solution!"

For the first time since the wager began, Muireann felt like the couple stood a chance. Even the Na Fir Ghorm had to honor an eternal bond.

All the things I wanted to say to Anna swirled through my head from the time I heard the recorded phone message until the helicopter flew overhead. Now, I couldn't recall any of them. Sprinting up the path, my breathing drowned out the helicopter engines as it lifted off and soared out of sight.

She was here, on Dòchas. Anna.

I passed my house and stopped at the fork. The woods would be faster than the cliff-side trail, I decided. Just as I rounded the turn, I saw her. Well, more like I leapt from the path in an effort to not crash into her as she bolted out of the woods.

I stared up at her from where I'd landed in the brush. I'd never seen anything so wild or wonderful. Her hair was tangled with leaves from running through the trees and she was breathing hard from exertion.

We simply stared at each other, and I understood. Words weren't necessary. She was here for me. All of me.

I stood and pulled her close. She didn't resist or say a word, she simply folded into my body and melted against me, heart pounding in time to mine.

"I love you," I whispered into her hair.

"I couldn't stay away," she answered.

"Thank God. Anna, I'm so sor—"

She cut me off with a kiss. "No. No apologies. Not now. We both know it without saying it. I need you and you need me. That's all there is—all there'll ever be."

I entangled my fingers in the hair at the nape of her neck and kissed her. She was here, and real, and kissed me back with such passion, I grew dizzy. Nothing else mattered. I'd been given more time. I would live in the moment and savor every precious second as my dreams and reality intertwined.

A twig snapped behind me. I pulled away to find Edmond and Polly Byrne with Megan McAlister. Megan's face was filthy, broken by clean streaks caused by tears.

"Can we speak with you, miss?" Edmond asked. "We saw the helicopter, so we were on our way to the mansion to see you."

As if just startled from sleep, Anna blinked hard, catching her breath. I almost chuckled. The Byrnes' timing was as terrible as the Bean Sidhes'.

Anna took a deep breath, sighed, then shrugged. "Sure."

Edmond shuffled on the path, eyes cast down. "Well, it's kind of private." He shifted his gaze to me and then back to the dirt.

Anna squeezed my hand, then dropped it. "Okay." She walked down the path with him until they were out of earshot.

Polly shifted uneasily, avoiding eye contact with me. Megan, however, studied me from head to toe. "Are you really a demon?" she asked. "What's it like?"

I squatted down and whispered, "Do you like secrets?"

She grinned and nodded. "Uh-huh."

"You must promise not to tell anyone, okay?"

She bounced on her toes and nodded again. "I promise."

Polly's eyes narrowed as if she were trying to warn me not to frighten the child. I winked at her and her eyes flew open wide.

I leaned closer to Megan. "I'm not really a demon," I whispered. "I'm just a regular person like you."

She laughed.

"But that's our secret, right?"

She nodded. "I'm hungry," she said.

Polly gripped her shoulder. "Never complain. It doesn't make things better."

"Come along, Polly," Edmond shouted from down the path. Anna was making her way toward us.

Polly patted Megan on the head. "Be a good girl." Then she walked away to join her husband, leaving the little girl behind.

Polly was Katie McAlister's sister and only living relative, so it stood to reason that Megan had fallen under her care. Sadly, the Byrnes were also the least able on Dòchas to sustain another mouth to feed. Most certainly, Edmond had asked Anna to take his second charge on along with the first.

Anna crouched down in front of Megan. "Do you like pancakes with chocolate chips, Megan?"

The little girl tilted her head to the side. "I like cake and I like chocolate, so I'm sure I do."

"Do you know who Deirdre is?"

Megan nodded.

"Well, her room has two beds in it and she would love to have a friend come stay with her at the mansion. Would you like that?"

Megan pointed at me. "Can he come stay too?"

Anna met my eyes, and the world stopped. "I certainly hope he will."

Muireann retrieved Liam's shirt from the beach where she'd abandoned it. With humans' strange attitudes toward their skin, she thought it best she be prepared when she shed her pelt this time.

She'd seen Miss Ronan come and go from a cave under the house. Perhaps she could find Liam that way and tell him what he needed to do to protect himself and his female.

He had disappeared into the large dwelling with his female and a small, red-haired human earlier in the day, and she was certain he was still there. The trick would be finding him without Brigid Ronan discovering her.

Anna and I watched from the other side of the kitchen as Megan giggled and Deirdre formed a new shape from chocolate chips on the table. "This one is a square. Can you make one too?" Megan nodded and emulated Deirdre's square, periodically popping chocolate chips in her mouth.

"I've never seen a kid eat so much," Anna remarked, leaning into me. "She must have polished off eight pancakes."

I shifted on the stool and wrapped my arm around her. "She probably hadn't eaten since her mother died."

Anna shuddered. "Well, that's never going to happen again."

"You're a good person." I kissed her neck.

Miss Ronan dropped a pan in the sink with a bang and turned on the faucet full force.

Anna turned in my arms so that she faced me. "I hate to break this to you, but I don't think Miss Ronan likes you," she whispered.

I gasped. "I had no idea! I'm completely crushed."

She wiggled closer, leaving me one step short of insane. "But *I* like you." She put her mouth to my ear. "A lot." She nipped my earlobe.

Miss Ronan cleared her throat and dropped a rinsed pan on the stainless steel countertop.

Anna giggled. "Let's go," she whispered. "Before she breaks something."

That suited me fine. The most likely thing to break was my sanity. Anna was making me crazy. She placed her slender hand in mine and pulled me from the kitchen without a word to Miss Ronan.

The midday sun streamed in through the stained glass, giving her bedroom a dreamlike quality. Honestly, even without the colored shafts of light, I felt as though I were in a dream.

"I missed you," she said, dropping my hand.

"And I you."

"No." She pulled the bottom of her shirt nervously. "I mean . . ." She took a deep breath. "Liam, it was weird. It was like I couldn't breathe or think. Like I was a zombie or something."

I sat on the edge of the chaise lounge and waited for her to formulate her thoughts into the words I had been searching for myself.

She paced from her suitcase by the bed to the door and back as she spoke. "We have something really strange and powerful going on here, you know? My feelings for you are so intense, it's overwhelming. It's like this crazy island of yours. I can't control it. And it scares me."

I stood. "Maybe we should stop trying to control it. Perhaps we should just give in to it."

She crossed her arms over her chest, trembling.

"I realized something while you were gone." I moved several

steps closer. "It happened when I was certain you had never loved me and had left me forever."

She opened her mouth to protest but said nothing when I held my finger up.

"I know that never happened, but at the time, I thought that it had."

She nodded and sat on the edge of her bed.

I sat next to her. "What I realized was that I could never love anyone but you. Ever. My heart is yours forever, Anna. I don't have a choice in it. You are the other part of me."

A tear rolled down her cheek and I wiped it away with my thumb.

"And I owe you an apology," I continued. "I doubted you, and that was unfair. I was wrong, and I'm sorry. I'm also sorry that you were hurt. Miss Ronan misunderstood the situation."

She brushed her hair behind her shoulder and met my eyes. "What was the situation?"

I shifted to where I sat higher on the bed. "The girl she told you about. She has unusual behavior. It wasn't what it looked like."

She raised an eyebrow. "I figured Ronan had just made it up to piss me off. Then Deirdre told me about it and I believed her. After I cooled off, I decided Ronan forced Deirdre to tell me a story to drive us apart. So, there really was a girl?"

My stomach churned. "Yes and no."

Her other eyebrow shot up.

"She's not really a girl. She's a Selkie."

For a moment, I thought she was angry, but her brow relaxed and she took a deep breath, shaking her head. "Honestly, Liam. I'd like to think you're delusional or screwing with me, but I think you're serious."

"Francine can clear a lot of this up for you. She had much more interaction with her than I did."

"Not according to Miss Ronan."

"Ronan is the one who planted the fake letter from you to Nicky saying you were bored with slumming and coming back to him."

Anna covered her mouth. "Oh, God."

"We've both been played, Anna. And honestly, I'm convinced we're part of some larger scheme."

"It's just Ronan being a bitch," she said, pushing to her feet.

"No. It's more than that. The Selkie couldn't tell me who sent her or why, but she said her objective was to help us stay together. Why would an Otherworlder be compelled to protect us?"

She paced the room again. "Wow. I feel like I've ODed on eggnog again."

"I know it's hard to grasp, but it makes sense."

Throwing her arms over her head, she made a frustrated groan. "None of this makes sense. I don't even know what's going on anymore."

"Here's what I know." I stepped in front of her and pulled her to me. "The *only* thing I know is that I love you and want to spend every moment with you if you'll allow it."

"That's why I'm here. We're getting out of here together with Deirdre and Megan as soon as the big chopper is available to fly us away from this awful place. We're going to be together away from demons and funeral pyres and creepy blue guys and screaming invisible women and starving children and all the other twisted, screwed-up things on this island. Just you and me." She ran her fingers through my hair. "I love you, Liam MacGregor, and all of the creepies in the world can't change that."

A scratching sound from behind me sent a tremor of terror down my spine. "Shhh. Listen," I said. "Did you hear that?"

Anna held her breath.

There it was again: a light tapping sounded from the other side of the secret panel.

"Oh, God," she whispered, backing away toward the door.

I crossed to the panel and put my ear against it. "Hello?" I said.

"Liam?" was the response from the other side.

I shoved the dresser I had placed in front of the panel aside and pulled the picture from the peg next to it. I pushed up on the peg and the panel clicked. I ran my fingers in the opening and released the second catch. "Anna, I'd like you to meet the Selkie I told you about." I swung the panel open to find Muireann drenching wet and shivering in my T-shirt.

"Hi, Liam's female!" Muireann entered the room without invitation. Anna took a step back. "I'm glad you returned."

Anna stood still, jaw open.

"How did you know about the passage, Muireann?" I asked.

"I went in the cave Brigid Ronan uses to talk to the Na Fir Ghorm. I used my human ears to hear you. Oooh. This is so pretty. It's like a sunrise, a sunset, and a rainbow all in one place." She ran her fingers over the stained glass.

"She's in your shirt," Anna muttered, still stunned.

"Yes. Liam gets all nervous when I only wear my human skin. He covers me up," Muireann said, wandering the room. "He made me wear this last time, so I wore it again."

I needed to get her to focus. "Muireann, why are you here?"

"Oh, well. I came to warn you and give you a trick."

Anna slumped down onto the bed, eyes still trained on Muireann.

"Warn us against what?" I asked.

"Well, I can't really say because I'm not allowed, but you need to be really careful." She picked up a vase from the table at the end of the chaise lounge and held it to the colored light coming through the stained-glass window. "You are only in danger for a few weeks more, so we have devised a trick to undo it."

I took a step closer to her. "Undo what?"

She clamped her hand over her mouth.

"Okay, what trick, then?" I asked.

Almost too quickly, she trotted over to Anna, who stiffened. "Do you love him? I mean really love him like I do?"

Anna shot startled looks from me to Muireann. "I love him *more* than you do."

"Great. And I know he loves you because he refused to mate with me."

Anna jumped to her feet. "He . . . what?"

"So, here's what you need to do. You need to become bonded for a moon cycle and a day so that they will leave you alone so they don't hurt or kill you and you can be together."

I took her by the shoulder. "Who?"

She covered her mouth with her hands. "Oops."

I turned her shoulder loose. "What do you mean by bonded?"

"I really like lamps." She skipped to the nightstand and switched the lamp on and off and on and off. "I got to play with one when I spent the night here."

Her attention was so scattered it was hard to keep up. "Muireann, please focus. What do you mean by bonded?"

She moved away from the lamp and ran her fingers over the bedcover. "Well, it's like your ancestors' handfasting ceremony but better because it works soul deep and into the Otherworld too. You can choose the amount of time you wish to be bonded from a moon cycle to eternity. We're not really supposed to share it with humans, but this is a special case and I got it okayed from higher up."

"Who is higher up?"

"Well, the Bean Sidhes said it was okay." She covered her mouth. "Oops."

"You can talk to Bean Sidhes?" Anna said.

Hands still over her mouth, Muireann nodded. She pulled her hands from her mouth and studied them, wiggling her fingers, smiling. "I need to go now before I make more mistakes. If you want to do this, meet us on the beach outside the tunnel just after sunset. Bye!"

After she slipped out the panel and pushed it shut, I slid the dresser back in place.

"This is worse than eggnog-induced delirium." Anna shook her head. "Wow, that was weird."

I sat on the edge of the bed and closed my eyes. This was not simply Muireann being whimsical. Something wanted to hurt or kill us to keep us apart and she was trying to help us.

Anna chuckled. I opened my eyes to find her still staring at the hidden panel. "You refused to 'mate' with her?"

I nodded.

She laughed. "Even when you thought I was home screwing around with Nicky?"

Her laughter unnerved me slightly. "There is no one else for me. Only you."

"She's very pretty. Striking, really. If she weren't some freaky paranormal creature, she could be a model."

"That's irrelevant. I love you."

She wrapped her arms around my neck and kissed me. "Let's do it."

"Do what?"

"The bonding thing she talked about." She ran her hands down my back and up again, causing my breath to catch.

"Anna, it's serious. It's marriage, only into the next world as well."

She dropped her hands. "So, you don't really love me *that* much?"

"My God. It's . . . Yes. Yes, I do. It's you I'm thinking of."

She plopped down on the bed. "I sat through my brother's wedding, and all I could think about was how much I wanted to be with you. How superficial everything seemed compared to my feelings for you." She stared right into my eyes. "Let's do it."

I couldn't believe she would even consider this. "There's no backing out once it's done until the specified time is up."

She crossed her arms over her chest. "Do you anticipate remorse?"

"Yes. You could have anyone."

"But I want you." She stood and moved directly in front of me—so close that if she had leaned forward, we would have touched. "Do you think you're going to want to back out?"

"No."

"Then you think for you, and I'll think for me." She ran her hands under my shirt and up the skin of my back. "Right now, I don't want to think at all. I just want you to kiss me."

34

If you will have faith in me, *I can and will satisfy your wildest desires.*

—Edgar Allan Poe,
from a letter to Helen Whitman, 1848

uireann waited at the water's edge, never taking her eyes off the cave entrance. She kept still and low, only the top of her head, eyes, and nose above water. She didn't want to be seen by the Na Fir Ghorm or even her pod mates, for that matter.

In the faint light from the setting sun, she could see Liam's shirt draped over the rock where she had left it. An involuntary shudder rolled through her. She dreaded shedding her pelt and being cold again. She never felt cold in her seal form, but the water made her human form numb and achy.

Maybe they weren't coming. Maybe she had said something wrong when she spoke with them. The human world was confusing. They spoke in riddles and hid themselves. Her stomach turned over. Maybe his female didn't love him enough to commit her soul to his.

Finally, movement came from within the cave. They had decided to go through with it after all.

Muireann's heart stopped when Brigid Ronan emerged from the opening.

I locked Anna's door after returning with two more candles from her uncle's room. Miss Ronan hadn't interrupted us, which was surprising since the sun had set and I was forbidden to be in the house after dark.

"We're in a hurry, Anna," I said. "We let time get away. It's already past sundown, which is when we were supposed to meet Muireann."

Anna appeared in the doorway of her bathroom, and I was spellbound. She wore the silver dress from Bealtaine and her hair was piled up on her head, exposing her lovely neck. "Muireann will wait." She smiled. "I have something for you. I got it from my uncle's closet while you showered."

She reached into her closet and produced a black suit jacket. "There's also a shirt, pants, and a tie." After pitching the jacket onto her bed, she produced the other items and laid them out beside it. "We should dress up, don't you think?"

We would only be bound for a month and a day, but I still wasn't certain Anna understood the seriousness of it. "You're sure about this."

"I've never been more sure of anything in my life." She unbuttoned my shirt and pulled it off, replacing it with the white, stiff shirt from her bed. Deftly, she buttoned it all the way down in the time it would have taken me to manage one button. "I'll leave you to the rest," she said, disappearing back into her bathroom.

I pulled on the pants and jacket. The pants were a bit loose, but they stayed up. The tie was another issue entirely. I'd seen plenty of them in the newspapers and tabloids, but I'd never laid eyes on one myself. After draping it around my neck, I tapped on the door frame of her open bathroom door. She put the top on her lipstick and smiled at me in the mirror. "You look so handsome. Like James Bond."

I wondered if we lived to be old, would she always have

this effect on me? Would I forever be held breathless when she smiled? Yes. Undoubtedly I would, I decided, as she tied the necktie while standing so close I could feel the heat radiating from her skin warm my own. Part of me felt unworthy of her, yet I also knew that no one would ever love and treasure her the way I did. Perhaps that part of me outweighed my deficits adequately enough to make me deserving. I would certainly endeavor to spend the rest of my days proving not only to myself, but to her, that I was worthy of her.

We found the trapdoor leading to the lower level of hidden passageways easily, and Anna descended first. "How do we know which way to go to find the way out to the sea?" she asked. "There are three directions we could take from here."

I watched my candle flutter, the flame leaning toward me and slightly to the left. Any breeze or air movement had to come from the tunnel leading to the outside. "It's this way," I said, taking the tunnel ahead of me to the right.

"Man. I get all turned around down here. I'm glad you know where you're going."

"James Bond always knows where he's going."

As we proceeded, the salty smell increased, confirming I was correct. The tunnel curved slightly to the left and took a sharp left turn around a large boulder. Before we made it all the way around the boulder, a golden cloud appeared in front of us. It materialized into a beautiful, shimmering woman.

"Oh, crap," Anna said. "Not this again."

The figure held a finger to her lips, then blew out our candles. As quickly as she had appeared, she was gone, leaving us in total darkness.

Anna stomped her foot in the dirt. "What the h—"

I put my candle in my teeth and covered her mouth. She immediately fell silent. I peeked around the boulder. From farther down the tunnel the round beam of a flashlight swung to and fro. Someone was coming our way. I crammed the candle in my pocket and pulled Anna back in the direction from which we had come. After wedging into a crag in the wall that I had noticed behind the boulder, I pulled her in tight against me.

There was no sound other than our breathing and no light for what seemed like forever. Just as I decided the person had gone back the other way, the light arced across the stone on the other side of the tunnel. The person was close, probably just on the other side of the boulder. I felt Anna take a big breath and hold it. I did the same.

With a slight crunching underfoot, the person passed us, light trained on the ground. The shape was unmistakable.

Anna let her breath out soundlessly once Miss Ronan had passed around the curve out of view. I nudged Anna, and she stepped from the crag. I pulled her with me around the large boulder and leaned against it until my heart stopped pounding. I removed the candle and the lighter from my pocket and lit it. "We only need one," I whispered.

Almost running, we proceeded through the tunnel until a light appeared ahead of us. Moonlight. I blew out my candle and enjoyed the cool wind on my face. My relief ended abruptly when we stepped outside.

"Oh, my God," Anna said, staring at the whirling golden clouds over our heads.

"You should tone it down a bit so the Na Fir Ghorm d-don't see you," Muireann said from our right. She wore my shirt and was shivering.

"Tone what down?" I asked.

"Oh, hi, Liam, and Liam's female." She gave us an awkward, closed-fingered wave. "I wasn't t-talking to you. I was talking to the B-Bean Sidhes."

The clouds reduced in size to small puffs the size of my out-stretched hand.

"I was afraid you weren't c-c-coming. Then I *was* afraid you w-were coming. Brigid Ronan was wandering around out here and it c-could have been bad." Her body shuddered. "How do you stand b-b-being c-cold all the time?"

"We're not cold. You're cold because you're wearing a wet shirt," I said.

"Oh." She ripped the shirt off over her head. "Now I'm not."

I cast my eyes down and Anna gasped.

"I'm still c-c-c-cold. You were wr-r-r-ong."

I slipped off the jacket and passed it to Anna.

"Here, put this on," Anna said quietly. When I looked up, she had buttoned the jacket, which hung halfway down Muireann's thighs, and was rolling up the sleeves for the trembling Selkie.

"When I sh-sh-shed my pelt the first time, I g-g-got really cold and Francine had Liam lie s-skin to skin with me. It worked very well."

Anna finished the second sleeve and smiled over her shoulder at me. "I bet it did."

The cliff rose straight up from the beach in a sheer wall of stone. The tunnel was clearly man-made, judging from the perfectly round opening, as opposed to some others in various places around the island that had been carved over time by the tide. The small beach was cut off from the rest of the shoreline by dense vegetation butting up to the enormous boulders on either end of it. The only way to reach it would be by boat or through the tunnel.

"I feel much better now." Muireann reached out and touched Anna's dress. "Pretty," she said.

The Bean Sidhes began making noise that sounded more like a chant than a scream, though it was still uncomfortable.

"Okay," Muireann said. "I've never seen a human handfasting ceremony or an Otherworld bonding, so they are going to tell me what to do."

"You can understand them?" Anna asked, sliding her candle into the pocket of the coat Muireann wore.

"Yes. They speak an ancient language known only to the Otherworld." She shoved her hands into the pockets of the jacket and stared up at the chanting puffs of gold. "They want to be sure you understand what you are about to do."

"Only in general principle," I said. "Handfasting vows are terminable and sometimes used on a trial basis among my people. How does this differ?"

Anna slipped her hand into mine.

The chanting increased in volume, as if they were speaking in unison. Muireann nodded.

"Well, it's pretty much the same, except it's deeper. Instead of it just being a promise made with words, it's a comingling of your spirits. See, even if you split up in human terms, your souls are mixed together, so the bond will carry over into the Otherworld." She paused and listened again. "They want me to give you a way to understand it that will make sense."

The chanting continued and Muireann appeared agitated. "Okay, I'll tell them, but we need to get this done before we are discovered." She gestured to the golden forms swirling overhead. "They say your soul is like water. Formless. It conforms to whatever shape it is in. So imagine you have two cups and a pitcher. The cups are full of water. You pour them both into the pitcher and then pour from the pitcher back into the cups. The water from each cup, once unique, has been mixed. It is impossible to sort it back out again. That is what will happen with your souls. You will be part of each other until the end of the term."

She stared up at the Bean Sidhes. "Okay, okay. They also want you to know that since you are *anam cara,* you have already experienced what it will feel like to some degree." She stomped her foot. "Enough already. They get it." She stared from me to Anna. "So are you good with this? A bonding of the minimum month and a day will be sufficient."

Anna squeezed my hand and smiled when our eyes met. The fact that she would even consider such a proposition nearly drove me to my knees. "I'm in," she said.

Unable to form words, I simply nodded.

Muireann grinned. "Great." She tipped her face up to the golden wisps. "Now what?" She covered her mouth. "Oops. I forgot." She turned in a circle, searching the beach for something. "I was supposed to tell you to bring a cord. Something to bind your hands with." She huffed. "I guess the pretty window and the lamp distracted me."

Anna slipped the tie off from around my neck. "How about this?"

Muireann grinned and clapped. "Oooh. Perfect!" She snatched it from Anna and held it up in the air. "Now what?" She nodded. "Okay. Now this is the part where you face each other and clasp right hand to right hand and left to left, crossed over . . . yes. Just like that." She skipped around us like an excited child. The Bean Sidhes chanted louder and took the forms of women. Muireann put her fingers in her ears. "Oh, this is great. I can't do this in my seal form," she yelled. "Here's the good part. We are going to keep it really simple and short." She put the ends of the tie together and put it folded in half over our hands. "Now, you humans do this differently. You do a lot of stuff for show. All I need is for you to tell me why you are here. You first, Liam."

I stared at the bloodred tie draped over our clasped hands. "I am here to be bonded to Annabel Leighton."

Muireann drew one end of the tie through the loop hanging across the other side and stared at Anna. "And?"

"I'm here to be bonded to Liam MacGregor." Anna too was staring at our hands.

Muireann pulled the other end of the tie through the loop and pulled down on both ends, tightening it. "Why?"

I had expected to repeat phrases and answer yes-and-no questions like in the handfasting ceremonies I'd attended in the village. The why of this was far too complex to put into words.

"Liam. This is the part where you state why you want to bonded to her body and soul. It's a requirement," Muireann said, stomping her foot. "You can't just stand there."

Anna's smiling flawless face in the moonlight gave me words. "I want to be bonded to her because I love her. I've always loved her and I always will. And the very fact that she would stand here and agree to be bonded to me makes me the happiest person on earth."

Anna lowered her eyes to our hands while Muireann tied a knot in the ends of the tie under the loop, then ran the ends up and over the loop again. Muireann grinned and bounced up and down, then looked expectantly at Anna.

When she raised her eyes, my heart stopped. She took a shuddering breath, never taking her eyes from mine, addressing me directly. "I want this because when we're apart, I can't breathe. You're like oxygen. You love me for who I am and you let me be who I am, which no one has ever done before. I can't imagine life without you. I don't want a life without you. And I will do everything in my power to never be without you again."

Time stopped. Nothing could surpass this moment. Pure exquisite emotion flowed through her hands to my heart.

"How long a term?" Muireann whispered. "You have to specify a length of bonding."

I was too overcome to answer. I couldn't even draw breath.

"Forever," Anna said, still staring into my eyes. "Forever, Liam."

I shook my head. She didn't understand. This was real. Irrevocable. "You only need to do this for a month and a day."

Her hand trembled in mine. "What don't you understand, Liam? Look around. We're on a beach with a Selkie and floating golden magical screeching things. This isn't business as usual. This is meant to happen. Fated. I want you forever. If you don't want me, tell me now. Don't screw around with me. Don't keep anticipating my needs or predicting my future regrets. I know what I need and want. What do *you* want?"

"Oh! Oh, I really like her," Muireann said. "No wonder you told me you could love no one else."

The Bean Sidhes had fallen silent, leaving only the lapping of the sea and my breathing to accompany my racing mind and heart. Surely this was a dream. A marvelous dream from which I would wake at any moment because it was too perfect to be real.

"What is it going to be, Liam?" Muireann asked.

I stared at the girl I had loved all my life, her pale skin and raven hair reflecting the moon, far more beautiful than a dream could be. There was no other sane response. "Forever," I whispered.

Muireann squeaked in delight and tied the loose ends together again. "Okay, this is the part where you pledge yourselves to each other for the amount of time you have agreed upon."

The Bean Sidhes chanted and Muireann translated. "So as this knot is tied, your souls will be likewise bound upon your declaration to make it so." She nodded to me.

I stared into Anna's blue eyes. "I wish to be bound to you forever. In this life and whatever comes after."

"Yes, forever. Eternity," Anna said, and at the moment the words were uttered, a gale-force wind swept around us, lifting sand and smaller particles with it to where we were forced to close our eyes. Anna buried her face in my chest, our bound hands clenched tightly. It felt as though the ground beneath us had shifted or fallen away completely and we were falling end over end. The Bean Sidhes' cries sounded distant and the temperature dropped to where our teeth chattered. Just when I thought I could no longer bear it, the earth around us became solid again and a complete wash of warmth filled my body. I opened my eyes. We were on our knees, hands still bound.

"Wow," Anna said. "That was trippy."

Neither Muireann nor the Bean Sidhes were anywhere in sight. The jacket was laid over a rock and the sopping T-shirt was still in a heap on the beach where it had been discarded.

"So, what do we do about this?" Anna lifted our bound hands.

"We try to extricate ourselves without breaking the knots." Which would be difficult with my useless hand.

She made her snort-through-her-nose sound. "Supernatural Celtic creepies' version of a Chinese finger trap, huh?" She looped her finger through the section around my right wrist and pulled some slack. "Can you pull your hand out?"

It worked, and with the removal of that hand, the rest became looser and slipped off easily.

"Okay," she said in a voice imitative of Muireann's, "this is the part where we sneak back into the house and we celebrate all night long, right?"

I answered by passing her the candle from the jacket I had just slipped on.

The way back up the tunnel seemed half as long as it had

been on our way out. We could hear banging and Miss Ronan shouting before we even entered her room. "Miss Leighton. I have strict orders from your parents that Mr. MacGregor is not to be in this house after nightfall. Stop ignoring me and open this door."

I shoved the dresser back in place in front of the hidden panel, leaned against it, and pulled Anna to me.

"He must leave!"

Anna's body molded to mine. A perfect fit in all ways. I captured her mouth in a kiss.

"Open the door! I'll call your parents. They won't like this."

Whatever had occurred during the bonding had left me single-minded. I wanted Anna—I needed her. And I certainly wasn't going to let Brigid Ronan get in the way. Anna groaned as I pulled away. "Hold that thought," I said.

When I opened the door, Miss Ronan gasped. "You are wearing his clothes again." Her eyes narrowed. "How dare you! Leave this minute."

I kept my voice low and level, leaning down to meet her eyes directly. "I understand and appreciate your position, but let me make mine perfectly clear. I'm not leaving tonight. If you feel compelled to report this to Anna's parents, by all means, do so. If your intention is to bodily eject me yourself, attempt it now. Otherwise, I want you to go away and not bother us again. Have I made my position clear to you?"

Her face flushed red. "You have no idea what you are doing. What kind of danger you are in. Both of you."

I stood up straight, fighting the urge to shout, keeping my voice barely above a whisper. "Every day I live is an unexpected gift. I've been in danger from the moment I was born. You've made sure of that. Go now, and leave us be."

Her mouth opened as if she were going to protest, but she clamped it shut, spun around, and stomped down the stairs.

I locked the door, feeling unstoppable. Brigid Ronan had backed completely down and I faced a night alone with the most perfect human being on the planet. Even if the Cailleach took me this very night, I had succeeded in taking control of my life and getting what I wanted. And at that moment, more than anything in the world, I wanted Anna Leighton.

Anna grinned. "Wow, Liam. Well done."

I ran my lips along her neck and she wrapped her arms around me. "I do other things well too."

She took my face in her hands. "Wait a minute. Is this the same guy who told me he was terrified?"

"No. That was someone entirely different," I said. "Now that I have your love, I've nothing to fear. Not in this world, or the one that comes after." I switched off the light and the moonlight that streamed through the stained glass danced across her skin in a dreamlike kaleidoscope. "With you, I'm completely within my comfort zone."

35

"Villains!" I shrieked, "dissemble no more!"
—Edgar Allan Poe,
from "The Tell-Tale Heart," 1843

Muireann was thrilled. She had finally done something to help her Liam. Something that would keep him safe from the Na Fir Ghorm. What good would it do to split them apart if their souls were bound forever?

Forever! She twirled around and took another breath before diving under. Liam's female was strong and wonderful and worthy of him. Surely now, the Na Fir Ghorm would drop the wager. The Bean Sidhes said they didn't even care about winning; they just didn't want the Na Fir Ghorm to hurt the humans.

Muireann swam to the entrance of the cave and let air out through her mouth. She wished she could breathe and speak underwater like the Na Fir Ghorm. In the darkness, she couldn't see the column of bubbles rising to the surface, but she could hear it. She hoped the creatures inside the cave could hear it too because there was no way she was going to swim inside.

It worked. One of them came to the entrance. "The Selkie has hailed us," he called into the cave.

Releasing all of her breath while that deep made her a little light-headed, but she didn't have time to waste. Empty lungs stinging, she shot to the surface and sucked in the sweet air.

She needed to get to the island so that she was not out in open water when they emerged from their cave. Even though the Otherworld laws forbade them to kill her, the Na Fir Ghorm had never been ones to adhere to rules. Hopefully, they would listen to logic.

The Bean Sidhes hovered above the rocky ledge, waiting. Muireann propelled out of the water, landing on her belly with an *oof.* She shuffled and wiggled away from the water. Legs would have been helpful at this moment, she thought as she turned to face her enemy. "They are coming," she said to the nebulous golden forms overhead.

Their only acknowledgment was an increase in brightness.

The moon had reached its high point and the air was almost still. Muireann scanned the water. They should have emerged by now.

Then, one at a time, heads popped through the water's surface, only feet away from the ledge. "Why have you interrupted us?" the leader asked. He tipped his face up toward the Bean Sidhes. "Ah, I see your allies are not hiding and spying this time."

Muireann took a deep breath, gathering her courage. "I've gathered you here to make one final plea for resolution. The Bean Sidhes are willing to let the wager go, dropping it entirely, in an effort to spare the humans any more hardship."

"You must know something we don't. You must be aware the humans are too weak to prevail, so you are trying to help your friends out by mediating and begging a truce." He put his clawed, webbed hands on the ledge and pulled slightly out of the water. "We will not back down."

"Why? They have proven themselves worthy. They have endured and passed every test. Leave them alone," Muireann pleaded.

The leader lowered himself back into the water, smiling. "You are in love with the human male." He laughed. "It just gets better and better! Now when we break him completely, we will be breaking you as well, you meddlesome, worthless creature."

"They are bonded," one of the Bean Sidhes shrieked.

The Na Fir Ghorm bobbing at the surface exchanged glances. The leader stared up at the Bean Sidhes. His expression transformed from surprise to rage. "How dare you!"

This was why Muireann had asked the Bean Sidhes to let her do the talking. She had hoped to not let the Na Fir Ghorm know about the bonding unless it was absolutely necessary. Since the female had returned and the couple was reunited, she had hoped the Na Fir Ghorm would see the strength of their love and simply allow the wager to be dropped. The bonding was the last resort. The secret weapon.

"They are ineligible," he shouted.

Muireann moved closer to the ledge. "No, with his lineage, they qualified."

"How came they to be bonded? Who witnessed it?" he asked.

One of the Bean Sidhes materialized from a cloud in her female form. "We witnessed it."

He slapped his hand on the surface of the water. "Who officiated? If it was Brigid Ronan, I'll see to it she dies a miserable human death."

Another Bean Sidhe joined in form with the first. "Who officiated is of no matter. What matters is that they are bonded for all time. Whatever happens, they cannot be separated."

"You broke the rules of the wager by interfering in this manner. We claim victory."

"We interfered no more than you did with the fake letter and the Selkie going ashore. You also have not informed us of each test as you initiated it. Since they are bonded, the wager is no longer valid."

The leader grinned and Muireann shuddered. "The test was of human love, not the inclination of the immortal soul. Despite this little setback, their human love can still fail. We intend to make that happen."

"Please let them live in peace," Muireann pleaded.

"With the added pleasure of watching the Selkie suffer along with them."

"What do you intend?" a Bean Sidhe asked.

"Well, they overcame obstacles already in place—differences in lifestyle and interests as well as the disapproval of her family. Then they withstood more difficult tests of distance, jealousy, and infidelity." He shrugged. "We've no choice but to move on to physical trials."

Muireann's heart stopped when she considered the horrible range of possibilities.

"What manner of trial?"

A grin spread across his face. "Sickness. The moment one becomes weakened and a burden rather than a pleasure to the other, the human love will snap as easily as a fishing line."

"No!" Muireann hadn't intended to blurt it out, but the thought of her Liam suffering illness was too much. "Please don't do this."

The leader laughed. "You are soft, Selkie. Your love for this human male is amusing."

She trembled.

"Very well then. We shall spare him."

She almost fainted from relief.

"We'll strike the girl instead."

This was almost worse. Liam would rather be afflicted himself than watch his female suffer.

"Let this go," a Bean Sidhe cried. "This is not a fair wager. Torturing them is not a test of love. It is wrong and outside the rules of the Otherworld."

"Fair? Did you say it's not fair?" he shouted. "There is a human saying that applies: 'All is fair in love and war.'" He turned to look at his clan and then thrust a fist into the air. "This is war!"

36

The wind came out of the cloud by night
Chilling . . . my Annabel Lee.

—Edgar Allan Poe,
from "Annabel Lee," 1849

*T*he sea was eerily placid and the air unseasonably still. The morning sun, as if to make up for this ominous condition, threw golden ribbons across the water, creating brilliant sparkles that reflected off Anna's skin.

She had surprised me with a picnic breakfast on a large flat boulder near the end of the jetty. She lay on her back on the checkered blanket, eyes closed, listening as the waves gently caressed the rocks around us.

I would never tire of looking at her. Lying on my side, I skimmed my fingers down her arm. She smiled. No one had ever been as happy as I was at that moment.

A boat horn sounded to the north. It would certainly be the supply boat we had been expecting for days. I sat up. "I need to go help Francine."

Anna rolled to her side and draped her arm over my lap. "No, you don't."

"Okay, I'll rephrase it. I *should* go help Francine."

She opened her eyes, which were as clear and blue as the sea surrounding us, and my heart stuttered. No love had ever been greater than ours. I was certain of it.

"How will I manage?" she teased, running her hand under my shirt.

I grinned. "With great fortitude and conviction." Which is what it would take to force me to leave her at this moment. The boat horn blew again, announcing its arrival in the harbor. "I'll come back as soon as it's been unloaded and reloaded." I removed her hand from under my shirt and kissed the inside of her wrist. "Hold that thought."

She grumbled and rolled again to her back, frowning.

Reluctantly, I stood. "Do you want me to help you carry things back to the house?"

"No, it's just a basket and a blanket." She opened her eyes. "Unless having you help me would keep you from going to work . . ." She winked.

The thought of leaving her was painful, but actually walking away was worse. I looked back when I made it to the base of the jetty. Lying there in the sun with her hair fanned out on the blanket, she was as beautiful as any angel. The emptiness and sorrow I felt at parting wasn't due to any premonition or sense of dread; it was simply feeling as though I was missing part of myself—a critical part. Perhaps this was the result of the bonding. Maybe it was simply love in its purest form.

Muireann spotted Liam as he entered the harbor. He didn't stay long in Francine's store before he came out to where a boat had moored to the dock. For a while, he helped two men unload boxes and crates from the deck, then reloaded it with items as Francine marked on a piece of paper.

She needed to warn him of the Na Fir Ghorm's plan but didn't really know what to warn against. How did a human become ill? She would shed her pelt and tell him all she knew as soon as the boat left, she decided.

Thunder cracked from the northeast. Strange, she thought, since the weather was sunny and clear.

The men from the boat studied the sky. "Weird," one said. "There are no thunderclouds and no storms predicted."

"Let's load up quick," the other said. "Better get moving in case something churned up unexpectedly."

Muireann was pleased. She wanted them to go away as soon as possible so that she could talk to Liam. She slipped from behind the boat around the bow to get a better look at him. He paused and stared at her. He let the device on wheels he was pushing rest against his waist. "Is that you, Muireann?"

She nodded and he smiled. If only he could understand her in her seal form, this would be so much easier. Despite the fact that she swam in agitated circles, he continued to smile, then resumed pushing the item on wheels to the boat. She had to be sure he didn't go back into the store after the boat left. She didn't want to have to go up on land for fear the Na Fir Ghorm were watching.

After way too much time and many more trips, Francine wrote on a piece of paper the first man handed her and he thanked her. Thunder cracked again, and from the direction of the large dwelling, black clouds hung low in the sky.

The boat pulled away, and as soon as Muireann was certain the men on board wouldn't see her, she moved to the stairs and stripped her pelt below her shoulders. "Liam!" she cried just before he entered the back of the store. "Liam!"

Francine grabbed his shirt. "She's trouble, I tell you."

He removed her hand. "No. She's helping me. Something's wrong."

A crack of thunder split the sky and Liam flinched, then

ran to where Muireann clung to the stairs, only half transformed.

As he kneeled down, the black clouds expanded and blocked the sun, causing it to appear as though it was dusk.

"I'm here to warn you," she said. "You need to protect your female. They intend to cause her harm."

Lightning shot through the sky, making everything stark white before it fell back into dusky darkness.

"Who?" he yelled over the rumbling thunder.

She had nothing to hide any longer. "The Na Fir Ghorm. They made a wager with the Bean Sidhes. You and your mate are the objects of the wager. They'll hurt her, Liam. They'll kill her."

"Dear God." He ran his hand through his hair. "What else do you know?"

The Bean Sidhes' shrieks drowned out the cracks of thunder. "Go now!" one screamed. "This is our fault!" cried another. They swirled around him in a tight circle screaming warnings and laments.

Liam shot to his feet. "What is it, Muireann? What are they saying?"

She could hardly see him through her tears. "They say you must go to her now and they blame themselves. I'm so sorry, Liam."

The tortured look on his face would haunt her, she knew, until her last living breath.

I'd never run so fast in my life. What had been a sunny day transformed into inky night, broken by terrifying flashes of lightning and deafening thunder. As I neared Taibhreamh, stinging sleet showered down, making the path slick with ice and almost impossible to traverse. The air had become so cold, my teeth chattered. This was no ordinary storm. It was Otherworldly.

Near blackness had enveloped our tiny island, and the precipitation reduced my visibility to almost nothing. I prayed that Anna was safely in the mansion, tucked in her warm bed, watching a movie on her iPad. Something deep inside me knew this was remote. Far down in my soul, I felt her distress. I tripped on something in the path, tangling my foot in it. I reached down and grabbed the ice-coated picnic blanket that must have blown up here in the gale-force wind. *Anna*.

"Where is she?" I shouted at no one. "Help me!" I screamed to the darkness.

The trail to the jetty was off to the left, but in the darkness and punishing sleet, I couldn't see it. I crawled on my knees, feeling for it with numb, cold fingers.

Lightning crackled in webs through the sky, and the jetty became visible. All around it, a dozen or so creatures that appeared to be human-like twirled in the waves with their arms raised to the sky. Anna was nowhere in sight. "Anna!" I screamed. It had to be the Na Fir Ghorm. Only this time, it appeared they had claimed her. "No!" Again, lightning flashed, illuminating the jetty. I saw her just a few yards out from the base on the beach at the water's edge. "Anna!"

Slipping and sliding more than anything else, I descended the trail, clothes and skin shredding on the rocks and vegetation.

In darkness, I stumbled to the base of the jetty and headed to where I had seen her. My feet stung as if perforated by needles and my breath came in shuddering gasps through chattering teeth.

"Anna!" I screamed, helpless in the darkness to locate her. I found the water's edge, not by sight or feel because my feet were too numb with cold, but by sound. I heard my boots splashing.

I knew she was somewhere just ahead of me. Not wanting to kick her accidentally, I crawled on my knees, hand outstretched in front of me. There. As cold as the water, I found her, stiff and rigid as a corpse. "Demons!" I shouted. "Devils!" They had conjured this storm.

I pulled her into my lap and felt her neck. A flutter of a pulse flickered below my numb fingers. Perhaps it was my own pulse instead. "No!" I screamed.

As quickly as they had come, the clouds dissipated. I squinted as the sun streaked through holes in their dissolving forms. Melting ice covered the beach. In my arms, Anna appeared like a painting in which the colors were all wrong. Her lips had a sickly bluish hue that I'd never seen in nature. Ice clung to her tangled hair. "No," I sobbed, still rocking her body against mine. "Why didn't you take me?" I screamed. "Why not me?"

Miss Ronan got to me first but said nothing. Francine had plenty to say even before she had reached the base of the jetty. Things I'd never heard come from her lips before.

"We've got to get her warmed up," Francine said when she reached me. "Lad, turn her loose."

I folded in tighter around Anna, racked with shudders.

"Liam, listen to me," Francine said, pulling on my good arm, looped around Anna's chest. "You must let us take her or she'll die."

"No." I couldn't let her go.

"You're not thinking straight, Liam. Let us help her."

Somewhere far away, my reason called to me and drew me back. I released my hold on Anna and she was immediately pulled away. Francine patted her back hard.

"She's near death. Her breathing is too shallow to issue water from the lungs," Miss Ronan said.

"Take her legs," Francine ordered Miss Ronan. "Can you walk, lad?"

"Yes," I answered, stiffly getting to my feet.

"Of course he can," Miss Ronan barked, following Francine up the beach with Anna stretched between them. "He was only cold a short while."

Deirdre met us at the door. "I've already heated the water bottles and collected the blankets like you told me to do, Miss Ronan," she said as the women hauled Anna into the kitchen.

"Put a blanket on the floor, Deirdre," Miss Ronan said, lowering Anna's feet. "Then get me a knife from the wall. A small one." She nodded to Francine. "Lay her down. We need to get her off her back as soon as possible in case she got water in her lungs."

A knife in Miss Ronan's hands was terrifying. "What are you going to do?" I asked.

She stared up at me with a look so full of malice I shuddered. "Shut up."

"Liam, lad. Go strip out of your wet clothes and wrap in one of those blankets," Francine said, gently cradling Anna's head as she lowered it to the floor.

I did so as quickly as possible, then sank to my knees at Anna's side. Miss Ronan took the knife from Deirdre and held it up to me, as if taunting. Then she ripped it through the front of Anna's shirt and down both legs of her jeans.

"Bring a blanket," Miss Ronan ordered Deirdre. She rolled Anna onto it on her side. "You too," she commanded, eyes boring into mine.

"Me too what?"

"He isn't warm enough to help her. You should use the girl," Francine said.

Ronan glared at her. "How stupid are you? With his blood, he is already fully restored. We need him. His touch and voice will encourage her to fight." She returned her attention to me. "Do as I say. Get next to her now."

She ripped the blanket from me and I lay next to Anna just as I had done with Muireann. Only unlike Muireann, Anna was cold as ice all over. Francine put a blanket over us, casting aside the wet one in which I'd been wrapped.

"Bring me the water bottles," Miss Ronan ordered. Deirdre scampered to the sink to retrieve them.

Francine brushed hair from Anna's face. "Poor little thing. You hang in there, now."

Miss Ronan pressed a flat rubber bladder filled with warm water against Anna's chest and I held it in place. She put another between her upper thighs.

"Here, hand me one and I'll put it on her feet," Francine said to Deirdre.

"You'll do no such thing," Miss Ronan ordered. "She's too far gone. You'll kill her. It will cause her heart to stop." She stood and shook her head. "She'll likely die anyway."

A sob escaped me.

"Go ahead and cry," she said. "This is all your fault."

"I'll not be lettin' you brutalize the boy, Brigid," Francine said, her accent thick.

"He's just like his mother. I warned him. I practically begged him to leave, but he refused. Now this." Miss Ronan crossed her arms over her chest. "It should have been him."

"Yes." My voice broke. "It should've been me. If only it had been." Unlike Muireann, Anna didn't tremble or shiver. "Are you sure she's alive?"

Miss Ronan placed her hand over Anna's neck. "Yes, but barely." She squatted down close to our heads. "You need to say whatever you can to encourage her to hang on to life. You're the only thing that will bring her back at this point. Isn't that ironic since it's your fault she's near death to begin with?" She stood and joined Francine and Deirdre on the other side of the kitchen.

Anna's leg twitched and my heart leapt. "I'm here," I whispered in her ear. "I'll always be here." The leg twitched again. I continued to whisper to her for a very long time until Miss Ronan changed out the bottles for warmer ones.

"Her color is better," Francine said. "Pale, but the lips are no longer blue."

A tremor racked Anna's body, then another. Panic caused my heart to race.

"Ah, there we go. She has enough circulation to contract the muscles. She'll warm up soon," Ronan said.

Then it sounded like Anna choked. Ronan dragged her from me and patted her back. It was more like she beat her back, but within a short time, Anna coughed up liquid, then vomited. Francine blocked my view, so it was hard to tell exactly what was happening. I sat up.

"Yes," Miss Ronan said. "That's it, Anna. Get that seawater out." A look of joy crossed her features. "She's going to live."

Anna coughed, gasped for air, then coughed again, and Francine held a towel under her mouth. "Poor darlin'," she cooed. "You are doing great. Just great."

Shuddering, eyes still shut, Anna moaned. It looked like her lips formed my name, but no word was uttered. "I'm here," I said. "Forever."

It wasn't until the next morning the fever started.

*We tremble with the violence of the conflict
within us,—of the definite with the indefinite—
of the substance with the shadow.*

—Edgar Allan Poe,
from "The Imp of the Perverse," 1845

ny news?" Keela asked, pulling herself up on the jetty to join Muireann.

"No. Nothing."

Keela put her chin on her sister's back. "They will be fine."

"I'm not so sure. This is the second day Liam and his female have not come out," Muireann said. "The one called Francine left this morning in a hurry. She went to her store but hasn't come back yet."

Keela scooted farther up on the jetty. "Why don't you swim to the harbor, shed your pelt, and ask her what is happening? You have spoken with her before, right?"

She shook her head. "I've spoken with her, but she would not be friendly. She blames me for this."

Rolling to her side, Keela sighed. "You are partially to blame, are you not?"

Muireann slid into the water without answering, heart heavy with guilt.

"The doctor should be here anytime now," Francine said, putting a cool rag on Anna's forehead. "Her parents answered when I called first thing this morning and said they were unable to come because of some business something or other with their family lawyer, but they would send the doctor immediately and would come as soon as possible if he thought they should."

Anna shivered, not from cold, but from the raging fever that had consumed her body.

"She's been like this for over twenty-four hours," I said, retreating to the bathroom to pull on my jeans Francine had brought back from the shop. "This is bad."

Francine opened Anna's suitcase and rummaged around. "Yes, it is. But doctors from the mainland have miracle cures. You keep heart. She'll be fine." She pulled out a silky nightgown. "Here we go. It's the most modest one she has. They certainly dress differently in her society." She smiled at me.

I tried to smile back but failed.

"We need to shower her off. The cool water will help. Do you think she'd mind if you helped me?"

I pulled the shirt on over my head. "Of course not. We're bonded."

She gasped. "Truly?"

Now I really did smile. "Truly. Muireann performed a handfasting ceremony night before last."

Her grin grew even wider. "An Otherworld bonding!"

I nodded.

"Oh, lad. Why didn't you tell me when you came to unload the boat?" She folded the gown over her arm.

"I had planned to, but the storm came up."

"Liam," Anna muttered. Her eyes fluttered open. "Lawyer."

I looked at Francine, who shrugged.

She closed her eyes again. "Need papers. For the girls. Promise."

I had no idea what she wanted of me. "I promise."

"She's delirious," Francine said. "We need to cool her off. Help me get her to the shower."

It wasn't long after we had showered Anna and changed the sheets we heard the helicopter.

The doctor was a gray-haired man wearing a bright blue short-sleeved shirt and tan pants. He came to Anna's room immediately while the helicopter pilot waited in the kitchen.

He placed a large black bag on the bed next to Anna and put his hand on her forehead. "How are you, Annie?"

She moaned and shook her head.

He tugged the top to his bag open. "So you're Liam."

I nodded.

"I'm Dr. Jackson. Her parents told me about you. So did she." His gray eyes met mine briefly as he pulled items out of the bag. "I've known her since she was a baby. You must have made quite an impression on her if she left home to come back here."

I didn't answer for fear of saying the wrong thing. He put a stethoscope in his ears and placed it to Anna's chest. Even though I'd never seen medical instruments, I'd read enough newspapers and magazines to recognize it. He scowled and rolled her to her side. "Breathe deep for me, Annie," he said. She coughed. He moved the end around on her back while he listened.

"The woman who called the Leightons said she had fallen in the water and had become severely chilled."

"Yes."

He shook his head. "Breathed in some water, maybe?"

I nodded.

"Did she vomit?"

"Yes."

"Might have inhaled some of that too." He put the stethoscope back in the bag and pulled out several white plastic packages of different sizes. "I'm going to give her some fluids and antibiotics. It looks like she has aspiration pneumonia. You were smart to contact me. We got it early and she'll be fine."

I let out the breath I'd been holding.

"Can you hold her arm for me?" he asked, pulling the wrapping off what looked like a small, clear version of the water bottle I held against her to warm her up.

I walked around the bed near the arm he indicated.

After tying what looked like a large rubber band on her upper arm, he unwrapped a piece of plastic with a needle sticking out of it and turned her arm over wrist up. Anna groaned. "You'll be better soon, Annie," he said. "Hold here and here," he said, indicating her wrist and behind her elbow.

I held her wrist. He looked up at me, taking notice of my left arm hanging limp at my side. "That should be fine." He wiped the inside of her elbow with a piece of cotton and stuck the needle straight into a blood vessel visible through the surface of her smooth pale skin. I winced. He looked up at me again after he taped the needle with the plastic bit on the end to her arm. "Have you never seen this done before?"

"No. We don't have a doctor on Dòchas."

"I figured as much. It explains your arm."

All my life I thought a demon failing to put my skin on correctly was the reason for my useless arm. Since Anna, I knew no such demon existed. "What caused this?"

He hooked the bag of liquid to her headboard and ran a tube to her arm, fitting it into the end of the plastic. "Were you born with it?"

"Yes."

He turned a round wheel in a blue plastic housing partway

down the tube. Drops of the liquid fell into a clear cylinder far-ther up the tubing. "Was the birth traumatic? Is it possible your collarbone was broken during the delivery?"

The birth had certainly been traumatic—especially for my mother. A broken collarbone was possible. "Yes."

He watched the drips in the cylinder for a moment, then stood and touched my neck and shoulder. He lifted the bad arm and ran his hand over my shoulder to my neck again. "I'm pretty sure this is Erb's palsy. You're lucky. Most people who have it suffer at least partial paralysis on an entire side of their body. I've never seen an arm in isolation before."

"What exactly is it?"

He closed his bag. "When you were born, you suffered an injury. If you had been born in a hospital, a surgeon would have performed a procedure and restored use of your arm. Since you were born here, without medical intervention, paralysis occurred."

I had already reached the conclusion a demon was not the cause of my disability, but hearing it from someone who was an authority brought me considerable relief. I was not and had never been a demon.

"I'll need to keep an eye on Annie for a day or so. Who do I see about that?" He put his black bag on the seat under the stained-glass window next to the stack of books saved from my shed.

"Miss Ronan is in charge of the house," I said. "Shall I get her for you?"

He shook his head. "No, you stay here with our girl. She should be feeling much better soon and would probably like it if you were here." He studied me a bit longer. "I sat with her at dinner at the wedding reception. She spoke of nothing but you. She's changed. I attribute that to your friendship." He nodded and closed the door behind him.

"Liam," Anna said. "Stay."

"I'm here," I said, lying beside her.

"Forever," she whispered.

Muireann hadn't seen a single Na Fir Ghorm since the storm. As night fell, she repositioned herself off the beach where the couple had become bound so she could watch the house and the cave.

Not long after darkness fell, her location proved to be the right choice. Brigid Ronan, flashlight in hand, hurried to the end of the boulder where she had met with the Na Fir Ghorm before. This time, Muireann was determined to listen. The Na Fir Ghorm usually swam as deep as possible, only coming to the surface when they had to. Swimming a wide circle, she zipped just under the surface, coming up on the back side of the boulder.

Brigid Ronan paced from one end of the flat outcropping of stone to the other, flashlight swinging loosely by her side. Her usual calmness was gone. Muireann had never seen her like this.

"News?" a Na Fir Ghorm demanded immediately upon breaking the surface. Muireann scooted farther to the far side so he would not see her.

"None," Brigid Ronan answered, switching her flashlight off. "They have only grown closer. I beseech you to abandon this. The Bean Sidhes will not hold you to the wager. They will willingly let go."

"Never. We will move to the next step."

Muireann's breath caught when Brigid Ronan began to weep. "No. I beg of you, no."

"You owe us a debt. We made a bargain. You agreed to do our bidding."

"I don't want it—any of it if it means her life. Take the boy's," she begged. "He's the one you want."

Muireann couldn't see the Na Fir Ghorm from where she hid, she only had a view of Brigid Ronan, but she could hear the smile in his voice. "What better way to destroy him than by destroying her?"

Brigid Ronan fell to her knees. Long after the Na Fir Ghorm departed, she continued to weep.

38

Her high-born kinsmen came
And bore her away from me.

— Edgar Allan Poe,
from "Annabel Lee," 1849

*Y*ou're fever free, Annie. How are you feeling?" Dr.
Jackson asked, pulling the stethoscope from his bag.

Anna coughed. "Better." Then she coughed again.

He placed the stethoscope on her back. "Take a
deep breath for me."

After a slow inhale, she coughed.

"You're going to be doing that for a few days—maybe
weeks," he said, taking the stethoscope from his ears. "You'll be
fine, though. You're fully hydrated, so I'm going to disconnect
the IV, okay?"

She nodded and took the handkerchief Deirdre offered her.

He pulled the tube out of the cylinder on her arm and threw
the almost-empty bag and tubing into the trash can.

Feeling utterly useless and helpless, I paced back and forth
at the end of the bed while he pulled the needle from her arm
and dropped it in a container in his bag. He taped gauze over
the place he had inserted the needle.

"All done," he said. "Do you have any questions or need anything else? I've left instructions with your housekeeper along
with some cough medicine should you need it."

Anna sat up. "Yes. I need something. It's really important." She held the handkerchief over her mouth and coughed. "Deirdre, in my purse on top of my luggage, there is an envelope. Please get it for me. I also need Miss Ronan."

"I'm here." Miss Ronan stepped in the room. She must have been lurking right outside the door.

Anna shifter higher in the bed. "I need Polly and Edmond Byrne right away. Could you get them?"

Miss Ronan's expression remained the same with the exception of a slight lifting of the eyebrows. "They are already on the grounds working in the gardens. Would it be acceptable for me to send Mr. MacFarley to fetch them?"

Anna nodded. "Yeah, that's fine. Ironically appropriate, actually."

Miss Ronan left as Deirdre handed Anna a large envelope.

"Dr. Jackson, I need you to witness something." She opened the envelope on her lap and pulled out a document consisting of several pages. "Deirdre, will you please go find our pilot, Mr. Jennings, and tell him we need him to notarize a document?"

"No-tar-ize," Deirdre sounded out. "Yes, miss." She scurried out the door.

"I'll leave you to your business," I said, feeling totally out of place.

She smiled. "You can stay if you want to. It's about Deirdre and Megan. When I was home, I set up a trust fund for Deirdre. I also talked to Suzette's parents and they agreed to take Deirdre in. I'm sure they'll take Megan too. The girls will never have to worry again. They'll be in a loving home and will go to the best schools."

Polly and Edmond entered the room. Both were out of breath and red-faced.

"I hear the library calling," I said, slipping out the door. Brigid Ronan, rigid as stone, stared at me from the bottom of the staircase.

"Thank you for helping Anna," I said. "The doctor says she's going to be okay."

She neither moved nor spoke. Something about her demeanor sent tremors through me. I forced myself to remain controlled as I descended the stairs and made my way to the library.

Once inside, I took several deep breaths to calm myself. I flipped on the light and sat on a tapestry chair nearest the window. With sunlight streaming in, it would be the perfect place to read a book. I wondered if my mother had sat in that very chair reading. I pictured the portrait of her with her haunted expression and the spotted fur wrap draped over her shoulders. My breath caught. She wore the spotted fur of a harbor seal.

I closed my eyes and recalled her tortured face and her enormous brown eyes . . . like Muireann's . . . like Miss Ronan's. A wave of nausea passed through me. Like *mine*.

It made sense now. My mother had appeared out of nowhere. No one knew her. Well, *someone* had known her. Someone else I resembled.

Gooseflesh traveled up my arm, and the hair on the back of my neck prickled. I didn't have to turn around to know Miss Ronan was in the room. "My mother was a Selkie," I whispered.

She said nothing, but the rustling of her skirts let me know she was moving around the far side of the room. I turned to find her studying me.

"And my father was Francis Michael Richards."

She stopped short. She had been in this house for twenty-five years, seven of them spent alone with Anna's uncle before my mother arrived. Another piece of the horrible puzzle slipped into place.

"And he was your lover too, which is why you hate me."

For the longest time, she stood stone still with the exception of the heaving of her chest with each desperate breath. She lifted her chin, her voice low and level. "I hate you for many more reasons than that."

I sat still long after she left the room, allowing this new information to mesh with the old, raising more questions than it answered.

Dr. Jackson stepped into the room. "I'm heading out now. Annie will be feeling much better soon, but make her rest." He extended his hand and I stood. "It was good to meet you, Liam."

I shook his hand. "Likewise. Thank you."

He smiled. "She tells me you'll be coming back to the city with her. She's very excited about it."

"Me too."

The helicopter motor roared to life outside. "Take care of her," he said, patting me on the shoulder. "See you in New York."

Through the library window, I watched as the pilot helped Deirdre and Megan into the helicopter. Once Dr. Jackson was inside, they lifted off. The girls had made it. They were safe on their way to a new life free from the dangers and oppression of Dòchas.

Like I would be soon, leaving my miserable past behind forever.

I had an irresistible urge to run to Anna's room and tell her what I had found out, but I decided that it would be prudent to wait until she felt better.

Maybe she'd like it if I read to her. I pulled the volume of Tennyson poetry from the shelf that matched the one from my shed. I flipped open to the table of contents. Pressed neatly in the pages was a sheet of paper. I unfolded it and read it several times. It made no sense. Maybe someone had made notes while reading.

I read it out loud. "'It is where my spirit found escape.'" I shrugged and placed it on the desk.

Anna smiled when I entered her room. "They're gone," she said. "I did it! I really did it."

I climbed onto the bed next to her. "Indeed you did. They'll be grateful the rest of their lives." I brushed her hair from her forehead. "How are you?"

"I'm great."

I flipped open the book. "Yes, you are."

Muireann felt completely helpless. She had seen the flying machine arrive yesterday and the two men get out. Then they left this morning with the two young villagers. She had not seen Liam or Anna since the Na Fir Ghorm created the storm, and Brigid Ronan had not returned to the beach since her last meeting with them.

She considered shedding her pelt and sneaking back inside the dwelling but was afraid she would do something wrong or get caught by Brigid Ronan.

So, she waited. And waited. And waited.

Just before sundown, the machine returned, bringing with it a finely dressed woman and man.

I didn't hear the helicopter arrive, so I was completely taken by surprise when Anna's mother turned on the light. I'd fallen asleep on top of the covers with the book on my chest, Anna's head on my shoulder. I'd seen lots of pictures of the wealthy heiress in the tabloids. She always looked perfect, just as she did now with her blond hair and green dress.

"I told you he was not to be here after dark," she said to Miss Ronan as if I were not in the room.

"He was not amenable to that request," Miss Ronan replied.

Anna's mother approached the bed. "Imagine that."

I tried to sit up without disrupting Anna. She startled awake and sat bolt upright. "Mom," she gasped before breaking down into a coughing fit.

Her father entered the room and stood next to her mother, arms over his chest as he stared into my eyes in some sort of challenge.

"Hey, Dad," Anna said, handkerchief still to mouth.

"We need to talk to you in private," her mother said.

I shifted to get out of bed and Anna grabbed my arm. "Anything you want to say to me, you can say in front of Liam."

Anna released me and I stood, extending my hand to her father. "I'm Liam MacGregor."

He looked at my hand but made no move to shake it. "I know who you are," he said.

I lowered my hand. "Maybe I should go."

"Good idea," her father replied.

Anna threw the covers off. "Liam, wait. Just wait downstairs, okay? I don't want you to go." Again, she degenerated into uncontrollable coughing.

I nodded and left, closing the door behind me. A lump formed in my throat. All my life, I'd battled discrimination. This was no different, just more personal somehow. I slumped down onto the top step. This would be my lot no matter where I lived.

At first their voices were low but still discernible through the closed door.

Anna's mother spoke first. "We met with the lawyer this morning to go over some company business and he told us you had been there when you were home. He said you have asked him to find an agent for that village boy's art."

"His name is Liam," Anna replied, "and yes, I did. He's extremely talented."

Her mother cleared her throat. "He also said that you had gotten the trust paperwork in order and that you changed your will."

Anna replied, but I couldn't make out her response.

"You changed your will so that your money will be completely thrown away," her father said.

"You have no idea what I did," Anna responded before coughing. "The lawyer's not allowed to tell you anything about it."

"You are giving it to that boy, aren't you?" her mother almost shouted.

My stomach dropped. Surely she hadn't done such a thing. I gritted my teeth and closed my eyes, fighting the urge to throw up.

"Is that why you're here?" Anna's voice was shrill. "I almost died and you're here because of that?"

"You would leave hard-earned Leighton money to *him*? Honestly, Anna, have you lost your senses?"

"No! I've come to my senses. And *you* didn't work for that 'hard-earned' money. You inherited it through Grandpa just like I did. And you've totally missed the point. I almost died!" There was a long pause before she spoke again. "The money didn't almost die. *I* did."

"You're right," her father said, tone softer. "And we're relieved you're okay. We were very worried. We can talk about this later. We're going to go unpack."

"Say your good-byes to Mr. MacGregor," her mother said. "The three of us will be leaving in the morning. Dr. Jackson says you will be okay to travel then."

"Not without Liam," Anna said as her father opened the door.

I stood and they passed by me to descend the stairs, not sparing me a second look.

I slipped into Anna's room and pushed the door shut behind me.

Leaning back against the headboard, eyes closed, she looked fragile and tired. "I'm not leaving with them," she said.

"Do you need anything?" I asked, sitting on the edge of the bed.

She opened her eyes and smiled. "You."

I took her slender hand in mine. "I'm completely yours. Regardless of where you are."

"I'm not leaving."

The Cailleach's reach might be infinite, but the Na Fir Ghorm wouldn't be able to hurt her again in New York. "Perhaps it would be best if you leave, at least until you're well."

Her brow furrowed. "My parents will change their minds. They're just pissed off right now. They won't make me leave. I just need to talk to my dad after they calm down."

I squeezed her hand. "Anna, I wasn't thinking of them."

She sat forward. "You know the blue guys were there when the storm came then. That they did that by magic or something to hurt me."

"Yes, I do."

"It won't happen again. I'm going to stay inside the house until we leave. *Together.*" She placed a hand on the side of my face. "There's not room for both of us and my parents on the helicopter, so I'll have it turn right around after dropping them off to come back and pick us up."

She leaned back against the pillows piled against the headboard. "We'll be free of this place. My parents will warm up to it. They have no real say anyway."

For a brief, shining moment I allowed myself to believe this dream. To imagine us living together free from the darkness and misfortune that had followed me my entire life. "I love you, Anna." The words were pitifully inadequate.

"I love you too," she whispered. "And nothing and no one will ever keep us apart."

The door cracked open and Miss Ronan cleared her throat. "The Leightons asked me to tell Mr. MacGregor it is time for him to leave now."

I stood. "I'll see you tomorrow."

"I don't want you to go," Anna said.

"It's only for one night. When you wake up, I'll be here."

She smiled. "Okay. Come back ready to leave this crappy little island forever."

"Forever," I repeated before leaving her room, heart so full, I was certain it would burst.

I couldn't bring myself to go home. Instead, I watched from an outcropping of boulders overlooking the front of the mansion. The great stone beast of a house seemed to watch me back, its great gaping mouth mocking my insignificance and inadequacies. "She loves me," I said, as if it could hear me. "And nothing in this world or any other can change it."

Sometime well before sunrise, Miss Ronan strode calmly from the house and took the trail to the harbor. She strolled back later and disappeared into the house. Perhaps she was unable to sleep and had gone for a walk.

Just after sunrise, the small helicopter landed in the clearing in front of the mansion. A man I'd never seen before got out and entered the house. The pilot remained in the craft.

For several hours, no one came or went. Maybe the man was the lawyer and he would clear up the issues between Anna and her parents.

"Come back ready to leave this crappy little island forever," she had said. A silly grin spread across my face. For the first time, I was ready. Regardless of the difficulties learning the nuances of her world presented, they were preferable to this. And I would be with Anna.

The man who had arrived in the small helicopter came out of the house. He now wore the black robes of a priest. Perhaps he had come to counsel the family.

Her parents emerged, carrying their luggage. The pilot followed, lugging Anna's huge suitcase. Anna didn't join them. Maybe she was sending her things ahead.

Once the doors were closed, the large helicopter took off, followed by the small one.

Just as I stood to return to the mansion, Miss Ronan appeared from around the side of the house. She ran up the porch steps and disappeared inside.

No one answered when I knocked on the doors. I pounded harder. Nothing.

I rounded the left side of the house and pulled on the first set of windows, but they were locked. The next set was locked as well. The third would be harder to access as it was higher and behind a prickly hedge. When I went behind the hedge, there was a step stool. Grateful for the good fortune, I stepped up and found the window unlocked. It slid open easily and I climbed into the room in which we had found Connor MacFarley with Deirdre. He must have failed to return to retrieve the stool. I pulled the window shut behind me.

Consumed by an inexplicable sense of dread, I held my breath. The mansion was like a tomb. No sound from anywhere, it was as if the evil in the house were waiting to overtake me when I least expected it. Silently, I climbed the stairs, then pushed Anna's door open. My heart skipped a beat to find her bed empty and neatly made. The dresser was back in its original place, no longer obstructing the hidden panel. Even my books were gone from the window seat.

"Anna?" I called, peeking into the bathroom. It was as if she had never been in there at all. Were it not for the faint smell of lilies clinging to the air, I would think the whole thing had been a dream.

"Anna?" I called louder.

Perhaps she felt good enough to go downstairs. I found the kitchen empty as well as the dining room.

A loud thud followed by another came from the opening under the staircases. Someone was in the library. I smiled at the prospect of seeing Anna again. My smile dissolved when I entered the room. Miss Ronan was pulling books from shelves as if she had gone mad. Left and right, she shoved them from their resting places in a trancelike frenzy, her hair falling in disarray from its usual tight twist.

"Where is Anna?"

She froze and straightened, back to me. "She is resting," she said, not turning around. "She does not wish to be bothered right now."

"Where is she?"

She turned. "I'll take you to her, but first you must tell me where you found this. It was on the desk when I came to replace the books from Anna's room." She pulled the piece of paper that I had found in the volume of Tennyson out of her pocket.

"In a book."

"Which book?" Her hand trembled, causing the edges of the paper to flutter.

"A volume of poems by Tennyson."

She nodded. "The red one." A strange, wistful look crossed her face. "She loved that one."

I took another step into the room. "Who?"

"Your mother." Her brown eyes met mine. "My sister."

39

Hearken! and observe how healthily—how calmly I can tell you the whole story.

—Edgar Allan Poe,
from "The Tell-Tale Heart," 1843

Numb, I sank into the chair by the window, the very one in which I had imagined my mother reading.

"She came here to save me," Miss Ronan said, folding the paper and returning it to her pocket. "We grew up in an educated and powerful clan that resides far up the Canadian coast. More and more of my pod were turning from the old ways and adopting the easier, simple life of the seal."

She grabbed several books and shoved them to the floor. "This troubled my father, who was their leader. Being the oldest of his offspring, I went in search of an island we'd heard of on which the villagers still honored the Otherworlders. Once it was found, I would return and lead my people to it."

She laughed, and my stomach churned at her crazed demeanor.

"Fine dream," she said. Another pile of books hit the floor. "When I arrived, I saw a human male on the jetty—a fine, strong, beautiful male who intended to throw himself into the sea. The Na Fir Ghorm, of course, were there to help him with this effort. I shed my pelt and kept him from destroying himself."

The look on her face softened as she stared out the window. "Never had there been so tragic a creature. He had lost his beautiful wife and was completely broken. I thought I could fix him."

The sharpness returned to her voice. "I lived with him for several years and fell hopelessly in love with him, thinking he returned my love." She flung a stack of books from the shelf. "He didn't."

My muscles tensed. She was surely on the brink of insanity.

"I longed to return to my pod, but he had found and hidden my pelt, which made me his prisoner." Another pile of books hit the floor. "Years later, my dear sister came in search of me, fearing rightfully that I had been captured. My father sent with her an amulet bestowed on our pod by Manannán mac Lir himself that gave the wearer immortality to use if either of us needed it."

She leaned against the desk, staring over my head as if she were witnessing the events as she recalled them. "I should have sent her away the moment she arrived, but I was overjoyed to see her. As we embraced by the sea, Frank took her pelt from where she had abandoned it at the water's edge."

I held my breath as she cleared several more shelves with terrible violence.

"He told me he did it for *me*. He wanted me to have company, and being in love with him, I believed him. He let us spend time together and we were happy. She told me all about my family and we talked about what it would be like when we returned to them. I had dreams to escape this island." Her eyes met mine. "Just like you do."

She rolled a ladder attached to a brass rail at the top of the bookcases to the next bank of shelves and climbed it. "He moved her from my room to the one next to it telling me it was so that he could be with me at night again." She shoved half of the shelf off and the books crashed to the floor, startling me enough to cause me to jump to my feet. "But he never came to me." More books cascaded down. "He went to her instead. But she didn't want him." She slumped against the ladder. "I could hear her screams through the wall. I tried to get in to help her, but the door was locked."

After several shaky breaths, she moved down the ladder to the next shelf. I took a couple of steps closer to the door.

"The next morning, he began calling her by his dead wife's surname, MacGregor. He told me if I tried to interfere again, he would kill her. He told her that if she ever screamed or resisted him, he would kill me." A tear rolled down her cheek. "She never uttered another word from that day forward."

She cleared that shelf and the one under it, not speaking.

"What are you looking for?"

"Her pelt." She rolled the ladder aside and emptied the one at eye level. "The note you found was the clue to where she hid it."

"I thought Frank took it."

"He did, but he got sloppy. He fell in love with her the way I had fallen in love with him. One day he insisted on painting her wearing her pelt over her shoulders and she saw where he hid it. She later recovered it and stashed it where he would not find it."

She took several books and slammed them on the desk. "She wouldn't leave. I begged her to go, but she remained because of me." She kicked some books out of her way. "She offered her pelt to me, but there was no way I could leave her with him. It was my fault she was his prisoner."

I tried to recall the wording from the paper, but couldn't. "What makes you think it's in here?"

"The clue on the note, but it's hard to believe. I don't think she was ever in this room alone. He always came with her. And he locked her in her room at night."

She knocked the books off the next shelf down.

"What exactly does the note say?" I asked.

"It is where my spirit found escape," Miss Ronan recited from memory. "This is the only place she found escape. Through these books."

Again, I imagined her reading in the chair near the window. I studied it from where I stood near the door. It was the only soft surface in the room. It was certainly where she would have read and found escape. Ronan was thinking too broadly.

As she continued to unload the shelves, I made my way casually back to the chair and stared out the window. I didn't want to help her to find the pelt, but I wanted to locate it in case it could be used as a bargaining tool. I was certain she was behind Frank's murder and perhaps my mother's as well.

"What happened next?" I asked, hoping she was still in a talkative disposition.

"She came up pregnant, of course." She shoved books out of her way with her foot. "Frank was pleased. So pleased, he lavished her with gifts. Then he got word the family was coming. He was only allowed to stay here by their good graces. He was afraid they would discover what he had done and throw him out, so he asked me to move her from the mansion temporarily until the season was over. I was thrilled to do so because it got her away from him."

I lowered myself into the chair as she moved the ladder to the next bank of shelves.

She climbed several rungs. "He sent for her at the onset of the weather because he knew the family would not come back until spring." Miss Ronan gave a sharp laugh. "She refused to come back. He could not have her bodily removed without the villagers figuring out what had happened. They believed she had been fired because of her unfortunate condition, and he was worried they would tell the family somehow. He was forced to leave her there."

When I was sure she wasn't watching, I ran my fingers under the edge of the seat. Sure enough, there was a torn spot.

"When her time came to have the baby, she tried to get to me but only made it as far as the edge of the woods. I heard her screams from the porch. I ran as fast as I could, but by the time I reached her, it was too late. She spoke to me for the first time since that horrible day and she begged me to save you. So I did, praying you were Selkie, but you weren't."

She turned her back to climb the rest of the way up the ladder. I stuck my fingers in the hole in the lining under the chair and felt silky fur within. The pelt had been stuffed into the cushion from underneath.

"You were in there wrong and wouldn't come out," she said, "which is why she died. Once she no longer lived, I had no other choice. I did what it took to get you out."

I put my hand in my lap. "So you made the claw marks, not me."

She said nothing as she dumped the contents of another shelf.

I stood. "I'm not a demon, you are."

Still on the ladder, she twisted to face me. "No. You are the worst kind of demon. You are a sickening reminder of what he did. His evil has passed straight down to you and I won't allow him the joy of ever seeing your face. You even look like him."

She turned away and grasped the ladder, sobbing.

A horrible realization hit me and tingles crawled under the surface of my skin. He was still alive somewhere in this house. "Where is he?"

"I don't know!" she screamed.

I backed toward the door. "What happened?"

She climbed down the ladder and grabbed twisted finials on the back of the desk chair. "Sometimes it's impossible to stop loving someone. No matter how horrible he is, you just can't stop."

She sat in the chair and buried her face in her hands. After some deep breaths to compose herself, she continued. "Six years after my sister died, it was clear he didn't love me and would never love me, despite my feelings for him. I offered him the amulet in exchange for my pelt. Immortality for freedom." She took a shuddering breath. "He then informed me that he had destroyed my pelt."

She folded her hands in front of her on the desk, the distant, crazed look returning. "I planned my revenge for weeks, waiting for the family to leave." She met my eyes. "That's the summer you met Anna."

After pulling several hairpins from her unraveled twist and dropping them on the inky surface of the mahogany desk, she ran her hands through her hair. "I put him in a place where he would long for the light the way I yearned for the sea. I would leave him in there as long as he had held me captive to that point. Thirteen years."

She was undoubtedly mad and capable of terrible acts. Fear flooded my body in a nauseating rush as the implications of her insanity crystallized. "Where is Anna?" I whispered.

As if I hadn't spoken, she continued. "I made a bargain with the Na Fir Ghorm. If they would lock him up in a place with no light for thirteen years, I would do their bidding for the duration." She laughed and stood. "With the amulet on, he could not die. He could only suffer . . . like me." Purposefully, she rounded the desk and stopped right in front of me. "Like you."

I grabbed her arm and gave her a shake. "Where is Anna?"

"She's sleeping," she calmly replied.

Staring into her glazed eyes, I had no doubt she had fallen into madness. "Where?"

She remained completely calm—eerily and unnaturally detached. "Something happened in the night and she never awoke. The priest came this morning and they buried her in the family crypt behind the house."

40

And so, all the night-tide, I lie down by the side
Of my darling—my darling—my life and
my bride,
In her sepulchre there by the sea—
In her tomb by the sounding sea.

—Edgar Allan Poe,
from "Annabel Lee," 1849

I shoved Miss Ronan away and sprinted to the front doors, ripping them open as the pain ripped my heart apart. I ran around the corner of the house and past the fountain to the back side of the mansion. I'd never been behind the structure.

Three crypts stood side by side. All three structures were constructed from slabs of weathered white marble with thick, arched iron doors that overlapped, meeting in a sharp point. Heavy locks held the doors in place. Carved angels in various stages of mourning stared down in mock empathy from the apexes of the crypts' roofs.

"Anna!" I screamed, mindlessly yanking the doors of the first structure and then the second. "Anna!"

Flowers lay strewn on the step of the third one. Lilies. She had to be in there. I pounded my fist on the doors and they clanged under my blows. "Anna!"

Terror-induced delirium collided with my rational thought, driving reason into oblivion. Surely this was a nightmare from which I would awaken at any moment. Anna had been fine when I last saw her. The doctor said she was going to be well in a few days. I banged on the doors again as if I expected her to rise from death and throw them open from within.

My Anna was inside the crypt, locked away from me.

Dead.

I'd never hear her voice or her laugh. Never touch her body or breathe in her lily scent again. I slumped down, laying my cheek against the cool metal door of her tomb. "Anna," I whispered.

The sea wind gusted and a gull called from overhead as if the world, unlike my heart, had not just shattered into millions of irretrievable fragments.

"A craftsman will be flown in to carve her name next week," Miss Ronan said from behind me.

It was impossible to breathe. My thoughts whirled in an incoherent tangle through my brain.

"This was where Frank was to be laid to rest," she said. "Suiting, don't you think?"

Suiting? I stumbled to my feet, discordant rage pounding at my brain, begging me to grab her. To hurt her. "You're behind this. You killed her, didn't you? You're in with them on this wager?"

She held up her hands. "No. I didn't kill her. Otherworlders are forbidden to kill humans." She shook her head. "I warned you, didn't I? I didn't kill her, you did. With your selfishness. I told you to stay away, but you just kept coming back."

The rage subsided, displaced by a sorrow that caused my body to ache as if I'd been thrown against the rocks by the waves. A sob welled up in my throat. If only Anna had stayed in New York. "Who has the key?" I asked. "I need to see her."

Miss Ronan turned and headed away, loose hair whipping in the sea wind.

"I have to see her!" I shouted to her back, unable to move. When she disappeared around the corner of the house, I slumped down on the marble stoop, no longer able to stand.

My misery was all consuming, reaching deep within and ravaging everything in its path. No part of me, body or mind, was spared from its devastating power. The pain had no ebb or flow. It was a constant ever-increasing knell in my chest, timed to the beating of my broken heart. "Anna," I whispered again.

Too overcome to move, I remained huddled at her crypt door begging death to take me as well. But death was deaf to my suffering, and so I remained like this until well into the night.

Lying on my back, I could imagine Anna looking down at me from the stars that winked between clearings in the night clouds.

"Anna!" I screamed to the sky.

I rolled in a ball on my side, fighting the pain in my chest that threatened to rip me apart.

"Liam."

It was faint and sounded as if it rose from the very earth itself. I was dreaming awake. "I love you," I whispered. A tear made its way to the ground under my cheek.

"Liam," her voice called again from my foggy imagination.

"Yes, I'll be there soon," I answered.

"We should not have moved the girl," one of the Na Fir Ghorm said.

"Shut up," the leader replied. "Ronan will now be indebted to us again. She was very useful in helping us with the wager."

Muireann shot to the surface, gulped air, and returned to the cave opening.

She missed the first part of what one of them said, but it ended with, "He still loves her, so we have lost anyway."

"It isn't over," said the leader. "When we send the Selkie this time, he will have no reason to resist. Human lust will dissolve any love that remains. He thinks her dead."

This was totally news to Muireann. She had seen the flying machines come and go delivering and taking strangers away, but she had no idea what had occurred. So it seemed Anna wasn't dead, but Liam thought she was and the Na Fir Ghorm had moved her somewhere. Where?

"Why didn't you retrieve the amulet?" the leader asked.

"We needed to get in and out as quickly as possible. Crossing the beach in daylight is risky. We almost couldn't move the boulder even with all of us pushing. We called, but the male locked within didn't answer. It was too dark to see inside. We just put the girl in the pit and sealed it back up before Brigid Ronan's sleeping potion wore off."

"Go find the Selkie," the leader said. "We're sending her up again."

Muireann bolted as far away from the cave as possible. She needed to get to Liam and tell him what she knew. She surfaced and took a deep breath. The full moon gave her a clear view of the large dwelling. Most of the lights were off.

And then she saw him. As if in a daze, he stumbled along the trail toward the jetty.

She darted along the edge of the rocks, barking. He didn't even look over at her.

Tripping and falling, he made his way over the jetty toward

the end. She needed to transform to get his attention but was certain she wouldn't be able to climb on the jagged, slippery rocks with her human legs.

She swam to the end and waited, knowing that would be her best chance. Hopefully, he wouldn't plunge off the side before he reached her.

A shooting pain seared the flesh of my calf when I lost my footing again and slammed into the sharp edge of a rock. I just needed to make it to the end of the jetty. Then I would be with her. "Anna!" I shouted. This time, I didn't hear her faint call in return.

Finally, I reached the end. "Anna!" I shouted again. I stumbled to a rock closer to the water. It would be awful to only knock myself unconscious and not make it to the sea. I was determined to never wake up without her again.

"Stop!" a girl's voice called. "Liam, no!"

I teetered on the edge of the rock, taking a step back to check my fall. Shaking my head to clear it, I focused on Muireann's face. She had half transformed and shouted to me from the water. "Anna's not dead. Do you hear me?"

Another trick by an Otherworlder. She was probably in on the wager too. I moved back to the edge of the rock near the water.

"No! Liam. Brigid Ronan gave her a sleeping potion. She's not dead. They moved her to another location."

As if slapped in the face, I sobered from my stupor. "Where?"

"I don't know. They called it a pit. It was in a cave under the house."

Every sensation was heightened as adrenaline coursed through me, pushing the misery aside and replacing it with hope. "Can you help me?"

"Yes!" she said. "I'll meet you on the beach where the two of you were bonded."

41

*Fearful indeed the suspicion—but more fearful
the doom! It may be asserted, without hesitation, that no event is so terribly well adapted to
inspire the supremeness of bodily and of mental
distress, as is burial before death.*

—Edgar Allan Poe,
from "The Premature Burial," 1844

Heart full of hope and light-headed, I collected
candles and a lighter from the dresser in
Frank's bedroom and a thick bathrobe from
his closet for Muireann so she wouldn't be
cold. I draped the robe over my shoulders, stuffed the extra candle in my back pocket, and lit the other one before opening the
hidden panel from the room.

I located the trapdoor to the lower level and descended into
the musty-smelling darkness. Taking the tunnel I had traveled
with Anna, I made my way around the large boulder we'd hidden behind at the turn and ran to the beach. Muireann stood
shivering at the cave entrance.

She looked over her shoulder at the water as I wrapped the
robe around her. "One moment," she said before running to a
grouping of rocks. She grabbed a pelt from behind it and ran
back. "I don't want the Na Fir Ghorm to steal it or anything.
They're looking for me right now."

"Why?" I asked, lighting a candle I held in my teeth.

Again, she looked back at the beach. "They want me to come try to seduce you again."

She hesitated when I held the candle out to her. "That's fire," she said. "It's dangerous. I don't want it."

"The tunnel is dark. We need to be able to see. It creates light."

"I have a better idea." She closed her eyes and chanted in a strange language. "We need to wait here for just a moment," she said.

"Why do they want you to seduce me?"

She tilted her head and stared at the flame in my hand. "So they can win the wager."

The wager again. I blew out the candle. "What exactly is the wager?"

"That human love is frail and will falter in the face of adversity."

Rage welled up from deep inside my chest and my face grew hot. "That's what this is about? It's a bet over whether love will last? Anna could be dying because of a stupid bet like that?"

She nodded and pointed at the sky. "Look, here they come. They'll light our way. No need for dangerous fire." She tilted her head up to the golden clouds swirling overhead. "His female is in the tunnel somewhere. Please help us find her."

The Bean Sidhes grew bright and created a golden light that cocooned us and lit our path as we traversed the tunnel. "Anna!" I yelled.

"They mentioned a boulder and a pit," Muireann said, running to keep up with me. "Ouch." She stopped and pulled a rock from the bottom of her bare foot.

I slowed to let her keep up without running. "Anna!" I shouted again.

Almost dreamlike, there was an answer. "Liam."

It came from just up ahead where the tunnel took a sharp right turn around the boulder. The boulder! My heart soared.

"Anna!" I shouted.

"Liam," her beautiful voice answered. "Help me."

I stopped at the boulder, desperately running my hand along the edge where it met the wall. "I'm here. Where are you?"

"D-don't know."

Her voice came from underneath the huge stone. I dropped to my knees and dug at the ground at the base of it. It was solid rock with loose pebbles around it. No matter how hard I clawed, I would never break through.

"Hang on. I'm right here." I stood and put my shoulder to the stone and pushed. There was no way I could move it. "Muire-ann, I need you to go get help. Please go tell Francine what has happened and have her bring men to come move this—as many as she can find. Anna is underneath. Please hurry."

"I will get there much faster swimming." She ran, a Bean Sidhe lighting her way, in the direction of the beach.

"Anna?"

Her voice drifted up from the far side of the boulder. "Please h-hurry. N-need you."

I crawled to the other side and ran my fingers along the bottom of the huge stone and found a gap between it and the floor. "Could you light this?" I asked a Bean Sidhe.

Anna's slender fingers slid up through the crack, guided by the light. "L-Liam. I love you. P-please know that."

I placed my hand over her fingers. They were as cold as the ocean. "I love you too. We're going to get you out of there."

"No. T-t-too late. Water. Love you."

The water had been halfway up the beach, which meant it was high tide. The water had probably risen almost to the top of the pit in which she was imprisoned. Panic slammed into me like the waves on the jetty. If I didn't get her out soon, she would become too affected by the cold water to stay conscious and she would certainly drown. I couldn't lose her again. I had to persuade her to fight for life. To stay.

"Anna! Listen to me. Just hang on a bit longer. Men are coming to move the boulder. Just stay conscious and above water." I squeezed her fingers. "Anna!"

Her fingers twitched. "So c-c-cold."

"I know. We'll have you right out."

Her voice was so faint I had to put my ear to the crack to hear it. "No. I'm warm now. It's all good. Sleepy."

"Anna. No. Stay awake. Stay with me."

"Always with you. Love you . . . forever." Her fingers went limp.

I clutched onto her even tighter, as though somehow I could keep her very soul from exiting if I just hung on hard enough.

Then time stopped. All sound and light disappeared, leaving me with nothing but the feel of her cold fingers and her last word repeating over and over through my mind. "Forever."

An unbearable ache consumed me entirely. I opened my mouth to scream, but no sound came out. It was as if a part of me had been removed. A significant part. Anna's part.

I crumpled over and ran my lips over her knuckles. "No. God, no."

But the vast, hollow emptiness in my chest confirmed what I already knew. No matter how hard I clung to her, I could not hold her here. She was gone. I'd lost her again.

I released her fingers and they slipped away through the crevasse into darkness.

42

The agony of my soul found vent in one loud,
long, and final scream of despair.

—Edgar Allan Poe,
from "The Pit and the Pendulum," 1842

Shouting came from up the tunnel toward the house. "This way," Muireann called, running in from the ocean entrance.

Standing, I stumbled away from the boulder, falling against the opposite wall, holding it to support me as voices bounced and skittered over the stone walls of the tunnel and then scattered through my brain.

Pa reached me first. "Son. I'm so sorry. We'll get her out."

I couldn't even form the words to tell him it was too late. Most of the men from the village were there: Mac, Ron, Edmond, and others. Everyone pitched in to push the boulder off, and before long it tumbled to its side, revealing a gaping hole almost full to the top with water. Anna rested primarily submerged on a shallow slope near the opening. I turned away as they pulled her out.

"She's gone," someone said. It sounded as if they were far away. Their voices echoed and overlapped in my mind as they spoke to one another.

"Frank!" Miss Ronan yelled from the edge of the pit. "Oh, dear gods of the ocean. What have I done?" Falling to her knees, she crumpled into a heap, her long hair dipping into the water. Her body shuddered with such violence, it appeared she would rattle apart into pieces.

A Bean Sidhe floated over the top of the pit and through the clear water, human bones were visible. Frank. Something gold glimmered against the edge.

"He took it off!" Miss Ronan screamed, tearing at her hair. "He could have lived forever, even underwater. I never imagined he'd take it off. I just wanted him punished." She crossed her arms over her body and rocked.

"She killed the girl. She killed them both," Pa said.

"No!" Miss Ronan jumped to her feet but was caught by Francine, who held her around the middle from behind, pinning her arms to her sides. Like a feral animal she struggled against Francine, writhing and kicking. "Anna wasn't meant to die," Miss Ronan shrieked. "Her parents were supposed to take the body home for burial, and she'd wake up. But they insisted on putting her in the family crypt." Her eyes darted from one villager to another like a cornered beast's. "I couldn't have her screaming where Liam could hear her, so I had her moved. She was to be fed and kept alive by the Na Fir Ghorm, then released when the term of the wager was over. She wasn't supposed to die." As if her bones had dissolved, she went limp, and Francine loosened her grip, letting her slide to her knees, sobbing. "The Na Fir Ghorm did this on purpose."

"Let's get the girl out of here," Mac said. The men helped him carry Anna toward the beach, leaving only Francine, Pa, Muireann, and Brigid Ronan.

Muireann, tears streaming down her face, moved to the edge of the pit. Eyes wide, she tilted her head and studied the glimmering object in the water.

Wordlessly, she dropped her robe and slipped her feet into

the back flippers of the pelt, crouched over, and stretched the pelt over her head.

Brigid Ronan screamed, and when I looked back, Muireann's seal form was complete and had slipped into the water. She returned to the surface with the gold object in her mouth. In her cumbersome seal body, she couldn't climb out of the pit, so she bowed her head and human arms pushed through a slit in the belly of the pelt. Soon, Muireann's full human form emerged. The amulet still in her mouth, she pitched her pelt out of the pit and began to climb up after it.

Before anyone could react, Brigid Ronan broke free from Francine and grabbed the pelt. "It wasn't supposed to happen this way," she said, backing away, pointing a shaking finger at me. "You were the only one who was supposed to die." As Francine lunged for her, she bolted out of reach, running through the tunnel toward the beach.

"No!" Muireann's scream ricocheted off the walls. "No! My pelt!"

I couldn't let Ronan get away. I sprinted after her but was too late. When I reached the beach, she had already transformed and plunged into the sea.

Catching my breath, I stared out over the water where Miss Ronan had disappeared, unable to fight off the delirium clouding my mind. The familiar sounds of the ocean seemed foreign, the rush of wind on my face abrasive.

"I'm sorry about your girl, son," Pa said from somewhere behind me, his voice skipping through my brain like a stone across water. "I'm sorry about a lot of things."

Francine wrapped her arms around me. I felt her, but still moved in a daze. Everything seemed far away. "You are bound, lad. You'll see her in the next world."

Again, the memory of Anna's voice filled my head. "Forever."

Forever, I repeated in my mind.

It wasn't until I turned around that the fog lifted from my brain and I found my voice. Anna lay on the beach, the moonlight reflecting off the gauzy silver fabric tangled around her limp body. The last time she had worn that dress, we were bound for all eternity on this very beach.

I fell to my knees and pulled her to me.

Folding over her body, the pain of my very soul issued forth in scream after scream, proclaiming my despair to every living creature in this world and the next.

The boundaries which divide Life from Death
are at best shadowy and vague.

—Edgar Allan Poe,
from "The Premature Burial," 1844

uireann had never witnessed agony like Liam's. Her heart ached inside her human chest, but she knew there was nothing she could say or do to help him. Like the tide, his sorrow had to run its course before it would subside.

The villagers, save for Francine and the human he called Pa, left through the tunnel.

Liam had stopped shouting and now simply rocked, holding his dead female to him.

Francine approached and squatted down facing him. She brushed his hair from his eyes. "Anna loved you, lad. That's more than most people get from life. True love."

"It was more than love," he said, still rocking. "I . . . I . . ."

"I know," she whispered, kissing his cheek. Pa patted his shoulder and then left through the tunnel with Francine.

For the longest time, Liam was silent. He caressed Anna's face and simply stared at her. Then something in him changed. Gently, he laid her down and stood, staring over the water with his good hand clenched in a fist.

His rage was as terrible as his despair, and just as painful to watch.

"Why?" he screamed to the sea. "Why her? Take me instead!"

A gray head popped up a few dozen yards from shore. Then another. Yellow eyes peering from blue faces. More joined them. From thin air, the Bean Sidhes materialized in their nebulous cloud-like forms, floating just above the surface.

Liam paced the water's edge. "It was a bet? A wager? You murdered her for that?"

Muireann ran her fingers over the raised gold crest of Manannán mac Lir on the amulet, hating the Na Fir Ghorm as they gloated from the water at Liam's suffering.

The metal warmed under her touch. That was it! Manannán mac Lir was the ruler of her people—of all ocean-dwelling Otherworlders. He had the ability to restore life to the dead; she'd heard stories of it since she had been a pup. She rubbed the amulet with her fingers. "Please come to us, great Manannán mac Lir. We need you," she whispered.

Lightning crackled in the clouds above, and the amulet grew hotter still.

"Please," she said, a little louder.

A bolt of lightning slammed into the water just behind the Na Fir Ghorm, and where it had struck, a huge horse bearing a rider now stood, appearing more gaseous than solid. The beast strode across the surface of the sea and halted at the waterline, its rider so terrifying, Muireann trembled.

Liam, halfway down the beach, stopped pacing and stared but showed no fear, perhaps because he had nothing else to lose.

Muireann marveled as the transparent figure of a warrior in armor solidified before her eyes. His stallion did the same as it snorted and pawed the surface of the water.

Manannán mac Lir turned the beast in a full circle, deep-set blue eyes traveling from creature to creature and stopping to rest on Muireann. He crossed his arms over his chest and said nothing.

Fear felt the same in human form as it felt as a Selkie. Her stomach churned as she struggled to inhale. "Please," she said. "Please help us."

Again, the warrior surveyed the scene. His eyes came to rest on the dead girl on the beach. He gestured to Anna. "Is this why I was called? A dead human?" His deep voice rumbled like distant thunder.

Muireann swallowed hard and nodded.

He dismounted and Muireann cringed. "In what manner did she die?" he asked.

"She was murdered!" Liam shouted. "Murdered by all of them." He gestured wildly with his good arm to the creatures in and above the ocean. "They made a wager and used us as pawns for their amusement. They killed her for sport!"

Thunder rolled through the sky as Manannán mac Lir turned his attention to the Na Fir Ghorm and Bean Sidhes.

"We killed no one," the Na Fir Ghorm leader announced, his voice shrill. "The Selkie Brigid Ronan did."

"Are you this Brigid Ronan?" he asked Muireann.

Unable to find her voice, she shook her head.

"Where is she?" All the creatures cringed as lightning split the sky.

"She's gone," Liam answered. "She stole Muireann's pelt and escaped. But they"—he indicated the Bean Sidhes and the Na Fir Ghorm—"are as responsible as she. More so, even."

Muireann slid off the rock and took a deep breath. "No. The Bean Sidhes are not at fault."

"Tell me then, little Selkie, what happened."

As Muireann told the tale, thunderclouds thickened overhead, and by the time she had finished, lightning struck all around, stopping just short of the water. She assumed the weather was an extension of Manannán mac Lir's emotions, since it intensified when his expression grew darker.

"Enough," he said, cutting her off mid-sentence as she reached the point when Anna's body was brought to the beach.

He stood very still and closed his eyes briefly before speaking. "Bean Sidhes, your involvement in a wager using humans as players was foolhardy and wrong. Your motives were not malicious, however, so I am granting you a reprieve. You have accomplished your task of exposing the wrongful deaths of the two humans. I will allow you to cross through the veil to the other side and join your loved ones there."

The six clouds took human form and shone brilliant gold. A bright white light shimmered just at the horizon, expanding toward the heavens in a thin vertical line that widened momentarily like a curtain being opened. The Bean Sidhes disappeared and the line narrowed into nothing but the night sky once again.

Muireann, still clutching the amulet, returned to her rock and cowered against it, dreading the judgment she would receive for her participation in the wager. She sighed with relief when he next turned his attention to the Na Fir Ghorm.

"Your part in this, however, was despicable and malicious. I can find no redeeming motivation behind your acts."

The Na Fir Ghorm exchanged looks, many of them shuddering to the point that ripples radiated around them in the already-turbulent water.

Manannán mac Lir raised his arms in front of him at shoulder level, the bronze bands around his upper arms glittering in the light of the setting moon. "You are from this moment forward banned to the deep ocean, where you will never have human contact again." Lightning shot from his fingertips in a wide fan, and as if they had never existed, the water's surface was clear of the horrible creatures.

Liam had moved back to Anna's body and was again holding her to him, no longer taking notice of anything else.

Manannán mac Lir strode to Muireann and held out his palm. "To prevent it from being abused again, I will take the amulet back." She placed it in his hand and he smiled at her. "It is unfortunate, little Selkie, that your pelt was taken. I have no remedy for you. I wish you a long and prosperous human life full of joy and love."

His words felt like a blow to her chest. Love and joy was what Liam and his Anna had shared.

Manannán mac Lir mounted his horse and jerked the reins, turning the beast toward the sea.

"No, wait!" she said. "What about the girl? There are countless stories of you restoring life to the dead." Tears streamed down her face. "Please."

From atop his horse, he stared down at the pitiful couple. "I'm sorry, she is but a mere human. Her soul has long taken flight. There is nothing I can do."

*E*ven in death, Anna was beautiful—her perfect flawless skin so pale, offset by her raven black hair. Long lashes fanned over her cheeks and a serene, almost-pleasant expression graced her features. My Anna. Forever.

I stared up at the fierce Celtic god of the ocean as he looked down on me with pity. There was nothing he could do, he told Muireann. I had expected as much. Why would the Otherworld give me relief when the human world would not?

Poor Muireann wept and ran to him atop his great stallion. She reached up and pulled on the edge of his kilt. "My life for hers," she said. "I know it can be done. I've heard of your generosity in this regard. I will gladly die to restore her life."

There was no room in me for more pain. Numb, I hugged Anna's cold body tighter, unable to even conjure coherent thought.

"Why would you do such a thing?" he asked.

"Because I love him."

He dismounted and took her face in his hands. "Sweet child," he said, wiping a tear away with his thumb. "Were she of the Otherworld, I could do such a thing. But she is human, and therefore I cannot."

"They are bonded," she said. "Otherworldly bonds."

He smiled. "Then they will be together. She waits for him just on the other side. She will continue to wait until he comes to join her. My power isn't needed."

With that, he swung his leg over his horse and galloped out over the surface of the water, disappearing in a bolt of lightning.

Muireann sank to her knees in front of me, fiddling with the sash on the bathrobe.

She had been willing to die for me. For Anna.

"Thank you," I said.

"Human tears burn the eyes," she said, brushing hers away. "It's a good thing you have hands to wipe them off. I suppose I'll have to get used to it since I'm stuck this way."

Something caught my eye over the water where the horizon would be when the sun rose. Just a flicker of light, then it was gone.

"You aren't stuck," I told her, shifting Anna off my lap and setting her head down gently. Again, a fleck of light glittered on the horizon momentarily.

"But Brigid Ronan took my pelt."

"My mother's pelt is in the mansion. It's stuffed inside a needlepoint chair in the library. The room with all the books." The light seemed closer and brighter this time. I stood and squinted to bring it into focus. It vanished.

"What is it?" Muireann asked, staring up at me.

"It's . . ." I held my breath and waited for it to reappear.

"Liam." It was a whisper, just as faint and fleeting as the light over the water had been.

Surely this was madness. I stared down at Anna's lifeless body.

"Liam," her voice whispered again. It came from the direction of the sea.

I ran several steps toward the water. "Anna!" I called.

The sun had just begun to define the horizon. Halfway between the water's edge and morning's fuzzy white line was a silver form just over the water. It was too far away to make out. "Anna," I called again.

Muireann joined me. "What is it?" she asked.

I pointed to the form that was getting closer to us. "Just there on the water. A light. Do you see it?"

She shook her head. "No."

As it got closer, I could make out its form, but not the face. It was a girl, sheer and shimmery and gauzy like the material of Anna's silver dress.

"Liam."

And she spoke with Anna's voice.

My heart hammered and I gasped for breath. "It's her! Don't you see her?"

"It's Anna?" Muireann asked.

Anna's face came into view as she hovered maybe fifty feet out from shore. She held her arms out toward me. "Liam," she said. "Forever."

"You don't see her? Hear her?" I asked, stumbling to the waterline.

Muireann answered, but I only heard Anna's voice calling my name.

I waded into the water toward Anna's open arms, ignoring the cold seeping into my legs from the frigid Atlantic Ocean.

Anna smiled and my heart soared.

"Liam. I love you," her beautiful voice whispered.

"Anna," I called.

"Yes, Liam," she said. "I want you forever."

Forever. I closed my eyes.

"You are almost here," she said. It sounded as though she were right next to me.

And all at once, the water became warm. So very warm. I felt buoyant. As light as air.

"Love makes you feel as though you can fly," she whispered. "Fly with me, Liam."

I opened my eyes to see her lovely face as she enveloped me in her arms.

"Forever," I said as the sun broke over the horizon.

"Forever," she whispered as her lips met mine.

Acknowledgments

The work of Edgar Allan Poe has affected and fascinated me since I first read "The Tell-Tale Heart" in elementary school language arts. It has been a delight and honor to work on a book based on "Annabel Lee," one of the most hauntingly beautiful poems I have ever read. That said, I wish to thank Edgar Allan Poe, first and foremost, for his overwhelming genius and contribution to literature.

I also would like to thank my agent, Ammi-Joan Paquette, and the crew at Erin Murphy Literary Agency for seeing through my BS and believing in me. Those unscheduled phone calls? You know you love them, Joan.

The professionalism and talent at Philomel blew me away again. Love to Jill Santopolo for the props when I needed them most and for the excellent advice and guidance. Thank you to Julia Johnson and Karen Taschek for making my work shine and to Linda McCarthy and Amy Wu for making the book beautiful.

When the "winged seraphs of heaven" and the "demons of the sea" needed an Otherworldly incarnation, Robert Cremins stepped in to help me discover their identities. Thank you for the time spent discussing things Celtic over lattes, Robert.

Love and gratitude to Kari Olson, YA guru and speed-reader extraordinaire, for her keen eye and excellent input—also for her nagging and harping at me to send the next chapter. Put the taser away, Kari. As you can see, I finished it.

I'm grateful for the expertise and time shared with me by Victoria Scott, Lindsay Marsh, Heather Dyer, and Patrick MacDonald. You guys are the best!

And of course, gratitude beyond words to my husband, Laine, and my kids, Hannah, Emily, and Robert, for putting up with my brooding and angst. Sunshine and bunnies in the next one, I promise.